The Year of Shadows

CLAIRE LEGRAND

SIMON & SCHUSTER BFYR

New York   London   Toronto   Sydney   New Delhi

Also by Claire Legrand

The Cavendish Home for Boys and Girls

SIMON & SCHUSTER BOOKS FOR YOUNG READERS
An imprint of Simon & Schuster Children's Publishing Division
1230 Avenue of the Americas, New York, New York 10020

Text copyright © 2013 by Claire Legrand
Illustrations copyright © 2013 by Karl Kwasny

For information about special discounts for bulk purchases, please contact Simon & Schuster Special Sales at 1-866-506-1949 or business@simonandschuster.com.
The Simon & Schuster Speakers Bureau can bring authors to your live event. For more information or to book an event, contact the Simon & Schuster Speakers Bureau at 1-866-248-3049 or visit our website at www.simonspeakers.com.
Book design by Lucy Ruth Cummins
The text for this book is set in Cochin.
The illustrations for this book are rendered in ink, watercolor, gouache, and Photoshop.
Manufactured in the United States of America
0713 FFG
2 4 6 8 10 9 7 5 3 1
Library of Congress Cataloging-in-Publication Data
Legrand, Claire, 1986–
The year of shadows / Claire Legrand. — 1st ed.
p. cm.
Summary: Forced to move into a haunted concert hall with her distant father, "The Maestro," and aging grandmother, Nonnie, twelve-year-old Olivia, and classmate Henry try to lay to rest ghosts tied to the Hall's past before time and money run out.
ISBN 978-1-4424-4294-8 (hardcover)
ISBN 978-1-4424-4296-2 (eBook)
[1. Ghosts — Fiction. 2. Haunted places — Fiction. 3. Orchestra — Fiction. 4. Family problems — Fiction. 5. Fathers and daughters — Fiction.] I. Title.
PZ7.L521297Ye 2013
[Fic] — dc23
2012034667

FIRST EDITION

For the music teachers, mine and everywhere —

—and for Mom, my anchor

Acknowledgments

This is, for many reasons, a special book to me. My own experience as a musician is one of these reasons (I used to be a trumpet player, but I was not much of a charmer); my mom's bout with cancer, which colored the writing of this book, is another. I therefore have many people to thank:

First, for her unwavering support, keen insight, and priceless phone chats, my agent, Diana Fox; my brilliant and enthusiastic editor, Zareen Jaffery, who asks all the right questions; the whole team at Simon & Schuster, especially the ever-helpful Julia Maguire, Lydia Finn and Paul Crichton, Katrina Groover and Angela Zurlo (oh, so many thanks for your fine-toothed combs!), Bernadette Cruz, Michelle Fadlalla; art director Lucy Ruth Cummins, for making my books look beautiful; Karl Kwasny, for his delightful illustrations; and Pouya Shahbazian and Betty Anne Crawford, for spreading the word.

To my writer friends, inspiring and encouraging— Alison Cherry, Lindsay Ribar, Lauren Magaziner, Tim Federle, Leigh Bardugo, Trisha Leigh, Emma Trevayne, Stefan Bachmann, Katherine Catmull, Ellen Wright; the Apocalypsies, for their relentless support; and especially to Susan Bischoff and Kait Nolan, writerly soulmates. To the bloggers, librarians, fellow writers and readers, to Twitter and Tumblr and all the online bookfolk who make the day-to-day fun and offer such lovely support—thank you.

I would not be who I am today without my musical background, so I must give the warmest thanks to a few special music teachers over the year—Kristen Boulet, John Light, Irene Morris, Asa Burk, J. R. Stock, Nicholas Williams, Dennis Fisher, Maureen Murphy, Mike Sisco, Ellie Murphy, Marty Courtney, and John Holt, all of whom challenged and inspired me. Thank you to Andrew Justice, Maureen Murphy, and Jonathan Thompson, for helping me program the City Philharmonic's season. Special thanks must go to the Dallas Symphony Orchestra and Maestro Jaap van Zweden, in whose beautiful music hall I first saw Olivia and Igor; and to Ryan Anthony, trumpeter extraordinaire and Richard Ashley's real-world namesake.

To Dr. Alan Munoz—"Dr. Birdman," to Olivia—and the staff at Medical City Hospital in Dallas, for taking such good care of my mom; to my friends and family, especially those who helped us through dark times—Pati Gann, Judy Roumillat, Pat Peabody; to Battleship Legrand—is it Destin time yet?!—to Ashley, Andy, my wonderful stepmom, Anna, and my unstoppable dad, W. D., all of whom I miss every day; to my dear friends Starr Hoffman, Beth Keswani, Melissa Gann, Brittany Cicero, and Jonathan Thompson—my rocks, my lifeboats; and to Matt, my love, master untangler of plot knots.

Lastly, to Drew, and to Mom—thank you, miss you, I love you. We made it.

PART ONE

THE YEAR THE GHOSTS CAME STARTED LIKE THIS:

The Maestro kicked open the door, dropped his suitcase to the floor, and said, *"Voilà!"*

"I've seen it before," I said. In fact, I'd basically grown up here, in case he'd forgotten.

"Yes, but take a look at it. Really look." He said this in that stupid Italian accent of his. I mean, he was full Italian and all (I was only half), but did he have to sound so much like an Italian?

I crossed my arms and took a good, long look.

Rows of seats with faded red cushions. Moth-eaten curtains framing the stage. The dress circle boxes, where the rich people sat. Chandeliers, hanging from the ceiling that was decorated with painted angels, and dragons, and fauns playing pipes. The pipe organ, looming like a hibernating monster at the back of the stage. Sunlight from the lobby behind us slanted onto the pipes, making them gleam.

Same old Emerson Hall. Same curtains, same seats, same dragons.

The only thing different this time was us.

And our suitcases.

"Well?" the Maestro said. "What do we think?"

He was on one side of me, and Nonnie on the other. She clapped her hands and pulled the scarf off her head. Underneath the scarf, she was almost completely bald, with only a few straggly gray hairs left.

The day Mom disappeared about nine months ago, just before Christmas, Nonnie had shaved all her hair off.

"Oh!" Her wrinkled face puckered into a smile. "I think it's beautiful."

My fingers tightened on the handle of my suitcase, the ratty red one with the caved-in side. "You've seen it before, Nonnie. We all have, a million times."

"But is different now!" Nonnie twisted her scarf in her hands. "Before, was symphony hall. Now, is home. *È meglio.*"

I ground my teeth together, trying not to scream. "It's still a symphony hall."

"Olivia?" The Maestro was watching me, smiling, trying to sound like he really cared what I thought. "What do you think?"

When I didn't answer, Nonnie clucked her tongue. "Olivia. You should answer your father."

The Maestro and I didn't talk much anymore. Not since Mom left, and even for a couple of months before that, when he was so busy with rehearsals and concerts and trying to save the orchestra by begging for money from rich people at fancy dinners that he wouldn't come home until late. Sometimes he wouldn't come home at all, not until the next morning when Mom and I were in the kitchen, eating breakfast.

Then they would start yelling at each other.

I didn't like breakfast much after that. Every time I looked at cereal, I felt sick.

"He's not my father," I whispered. "He's just the Maestro." I felt something change in that moment. I knew I would never again call him "Dad." He didn't deserve it. Not after this. This was the last straw in a whole pile of broken ones.

"*Ombralina . . . ,*" Nonnie scolded. *Ombralina.* Little shadow. It was her nickname for me.

The Maestro stood there, watching me with those black eyes of his. I hated that we shared the same color eyes. I could feel something building inside me, something dangerous.

"I think I'm going to throw up," I announced.

Then I turned and ran outside, my suitcase banging against my legs. Out through the lobby, past the curling grand staircases and the box office window, and onto the sidewalk. Right out front, at the corner of Arlington Avenue and Wichita Street, I threw down my suitcase and screamed.

The traffic sped by—cars, trucks, cabs. People pushed past me—office workers out for lunch, grabbing sandwiches, talking on their phones. Nobody noticed me. Nobody even glanced my way.

Same old Emerson Hall. Same curtains, same seats, same dragons.
The only thing different this time was us.
And our suitcases.

Since Mom left, not many people noticed me. I wore black a lot now. I liked it; black was calming. My hair was long, and black too, and shiny, and I wore it down most of the time. I liked to hide behind it and pretend I didn't exist.

I couldn't decide if I wanted to cry or hit something, so I turned back to Emerson Hall's double oak doors. Stone angels perched on either side, playing their trumpets. Someone had climbed up there and spray-painted the angels orange and red. I squinted my eyes, trying to imagine the Hall's blurry shape into something like a home. But it didn't work. It was still a huge, drafty music hall with spray-painted angels, and yet I was supposed to live here now.

"Might as well go back in." I kicked open the door as hard as I could. "Not like there's anywhere else to go."

Our rooms were two empty storage rooms backstage: one on one side of the main rehearsal room, and one on the other side. There was also a cafeteria area with basic kitchen stuff like a sink, microwave, mini-fridge, and hot plate. It used to be for the musicians, so they could break for lunch during a long day of rehearsals.

Not anymore, though. It was our kitchen now.

The Maestro, Nonnie, and I hauled our suitcases backstage — one for each of us, and that's all we had in the world, everything we owned.

The Maestro disappeared into the storage room that would be his bedroom and started blasting Tchaikovsky's

Symphony no. 4 on the ancient stereo that had been there for years. The speakers crackled and popped. Tchaik 4—that's what the musicians called it—was the first piece of music on the program that year. Rehearsals would start soon.

Nonnie carefully arranged her suitcase in the middle of the rehearsal room, surrounded by stacked chairs, music stands, and the musicians' lockers, lining the walls. She perched on her suitcase and waved her scarf at me. Then she started humming, twisting her scarf around her fingers.

Nonnie didn't do much these days but hum and twist her scarves.

I sat beside her for the longest time, listening to her hum and the Maestro blast his music. I felt outside of myself, distant and floaty, like if I concentrated too hard on what was happening, I might totally lose it. The tiny gusts of ice-cold air I kept feeling drift past me didn't help. *Great,* I thought. *It's already freezing in here, and it's not even fall yet.*

This couldn't be happening. Except it was.

Nonnie and I each had tiny cots that came with sheets already on them. I wasn't sure where the Maestro had bought them, but I didn't trust strange sheets, so I took them down the street to the coin laundry and remade the beds.

That put me in an awful mood. Buying the detergent and paying for the laundry had cost us a few bucks, and every few bucks was precious when you didn't have a lot to begin with.

 8

Nonnie and I also each had a quilt. Mom had made them during one of her crafty phases when she'd spread out all sorts of things over the kitchen table after dinner—fabrics, scissors, spools of thread, paper she'd brought home from her office.

The Maestro came into our bedroom while I was spreading out the quilts over our cots.

"You should get rid of those ratty old things," he said.

"This is my and Nonnie's bedroom." I kept smoothing out my quilt, not looking at him. "And you should get out."

He was quiet, watching me. "I have some money for you. If you want to go get some things for your room, school supplies. School starts soon, doesn't it?"

"Yeah." I took the crumpled twenty from him. "You should get out."

After a minute, he did.

When the beds were made, I found some boxes in the rehearsal room that didn't look too old or beat-up. I also found a couple of old pianos, rickety music stands, chairs with shattered seats. All the broken stuff.

I refused to live out of my suitcase. It was too depressing. I stacked my clothes in one box and Nonnie's clothes in another box and arranged them at the ends of our beds, on their sides with the flaps like cupboard doors. Then I shoved our suitcases under the beds so we wouldn't have to look at them.

I lugged a couple of music stands to our bedroom and put them beside each of our beds, lying their tops flat like trays, so we could have nightstands. On my "nightstand," I carefully arranged my sketchpad and my set of charcoals and drawing pencils. It all looked so sad, sitting there next to my fold-up cot in my bedroom that had ugly concrete walls because it was never meant to be a bedroom.

Nonnie came up behind me and hugged my arm. She could always tell when I was upset.

"Maybe we need more color in these rooms," she suggested.

"Yeah. Maybe."

I couldn't stop thinking about our old house uptown, the pretty red-brick one with the blue door. The one we'd had to sell because the Maestro had taken a pay cut and we couldn't afford to live there anymore. Because the orchestra didn't have any money, so the Maestro couldn't get paid as much as he used to.

Because he'd auctioned off everything we owned so he could plug more money into the orchestra to keep it alive.

I hated the orchestra, and Emerson Hall, and everything associated with either of those things—including the Maestro—more than I could possibly put into words.

So I drew the hate instead. I drew everything. That's why my sketchpad got a place of honor right beside my bed.

"I'll be back later, Nonnie." I shoved the Maestro's money into my pocket, tied one of Nonnie's scarves over my hair, and slammed on my sunglasses—the glamorous, cat-eyed ones Mom had bought for me. Like those actresses from the black-and-white movies wore, like Audrey Hepburn and Lauren Bacall. Mom loved those movies.

"They're so elegant," she'd say, hugging me on the sofa while we sipped milk through crazy straws. "You know? The way they talk and walk and dress. It's like a dream."

"Uh-huh." I didn't get what the big deal was about Cary Grant. I thought he talked kind of funny, honestly. But I'd say whatever Mom wanted to hear.

It made me kind of sick, to think about that now. How did I never see it, right there in front of me? That someday she would leave me?

I shut my eyes on that thought and pretended to squeeze it away. I didn't like feeling mad at Mom, like if I got too mad, she'd sense it. She'd be right outside with her suitcase, ready to come back to us, and then she'd feel how mad I was and change her mind. She'd walk away, forever this time.

It was easier to get angry at the Maestro. After all, if it wasn't for him, Mom might still be around.

"Where are you going, *ombralina*?" Nonnie asked as I headed out the door.

"Shopping."

If the Maestro wouldn't take care of us, I would. And if he wouldn't give me and Nonnie a real home, I'd do my best to make us one.

There was this charity store right off Arlington at Clark Street. It had a soup kitchen and a food store, clothes, and household goods. I walked there as fast as possible, huddling beneath my scarf and sunglasses. If I had to go there, no way was anyone going to recognize me. The thought of going there made me want to smash things, or maybe just huddle up in Mom's quilt and never come out.

I'd never had to shop at a charity store before. No one I knew had ever had to either. I'd have to go back to school in two days being the girl who shops at a charity store. On top of the girl whose father is going crazy, who draws weird pictures all the time, who lives in a symphony hall like some kind of stray animal.

The girl whose mom left.

CHAPTER 2

*T*HIS IS WHAT I GOT AT THE CLARK STREET charity store:

1) a pack of multicolored construction paper, for decorating our ugly gray walls

2) soup, pasta, milk, bread, a bag of potatoes

3) two pairs of flip-flops for me and Nonnie, for when we showered at the Y a couple blocks over (there weren't any showers at Emerson Hall, just toilets with rust around the rims)

4) for Nonnie: a new green scarf with gold flowers on it

5) for school: a couple of spiral notebooks, folders, pens, pencils

I felt a little bad about buying the scarf for Nonnie. I guess it wasn't totally necessary; she had dozens, and I could have used that money to get some spiral notebooks with designs on them instead of the plain ones. But Nonnie didn't have a lot going on in her life. She played with her scarves and slept and read the three books she owned over and over, and played Solitaire with a deck of cards that had a bunch missing, so

I'd had to re-create the missing ones on index cards.

Plus, Nonnie was so small. She seemed smaller, older, and more wrinkled in the buzzing fluorescent lights backstage at Emerson Hall than she'd ever seemed before. It scared me. Kind of like how I got scared when I let myself think about where Mom might have gone. Was she happy? Or was she small and lonely, like Nonnie would be if she didn't have me?

The day before school started was a Monday. After lunch that day, I went to The Happy Place, a tea shop across the street from the Hall.

Mom started taking me there for muffins and juice when I was little, and I'd kept going even after she left. It had bright yellow walls, a bright orange door, blue lamps, and THE HAPPY PLACE written in swirly black letters above the door. On either side of it was Antonio's Shoe Repair, which had been boarded up for over a year, and a dingy gray apartment building, so The Happy Place stood out like sunshine.

"Mr. B?" I called out, stepping inside. Gerald the parrot cawed at me from his perch in the corner. I waved at him and he bobbed his head, dancing around on one leg.

Mr. Barsky popped his head up above the counter. "Why, Olivia, *ma belle*! *Bonjour, ma petite belle!* And how are you zis fine Monday?"

Not even Mr. Barsky's silly fake accents could make me smile today. See, he used to be an actor. He'd never "made

14

it," as they say, but he claimed accents were his specialty, so he put on these accents all the time and pretended to be different characters. This guy, the French guy, was Ricardo.

"Isn't 'Ricardo' a Spanish name?" I'd asked him once.

He'd leaned close and waggled his eyebrows. "Ricardo is . . . a mystery, Olivia."

"Hey, Ricardo," I said, slumping onto a stool at the counter.

"Why, whatever is ze matter, mademoiselle?" Mr. Barsky flung his towel over his shoulder and started rummaging through the pastry displays. "When people wear expressions like yours, I always say, ah! Time for *une crepe*! Or, *un biscuit chocolat*!"

Mrs. Barsky came out of the kitchen with a big steaming pitcher. She clinked when she walked because she liked to wear miles of beads around her neck. Today they were a shiny ocean-green color. Her hair was silver and stuck up everywhere, and her nails were painted ten different colors, one for each finger.

"Olivia!" Mrs. Barsky said. "What a pleasure. It's been a while. What'll it be? Raspberry tea? Mango juice?"

"Actually, I can't have anything." I looked around, starting to sweat. There were only two other people here, two guys by the window chatting over some book. "I was wondering if I could work here? Just for a while, maybe."

I didn't want to keep waiting on crumpled twenties from the Maestro. Besides, who knew how long he'd keep giving them to me?

The Barskys looked at each other, and then at me. Mr. Barsky closed the pastry case.

"You need a job?" Mrs. Barsky asked.

"Well. Yeah." I cleared my throat, trying to figure out how I could somehow melt into the cracks in the floor so no one would ever have to look at me again. "See, we sold our house this summer. We moved into the Hall, backstage, and we just have these suitcases, and the orchestra's running out of money. You know, with The Economy and everything."

I wasn't too sure what The Economy involved, but everyone had been talking about it lately, and I knew it was something about no one having any money. Whenever grown-ups talked about it, a shadow fell over them, like they'd just heard terrible news.

"Oh, Olivia." Mrs. Barsky said that in this sad, sighing voice. I couldn't look at her. Instead, I pulled one of my charcoals from my bag and started scratching a doodle on a napkin. I took my charcoals with me everywhere.

"It's just that I have to buy groceries, you know? And things for school, probably. And the Maestro doesn't help too much. I can wipe off tables." I dug the tip of my charcoal into the napkin. "I can wash dishes, sweep. I could probably bake cookies or something too."

Mr. Barsky put his hand on my hand so I had to stop drawing. "Of course you can work for us, Olivia," he said, with his normal voice, which was warm and scratchy like wool. "We'd be glad for the help. How does twenty dollars a week sound? You can come in after school."

I cleared my throat. "I can only come in Mondays through Thursdays. Once the season starts, I've got to be around on concert nights. Nonnie likes me to be there."

"Of course," said Mrs. Barsky.

"And I can probably only stay for a little bit after school." My voice got quieter and quieter, until I almost couldn't even hear myself. "You know, because of homework, and I've got to make dinner and get Nonnie ready for bed. And I've got to have some drawing time."

I didn't feel bad talking about drawing to the Barskys. I used to go to The Happy Place all the time to draw. The green star-shaped table in the corner was my spot. Sometimes Mr. Barsky would waltz by between serving people and leave me an oatmeal raisin cookie.

"How about just half an hour after school?" Mrs. Barsky suggested. "Maybe forty-five minutes if it's busy and you don't have too much homework?"

"Perfect," I whispered. "Thanks."

Mr. Barsky patted my hand, and Gerald squawked because new people were coming in, some college kids from the university. I dug out my sunglasses and shoved them on so maybe they wouldn't look at me.

"Here," Mrs. Barsky said, on my way out the door. She put a twenty-dollar bill into my hand and folded my fingers over it. "Consider it a signing bonus. Go get yourself something nice, all right? A pick-me-up?"

I shifted back and forth from one foot to the other. If I didn't get out of there that very second, I'd start crying like some kind of pathetic baby.

"Thanks, Mrs. B," I said, and hurried out the door.

The only good thing about living in the Hall is that it had lots of staircases and sculptures and weird architecture I could use to practice drawing.

I shoved the Barskys' twenty-dollar bill into my clothes box, beneath my underwear where nobody would go looking for it. Then I headed for the grand staircases in the main lobby. Today I planned to practice drawing steps, and the ones on the grand staircases were tricky because they curved.

On my way through the west lobby, I peeked inside the Hall's propped-open doors.

A bunch of people were milling around onstage, chatting and setting out their music, blowing warm air into the cold metal tubes of their instruments.

The musicians were back.

Summer was off-season for the orchestra, like how football teams don't play in the spring. Some orchestras still had concerts during the summer, but special ones, like pops concerts and concerts for kids.

We didn't have the money for things like that, though. Instead, the Hall had stayed locked up all summer, except for when the Maestro came here to root through the music

18

library and "get some peace and quiet." I'm not sure what he needed peace and quiet for; our house had been quiet ever since I woke up the morning Mom left, when I'd found the Maestro sitting at the kitchen table with a cup of cold coffee and his head in his hands.

Normally, I'd have gone to say hi to the musicians—given Hilda Hightower a hug, let Richard Ashley ruffle my hair, which always gave my stomach these weird floaty flips because he'd smile at me when he did it.

But not today. Today, I stayed in the shadows. If the musicians didn't already know about us selling the house and moving backstage, they'd know soon. And I didn't want to see them looking sorry for me, or hear how awful it all was, or—even worse—how everything would be okay.

I heard voices coming from around the corner, and slid back against the wall behind a pillar. The Maestro and Richard Ashley entered the Hall from the lobby.

"Maestro," Richard was saying, "you can't be serious." He looked furious. "This is no place for a twelve-year-old girl to live, much less an eighty-year-old woman."

"I had no choice," the Maestro said.

Some of the musicians onstage paused at the commotion. The Maestro clapped his hands. "What are you staring at? We start in five!"

"Maestro. *Otto*," Richard whispered. "Are things really that bad?"

"Yes." The Maestro ran his hands through his oily black

hair. "If this season goes as badly as last season . . . I don't know what will happen. The numbers don't look good. Donations are down. Even our regulars don't have money to give these days." He shoved his hands in his pockets. "We just need a year. A year to get back on our feet. Things will get better. Next year will be different, and I'll move Olivia and her grandmother back uptown. We just need a little time."

"Do you really think things will change this year?" Richard said.

The Maestro looked at him, not saying anything. Then he headed for the stage.

When he was gone, Richard sighed. I must have moved or something, because his eyes narrowed and he peered behind my pillar.

"Olivia!" He flashed me a smile, the one Mom had always said to watch out for, because it was "pure trumpet player," and trumpet players could be real charmers, whatever that meant. "How was your summer?"

I wanted to shrivel up and die. I could tell he was worried I'd heard him and the Maestro talking; his voice sounded bright, and too happy. Why had I let him *see* me?

"You know. It was all right." I folded my arms over my sketchpad and hugged it tight. "I drew a lot."

"I would expect nothing less from my favorite artist. You'll have to show me your new work sometime."

My cheeks turned hot. "Okay."

"So, Olivia." Richard got this weird look on his face. He cleared his throat and looked back at the stage. I saw Hilda Hightower polishing the bell of her French horn. I saw Michael Orlov wheeling out his double bass. Hilda waved at me. I waved back and hoped they wouldn't come over. I started inching away.

"I just want to check on you," Richard said.

"About what?"

"Your dad told us what happened this summer. With your house, and the move."

My stomach flipped, but not in a good way. "Oh. Yeah."

"I'm so sorry to hear about this, Olivia." Richard squeezed my hand. "I really don't know what to say. Your dad said you're living backstage now."

It was even worse hearing it said out loud, but I would *not* cry in front of Richard Ashley. "Yeah. That's right."

"It's *not* right, though. Don't you have family or friends you could stay with?"

I'd thought about that before. "No. The Maestro's family is in Italy, except for Nonnie, and Mom's family . . . they don't talk to us. They've never liked us. They didn't want Mom to marry Da—the Maestro. And the Maestro doesn't have friends." My fingers tightened around the edges of my sketchpad. "He doesn't keep up with people. All he can think about is the orchestra."

Richard got quiet for a minute, and then he put his hands on my shoulders. Normally this would have sent my stomach into floaty-flip overload, but now it just made me feel sick.

"Olivia," Richard said, "I know you probably don't like us a whole lot right now, but we're here for you. You know that, right? The whole orchestra is here for you and your dad and your grandma."

That was too much. The orchestra was *here* for me? The orchestra was the whole reason this was happening.

I shrugged him off me. "Yeah, I know."

"If you ever need to talk to someone, you can always talk to me. Okay?" He held up his fist for our secret handshake. *"Capisce?"*

I shook my head and looked away. "Yeah, okay."

"What?" Richard put a hand to his heart. "No secret handshake? You wound me, madam."

"No." No stupid secret handshake. If he didn't stop talking to me, I was definitely going to cry.

"Maybe we can work something out. Maybe you can spend the night at Hilda's place now and then, or with any of the girls, really. They'd love to have you. It'd be like a slumber party. You could invite your friends."

"I don't have friends."

"Olivia. What can I do? Anything?"

He felt so sorry for me; I heard it in his voice. But it didn't make me feel better. It made me feel about two inches tall.

"Leave me alone," I whispered. "Please?" Then I hurried away in the other direction, into the main lobby and up one of the grand staircases. I threw myself down near the top, on a step with the carpet rubbed through to the wood under-neath, and yanked out my sketchpad.

"Slumber party." I wiped my eyes. That's what the Maestro had said too. *It'll be like a, what is the term? A slumber party. Every night, all of us backstage. It will be an adventure, Olivia.*

Why couldn't I stop sniffling? At least Richard couldn't see me up here. "Adventure. Yeah. Some adventure."

All I wanted was to go home—our real home, with the blue door and the yellow kitchen, and the creaky ninth step on the stairs that went up to my room. And Mom. Mom had to be there too, or else it was no good.

As I thought of our house a gust of cold rushed past me. It was the kind of cold that lingers, settling deep in your bones. I shivered and rubbed warmth back into my arms. I could have sworn someone was watching me; I felt eyes on my skin. But when I looked around, I saw only the familiar, dusty portraits of dead musicians on the walls and the faded angels on the ceiling.

And a black cat, staring up calmly from the lobby floor.

CHAPTER 3

*I*T WAS A FAT BLACK TOMCAT WITH CROOKED gray whiskers and patches of matted hair all over his body. His tail flicked slowly back and forth.

I slid my sketchpad back into my bag and started inching down the stairs. "Here, kitty, kitty. Here, cat."

At the bottom of the stairs, I put out my hand, knelt down, and waited. One of the Hall's front doors stood open. I must not have shut it all the way when I came back from The Happy Place.

"Thought you'd just come in and make yourself comfortable, huh?" I said to the cat.

His tail twitched. He butted his head into my fingertips.

"You know, some people might call that trespassing."

The cat watched me as I petted the scruff of his neck, like he couldn't believe he was actually allowing this to happen.

"You're kind of ugly," I said, tilting my head for a better look.

The cat narrowed his bright green eyes at me.

"And fat."

The cat yawned.

"But your hair is black. I like that." I pulled a section of my hair over my eyes. "See? Mine is too. You're a little shadow, like me. Nonnie calls me that, but in Italian. It's *ombralina*."

The cat got this expression on his face that looked exactly like someone saying, *Fascinating. And by that I mean, you're boring me.*

I sat back on my heels. "You have a great face, cat. Real expressive."

At least one of us does, he seemed to say as he flicked his left ear. He plopped down on his belly and stared at me through half-open eyes.

I plopped down on my belly too, watching him. "You have a home, cat?"

The cat started cleaning his paw. I figured he meant: *Not really. Here and there. Mostly nowhere.*

"Yeah. Me too. Well, my home is here, anyway. In the Hall. Which is basically nowhere because it doesn't count."

Why doesn't it count? If the cat could have talked, that's what he would have said. He would have sat there, just like this, and listened to me, and asked me all the right questions. His voice would sound kind of like Cary Grant's, all weird and halfway British. Mom would have liked that.

"Because I hate it here," I whispered. "The Maestro said

it would be an adventure, but it's not. It's just this prison. It's ugly and it's embarrassing."

The cat rolled over and looked at me upside down.

"Who's the Maestro?" I rolled over on my back too. Staring at him like this made my head hurt, but it was kind of fun. "Well, *technically*, he's half my DNA. But I don't like to think about that."

The cat blinked slowly, like he was already half asleep.

"I mean, I guess, yeah, he's my *father*." I made quotation marks with my fingers. "On paper, maybe. But not to me. I've disowned him, I guess you could say." I paused, tapping my feet together. "Everyone at school thinks I'm crazy these days, you know. Because of my clothes and because I draw all the time instead of talking to people. I guess by talking to a cat I'm proving them right."

I sighed. "I don't know what's worse, talking to myself or talking to a cat." I pulled the cat onto my chest. "Oof. You really are fat."

The cat's eyes narrowed. I'm sure he was just sleepy, but I took it to mean: *You're not a very polite hostess.*

"But we're still friends, right?"

His ears flicked. *Friends? That's presumptuous of you.*

I scratched under his chin.

The cat stretched out his neck and closed his eyes. *Oh. Keep that up and we may have something.*

I snorted. "You might be the cutest thing ever."

"Hey, cool," a voice said from above. "You found a cat."

I scrambled up into a sitting position and faced the voice: red hair, tons of freckles, stupid ears that stuck out.

Henry Page.

Ugh.

Henry's parents started dropping him off for concerts a couple of years ago, and eventually he'd begged his way into an usher job—just a part-time thing, and it didn't pay much, but you'd think it was heaven on Earth the way Henry took to it. Now he was one of the two ushers left. Everyone else had quit a long time ago, except for ninety-something-year-old Archie, who was basically a walking corpse.

Henry was in my grade at school. He played baseball and ran track. He made good grades because he studied a lot, but somehow he still got to sit at the popular table at lunch, which were two things I didn't think ever went together. But they did for Henry because Henry was perfect. His whole life was perfect. It was so perfect that I had to make a Reasons to Dislike Henry Page list and keep it in my sketchpad so I could look at it whenever I caught myself thinking that it might actually be okay to like him.

The only things that weren't perfect about him were his millions of freckles and the fact that his ears stuck out. One day last February, people kept coming up to me at school, saying, "Sorry about your mom, Olivia." "Man, that really sucks, Olivia." "Why'd she leave, anyway?" Someone had blabbed, and it hadn't been me. The last thing I wanted was for everyone to find out my family secrets. The blabber had to have been Henry, who was always hanging around the Hall and learning everybody's business. So I drew this picture of Henry looking like an elephant, with red hair sticking out everywhere and freckles all over his trunk and ears hanging to the ground. I'd labeled it DUMBO PAGE and hung it on Henry's locker.

All that had done was make people give me nasty looks instead of asking about Mom. Then they'd started ignoring me altogether.

See, that picture couldn't hurt Henry, even though it was the best elephant I'd ever drawn. Everyone at school loved Henry Page.

Everyone except me.

"Where'd you find him?" Henry said, bending down to pet the cat. The cat started to purr.

Traitor.

"None of your business." I slung the cat over my shoulder and stalked away, toward backstage. Sounds of the orchestra tuning drifted out through the Hall doors.

"So, I heard your dad talking to Richard earlier." Henry was hot on my heels.

"Go away, Henry."

"Something about your family moving backstage? It sounded pretty rough. Are you okay?"

"Go away, Henry."

But he wouldn't give up. "I'm really sorry that happened,

CLAIRE LEGRAND

Olivia. I don't . . . well, I know we're not great friends or anything, but did you want to go get an ice cream or something? Donatello's is having a back-to-school deal, and I just got my allowance."

I stopped so abruptly that Henry almost ran into me. We were in the west lobby, right by the cracked violinist fountain, which hadn't worked for years.

"Listen, Henry. Butt out, okay? Stop eavesdropping and sticking your nose into other people's business. Why do you care, anyway? Don't you know you're supposed to hate me?"

"Why am I supposed to hate you?"

I rolled my eyes. "Remember? That picture?"

"Oh. Right. The elephant." He shrugged. "Well, I don't hate you. I know you did it because you think I told everyone about your mom."

I stepped back. "What? How do you know that?"

"I just assumed."

"Well, you know what they say about assuming."

Henry rolled his eyes. "I didn't tell anyone, by the way. I don't know who did, but people would have found out eventually anyway. Lots of people have family problems."

"Oh, yeah? And what do you know about family problems, Mr. Perfect?"

Henry got this weird look on his face, but he didn't get a chance to answer. The orchestra started playing Tchaik 4 — those big opening notes in the French horns and trumpets that sound like the end of the world. And because I was a conductor's daughter, my brain recited to itself, automatically: *This is the Fate theme.*

Fate: when things happen to you that you can't control, also known as "destiny." Fate happens, and you deal with it the best you can.

The cat hissed at something behind me. The sound of it — and the sudden rush of cold around me — threw chills across my skin.

Behind me, the heavy metal door that led to the basement started rattling on its hinges, like someone was on the other side, trying to break it down.

"K EPLER NEVER LEAVES THE BASEMENT unlocked," Henry whispered.

Old Kepler was the cleaning guy, and Henry was right — Kepler never left it unlocked. He was obsessed with security.

"Don't want no hooligans down there," he'd grumble. Like there was something in the basement worth stealing.

But someone *was* down there now. Uneven steps stomped up the basement stairs. Dark shapes curled out from behind the door — along the sides, along the bottom. Long, thin, shadowy shapes.

Like fingers.

The cat clawed his way out of my arms and bolted away, yowling like crazy.

The basement door blew open, slamming into the wall. Arctic cold rushed out, nearly blowing us over. Then a second gust of icy air barreled past us from behind, hitting my arm and Henry's leg. That one *did* blow us over. My head thudded against the floor, knocking my teeth together. I looked up just in time to see a long, thin black shape seep into the darkness of the basement stairs.

Hovering there on the threshold, a dark shadow roiled. It wasn't an ordinary shadow, though. It looked heavy, solid, *real*. And it was shaped like a human — but a deformed human with a too-long neck and too-long limbs, shifting like a black puddle from one shape to the next.

"Olivia?" Henry tugged on my sleeve.

"No sudden movements, Henry," I said, my eyes fixed on the shadowy figure. More than anything, I wanted to draw it. But I'd have to get out of there alive first, and the feeling seeping off the shadow, like poison, was not good. It was wrong, it was *evil*. "Just back up, slowly."

"No, Olivia, *look*."

I turned around, and I saw the gray man.

He stood behind us. *Drifted* behind us. He had legs and feet, but they looked like you could blow them away with a good sneeze. He didn't have much of a face — a shimmering mass of gray smoke, shifting into shape after shape after shape — a long nose, then a bulbous nose, then no nose at all. His eyes were black, swirling holes the size of saucers. His mouth gaped open wide as a dinner plate, but he had no teeth, just a bottomless pit between his lips.

I opened my mouth to scream, but nothing came out. It was exactly like what happens in nightmares.

And it got worse.

The gray man rushed right at us. He reached us in the blink

of an eye, jerking forward like an old movie with bad film.

Then he was rushing right *through* us.

It shouldn't have been possible, but I felt the gray man oozing through us like a wintry breeze, except this breeze somehow got into my skin, my blood, my bones. I couldn't breathe.

I reached for Henry. He was doing the same thing, grabbing at me like he was drowning.

And the gray man wasn't alone.

More gray, smoky shapes rushed to join him. Three more, to be precise. As each one passed through us—like we were nothing, like *they* were nothing—I struggled not to pass out from the cold that squeezed my insides.

Together, Henry and I stumbled away, trying to run, before I realized the gray shapes were *herding* us toward the basement. Toward that shadow thing with its pointy black fingers. The shadow shrank back as we approached it. Then, it *shrieked*.

"What is it?" Henry clapped his hands to his ears.

I couldn't answer, watching the shadow shrink back down the basement stairs, in full retreat. Its awful screams wedged beneath my fingernails, in my teeth, shaking me to the core.

The basement door slammed shut.

Silence, except for the orchestra playing.

The shadow was gone.

The four gray figures, suddenly alone, flitted away like

scared rabbits—one into the ceiling, two through the wall, and one—the original gray man—sinking through the floor. Right before he disappeared, he winked at me.

Henry and I jumped to our feet and ran, shoving each other to go faster. Soon we were outside, tearing down the wide gray steps that led from the Hall down to Arlington Avenue, and then we were almost getting run over by a cab.

The wail of its horn brought us to a halt. The wind of its passing tires shot goosebumps up my arms. Suddenly, we stood in sunlight and skyscrapers. The spice of a nearby food cart stung my eyes.

"Watch it!" the cab driver shouted out his open window.

Henry put his hands on his knees, catching his breath. "What *was* that?"

I smoothed my fingers over my arms. Little red lines marked my skin from where the cat had clawed me. Then I felt something weird, a rough patch of skin. I turned my arm over and saw the black spot.

Right where the cold thing had slammed into me, knocking me to the ground, a splotchy black mark glittered in the sunlight. It almost looked like a burn, dark as that shadow by the basement.

"What the . . ." Henry inspected a similar black spot on his right calf. "Olivia, what is this?"

I probed the burn mark with one finger. It sizzled, colder than ice against my fingertip, the skin rough and scratchy.

"Olivia?"

Henry watched me expectantly. A new light shone in his eyes that I didn't like. I recognized that look. A few brave souls last spring, mostly new kids, had sometimes approached me in the cafeteria with that look in their eyes. They would think, "Could this be a new friend?"

One look from me was usually enough to dispel them for good.

Shadows, after all, don't have friends.

Especially not friends like Perfect Henry Page.

I gathered myself and drew down the shades. That's what I called it when I hardened everything about me from my eyes to the way I was standing, so people would leave me be. It's like when you draw down the shades of your window to keep out all the sunlight.

"I don't know what you're talking about," I said to Henry.

"Are you kidding me? We just saw—"

I shrugged. "I didn't see anything." Then I walked backstage alone. Henry didn't follow me. Maybe he was too scared to come back inside.

But he was right: We *had* seen something. For the rest of the day, I caught myself drumming my fingers against the burn. It stung when I touched it, but I couldn't stop messing with it, like when you just have to keep wiggling a loose tooth even though it makes your gums sore.

Something had left its mark on both me and Henry. And another *something* had saved us from whatever lay beyond the basement door.

I didn't know what this meant, but my sketching hand itched to find out. My head swam with images of shadow fingers and gaping black mouths.

What had happened? What had we seen?

One word kept whispering through my head as a possible answer:

Ghosts.

 I DIDN'T SLEEP MUCH THAT NIGHT. THE NEXT morning I'd have to go back to school, and I wasn't sure which was scarier to think about: school, or the ghosts.

Every time a sound rustled through the cracked door of my bedroom, or Nonnie shifted in her bed, I sat up, listening hard.

I kept seeing those shadow fingers curling out from underneath the basement door. The feeling of those gray, foggy shapes rushing through me lingered all through the night. I couldn't stop shivering. I couldn't stop thinking about Mom—what she would think, how she'd make me feel better.

I couldn't stop peeking at the burn on my arm either.

After a while, I got tired of tossing and turning, so I took a few deep breaths and headed into the kitchen. Underneath the flickering fluorescent light, I examined my burn.

Yes, there it was, glittering again. It caught the overhead light like I had a million tiny prisms embedded in my skin.

"Beautiful," I whispered. "It's beautiful."

"Olivia?"

I jumped, stubbing my toe on the sink. The Maestro stood just past the light, rubbing his eyes.

"What do you want?" I said.

"What are you doing up?"

"Nothing." I shifted my burned arm behind me. "Getting some water."

"Are you—?" He cleared his throat, slicked down his hair. "Did you have a bad dream?"

"My *life's* a bad dream."

Then I stalked past him back to my room. He didn't follow me.

I grabbed my umbrella from under my bed and tucked it into the sheets with me. If ghosts *did* come after me, it probably wouldn't do much good. But it made me feel better to have it, to hold it tight and pretend like it made me safer.

Sometimes you have to lie to yourself like that. Sometimes that's how you get through things.

The next day, when I woke up, the cat had returned.

He was cleaning himself, perched on the metal footrail of my cot much more gracefully than such a large cat should have been able to perch. I stared at him, too afraid to move because then he might disappear again. My heart still pounded from the night of strange dreams I'd had—dreams of gray shapes and black shadows and terrible shrieks.

Dreams of ghosts.

 38

Don't think this means anything, said the cat's bored expression. *I'm keeping you around as a curiosity, pet. This isn't romantic.*

"Don't go." I stretched my hand out one slow inch at a time. "Don't go, you weird cat. Please?"

The cat's whiskers twitched. *Of course I'm not going anywhere. If I were going anywhere, why would I have come here in the first place?* He sat down after circling once to inspect the area, then blinked at me. *Idiot.*

I smiled.

"Is a strange name, 'Weird Cat'," said Nonnie, from across the room. She sat up in bed, swaying, like someone was playing a waltz only for her. "Is that his name? *Gatto, gatto.*"

"Put your scarf on, Nonnie." I didn't like seeing Nonnie like that, without some kind of scarf on her naked head.

"Which scarf?"

"The yellow one with the blue polka dots."

"Oh, I like that one, Olivia!"

"I know."

"So, is that his name, *ombralina*? Weird Cat?"

I pulled on my boots to go use the bathroom. I had these scuffed black army boots I wore everywhere, and we couldn't trust the plumbing in this place. "I don't think so. That's kind of quirky, but it's not him."

"Igor."

"What?"

Nonnie smiled at me. Her eyes nearly disappeared in wrinkles. "His name. Igor."

"Igor?"

"Like Stravinsky!"

I made a face. "I am *not* naming him after a composer, Nonnie."

Nonnie clasped her hands under her chin. "I love Stravinsky! *Molte bene!*" Then she started to hum the trumpet solo from *Petrushka*.

I scowled. It was difficult to argue with Nonnie when she looked so happy. Plus, Stravinsky wasn't the absolute worst or anything. His music was odd and sometimes disturbing. I wondered if he had been a "little shadow" when he was a kid too.

"Fine." I sighed. "If you really think so."

The cat jumped down next to me, butting his head against my boot. *Well? Are we going to brave the plumbing together or aren't we?*

"Igor, Igor!" Nonnie cried, throwing up her hands.

And so, his name was Igor.

I walked to school alone, getting more nauseated with every step.

School wasn't always so bad. It used to just be school, with homework and people messing around in the halls and passing notes in class. I always decorated my notes with elaborate drawings and folded them into origami shapes, like Mom had taught me. Once, when Mr. Fitch had caught me passing a note, he'd taken it up and asked to see me after class.

"If I catch you doing this again, Olivia, I'll have to give you detention," he had said. "You need to pay attention. You need to take notes. Sixth grade is a big year, an important year. Do you understand?"

Every year was an important year, according to every teacher I'd ever had. It got exhausting after a while. "Yeah. I get it. I'm sorry."

Then he had sighed and turned the origami swan over and over in his hands. It had swirls and stars and forests all over it, like a quilt of sketches. "But this is quite beautiful, Olivia." He had handed the swan to me and smiled. "You should do something with that. You really should."

But now? Since Mom left? I think I became a shadow at school more than anywhere else.

People just didn't get me anymore. That's how I wanted it to be. I'd *made* it happen, in fact. It was embarrassing to be the girl whose Mom left her without even a good-bye. So I'd done my best to turn invisible. Like a sketch of me with my mouth sewn shut and my face scribbled over. That's what I had created. No hot, bubbly feelings spilling out. No humiliating family secrets blurted out by mistake. No random screaming fits. I felt like doing that a lot—just throwing my head up to the sky and letting a scream rip out.

But people generally don't approve of random screaming fits, even when they might be perfectly justified.

I even looked like a shadow. Short, skinny half-Italian girl with long black hair. Wearing my favorite striped socks (which I wore with everything) and my boots (ditto), whatever faded clothes I had left (I'd thrown out all the bright colors, keeping only the darks and the blacks), or whatever I found at the charity store. Shabby old jacket. Hair covering my eyes. Head buried in a sketchpad.

And now one of Nonnie's scarves tied around my arm to hide my burn.

I used to have friends. Not real friends, I guess, but the kind you sit with at lunch and sometimes have sleepovers with, the kind you pass notes to in class.

But friends don't stick around if you don't talk to them. Not even halfway friends do that. Some of them tried for a while: "Hi, Olivia. How'd you do on the test?" "Olivia! Can you do one of those pen tattoos on my arm?" "Olivia? Are you okay? I heard about your mom."

At first, I gave them one- or two-word answers. Then I stopped giving them any answers at all.

Before long, I sat by myself at lunch. I sat by myself in class, even though I was surrounded by twenty other kids. I was by myself everywhere. It was easier that way.

My sketchpad was a better friend than anyone else could be, anyway. As I turned off Gable Street and passed through the concrete courtyard of James S. Killough

Intermediate School, I held my sketchpad tightly to my chest. Like a shield.

For a few days, everything went just like it was supposed to. I went to school. Class. Lunch. I watched for Henry and went the other way whenever I saw that bright red hair. I kept my head down and scribbled notes as much as I needed to so my teachers wouldn't get suspicious. I went to The Happy Place after school and wiped tables and washed dishes. And the rest of the time, I drew.

Mostly, I drew ghosts.

I looked everywhere for them, every night—in the restrooms, in the rooms backstage, underneath every row of seats.

Nothing. Not one shadow finger, not one gray foot.

The picture I had of them in my head was pretty fuzzy, so I kept drawing them over and over, trying to capture the memory of them on the page. It wasn't working very well; it's harder than you might think to draw just the right amount of transparency, of driftiness. And those black eyes of theirs—I couldn't quite get them black enough.

But, ghosts or no, my burn stayed the same, dark and glittering.

Henry didn't talk to me for a whole week, although I always felt him watching me with this thoughtful look on his face, like I was his homework and he had to figure me out. The Maestro and the office staff, they all let him hang out at the Hall even when he wasn't working. He'd camp out in the middle of the floor seats and do his algebra problems like it was his living room couch or something.

The dork.

Then, the Thursday of the second week of school, Mark Everett decided I'd had enough time to myself, I guess, and started hollering at me across the cafeteria. Mark Everett was one of those boys who probably picked at scabs till they got infected. He just couldn't leave people alone.

"Hey, what's the deal, Olivia?" He was sitting a few tables away from me. Henry's table. "Why so gloooomy, Olivia? Why so *sad*?"

The boys at the table laughed, except for Henry. He just kept chewing his sandwich. Heads all across the cafeteria turned to see what was happening.

"You going to a funeral or something, Olivia? Why you gotta wear so much black, Emooo olivia? Get it?"

Mark was truly cracking himself up over there. I sat at my table, alone, and started drawing. I wasn't so hungry anymore.

A noise across from me made me look up. It was Joan Dawson. We'd gone to school together since kindergarten, but we'd never really talked or anything. All I knew was that Joan's family was rich, and that she liked to make signs and hold one-woman protests in the courtyard outside. You know, antiwar stuff and antifascism stuff, things like that. The teachers called her *precocious*. And sometimes, when they thought no one was listening, *obnoxious*.

Joan was usually by herself too. But she didn't seem to care. I tried not to care, but every now and then I could feel it creeping up on me, sending this awful, sinking, lonely feeling into the pit of my stomach.

"You shouldn't listen to them, you know," Joan said. She tossed her shiny brown hair like the way people do in magazines. Joan would have probably been popular, if she'd cared about things like that. "They're *plebeian*."

I frowned. "What does that mean?" Mr. Henry Perfect would probably know.

"It means common. Vulgar." Joan sniffed. "Anyway, don't worry about it. Okay? You're above all that. You're an artist."

"Whatever." I turned back to my drawing. Joan ate her salad in silence.

It was the most I'd said at school all week.

THE NIGHT OF THE OPENING CONCERT OF THE season, I crept up the west utility staircase like usual. A heavy metal door at the top marked the way to the catwalk, this black metal walkway that stretched from one side of the Hall to the other.

It wasn't that I liked listening to the orchestra or seeing the Maestro flail his arms around. It's just that the catwalk was my favorite spot to hide and spy and draw. I could see everything from up there—the different levels of seats, the aisles and exits, the choir loft, the pipe organ loft. The plaster of the ceiling peeling away in curls. The cobwebs stretching across the rafters.

Rails along the sides of the catwalk kept you from falling off. Crisscrossed metal gates blocked off where it wasn't safe to step.

Igor didn't mind the metal gates; he slunk around wherever he wanted to, purring the whole time. *I bet I could do this with my eyes closed, you know.*

"I'm sure you could. Show-off."

Ghost hunting with Heny is not what I had in mind.

Larry and the other stage technician, Ed, came up a few minutes later. I liked Larry and Ed. They kept to themselves; they never asked a lot of questions. If they knew about where I lived now, they didn't show it.

"Here to watch the show, eh, Olivia?" Larry said.

"I guess." I rested my chin on my sketchpad and pressed my face to the railing. Below me, tonight's audience was starting to trickle in. Most of them wore normal clothes, but some of them, the die-hards, wore furs and gowns, jewelry that blinked at me like stars.

There weren't very many of them. Part of me wanted to be happy about that; I knew such a small audience would embarrass the Maestro.

The other part of me, deep in my gut, felt afraid and kind of sick. I thought of Nonnie, tiny and frail, legs thin as a bird's. I'd settled her on a chair by the television monitor in the rehearsal room. The monitor showed everything happening onstage. That's how she liked watching the concerts.

What if anything ever happened to her? What if she got sick?

I chewed on my lip, staring down at the empty seats. We needed a big audience, not a small one.

We needed the money.

The musicians drifted out onto the stage. After the week of rehearsals they'd had, they didn't even chat or make jokes with one another. When they started warming up, it seemed like someone had turned down the volume on a giant remote control, like they were afraid to play too loudly. I saw people seated in the dress circle, the die-hards in their furs and coat-tails, whispering to each other behind their programs.

I'm sure everyone had heard the rumors—about the lack of money, about how there were fewer concerts this year, about Maestro Stellatella living in the back of the Hall and how the orchestra was generally going downhill.

Probably most of them had come tonight just to see if it was true, like when you see a car accident, and you feel bad about looking but you just can't help it.

When the Maestro walked out and the orchestra stood to acknowledge him, I heard barely any applause from the audience. When the orchestra sat back down, their chairs squeaked, instruments clanging against their music stands.

Scanning quickly, I found Richard Ashley's sandy brown head in the back row. He looked like anything but a charmer at the moment. His ears were red. He was sweating. I wished I could reach down and hide him from everyone's stares.

The Maestro raised his hands, and the concert began.

Normally, I would have jammed on my headphones and listened to what Nonnie called my "angry music" while I sketched the night away, but tonight I would be on the look-out for ghosts. The first time I'd seen them had been during the orchestra's rehearsal. Maybe they'd show up during the concert, too.

Even as I thought the word *ghosts*, my burn twinged, like

it was hungry, like it was ready to jump right off my skin.

First, they played *Francesca da Rimini*, by Tchaikovsky. That piece is actually all right, as orchestra music goes. It's about Hell, and ghosts who have to live there and can't ever leave.

At intermission, I shared peanut butter and jelly sandwiches with Larry and Ed, and then the second half of the concert began. Larry and Ed left me for a bathroom break, and I used this opportunity to pace the catwalk, careful not to ripple the curtains.

I paced until my calves were sore from tiptoeing and my eyes burned from squinting. But there was nothing—no ghosts, no shadows beyond the normal ones.

With a huff, I sat back down on the catwalk, glaring at the Maestro's shiny black head below me.

I hoped he never figured out I was up here for every concert. He'd think I came for the orchestra, to marvel at his conducting skills. He'd think I was supporting him.

What a joke.

Just as the trumpets started blaring their fanfare onstage, someone tapped me on the shoulder.

I whirled around, barely suppressing a scream.

"Hello," Henry said, waving.

Igor jumped down from the railing. *It appears you've been found out.*

I impaled a piece of sketch paper with my sharpest charcoal. "You're not allowed up here, Henry."

Igor yawned. *You're not allowed up here either, you know.*

"I'm allowed anywhere I want."

Igor batted lazily at a fly. *Fair enough. That's always been my life philosophy.*

"Are you talking to your cat?" Henry asked.

"No, stupid, I'm talking to you. What are you doing up here?"

Henry took out a pair of goggles from his pants pocket and put them on. "I came up here to help you. Those ghosts or . . . whatever. I've been totally freaked out ever since then. I haven't been able to study or concentrate at baseball practice. If I don't figure out what they are, I'll go nuts. You know?"

I stared at him. Those thick goggles, combined with his usher's tuxedo, made him look ridiculous.

"You came up here to help me . . . what, exactly?"

"Look for the ghosts. That's why you're up here, right?" Henry peered over the railing and then turned quickly back. "Oh wow, we're high up."

Igor yawned once again. *He's quick, this one. Quick but with horrible fashion sense.*

"Ghosts?" I said. Ghost hunting with Henry is not what I had in mind. "What are you talking about?"

"You know, from last week when we got those burns and we saw those foggy people that looked like ghosts? That."

"Whatever." I turned to my sketchpad and pretended to draw. "You were obviously hallucinating."

"Yeah. Sure. And this burn on my leg is actually a bruise."

"Why do you have *goggles*, anyway?"

"For protection." He tapped one of the thick plastic lenses. "Ghosts are probably pretty unpredictable. And those shadow things . . ." Henry shuddered. "Whatever they are, I'm sure they're even worse."

Boiling mad, I shoved my sketchpad in my bag and stalked to the end of the catwalk. I sat down hard on one of the steps, staring at the black grating beneath my boots.

Igor sauntered over. *You throw truly marvelous tantrums, did you know that?*

"I'm not throwing a tantrum. I just want him to go away and leave me alone."

Igor slid against my leg. *Sounds like a tantrum to me.*

"I know what I saw. I know there were ghosts. Or at least, I think that's what they were. I just . . . Henry's not my friend."

Igor began cleaning his paw. *And why not? Goggles aside, he seems perfectly decent.*

"I don't want him to see . . ." I struggled to find the words. "Where I live. *How* I live."

Igor coughed up a disdainful hairball. *He's not stupid. He works here. He already knows you live backstage, he knows about your mother, and he hasn't made fun of you for it. So what's the problem?*

I turned around, glaring at Henry over my shoulder. He sat in the middle of the catwalk, goggles up on his forehead. He waved at me.

 52

"Ugh. Fine." I tiptoed toward him. Below, the orchestra had started the second movement. "Henry, if I search for ghosts or whatever with you this one time, will you leave me alone?"

Henry stood up, grinning. "You bet."

"I'm serious. This is it. We're not friends."

Henry saluted. "Strictly business."

"I mean it. This is not your chance to learn all about crazy Olivia so you can go back and laugh about it at school with Mark Everett and his minions. You got that?"

Henry raised an eyebrow. "Minions?"

"You know. Like evil servants."

"I know what 'minions' means. Unlike someone I know, I've made the honor roll three years straight."

I blushed. "Well, good for you, Mr. Smartie Snob. Can we just keep looking?"

"Mark doesn't have minions, you know. We've been friends a long time."

"Whatever. He has minions. I can tell."

Henry sighed and put his goggles back on. We searched in silence, the orchestra's music surrounding us. Every now and then, when they'd play out of tune or out of time, or someone would crack a note, Henry would cringe.

I didn't let myself cringe. I tried not to think about how Richard and Hilda and Michael and everyone must be feeling, how embarrassed they must be. Instead, I focused on the Maestro. I bet his ears were turning red. I bet he was burning up from the inside out with shame.

Henry and I searched every staircase. We crept through the green room and peeked behind its fraying floral couches. We even snuck into the sound booth, where Fran was recording the concert. She was not happy to see us there, but she let us each have a peppermint anyway. When we reached the rehearsal room backstage, I put myself between Henry and the door and pushed him away.

"All right, search is over. Now you hold up your end of the deal, and go away."

Henry raised his goggles. "But we haven't looked backstage yet."

"And you're not going to. This is private property."

"I come into the rehearsal room all the time," Henry said, frowning.

"Trespasser." Igor rubbed against my shoe, so I let him jump into my arms. "I could have you arrested."

Igor looked up at me. *That would be a sight to see.*

Henry drew himself up angrily, but before he could say anything, the rehearsal room door flew open.

Roger Fernandez, one of the violists, stormed out, jacket flying. "You're crazy, old man!" he yelled over his shoulder. He didn't even look at us before slamming open the backstage door and disappearing into the parking lot.

Henry and I stared after him.

"The concert must have ended while we were searching," Henry whispered.

 54

Oh. This would be good. Musicians yelling at the Maestro and even quitting on him? I couldn't miss this.

"Come on," I said, nodding at the door.

We stepped inside the rehearsal room. I immediately wished that we hadn't.

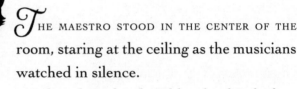

CHAPTER 7

*T*HE MAESTRO STOOD IN THE CENTER OF THE room, staring at the ceiling as the musicians watched in silence.

I found Richard Ashley by his locker. Henry, annoyingly, followed right behind me. "Richard?" I whispered. "What's going on?"

Richard put a finger to his lips and shook his head, but he put his other arm around my shoulders.

"I do not know what to say," said the Maestro finally. "That . . ." He laughed, but it wasn't a nice laugh. "My friends, that was not good."

I glanced up at Richard for his reaction. It was the first time I noticed how tired he looked, how many lines crisscrossed his face, how faded his tuxedo had become.

Then, out of nowhere, the Maestro grabbed the nearest folding chair and threw it against the wall.

Everyone jumped. Richard pushed me and Henry behind him, his hand tight on my shoulder. Igor growled softly.

The chair flew into an old set of wind chimes and sent them crashing to the floor. The racket lasted for centuries.

The Maestro turned his back to everyone, put his hands on the wall, and leaned his head against it.

I tried to clamp down on the panicked somersaults in my stomach, but it didn't work so well. Poor Igor must have been squeezed within an inch of his life.

Finally, the Maestro picked up the walkie-talkie at his belt. "Jeremy, if you'll come backstage, please."

"Be there shortly, sir," came Jeremy's static-lined reply.

For a brief, awful, wonderful second, I closed my eyes and imagined that Richard Ashley's arm on my shoulders was Mom's arm instead.

When the Maestro started having fits like this, right before The Economy changed, right before *everything* changed, Mom would make me a bedsheet fort and cut out stars from the scrap paper she brought home from the office. Once the fort was done, and the stars strung up, she and I would lie under the starry bedsheet sky. She would hug me and kiss my hair and tell me a story. I'd fall asleep to her fingers tracing shapes on my back, the Maestro's music floating up from downstairs.

"I was not going to tell you this," the Maestro said, staring down each of the musicians, one by one. "I was going to wait until later in the season. I thought, *Why upset them?* There was no need. But then you play like a high school group. Need I remind you, you're getting paid for this? You are *professionals*."

Jeremy, the box-office clerk, entered the room. He held a scrap of paper in his hands.

"I'm here, sir."

The Maestro waved his hand impatiently. "Tell them how many people were in the audience tonight. Tell them."

Jeremy paused. Mr. Rue, the president of the orchestra, came up behind him, hidden in the hallway that led to the east side of the stage. He crossed his arms over his chest, watching. Mr. Rue basically ran the orchestra; he decided where the money went, and hired and fired people, and was the Maestro's boss. They were old friends. Mr. Rue usually stayed out late after concerts, doing what Mom always called "The Big Schmooze." That meant sucking up to the rich people so they'd give the orchestra money.

Seeing Mr. Rue standing there spooked me. Why wasn't he out schmoozing? This was bad.

The Maestro pounded his fist against the wall. "Tell them, Jeremy."

"Okay, I'm—I've got it right here." Jeremy fumbled with the paper. "We had four hundred twenty-three people in attendance tonight."

"What was that, Jeremy?"

"Four hundred twenty-three."

Beside me, Henry slumped against a stack of chairs. Richard Ashley sat down heavily on the bench in front of us. I didn't want to be there anymore.

"And the total box-office receipts?" The Maestro paused. "How much *money*, Jeremy?"

"$21,008."

That might seem like a lot of money. But when you have

to pay over a hundred musicians and office staff, and keep the electricity on and keep the Hall itself from falling down, it isn't a lot of money at all.

A couple of the musicians said a bad word or two. One of the clarinet players started to cry.

Mr. Rue stepped out of the shadows, his bald head gleaming. Even his tuxedo looked rumpled. "What's the problem, ladies and gentlemen? What happened tonight?"

No one had anything to say.

"I know it's hard. What with the current state of the economy, you've already taken pay cuts. And with the Hall in its current condition . . ." Mr. Rue waved one hand at the ceiling. "I know *I* wouldn't want to perform under these circumstances. But if ticket sales don't go up—*drastically*—by the end of the season . . . I don't know what will happen. We may have to shut down. Pull the plug."

The Maestro stalked out. The sound of his slamming bedroom door echoed through my bones. Nobody moved for a long time.

Mr. Rue rubbed his forehead, his eyebrows creasing sadly. "I'm sorry to be the bearer of bad tidings, everyone. I wish I didn't have to be."

Richard Ashley squeezed my shoulder. I looked at him and felt instantly better. Richard always knew just what to do and say, in any situation. It was part of his charm. That's what Mom always said, right before rolling her eyes.

"Richard?" I said. "He's not serious, is he?"

"Yeah, Olivia," he said, turning away, like he couldn't stand looking at me anymore. "I think he is, kiddo."

As everyone drifted out into the parking lot, Mr. Rue found me and patted my arm. "It will be all right, Olivia, somehow. Trust me. Trust your father. Hmm?"

My throat was so pinched I couldn't get out what I wanted to say:

Why should I trust the Maestro? He'd torn our family apart.

Right before Henry left with Richard for his ride home, he pressed a folded-up note into my hand. It said only: *This isn't over. Not to sound creepy. I just mean, I know we didn't find the ghosts tonight. But we will. See you at school.*

I folded up his note and slipped it under my pillow. For a long time, I stared at the ceiling, thinking. Igor snuggled up next to me. Across the room, Nonnie breathed thin, rattling breaths. I snuck over and tucked my quilt around her so she'd be warmer. Those strange cold gusts were happening more and more now, ever since Henry and I had seen the ghosts. I didn't know what that meant, but it couldn't have been good.

By the time I settled back in bed, I'd made my decision: I would do it. I would find the ghosts, even if that meant teaming up with Perfect Henry Page. Two heads were better than one, after all, and I needed to find these ghosts. I *had* to. Maybe I couldn't fix everything in my life — maybe the orchestra was awful and we were poorer every day and Mom was gone and school was the pits, but this—I could do this. I could find the ghosts.

If I could make sense of ghosts, if I could solve that, I could solve anything.

Maybe if I figured out where this one puzzle piece went, I could find the rest of them and somehow put my life back together.

CHAPTER 8

THE NEXT MONDAY AT SCHOOL, THE UNTHINK-able happened: Henry Page sat with me at lunch.

There I was, minding my own business and sketching ghosts. A perfectly normal day.

Joan sat across from me. She'd been doing that a lot lately. "What are you drawing?"

I glared up at her through my hair. Even if I'd wanted to talk to her, I wasn't sure how to explain.

Joan calmly chewed her sandwich. "You look freaky like that. Like one of those Japanese horror movie girls."

"Thanks. I like looking freaky."

"Yes," Joan said thoughtfully. "You work very hard at it."

"What's that supposed to mean?"

Then Henry slid into the seat beside me.

It was like you could hear the entire cafeteria hold its breath. Henry Page—baseball star, track star, popular kid—was sitting next to Olivia Stellatella—homeless girl, daughter of crazy conductor, motherless artist.

"Hey," said Henry.

I shrugged. "Hey."

Henry opened the first of three milk cartons on his tray. The cafeteria let out its breath, and people started talking again. I wondered how much of the whispering I heard was about us.

"Hey, Joan," said Henry.

Joan sat there with her mouth hanging open.

Henry ate in silence. Eventually, Joan started doing the same. I hunched over my sketch so Henry couldn't see it.

"What are you working on?"

Behind Joan, Mark Everett and Nick Weber, this other boy from Henry's usual table, walked by with their lunch trays. Nick looked horrified, like he'd just seen some kind of alien. Mark looked angry.

I waved and flashed him a smile.

Henry raised his eyebrows at me. "Hello? What are you drawing?"

"Nothing."

"It's one of them, isn't it?" Henry craned his neck to peer at my paper.

I slammed my sketchpad shut. "One of what?"

Henry glanced at Joan. "One of . . . *you know*."

Joan leaned closer. "What's going on? Is something going on?"

"Nothing's going on," I said. "And I have to pee. If you'll excuse me."

I headed for the restroom. On the way, I dropped a piece

of paper into Henry's lap so Joan couldn't see. My stomach jumped when I did it, but it definitely was not because of Henry, no matter what anyone might think. It just felt nice to have a secret that was actually *fun* to hide.

I want to contact the ghosts, the note said. *For real. We can't find them, so we'll bring them to us. And I know someone who can help us. I've got a plan. Meet me in the courtyard after school, by the water fountain that doesn't work. P.S. We're still not friends, though.*

This thing between me and Henry, this ghost hunting thing—I didn't know what it meant, and I still didn't want him to be my friend. But maybe we could at least be partners. It would be, as Henry had said, "strictly business." Not friends. Partners. I could handle that. I could handle "strictly business."

Henry found me by the water fountain after school. I was watching Joan march in circles through the courtyard, holding up a posterboard and shouting out something about corrupt banks.

"Hey," Henry said. "So, what's your brilliant idea?"

By that point, I was pretty much bursting, but I tried to keep things cool, like partners would.

"I've started working at The Happy Place after school."

"Really? I didn't know that."

"That's probably because I don't tell you every little detail about my life."

Henry frowned. "If you're going to be rude, I'll just go

home or something. I've got lots of homework to do."

"This is more important than homework." I paused at the shocked look on his face and sighed. "Okay, okay. Sorry. I won't be rude, ever. Promise."

"Ha. Yeah, okay."

The fact that Henry thought I was incapable of *not* being rude hurt in a kind of surprising way, like when a bee stings you out of nowhere. "Well. I'll try, anyway."

"Fine. So, The Happy Place?"

"Yeah. Well, you know the Barskys."

Henry nodded. "Sure."

"So, they're really weird, right? I mean, I like them a lot, but they sell all this crazy stuff in their shop. New Agey stuff, you know? Crystals, incense, books about how to understand your dreams. But I think they actually believe in all of it. So I was thinking—"

A couple of girls walked past us, talking just loud enough to make sure we could hear.

"Do you think they're going out?" one of them said.

"Nah," the other one said, practically shouting it. "You kidding? Henry Page? With *her*?"

Henry's chest puffed up, but I shoved him out of the way and marched up to the girls myself.

"Why not with me? Because I'm *crazy*?" I waved my arms around and stuck out my tongue. "Ooga wooga booga!"

The girls gasped and jumped back.

"Psycho," they said. "Freak." Then they walked away,

shooting these awful looks at me over their shoulders.

Henry and I headed out the courtyard in silence. As we walked toward Arlington, it started to rain.

"Don't you have a raincoat?" Henry asked, after a minute.

"No," I snapped. "Too poor for a raincoat."

"Do you want my raincoat?"

"No way."

"Well, what about that charity store on Clark Street? You could maybe get one there."

"How about you go to the charity store and see how you like it? Then we'll talk."

"I do sometimes," Henry said quietly.

"Oh."

That's when I realized exactly how little I knew about Henry Page. Why would Henry shop there, too? Was it something about The Economy? Is that why he'd had to start working as an usher? Not because he loved music, but because he'd actually needed the money? I frowned at the sidewalk, suddenly embarrassed to look at him. I wanted to ask all those questions, but I'd never, not in a million years. Partners didn't pry into each other's personal lives.

"You're not, you know," Henry said, after a few minutes.

"Not what?"

"What they said. Freak. Psycho. You're not."

I didn't know what to say to that. *Thanks*, probably, but I couldn't get the word out. So I just kept walking, concentrating on the sight of my boots against the wet pavement.

"You promise?" I said.

"Promise what?"

"That I'm not a freak?"

"Sure, Olivia." He smiled at me through the rain. "I promise."

I didn't know what to do then, so I stuck out my arm and shook his hand. Firmly, like partners do.

The Barskys were busy with customers when we got to The Happy Place, so Henry and I started inspecting their shelves. They were full of voodoo dolls and plastic skulls, model dragons and incense burners decorated with Chinese tigers, candle holders painted with pink stars and salt-and-pepper shakers shaped like fat penguins.

Eventually Mr. Barsky made his way over to us.

"Olivia, my dear girl! How positively delightful to see you!" Ah. So today was Lord Winthrop, Mr. Barsky's English character. "And you brought a friend today!" He shook Henry's hand like Henry was the most interesting person in the world. "Tell me, my good man, dost thee desireth a spot of tea?"

"Mr. B, this is Henry. Henry Page. We go to school together, and he's an usher at the Hall."

"Ah, Sir Page, it is a pleasure, to be sure."

Henry looked mystified. "You too, Mr. Barsky."

"So, Mr. B," I said, "I have a question for you before I start work today. And for Mrs. B. It's really important."

Mr. Barsky swept himself into a bow. "I shall summon the missus at once. Oh, Mother Barsky!"

Mrs. Barsky came out from the kitchen, her neck draped with green beads. "David, I will only say this once: *Never* call me that again."

"Of course, sweeting. But if you will, Olivia has an important question for us."

"Hello, Olivia." Mrs. Barsky smiled. "And who is this?"

"Henry Page, ma'am." Henry offered his hand. "Pleased to meet you."

"Henry ushers at the Hall," Mr. Barsky added.

"Oh, that's wonderful, Henry. Are you a musician yourself?"

Henry's whole face lit up. "No, ma'am, not me. But I'm an enthusiast. Did you know, they say that music is one of the most important building blocks of—"

"So, my question," I interrupted. I did not want to hear one of Henry's lectures about the greatness and benefits of music. "Like I said, it's important. See . . ." I took a deep breath. "Henry and I, we need a way to contact ghosts."

The Barskys stared at me, and then at each other, and then back at me.

"Ghosts?" Mr. Barsky repeated.

"Yeah. We've seen some at the Hall . . ."

Mrs. Barsky leaned back against the counter. She wiped her forehead, gone pale. Beside me, Henry started to look really uncomfortable.

 68

". . . but we haven't seen any for a couple of days, so we thought . . ."

I trailed off. I had never seen the Barskys look so strange, like . . . well, like they had just seen a ghost. Mrs. Barsky looked especially frightened. Mr. Barsky put his arm around her.

Henry jumped in. "Olivia thought, since you sell the right kinds of things here . . ."

"Yeah, like all these candles and incense burners, and the weird voodoo dolls—"

"—that maybe you would know, or give us some pointers . . ."

Mr. Barsky cleared his throat. "You've really seen ghosts?"

"Yes," I said. "Well, we think so, anyway. One was tall and thin and—"

"Don't *describe* them to us," Mrs. Barsky whispered. "We don't want to know."

This was not the reaction I'd been expecting. "Why not?"

Mrs. Barsky considered me for a moment. "Listen carefully, Olivia. Contacting ghosts is no laughing matter. It's not fun and games. Strange, terrible things can happen when you delve into the world of Death."

A chill shot through me. My burn started pulsing, like something had woken it up.

Beside me, Henry said, "The world . . . of Death?"

The world of Death, I thought. A million sketches raced through my mind. "Do you know anything about it? The world of Death? What does it look like? Who can go there? Where does—"

Mrs. Barsky shook her head, covered her mouth, and disappeared back into the kitchen.

Mr. Barsky's face was grim as he pressed my money for the week into my hand. "You'd better just go home today, Olivia."

"Is Mrs. Barsky okay?" Henry asked.

"She's fine, she's just . . ." Mr. Barsky paused. "She's seen a lot. She *knows* a lot. Some people do, you know."

I didn't know, but Mr. Barsky basically forced us out, and that was that. In silence, Henry and I waited at the corner for the light to change. I guess neither of us knew what to say.

I wondered if Henry's brain, like mine, was too busy imagining what the world of Death looked like to bother with something like talking.

What would the world of Death look like?

   1) a long, winding, icy river full of drifting souls

   2) stars forever and ever, in all directions

   3) heaven (clouds, angels, golden gates)

   4) hell (fire, brimstone, demons)

   5) nothing

*H*OW TO CONTACT GHOSTS: IDEAS.

I sat back and stared at my paper. Mrs. Farrity, my English teacher, was talking about some book I hadn't read, and I was supposed to be taking notes. But how could I possibly be expected to take notes when thoughts of ghosts and Death and Mrs. Barsky's terrified face kept racing through my brain?

Henry had been avoiding me. I think Mrs. Barsky getting so scared about ghosts really spooked him. It had scared me, too, but not enough to get all dramatic about it or anything. In fact, it kind of excited me; it was an adventure, something to concentrate on that didn't involve school or money or Mom. Henry, on the other hand, had gone back to his popular table at lunch. He'd even turned and walked the other way the couple of times we'd seen each other at the Hall.

Not that I cared. Henry Page could sit at every popular table in the world, if he wanted to. In fact, it was a relief to have gotten rid of him and his stupid goggles and his stupid honor roll grades.

If neither Henry nor the Barskys would help me find the ghosts, I would have to do it myself.

Outside, rain pounded against the windows. The sky was black. It was almost October.

I ran through everything I knew about ghosts, which didn't count for much, but I remembered some things from books I'd read and from the couple of scary movies I knew about.

Write backward on steamed-up bathroom mirror, I wrote. I thought that sounded poetic.

Go into dark bathroom, close door, stare at mirror. Say Bloody Mary *three times in a row.* I remembered that one from when I was little, when I'd had friends over for the night.

Visit graveyard. Sit on graves.

Consult fortune-teller for help.

Visit funeral home? Consult owner.

Ouija boards?

Fake near-death experience.

I stared at that one. If I came close to dying, and therefore came close to being a ghost, would that make it easier to talk to them? It made sense to me, but I didn't know what *kind* of near-death experience would prove most effective, so I made a note beside it:

Research near-death experience stories. Find out which ones mention seeing ghosts.

Suddenly, my paper disappeared from beneath my hand.

"'How to Contact *Ghosts*'?" came Mark Everett's voice. He had my list.

"Graveyards, Ouija boards . . . near-death experiences?" He laughed. "Look at this! She's talking about *ghosts* now. First those freak drawings. Now this." He waved the paper around, rattling the air. I looked for Mrs. Farrity, but she was gone. It was only us kids. Some of them stood up or leaned forward to look. Some of them were laughing or whispering things. I didn't know what to do, so I just sat there, staring at my desk, my clothes shrinking around me.

On my other side, Joan Dawson leapt to her feet, grabbing for the paper. "You give that back to her!"

Mark Everett jumped back, hooting, and that hooting sound was so loud, so ugly, that I couldn't help it. I bolted out of my chair, right at him, and screamed as loud as I could.

Everyone jumped back. Mark tripped over himself and fell hard on his butt. Desks and chairs toppled over as people bolted away from me, and a couple of girls shrieked.

A door swung open, and Mrs. Farrity's voice barked, "*What* is going on here? I step out for one minute, and this is how you behave?"

A hush fell over the classroom. Mrs. Farrity's footsteps clicked over to where Mark stood. I heard her taking the paper from him.

I slid back into my seat and stared at my desk.

"Olivia," Mrs. Farrity began quietly. "What is all this?"

My hair slid forward, slipping over my eyes.

"Please, Mrs. Farrity," Joan burst out. It sounded like she might combust. "Olivia didn't do anything wrong. Mark's the one who took her paper, he just *snatched* it from her!"

"Calm down, Joan." Mrs. Farrity knelt by my desk. "Olivia? Olivia, I want you to look at me."

I did. Mrs. Farrity's face was full of frowns. "Olivia, this is quite serious."

"Okay." I wished that I'd worn long sleeves today, instead of my scarf. My burn felt completely exposed. Mrs. Farrity glanced at my scarf and frowned even more deeply.

"Is everything okay at home, Olivia?"

"Yeah."

"Why did you push Mark? Why did you scream?"

I didn't say anything. If I opened my mouth, I'd get myself into even more trouble. Anger stewed in the back of my throat.

Mrs. Farrity sighed.

"You're coming with me to Principal Cooper's office." She took my hand, her grip pinching my skin. "Mark, I'll deal with you later. And don't you think you can try something like that again. I'm sending over Mr. Hawthorne from next door. Do you hear me, everyone?"

"Yes, ma'am."

"Mrs. Farrity, *please*." Joan actually stamped her foot. "Olivia was just defending herself. She's well within her rights. This is completely unjust!"

"All right, Joan. You're coming too."

"Fine." Joan put her arm around me stiffly. "I *will* come, and I'll be her defendant. I witnessed everything. I know the truth."

In the principal's office, Mrs. Farrity whispered some things to Ms. Renshaw, who had a cloud of blond hair and gave us pieces of chocolate when Mrs. Farrity's back was turned. Then Mrs. Farrity filled out some papers and left, and Ms. Renshaw led us into Principal Cooper's office.

Principal Cooper watched me and Joan for a minute. We sat across from him in hard black plastic chairs. I don't know about Joan, but I stared at the ceiling, refusing to look at him. I didn't have anything to say to Principal Cooper. I hadn't done anything wrong.

"Well?" he said. "Why don't one of you tell me what happened?"

"Principal Cooper, my name is Joan Dawson," Joan said, breathlessly, "and I witnessed the incident myself. I'm here to offer testimony on behalf of the accused."

"Miss *Dawson*," said Principal Cooper. He rubbed his forehead. I got the feeling he and Joan had done this before. "Why don't you let Miss Stellatella talk first?"

Joan cleared her throat. "I, Joan Elizabeth Dawson, do solemnly swear—"

"Miss Dawson, that's quite enough." Principal Cooper called Ms. Renshaw to take Joan into the other room.

"Don't let him pressure you, Olivia," Joan hissed, digging in her heels at the door. "You're innocent!"

After Joan left, Principal Cooper's eyes crinkled tiredly at me. Was everyone tired these days? Richard Ashley, Mr. Rue, even me. I wanted Mom. I wanted to go home—to the home we'd had, the home where Mom had watched me draw like it was the coolest thing in the world.

The home before everything started to go wrong, when the Maestro still had dinner with us and let me sit on his lap while he studied his scores.

"What key is this in, Olivia?" he would say.

Four sharps. Easy as pie. "E major!"

Principal Cooper cleared his throat. "How are things at home, Miss Stellatella?"

I stared at his desk. "Fine."

"Are you sure?"

I opened my mouth, closed it, and opened it again. I didn't know what to say. I didn't know what he knew, and I couldn't say, *I live at Emerson Hall, in the back storage rooms with bad plumbing, and Nonnie is small, and Richard Ashley is tired.* I couldn't tell him about the ghosts or show him my burn. What would he say? What would he think?

Even worse, what would he *do*? Somewhere there was probably a law against kids living in music halls.

So I said nothing.

"I know about the Philharmonic," Principal Cooper said gently. "About the orchestra. I know it must be . . . difficult."

"It's fine," I said. "We'll be fine."

After a long time, Principal Cooper said something about a counselor and a letter home, but I wasn't really listening. They let me stay in the nurse's office for the rest of the day. They wanted to watch me, they said. When they pulled down my scarf to inspect my arm, they found nothing; my burn had disappeared. They asked me questions about my eating habits, and other things too, but my brain was too shocked to think. When they left me, I peeled back my scarf again.

Nothing. It was gone. I tried to find some sort of explanation, and couldn't, except for one: None of it had been real. We really had hallucinated the whole thing, me and Henry, like mass hysteria or something. The burns had never actually been there.

But when I got to The Happy Place after school, I checked again, just in case.

The burn was back, its black color slowly seeping back into my arm. Maybe it only showed up near the Hall. Maybe it faded when I left the Hall, for some reason.

Whatever it was, I was glad. I couldn't stand the thought of it all being a hallucination. I needed to find these ghosts, and I knew that, somehow, the burn connected me to them.

That night, I dreamed about the world of Death. It was black and glittering, like my burn. I walked into it through an archway of comets, and Igor was right beside me.

OCTOBER

*I*T WASN'T UNTIL A COUPLE OF WEEKS INTO October that everything clicked.

Wednesday morning. October 13. I woke up with my teeth chattering, like I'd been sleeping in a freezer. My breath puffed in little white bursts. So did Igor's and Nonnie's. I dressed fast, skipping around on the cold concrete floor.

"Stupid drafty old place," I muttered. "You'd think we lived in the Arctic or something."

Nonnie watched me happily from her cot, wrapped up in our quilts. "You're grumpy lately, *ombralina. Scontroso.*"

"Well, Nonnie, that's what happens when a girl gets moved from a house into a meat locker."

Nonnie clucked her tongue. "Is not so bad, now."

She was right; the temperature in the room had increased, and my breaths were back to invisible. I looked at Igor. "Weird, huh?"

He glared up at me from my rumpled sheets. *When will you stop talking so I can go back to sleep?*

"But not just today," Nonnie said, tying her scarf over her eyes. "You are strange all the days. You are distracted."

Guilt sank into my stomach. I *had* been pretty distant lately. All I could think about were the ghosts; I spent hours drawing them after work, hours I should have spent with Nonnie.

Nonnie peeked out from beneath her scarf. "You missed cards last night."

"I know. I'm sorry. It's just . . ." I sighed and plopped down beside Nonnie. "What would you say if . . ." I looked at Igor for reassurance, but he wasn't much help, already half asleep. ". . . if I told you I'd seen ghosts? And that I wanted to find a way to talk with them?"

Nonnie's eyes widened. *"Il fantasma. Lo spettro!"*

I patted Nonnie's arm. "Shh, shh. It's okay. I didn't mean to scare you."

"No, no!" Nonnie shook her head, grinning. "I saw *lo spettro* once. Once, when a girl. In old country. Oh, I was beautiful, *ombralina*! I wore lace scarves. Everyone said, 'She is so beautiful!'"

"I bet you were, Nonnie."

"There were parties, oh, so many parties. And at one party"—Nonnie held up her finger—"there was game. And we sat in a circle and lit candles. We spoke to *il spettro*. He was a pirate *capitano*." Nonnie grinned, leaned back against the wall. "He liked my scarf. He told me he did."

Chills skipped down my arms. "Nonnie?" I grabbed her

shoulders, gently. "You said you sat in a circle. You lit candles. And then you talked to ghosts?"

Nonnie nodded, moony-eyed. "*Il capitano*, he was in love with me, I think."

"Nonnie!"

She waved me away. "*Ombralina*, it was *la seduta*. *La spiritica*."

Spiritica. Spirits.

"Oh my gosh, that's it," I said. I jumped to my feet, yanked on my boots, and grabbed my jacket from the bed. Never in my life had I been so excited to get to school. "That's what we need! That's how we can contact the ghosts!"

A séance.

At lunch that day, I walked to Henry's table in the cafeteria and tapped him on the shoulder.

"What are you doing here, psychopath?" Nick Weber said. The others laughed, except for Mark Everett, who focused hard on his lunch. I think I'd really freaked him out that day, running at him like I had. The thought made me smile.

"Trying to decide what curse I should use on you," I said. "So many choices."

Nick flushed. "Shut up."

"Careful." I wagged my finger. "Henry, can I talk to you?"

Henry was watching me in that quiet honor roll way of his. "Sure."

"Henry," Mark hissed, but Henry ignored him. When we reached my customary table in the corner, Henry sat next to me like nothing had changed. He opened his milk carton.

"So, what's up?" he asked.

"We need to hold a séance."

Henry shook his head. "Gosh, I'm fine, Olivia, thanks. And you?"

I narrowed my eyes at him. "I'm fine. Now, can I continue?"

"Fine."

"Like I was saying, we need to hold a séance. I've been doing a lot of thinking"—*while you've been avoiding me*—"and I think it's the only way to contact the ghosts."

"Why?"

I hesitated. "Nonnie told me."

Henry raised his eyebrows. "Olivia, no offense, but . . . your, like, eighty-year-old grandmother?"

"So? What does that matter? A séance is a real thing. Look it up if you want. You can speak directly to the ghosts. Henry, we can find them, see where they're hiding!"

"I don't know . . ."

"A *séance*?" Joan appeared out of nowhere in the seat across from us. "Please tell me I heard you right. You're holding a *séance*?"

Henry and I glanced at each other.

"Are you okay?" Henry asked.

Joan was practically vibrating. "If you're holding a séance, can I do it with you? I know all about séances. I've even held a couple. You know, just stupid things at sleepovers, but I'm telling you, I know *everything* there is to know." She looked back and forth between us. "Please? How many people do you have so far?"

"Well," I said, "just me and Henry, but—"

"Oh, you'll never get it to work with just two people. No, you need three people. But no more than that. Just three."

"Are you sure you know all about séances?"

"Oh, yes. Absolutely." Joan paused. "Please, can't I help you?"

Joan had this weird look on her face, a twitchy, tight-lipped kind of look, and I got this feeling that she actually had no idea whatsoever how to hold a séance.

I also got the feeling that I'd been wrong about Joan. Maybe it was a little lonelier being a one-woman protester than Joan let on. Maybe she liked having someone to sit with at lunch, even if that someone was me.

Henry sighed. "Look, I don't even know what I think about having a séance in the first place. It seems kind of dumb."

Joan's eyes widened. "Oh no, it's not dumb at all. The spirits are all around us, just waiting to be contacted. Sometimes they even want our *help*. But some of them aren't very nice. That's why you need an expert to help you, someone who's done it before. Like me. So."

I put a hand over my burn. Whenever my skin got

goosebumps, my burn stung like crazy. "Some of them aren't very nice?"

"Just like some people aren't very nice. It's the same with spirits."

I took a long, hard look at Joan. I wasn't sure how I felt about Joan's supposed expert knowledge. Plus, Joan was someone completely outside the world of the Hall. What would she think about it? What would she think about how I lived?

But Joan was throwing this pitiful face at me, and I just couldn't say no. Plus, I wanted to contact the ghosts so bad it was like this hard knot in my stomach.

"Fine," I said at last.

Henry looked at me in surprise.

Joan squealed and drew out some paper and a pencil from her bag.

"But I'm the boss of this operation. Okay? You're the séance expert or whatever, but I run the show."

"Of course," Joan said. *Séance Instructions*, read the heading of her paper. "Now, where are we having the séance, and why?"

"At Emerson Hall. Henry and I . . ." I paused.

He threw up his hands. "Might as well just tell her now."

"Tell me what?" Joan whispered.

"We've seen ghosts. At the Hall. But only once, and we haven't been able to find them since, and we want to talk to them for real."

Joan took a deep, centering breath. "Oh my gosh, oh my *gosh*. That is so . . . oh my gosh." She bent over her paper and started writing frantically.

"What are you writing?" I said.

"A list of the things we'll need."

She finished with a flourish. We leaned closer to read it.

"A homemade Ouija board?" Henry said.

"The ones you can get at the store are just phonies," Joan said. "*Much* more powerful to make your own. Don't worry about it, I've got the supplies for that."

"Three white candles, a dish of water, a feather, incense, an important personal artifact . . . a hair from each of our parents?" I looked up in disgust. "Are you kidding?"

"I don't make the rules," Joan said.

Beside me, Henry shifted in his seat. "Would it not work if we didn't have . . . if any one of those items was missing?"

"It can still work, of course," Joan said quickly. "The important thing is that you have to really *want* it to work. From the bottom of your heart. The items are just there to help you focus."

I tried to imagine getting close enough to the Maestro to pluck a hair from his head. "Ugh. Fine."

"Fine," Henry said, but for the rest of lunch, he didn't say a word.

After school that day at The Happy Place, I finished refilling the sugar packets and leaned over the counter.

"Mrs. B?" Since that day Henry and I had brought up the ghosts, Mr. and Mrs. Barsky had been completely normal, like it had never happened. "Do you think . . . ? I need to buy some stuff. Could I get an employee discount?"

Mrs. Barsky looked up from where she was organizing the register. "What kind of stuff?"

I shrugged. "Just some candles and things like that."

Mrs. Barsky pursed her lips. I forced myself to meet her eyes.

Finally, she nodded. "All right, Olivia."

I picked out the things we needed: three white candles, sandalwood incense, and an incense burner. The money Henry and Joan had given me jingled in my pockets.

I put it all on the countertop. "This is it."

She scanned everything quietly, not saying anything until I was halfway out the door.

"Olivia?" she said. "Be careful."

I thanked her for the discount and left, fear and excitement crackling in my chest like tiny bolts of lightning.

CHAPTER 11

I PUT OFF GETTING ONE OF THE MAESTRO'S HAIRS until the night of the séance. I went to bed, wide awake, and waited. Beneath my blanket, I clutched my backpack, which held my supplies, including my important personal artifact—my sketchpad.

"Your brain is busy tonight, Olivia," Nonnie murmured from across the room.

"Go to sleep, Nonnie. I'm tired."

Finally, I heard the Maestro's footsteps coming down the hallway, shuffling through the kitchen, entering his bedroom.

It was time to make my move. I waited as long as I could stand and then crept out of bed. I paused at the door.

"Nonnie?" I whispered.

Nonnie mumbled, half-asleep.

"I'm gonna have my séance in a little bit. Remember? Like we talked about? But you can just stay in here, okay? Just keep sleeping. Everything will be fine."

"Bring me some radishes."

"Sure thing."

In the hallway, I stayed close to the wall. The concrete floor was cold on my socked feet.

Something brushed against my leg. I almost screamed until I saw two green eyes staring at me in the dark.

I sighed. "Igor, you've got to stop sneaking around like that."

He cocked his head.

"Don't give me that look. I'm serious." I continued toward the Maestro's room, gathering my insides together into one solid, fist-shaped knot. I could do this. I could slip into the Maestro's bedroom and pluck a hair from his greasy head while he slept.

But at his door, my hand on the knob, I froze. From beneath the normal noise of his music — he always slept with his music on — I could hear a strange sound.

It sounded like crying.

This made no sense. The Maestro didn't cry. The Maestro was made of stone and numbers and anger, and mostly he was made of music — cold, unfeeling, metal-tubed music.

But I could hear him crying. As I stood there, a sick feeling growing in my throat, I heard him say: "Cara."

Cara. Mom's name.

"Cara, *please.*"

I hurried back to bed. I couldn't banish the sounds of the Maestro crying, no matter how hard I pressed my ears to my head. Eventually, Igor found me and crawled into my arms, and I plucked a single black hair from his tail. It would have to do.

At midnight, I heard a knock on the parking lot door. I pushed it open and moonlight poured in.

Henry and Joan rushed inside. Behind them, their cab pulled away from the curb. The city was dark and quiet, except for windows in the high-up office buildings, where no one ever slept.

"You snuck out okay?" I said.

"Yeah," said Henry. "No problems here."

"Oh, yes," Joan whispered. "Daddy sleeps like the dead. And did you see? It's a full moon. Full moons are the absolute best for séances, they make everything more potent."

I shut the door behind them and turned the latch. "This way."

"I hope you have all your materials," Joan said from behind me in the dark. The light of my flashlight bobbed ahead of us.

"Candles, incense, matches," I said.

"Feather, bowl," said Henry.

"And I've got the Ouija board," said Joan. Her voice hushed on the words *Ouija board*. "And the hairs."

"Yeah, me too," said Henry quickly.

Joan had decided to hold our séance onstage. She said the pipe organ would provide *ambiance*. I led them there using an indirect route, so neither of them could see too much of where I lived.

When we entered the Hall, Joan grabbed my flashlight.

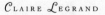

88

"Oh my gosh," she whispered, "this is *marvelous*." She ran around the Hall, pointing the flashlight up into the balconies, across the gleaming pipes of the organ.

We set up in a circle in the middle of the stage. Joan lit the candles and set up the incense burner. She whipped out a water bottle from her bag, filled up Henry's bowl, and drew a cross above the water with her finger.

I tried not to laugh. Joan wasn't a priest or anything; I doubted that cross would do much good, if we ever needed it.

A queasy feeling turned over in my stomach. *Would* spirits come for us? And would they be good or bad? Or was it even that simple, with spirits? I looked around at the dimly lit Hall. Shadows stretched everywhere. When Joan lit the candles, the shadows danced too.

Henry had started to sweat. I hoped I didn't look as nervous as he did.

"We'll sit in a circle," Joan said. "You right there, Olivia, and Henry, right next to her. Close enough to hold hands. I'll sit on Henry's other side."

I sat down, scowling at the floor. Maybe if I spat on my palms, we could skip the whole hand-holding thing.

"Hairs," Joan said, holding out her hand.

She dumped them into the bowl of water.

"Feather."

Henry handed Joan a ratty pigeon feather. Then she sat down beside me and set the bowl and feather in the middle of our circle.

"Place your personal artifacts in the circle," Joan said, spreading her arms, "and tell us why you chose them. I will go first."

She placed a tiny rag doll next to the feather. "This is Magda. My grandma made her when I was little. She reminds me of family and togetherness, and those are strong positive emotions, and positive emotions keep the evil spirits away." She patted Magda on the head, smiling. "Now you, Olivia."

Igor crept forward out of the darkness of stage left, his eyes wide. *Olivia, what are you doing? What is all this?*

His expression made me nervous, but I slid my sketchpad forward anyway. "This is my sketchpad. It's where I keep all my drawings. I take it everywhere I go."

"And?"

And Mom gave it to me and told me it was important to dream. Dreaming tells us who we are and scrubs away the bad days. I glared at Joan. "And nothing. That's it."

Joan sighed. "Henry?"

Henry slid forward a glass jar brown with age and dust and dirt and who knows what else. It rattled, but the glass was too dark to see inside.

"This is my . . . my jar," he said. "I keep important things in there, things that mean a lot to me. And . . . well, yeah."

"That's all you're going to say?" said Joan.

Henry nodded.

"Look, I hope you two are committed to this and have open minds," Joan said. "Otherwise it won't work."

"Joan, we're committed, we've got open minds, we're full of sunshine," I said. "Let's just do this, okay?"

"Fine." Joan thrust out her arms. "Grab my hands and bow your heads."

"Sunshine, Joan," Henry said, soothingly. "Sunshine, remember?"

Joan closed her eyes. "Yes. Positive energy. Positive . . ." She breathed in. "Energy." She breathed out.

We joined hands. We closed our eyes. Then Joan began to speak.

"*Spirits*," Joan called out, throwing back her head. She almost jerked my arm out of its socket. "We are here tonight to speak with you, and to offer our help, if you need it. Can you hear us? Are you there?"

Nothing. Complete stillness, except for the dancing fire and its shadows. I squeaked open one eye to look around and saw Henry doing the same thing. I shut my eyes before he could see me looking, and tried to concentrate.

"Spirits?" Joan called out again. "We are here. We wish to speak with you. Can you hear us?"

After a minute, Joan let go, sighing. "This isn't working."

Henry raised his eyebrows. "Shouldn't we try for a little longer than that? It's only been—"

"Listen, I know all about séances, and you don't want to

linger too long in any one position. You have to *rotate your methods*." She spun her hand around.

"Whatever you say."

Joan pulled out her homemade Ouija board and started rearranging everything. Igor perched on the edge of the stage and looked out over the empty Hall, into the shadows. His ears pricked forward; his tail stood straight out behind him.

He meowed softly. *Curiouser and curiouser.*

I looked out into the Hall too, but all I could see was the red exit signs. One of them flickered on and off, buzzing. Had it been doing that before? And the coldness settling into the Hall like an invisible fog, scraping goosebumps across my skin—how long had that been going on?

Slowly, Igor stood up. The hair on the back of his neck poofed. *Curiousest of all.*

"Come on, Olivia," Joan was saying. "We need your hands." She shoved our hands together onto the Ouija board's pointer, a piece of cardboard with a hole in the middle and plastic wrap stretched across the bottom of the hole. It distorted the letters, wrinkling them.

"Don't press down too hard," Joan whispered. "Just barely touch the cardboard. Close your eyes. Let out a long breath."

After I exhaled, the only sounds I could hear were my own racing heartbeat and the distant buzzing of the exit sign. Beside me, Henry pressed his knee against mine.

 92

"*Spirits*," Joan called out once more. "Tell us—*are you here with us?*"

Beneath our fingers, the pointer began to move. Henry cried out, and I bit down hard on my tongue to keep from doing the same.

"Don't stop," she hissed. "We're getting somewhere. Watch."

We did, staring at the pointer as it moved across the board—but what letter was it heading for? First *N*, and then *Y*, and then *Z*. That didn't make any sense.

I imagined stretching out my brain into the corners of the room, like tendrils. *Please let this be real.*

"Joan?" Henry whispered. "What's happening?"

"She's moving it herself, is what," said a voice from somewhere across the stage, a scratchy, dirty-sounding voice, like it had been scraped off the inside of a chimney.

We all froze, including the pointer. Joan stared past us. Her face went rigid.

"Olivia?" Henry's fingers dug into my knee. "What *is* it?"

I swallowed down the buzz of panic. Whatever it was behind us stood there, waiting. I wanted to run away and not look back; I wanted to turn around and face whatever it was.

I turned around.

It was the gray man, tall and thin, with black-hole eyes and a black-hole mouth. He was made of smoke and shifting light and patches of dark nothingness. His head was too large, and then it was too small. A nose flickered across his smoky face and was gone. He had feet, and then he didn't.

Igor batted at the gray man's wavering fingertips with his front paws. *What a delightful new toy! I must have it.*

"You know," said the gray man, his mouth stretching into a horrible smile, "you really don't need all that rubbish to talk to ghosts."

 94

PART TWO

JOAN MADE THAT SOUND LIKE WHEN YOU WAKE up from a nightmare and try to scream, but your voice gets stuck and instead comes out this terrified, whimpering whisper. Then she ran for the nearest exit.

That left me and Henry onstage. And Igor, and the tall, gray man made of smoke, and three more smoky figures behind him, emerging from the shadows.

Henry and I watched them come. Henry was shaking so badly, I thought he'd get up and follow Joan any second now, but I stayed put, even though my heart raced so fast I thought it would explode from my chest. We'd done what we wanted to; we'd contacted ghosts. I wasn't going to waste this opportunity.

Besides, Igor didn't seem too concerned with the fact that there were now four ghosts onstage. In fact, he collapsed in front of the gray man and showed him his belly.

"There's no need to be afraid," said the gray man. His smile gaped crookedly, and his stomach was a big patch of black. He put out one arm, his smoke-fingers curling eloquently. He had a strange, old-fashioned accent. "I am not here to hurt you, nor your cat. Nor you, Henry."

Henry made a tiny, scared sound. "You know me?"

The gray man cocked his head like a bird. "One does not spend years in a place without getting to know the people in it. We've been watching both of you for a long time."

Something clicked inside my head. "That cold air! That was you, wasn't it?"

The gray man's smile widened. "Precisely. And I think we're ready to trust you now. After all, you went through all this trouble. The least we can do is say hello."

The gray man turned his head around 180 degrees to look at the other gray figures behind him. "Wouldn't you agree, friends?"

The other three ghosts nodded, the smoke of their bodies rippling.

"I would," said one of the two smaller ghosts—a boy, maybe a couple of years younger than me. His gray had a bluish tint, his smoke-skin covered with dark, glowing patches. They looked almost like burns.

"And I think Tillie would agree too," the boy ghost continued. When he smiled, half his jaw fell away in a chunk of smoke and then came back together. "Of course, I only *think*."

"I agree," said the other small ghost—a bluish-gray girl with braids floating around her head. Smoke rose from her body as though she were on fire. "And I bet Jax does too."

The gray man nodded. "Tillie and Jax, they cannot see each other, you see. Or hear each other. It's quite tragic, really."

Jax, the boy, crossed his arms over his chest, and the girl, Tillie, spat a glob of churning black smoke onto the stage. It melted right through the floor.

"Don't be melodramatic, Frederick," said Tillie.

The gray man said, "Forgive me, I tend to do that. The result of working in the arts, I suppose. At least . . ." He frowned. "Maybe it was the arts. Or perhaps it was politics. Or perhaps agriculture. It's all rather fuzzy."

"The arts?" I whispered, trying to keep everything straight in my head.

The gray man, Frederick, nodded. He bowed, and then crumpled into a gray-and-black puddle on the floor, and then came back together again. Henry and I backed away, but the gray man only smiled.

"I apologize. Sometimes it is difficult to keep things together." He patted the remaining smoky bits of himself back into his body, straightening his smoke-jacket. "My name is Frederick van der Burg, and this is Tillie and Jax." He stretched his fingers out to the girl and boy ghosts. "And this"—he pointed to the fourth ghost—"is Mr. Worthington."

Mr. Worthington stared. His eyes and mouth were the largest, hanging open like gateways to some secret, dark place. His head didn't hang quite right, like someone had screwed it on wrong, and he was skinny as a bundle of twigs.

His shape was the hardest to make out in the shadows; he was mostly darkness.

"He's a businessman," Tillie said. "But he doesn't speak much."

I picked out a smoky fedora and business suit in Mr. Worthington's driftiness. It was strangely reassuring to see a ghost wearing a business suit.

"If he doesn't speak," Henry said faintly, "how do you know his name?"

Jax shrugged. So did Tillie. They started speaking over each other, but I could pick out most of it: "We've known him for a while. Besides, he's a ghost and we're ghosts. So we just . . . *know*."

"We only know *some* things, though," said Tillie.

"We don't know *everything*, though," said Jax.

"Just enough to get by," they both said, their words lining up almost exactly.

"Such interesting children, aren't they?" Frederick said. "If I had to be stuck with others, I'm awfully glad it's such interesting others."

"Children?" Tillie and Jax said. "We've seen more than you have, I'll bet."

Frederick laughed, a terrible sound that screeched down my spine.

"And what shall you bet, young ones? Eternity?" He held out one hand in a swirl of smoke. "Or eternity?" He held out his other hand. "As that's really all we have."

"Olivia," Henry whispered, inching closer. "Let's get out of here. Please."

"If we run, they'll just follow us."

"That's true," Frederick said. "But we wouldn't hurt you. I bet that's what you're thinking, isn't it?" In a whirl of wind, he rushed down to sit across from us and propped his head in his hands. "I remember loving ghost stories when I was a boy. How silly they were—harmless, I suppose, but silly and wrong."

"Why won't you hurt us?" I said.

Henry pinched my hand. "Don't *ask* him that!"

"Why would I want to hurt you? Why would any of us?"

I shook off Henry's hand. "Don't ghosts do that?"

Tillie and Jax settled in smoky pools on either side of Frederick. "Some do," they whispered in chorus.

"But there's no need to be frightened around *us*." Darkness dripped from where Frederick's teeth should have been. "You have my word."

He stretched out his hand—or smoke and darkness in the vague shape of a hand.

I narrowed my eyes at him. "How I am supposed to trust your handshake if you don't really have a hand?"

All of them laughed, except for Mr. Worthington—croaking, creaking sounds like rusty doors.

"Oh, I like her," said Jax, nodding.

"She's all right," said Tillie, smiling.

"How blunt of you, how charmingly forthright." Frederick

straightened the clump of smoky bowtie at his throat. "Let me just say that, once, I had a hand. Once, I had a lot of things. And I swear on all those things, those realnesses that were once mine, that none of us will hurt you. Ever."

He held out his hand once more. I glared at it.

"We are lonely," he said, quietly. "It is nicer than I can say, to talk to a real person and remember what it was like."

I examined Frederick's face for a few seconds, but it was hard to read a face that wouldn't stop drifting around.

"Look," Henry said, shoving past me, "why don't you just get out of here? You say you won't hurt us, so don't. Just leave."

"Henry, stop it," I hissed. "You wanted to find them."

"Yeah, I *did*."

"Well, here they are!" I put my hands on my hips. "Frederick, I've got some questions."

"Oh, I do love questions." Frederick, trembling, drifted away into pieces, like a pile of leaves blown apart by wind.

Tillie and Jax tugged at the pieces of him. Even Mr. Worthington helped. They patted Frederick back together, drawing the smoke-shape of him in the air with their smoke-fingers. I felt hypnotized; Henry's mouth hung open.

Whole again, Frederick muttered, "Thank you, friends, thank you most kindly. Now. By all means. Your questions, Olivia: Ask them."

"First, why are you here?" I said.

"We are here because we can't leave."

"We're stuck," said Tillie.

"We're bound to this place," said Jax at the same time.

"What *place*, exactly?" Henry asked.

"Emerson Hall." Frederick looked around at the Hall, his eyes lingering on the organ and the vaulted ceilings with their murals of crumbling paint. "It is our haunt. It was beautiful once. At least, I think it was. I seem to remember it once being beautiful."

"It's beautiful *now*," Henry said defensively.

I elbowed him. "Why here?"

"We left things behind, *before*," Frederick said. "Important things. And we left them here, somewhere on these grounds. And without them, we cannot move on. Without them, our souls are incomplete. They are our anchors. They represent things we did not finish, things that keep us from becoming whole, from moving on. They keep us here, in the world of the Living."

"*Before?*" I asked.

Frederick hung his head. Tillie and Jax looked away and, unknowingly, right at each other. Mr. Worthington stared.

"Before we—before we . . ." Frederick sighed. "Forgive me, the word can be difficult to say."

"Oh, come on, Frederick," said Tillie. "Before we *died*."

"It's hard for Frederick," said Jax, patting Frederick's shoulder with tiny puffs of smoke. "He's new. He hasn't been around as long as we have."

 102

"Frederick's new," Tillie explained, at the same time as Jax. "It's harder for him. We've been around longer, but not as long as Mr. Worthington."

So Mr. Worthington was the oldest of the group. That made a strange kind of sense. I did not let myself meet his dark, unblinking eyes.

"What did you leave behind?" I asked. "What are these anchors?"

"We don't know," said Frederick.

"What do you mean, you don't know?"

"We can't remember what they are."

"When we died," Tillie said, "we forgot a lot of things."

"Dying makes you forget things about living," said Jax.

"So," I said slowly, "these anchors are keeping you here in the Hall."

They nodded.

"But you don't remember what they are, and I guess you don't know *where* they are either?"

They nodded again.

Henry cleared his throat. "What happens if you *don't* ever find them?"

"Then we will remain here forever," said Frederick.

"We'll never move on," said Tillie and Jax.

"On?" Henry said. "On to where?"

The world of Death, I thought, remembering Mrs. Barsky's spooked face.

"The world of Death," Frederick said.

"That's where the Dead go," said Tillie. "But we're not quite Dead yet, not all the way."

"Only the Dead can enter Death," said Jax. "Those with complete souls. But we're only halfway there. Our souls are damaged, incomplete without our anchors. We're *not quite* Dead. We're in between."

"We're in between," whispered Tillie.

I tried to imagine being stuck in the Hall forever, never being able to leave. Or worse, if we did run completely out of money, being *forced* to leave. Living on the streets. Building a bed of newspapers for me and Nonnie under the East River Bridge.

It wasn't a nice thought, and for all I knew, it could happen.

I forced myself to feel braver than I wanted to. I didn't know what would happen to me—to Nonnie, to the Maestro and his orchestra—but maybe I could do something about these ghosts. Maybe I could help them.

"I have a question," Henry said. "You say you've been here for years. Why are we just now seeing you?"

"People only see ghosts when we allow them to see us," Frederick said. "It's a sort of built-in safety precaution, if you will."

"Why did you let us see you? We saw you a few weeks ago in the lobby, with those shadow things, and now today."

The ghosts looked at each other. Then Frederick chuckled sheepishly. "Oh, in the lobby. Yes, that was a . . . how shall I say it? A preliminary test. We had to show ourselves to you,

CLAIRE LEGRAND

see how you responded. Congratulations! You passed, and now here we are today."

"And these burns on our skin?" I held up my arm.

"An unfortunate side effect of communicating with ghosts, I'm afraid," Frederick said apologetically. "They should fade in time."

"Okay, so we're all talking now. What do you want from us?"

The ghosts seemed suddenly shy, their cheeks darkening. Were they blushing?

"We thought maybe you could help us," Jax said softly.

"We thought it was time to ask you," Tillie said.

"To find our anchors," they said together.

I frowned. "And how would we do that, exactly?"

"I'm afraid there's only one way for us to move on," Frederick began slowly. "We must first remember what our anchors are. Then we must remember *where* they are. And finally, we must find them and reunite with them. Then, and only then, can we enter Death."

"But you said you don't remember any of that," Henry said.

"In order to remember these things, we will need to be more alive. We will need to live through our last memories, relive our deaths." Frederick paused and looked straight at me, and in that second, I knew what he was going to say before he said it. "We will need to relive our deaths . . . through *you*."

  **13**

FOR A MINUTE, NO ONE SAID ANYTHING. THEN Henry totally lost it.

"What?" He backed away until he hit the wooden wall of the choir loft. "You mean possession, don't you? No way. No *way*."

Frederick clucked his tongue. "Henry, do calm yourself. You'll wake everyone up."

Possession. It made me think of scary movies and dolls that could talk.

"*Possession* is such an ugly word," Frederick continued. "It implies that we would own you, and that's not it at all. It would be a . . . sharing. You would see our memories, and we would use your minds to remember them."

"That's just ridiculous," Henry said. "Why couldn't you just, I don't know, think harder or something, and remember everything yourselves? Why would you need us?"

"Henry, Henry. We ghosts are only just floating! We can hardly keep all the bits of ourselves together, much less put our *memories* back together. Memory building is hard work, and I'm afraid ghosts just aren't very good at it. We're so very close to *un*being, to nothingness. We're not in your world, and we're not in the next one either. If we put our concentration into finding our memories and piecing them back together, we'd simply . . . drift away."

Henry shook his head against the choir loft wall, his eyes wide. "I am so freaked out right now."

"And I can't say I blame you for that. I understand this is a bit much to take in, but . . . what do you think?" Frederick turned to me. "Olivia? Are you still interested in helping us? You haven't said a word."

My mind spun around all kinds of questions and countless sketches. More than anything, I wanted to draw. I didn't want to forget anything that had happened that night.

"If we help you, you'd be inside our minds?"

Tillie and Jax nodded. "That's right."

"Would it . . . hurt?"

Mr. Worthington wrung the ends of his long smoke-coat in his hands. He shook his head, staring at the ground.

"It could," Frederick admitted. "We've seen . . . others do it to other humans. The results are not always pleasant. But it works so much better for everyone involved if the humans are willing. We would never share without your permission. We are not that type of ghost." Frederick drew himself up tall, ghost smoke quivering around him. "I promise you that."

"But it *could* hurt," I said. "Even if we give you permission."

"I'm afraid it very well might."

"And it's worked before? The other ghosts you knew who

did this, who shared with humans and found their anchors. They moved on?"

Frederick nodded excitedly. "Not all of them, but a good many, yes!"

Mr. Worthington jerked his way over to Frederick and tugged at his sleeve. He pressed his face against Frederick's ear, his black smoke and Frederick's gray smoke blending together.

"Olivia, this is insane," Henry said. "You're not really going to do this, are you?"

"Stop grabbing me, Henry."

"But, *Olivia*—"

"Mr. Worthington says," Frederick said, "that he also doesn't know if the sharing will hurt or not, the actual part where we get into your mind. But he does know that the dying . . . that will hurt."

"The dying?" Henry repeated.

"As I explained, you will relive our last moment with us, and you will die with us. You will feel what it is like to die."

"Are you *crazy*?"

"Quiet, Henry," I said. "After we die, then what? What happens after that?"

"Then we all return here, back to normal. You as humans and us as ghosts."

"So we wouldn't actually die, for real."

Frederick's jaw literally fell off. "Of course not." He

scooped up his jaw and patted it back into place. "I told you we wouldn't hurt you, and we won't."

"Except for the part where we're going to *die*," Henry snapped.

"Well, yes, except for that. But it's not really dying, just feeling like you are."

"Oh. That's much better, then."

"And what would we get out of this?" I said. "We fake-die and help you . . . for what?"

"Well, you would be helping us, first of all, which would be very kind of you," Frederick said carefully. He glanced at the others, clearing his throat. "Secondly, you would no longer have, shall we say, unwanted beings in your Hall. And it would be an adventure, wouldn't it?"

"You don't have to, Olivia," Jax said. He placed his fingers on mine, a brush of ice cubes. "We won't make you."

Tillie chucked me on the shoulder, a snowball's direct hit. "I wouldn't blame you if you didn't do it, Olivia. *I* wouldn't want to."

Mr. Worthington shoved his hands in his pockets. I wondered if he was trying to tell me something with those black-hole eyes of his. I wondered if he'd ever been as scared as I'd been lately.

I put up my chin like I knew what I was doing. "Henry and I need a moment."

Frederick nodded. "As you wish." Then he floated across the stage, taking the others with him.

"Well?" I whispered to Henry. "What do you think?"

"I think that if you're considering helping them, you're insane."

The word stung. "A freak, you mean? A psycho?"

"Come on, you know I don't think that. But how can we trust them? And how we do know 'sharing' with them won't . . . I don't know, scar us for life or something?"

I hugged myself. Henry made good points. "I guess we don't know any of that."

"And we barely know these ghosts, anyway," Henry continued. "I mean, I'd risk all that for *you*, but I don't think I would for them."

I blinked. "You'd risk getting scarred for life . . . for me?"

"Duh. That's what friends do."

"But I thought . . ." For a minute, I forgot the ghosts were even there. "I thought we were just partners. Strictly business."

Henry threw up his hands. "Sure. Fine. If that makes you feel better."

I wasn't sure if it made me feel better or not, though. I didn't know how to process the sudden calm I felt after hearing Henry say, so matter-of-factly, "That's what friends do."

Could partners be friends?

Igor patted my leg with his paw. *Your ghost friends are waiting, you know.*

I tried to shake my thoughts clear, but they were too muddled. Death. Ghosts. Broken memories. I couldn't make sense of it, not enough to make a decision.

"We need some time to think about this," I said slowly. Then I turned to the ghosts. "Meet me back here tomorrow at midnight, and you'll have your answer."

"Midnight." Frederick smiled dreamily. "How poetic of you. Important things always happen at midnight."

Henry muttered something angry and turned away.

Abruptly, Tillie kicked the Ouija board. Her foot went right through it, of course, but she didn't seem to care.

"What was that for?" I asked.

"Don't ever bring that board in here again," she said, looking around into the shadows. Beside her, Jax did the same thing; they were almost touching, but not quite. "They attract the wrong sort of spirits."

$\mathcal{T}$HE NEXT DAY AT SCHOOL, RIGHT AFTER HENRY sat down across from me with his lunch, I said, "So? Are we going to help them? What do you think?"

He shoveled a chunk of potato salad into his mouth and glared at me. "The same thing I thought yesterday. No. Way."

"Because you're scared."

"No, not because I'm scared. Because I don't really feel like fake-dying for ghosts who might turn us over to the Devil or something if they decide they don't like us."

"So . . . you're scared, then."

He stabbed his chicken patty. "Maybe."

"Me too."

"Really?"

"Yeah." I opened my sketchpad, turning past page after page of scribbled ghosts to find a clean sheet. "I'm not sure it's such a good—"

My stomach lurched. Five pages. Five clean pages left in my sketchpad, and I didn't have the money to get a new one. My vision narrowed to a blurry tunnel, centered on those precious five pages. Soon, I'd have to start drawing on whatever paper I could find—napkins, scrap paper from school, newspapers. The thought was humiliating; artists didn't draw on napkins and newspapers. They drew on fine paper in sketchpads.

I didn't let myself start crying, though. It would have messed up the paper, and I didn't have any to waste.

"You okay?"

I slammed the sketchpad shut and avoided Henry's eyes. "Yeah. It's fine."

"Ahem" came a quiet voice. It was Joan. She sat farther down the table than usual, right at the edge of the bench. She kept looking at us and then back at her lunch tray. "Ahem."

"Yes, Joan?" I said, irritated.

"I was wondering, please, if I could have my doll back."

"Can't hear you."

"I *said*," she almost shouted, frantically, "I want my doll back! My doll, Magda!"

People at nearby tables turned to stare.

"Oh, right." I took Magda out of my bag and slid her across the table. "Here. I threw the Ouija board away, though. The ghosts said it was bad—"

"Don't," she whispered through clenched teeth, "say—anything—about those—those *things*." She grabbed Magda and hurried away, dumping her whole untouched lunch tray into the trash can.

"For a *séance expert*," Henry said, "she sure does scare easy."

But I just stared after Joan, frowning. "That's right. She saw them, didn't she?"

"What?"

"Joan saw the ghosts just like we did. I guess that means they trust her, too."

"So what are you going to tell them tonight?"

I turned back to my lunch, picking at my bread crusts. "I don't know. It probably isn't a good idea, but . . ."

"But you're curious."

I looked up at Henry, and noticed a startling thing. His eyes were clear and open, like pools of blue water. Like the sky. Sky eyes. I'd never looked hard enough to notice before. Looking at them gave me the floaty, flippy feeling; I'd never felt that for anyone but Richard Ashley before.

"Yeah." I forced my attention back to my sandwich. "I'm curious."

"Well. If you *do* decide to help them—and I still don't think you should—I'll help them with you."

My head shot back up. "Really?"

"Really." Henry dug in for another glop of potato salad. "It's not safe enough for you to do it alone. I don't trust them."

This hot, tingling feeling raced up my arms, but I remained professional. "Maybe it isn't so bad being your ghost-hunting partner after all, Mr. Perfect."

He smiled at me through a mouthful of food.

That night, after Nonnie went to bed, I camped out by the rehearsal room door to let Henry in. He wouldn't be there until midnight, but I couldn't possibly stay in bed. My skin crawled with nerves; I hadn't decided what to tell the ghosts, and part of me was afraid of what they'd do if I said no. They'd promised they wouldn't hurt us, but what did a ghost's promise really mean?

As I was sitting there, huddled up in the dark with Igor in my lap and a flashlight under my foot, I heard someone stumble into the kitchen. The light buzzed on, bathing the hallway in harsh white light. I heard a heavy sigh—the Maestro's sigh.

"I thought he was asleep," I whispered to Igor.

Igor perked up. *Finally, something to do.* Then he leapt off me, darting silently into the kitchen.

"Olivia?" The Maestro poked his head around the corner. I tried to blend into the darkness. "What are you doing out there?"

I rolled my eyes and dragged myself over to him, arms crossed. "Nothing," I snapped. I needed to get him into his room and asleep before Henry showed up.

"I'm making chamomile tea, if you want any."

Chamomile tea. That was good. That would make him sleepy. "Great. I'm going back to bed."

But when I walked past the kitchen, a pile of glossy papers on the kitchen table caught my eye. I peered closer. I saw THE CITY PHILHARMONIC and shining pictures of the Maestro and the orchestra. The concert schedule for the rest of the year.

"What are these?"

The Maestro tried to scoop all of them into his arms, but the paper was too slick. The fliers slid everywhere, falling to the ground. "They're nothing. Just a little something."

I picked up one of the fallen papers. "They're fliers about the orchestra."

"I thought maybe if I put them around town, it could help. Even though it isn't much."

I stared at the paper in my hand. The ink was so bright, the paper crisp and shiny. "These must have cost a lot."

"Yes." The Maestro paused, hunched over, his arms full of fliers. He seemed afraid to look at me. "They cost a good deal."

"Where'd you get *that* money?" I threw the flier to the ground. "Did you sell Nonnie and not tell me?"

"How could you say such a thing?" The Maestro stepped toward me, and the pile of paper in his hands tumbled to the floor, skidding into the corners of the room. Igor chased after it, yowling.

The Maestro stood there staring at the fallen papers like it was this mess he could never pick up. He was as skinny as I was. He needed to shave.

"I think I might be going mad, Olivia," he said at last. He slumped into the nearest chair. "I think that I see things. I think that I see *her*. But when I look again, it is just a trick of the shadows."

 116

He looked up at me, wiping his face. It made him look so small, like a child, like Nonnie cuddling her scarves in her bed. Suddenly I couldn't breathe.

"You're pathetic," I whispered. "Mom's gone. She's not coming back."

The Maestro nodded. "You're right. You're right, of course." Then he wiped his face again, and then he got on his hands and knees, picking up each flier one at a time, stacking them neatly, like they were pieces of glass.

By the time Henry knocked our code on the rehearsal room door—da da da-da da . . . da da!—the Maestro had gone to bed.

"Well?" he said, as I let him in. He had this big lumpy backpack on his shoulders. "What's your decision?"

I kept thinking of the Maestro and his fliers, no matter how hard I tried not to. Hot lumps in my throat made it hard to breathe. He thought he saw Mom. He thought he saw her in the shadows. That wasn't possible. Unless he was crazy. Or unless . . .

A horrible thought occurred to me, so horrible I couldn't get the words out.

"Olivia? What's wrong? You're staring at me."

I spun on my heel and ran out onto center stage, Henry hurrying behind me, whispering for me to slow down.

"Ghosts," I hissed, once we got out onstage. I swung my flashlight around like a searchlight. "Get out here. *Now.*"

"Olivia," Henry said. "You don't order ghosts around. What's the matter with you? What're you gonna say?"

Before I could answer, Frederick, Tillie, Jax, and Mr. Worthington manifested right before our eyes. Henry staggered back.

I was too angry for surprise. I plunked a finger in the middle of Frederick's chest. Cold shot up my arm, turning my skin white as snow and my veins purple. I didn't care.

"You're messing with the Maestro. You're making him see things that aren't there. Aren't you?"

Frederick's expectant smile disappeared. "I beg your pardon!"

"Don't mess with him. I need him to stay sane. I need him to make money. Or else . . . or else . . ." I trailed off, shaking, with a fear so deep it was hard to stay standing. "I'll do it, okay? I'll help you move on. Just leave him alone. Leave *us* alone. And if you go anywhere near Nonnie, I swear I'll make you sorry."

Henry pulled back on my arm, and Frederick held up his hands. "Olivia, please! Slow down. We haven't 'messed with' your father, nor with your grandmother. Nor with you, for that matter. I don't know what your father saw, but it wasn't us."

I yanked my arm away from Henry, tears wobbling at my eyelids. My cheeks felt like they were on fire. "You promise?"

Frederick floated down to my level. Tillie, Jax, and Mr.

Before I could answer, Frederick, Tillie, Jax, and Mr. Worthington manifested right before our eyes.

Worthington hovered solemnly behind him. "We promise you, Olivia. Cross my heart and hope to . . . well, stay dead."

"Cross your human heart? The one you used to have?"

Frederick drew an *X* over his chest, leaving dark ripples in the grayness. "Absolutely."

Henry was staring at the ghosts hard. "*Did* Olivia's dad see something? Do you know what he's talking about?"

The ghosts looked at each other uncomfortably.

"It's possible we know," said Tillie.

"We might know something," said Jax.

"But you're not going to like it," they said together.

"What does that mean?"

Frederick's shoulders rippled darkly; his head drooped. "I suppose I should show you."

"Frederick, don't!" Tillie said.

"No, Frederick," said Jax.

"You'll scare them away!"

Mr. Worthington shook his head, staring at the ceiling.

"They deserve to know," Frederick said sharply. "Everyone, gather at the backstage door. Olivia, please switch off your flashlight. We'll wait there."

Henry grabbed my hand in the dark. I didn't mind one bit; Frederick's expression scared me. "Wait for what?"

"You'll see." Frederick shuddered; it felt like drizzling ice against my skin. "It won't be pleasant, and it's actually quite dangerous for us ghosts. But not with you close by."

 120

I didn't know what that meant, but I was too afraid to ask. The darkness had swallowed up my voice. We waited in the doorway for what felt like hours, Henry's hand crushing mine. Then the red exit sign at the back of the Hall flickered.

"There," Frederick whispered, pointing at the ceiling.

In the moonlight streaming through the high terrace windows, I saw shadows. Solid, twisting, vaguely human-shaped shadows like the ones Henry and I had seen that day in the lobby.

The burn on my arm stung with sudden coldness.

"We've seen these before," I said. "That day in the lobby, the first day we saw you."

"Yes."

"You said that was part of some test," Henry whispered furiously. "Were you lying?"

"Yes, and I'm sorry for that. But I didn't want to frighten you away before we could even explain ourselves."

I followed the shadows' flickering movement across the ceiling. It was mesmerizing. "What are they?"

Frederick exhaled, sending goosebumps down my back. "They are shades. Ghosts who could never find their anchors, who were never able to move on. Ghosts who were tempted into Limbo. We used you to drive them away, that day in the lobby. I apologize, but . . . they are much stronger than we are, and they wouldn't leave us alone."

I rubbed my burn. "They hit us. They left marks behind."

 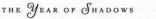

"They hate humans. They are terribly jealous of you, and yet they love you too," Frederick said quietly. "You have what they have forever lost: life. Mostly they stay away from you. The pain of remembering is too great. But sometimes they cannot help themselves."

I inched my head a bit farther out the door. The shades scampered across the ceiling, darting in and out of the moonlight like spiders. Darkness trailed off of their bodies like black fog. When the light hit them, they glittered. Like my burn.

"You said something about Limbo," Henry whispered. "What's Limbo?"

"There is the world of Death, where the Dead go," said Frederick. "There is the world of the Living, which holds the Living and the ghosts. Then there is Limbo, which is between the two. Once a ghost enters Limbo, it becomes a shade. It can travel back and forth between the world of the Living and Limbo. It can even touch things in the world of the Living, if it wants to. You see?"

One of the shades careened into a chandelier. The diamonds clinked and shuddered. Soft shrieks drifted down afterward.

"That doesn't seem fair," I said. "*You* can't touch anything."

"No, but at least I can perhaps move on someday. Sooner rather than later, if we have your help." He smiled shyly. "Shades, on the other hand, can never move on. Or at least,

I've never heard of it happening. They're not the best conversationalists, shades. I only know of them what we have managed to piece together through watching them. You see, in Limbo, their minds are clear. They remember that they have anchors, somewhere in the world of the Living. They remember that they would like to move on. But once in the world of the Living, they forget all of that. They become hardly more than mindless beasts, confused and vicious. Thus, they can never remember, and they can never move on. They can touch things, oh yes, but they can never find peace."

"How do you know all this?" Henry demanded.

"We told him," Tillie said, jutting out her chin. "And Mr. Worthington told us. And other ghosts told him. You have to study your enemy. We *know* shades."

"So shades are shades for eternity?"

Frederick nodded, his eyes fixed on the ceiling.

Eternity: forever, and ever, and ever; an endless amount of time.

I tried to wrap my brain around the idea. I'd heard that the universe was eternal too, spreading out in all directions, and if you tried to find the edge, you never would. You'd just keep on flying through space, *forever*.

I grabbed onto the door frame, suddenly dizzy.

"What do the shades want?" Henry said beside me. "Why are they here?"

"Shades exist wherever ghosts do," Frederick said.

"They hate us because we have what they can never have: a chance to move on. So they haunt us, try to lure us into Limbo."

At the word *Limbo*, the other ghosts shivered. Tillie and Jax had to hold Mr. Worthington together so he didn't fly apart.

"It is tempting, to go to Limbo with them," Frederick said softly. "It would be easier than resisting them. If I were a shade, I could touch things. I could feel a little of what it is to be alive again."

"Yeah, and then you'd be stuck that way forever," I snapped. "You'd be stuck as 'a little of' something."

At the sound of my voice, the shades on the ceiling scattered, fleeing into the corners of the Hall like roaches. One of them seeped into a crack in the wall and disappeared. Another snaked its way down one of the terrace columns and vanished into the floor.

Once they'd gone, Tillie exhaled, and it frosted my cheek. Jax, who had hidden himself behind Mr. Worthington, blinked up at me through Mr. Worthington's chest.

"I thought you deserved to know," Frederick said quietly. "Even if you aren't going to help us. These creatures live in your music hall, and they won't go away unless we do."

I pulled out of Henry's grip and started to pace. "And you think maybe they made the Maestro see things? Showed him things that weren't there?"

124

"It's possible. I've seen shades pull all sorts of nasty tricks on humans. It's the only revenge they can get, I suppose."

"Revenge?" Henry said. "We didn't do anything to them."

"You're alive, aren't you?" Frederick shrugged. "That's enough."

"Do *you* hate us?"

"No. And even if I wanted to, I wouldn't." Frederick smiled tiredly. "Hate takes too much effort, and we're hardly here as it is."

When I realized they were all watching me, waiting for my answer, I stopped pacing and made myself face them, looking deep into those freaky ghost eyes.

"I'll do it," I said at last. "I don't want those things, those shades, in here. I don't want them distracting the Maestro. I don't want them hurting Nonnie. And if helping you move on is the best way to do that, then . . ." I put out my hand. ". . . consider me your partner in crime. Or moving-on . . . ness. Whatever."

The ghosts stared at my hand like it was a heap of treasure.

"You're quite certain, Olivia?" Frederick whispered.

"Yes. Now let's shake on it before I change my mind."

Four ghost hands piled on top of mine—four clumps of ice-cold air, swirling through my fingers.

I glanced at Henry. He had this steely, quiet look on his face. Then he put his hand on top of all of ours.

"If Olivia's in," he said, "then so am I."

"To moving-on-ness," Frederick said. His grin was so big, his face literally split into pieces, cracking every which way like a giant spider.

"To moving-on-ness," we said, except for Mr. Worthington, who grunted something that sounded like "Mmmgrmph."

This was going to be interesting.

CHAPTER

15

$\mathcal{T}$HE NEXT NIGHT, ONCE AGAIN AT MIDNIGHT, Henry and I waited on the stage for the ghosts to show up. I couldn't sit still; I was too nervous.

We were going to try sharing for the first time.

Possession.

"Don't your parents care that you're here?" I sat on the edge of the stage, tapping my feet together. "How do you keep sneaking out?"

He shrugged. "I'm responsible. They trust me. They don't bother me too much."

I tried to get a good look at him, but he was turned away, hiding his face. Something about the way he talked about his parents seemed funny.

"How'd you get here tonight?"

"I walked."

"You *walked*? Out by yourself in the middle of the night?"

He grinned. "Concerned for my safety, huh?"

"Ha-ha." I paused, scuffing the floor with my shoe. I

felt suddenly very nervous. "Henry, what's in your jar? The one you brought for the séance?"

Henry glared at me. "It's none of your business."

I tried to hide how much that hurt me, deep in my gut. He was right; it wasn't any of my business. But he knew private things about me, things lots of other people didn't know — about where I lived, for example. It was only fair that I get to know something too.

I walked it off, pacing back and forth across the stage until the only thing left was nervousness. My skin turned hot, and then cold, and then hot again. I wiped my hands on my jeans.

Sharing, not possession, I reminded myself, over and over. Sharing was good. Everyone teaches you that.

Out of nowhere, Igor bounded up the stage-left staircase, which led up from the floor seats.

Henry jumped. I think he might have even said a bad word.

I tried not to laugh. "It's only Igor."

Igor pressed his head against my palm. *Only Igor? There's nothing "only" about me, pet.*

"I wonder if cats can share with ghosts."

Igor nipped my thumb. *You couldn't feed me enough fresh tuna to share with a ghost.*

"No way," Henry said. "We're not bringing a cat with us. Animals are unpredictable. You never know what they might do."

Suddenly, four grayish shapes popped out of the empty space in front of us.

"Boo," Tillie said, grinning.

Henry jumped back. "Oh my God."

"Oh," Frederick said, tilting his head. "Have we startled you?"

"No," Henry mumbled.

"Yes," I said. "Ground Rule #1: You can't just appear out of nowhere and freak us out like that. *Capisce?*"

"We can't help it," said Jax.

"We are *ghosts*, you know," Tillie said.

Henry had recovered himself. "Yeah, well, you aren't the ones getting possessed tonight. So just calm down with the ghost stuff, all right?"

Tillie turned upside down to gaze at Henry. "Henry? What's in your bag?"

"Oh." Henry flushed a little. "I brought an emergency kit. You know, in case something goes wrong."

"Oh?" The ghosts looked at each other, smiling.

"Yes." Henry emptied the contents of his bag for us to see: "A first-aid kit. A Bible. Some books about exorcism I checked out from the library. And one of those pay-as-you-go cell phones. You know. In case we need to call 9-1-1. Or a priest."

Frederick looked amazed. "A priest? Which priest?"

"All of them," Henry said grimly. "I've got the numbers of every church in the area."

The dark line of Jax's mouth rippled like a wriggling black worm. "So responsible, Henry."

"Wow, Henry, you thought of everything," said Tillie, smirking.

Henry flushed even redder. "I like to be prepared."

"I assure you, Henry," said Frederick, "you won't need any of that."

"But you said you've never done this before!"

"Well, you most likely won't need any of that."

"Most *likely*?"

"You'll just have to trust me." Frederick cleared his throat, a rumbly, echoing sound like a storm. "Now, if you'll please put those things aside and sit down."

The ghosts surrounded us, on four sides like the points of a compass. It suddenly felt very real that we were about to *share* with them. Even if it was only for a few seconds, and even if it wasn't real, we were about to die.

What would it be like? What would it *feel* like? Part of me was, well, dying to know.

Another part of me was shaking, screaming, panicked.

Henry held out his hand, and I took it. If there was ever a time to hold someone's hand, this was it. Together, we looked up at Frederick, who loomed driftily over us. His smile dripped down his face.

"I'll be going first, since I'm the youngest," he explained. "That is, I've been a ghost for the least amount of time. It will be easiest for you. The older the ghost, the more diffi-cult the sharing."

I chanced a look at Mr. Worthington. In the darkness,

I couldn't pick out the details of his face.

Igor sat next to him, watching us. *Don't be afraid*. That's what he would say, if he could, to make me feel better. His tail was twitching, though; he was on high alert.

Wisps of Frederick came to rest on our legs, our arms, our hair, sinking into us. A cold curl snaked into my ear.

"I shall try my utmost to bring us back to a useful moment, near the end of my life," he said. "I'll be with you the whole time. I'll be right here."

I squeezed Henry's hand tighter.

"Henry," I whispered.

He squeezed my hand back. "Right here, partner."

"We won't let anything happen to you," Tillie and Jax said, but their voices were muffled. There was too much Frederick smoke in my ears. My skin was tingling like crazy. I was sinking into black water, cold as ice.

"I'm sorry," Frederick whispered, just before it happened. His voice was everywhere—in my blood, in the hairs standing straight up on my arms, in the breaths I couldn't quite take. "I hope it doesn't hurt."

16

*I*T DID HURT. A LOT.

At first everything was quiet, like right before a storm when all the wind is sucked out of the world.

I couldn't move; I couldn't swallow or breathe or open my eyes. The only thing I could feel was Henry's hand gripping mine.

And cold.

Cold, everywhere. Cold rushing into me, through my mouth and nose, even seeping beneath my eyelids. Cold sliding under my fingernails. Cold freezing every hair on my body into silver needles.

I tried to scream. A harsh ringing sound drummed against my ears. Was it the sound of dying? It yawned, groaned, scratched my insides like ragged fingernails. I wanted to slam my hands against my ears and block it out. But I didn't move; I couldn't lose my hold of Henry's hand. If I did, I would drown in the cold; we both would.

Worse than the cold, though, was the feeling that I wasn't quite myself anymore. I was Olivia, yes, but I wasn't alone.

There was another person inside me, made of ice and smoke and a dark, heavy feeling, like my insides had been crammed too full.

Are you there? A faint voice, miles away. *Olivia? Henry? It's me.*

Frederick's voice. I struggled to listen more closely, but cold fog plugged my ears. Cautiously, I tried to shake out the muffled feeling.

Yes, that's good, whispered Frederick's voice. *Roll your head around. Stretch out your fingers.*

I did, with my free hand. I couldn't see yet, but I could still feel Henry's fingers; he wasn't going anywhere. At each new movement, fresh cold hit me, like when you creep out of bed on winter mornings.

Don't open your eyes yet. Can you speak?

I tried opening my mouth, which hurt. Beyond my eyelids shone a whiteness.

Don't speak with your lips, Frederick said. His voice was louder now; in fact, it sounded like it was coming from inside me. *Just try thinking things to me. It takes some getting used to, but it's much less confusing. Say something. It's all right.*

I concentrated as hard as I could, breathing in and out slowly. *Frederick?* My head felt full of splinters. *Where are we?*

Frederick sighed happily. *Oh, wonderful. You're coming around. Now you, Henry.*

That hurt, I heard Henry gasp out, from the corner of my mind.

If it makes you feel any better, the sharing was uncomfortable for me, too.

Actually, that did make me feel better.

Keep moving, keep speaking.

A few minutes later, I could feel my toes and fingers, my fluttering insides.

Henry? I whispered.

I'm here. His fingers squeezed mine.

Can we open our eyes, Frederick?

Almost, Frederick said, and I nearly screamed. He was too close. He was in my head; his voice was mine. I felt my lips move as he spoke. He was speaking through me, and in a strange way, I was speaking through him, too.

Henry, say something, I said, and I felt lips that weren't mine move too. And when Henry said, *Something, Olivia,* my lips also formed the words *Something, Olivia.* My voice echoed over his. So did Frederick's.

Ah, you're beginning to understand, said Frederick. *When we share, we share everything. I am your voice, and your voices are mine. My mouth is yours, my mind, my breath, and your mouths, minds, breaths, are mine, too. We are all one being, at the moment.* He paused. *Have you ever participated in a three-legged race?*

Very funny, Frederick, Henry said—and Frederick's voice and my voice said it along with him.

Well, I thought it was a good analogy. We must learn to think, speak, and do together, just like if our legs were tied together.

Can we at least try to concentrate enough to use our own voices? I said, squeezing my eyes shut again. *I can't stand this; we're all echoing over each other.*

Very well. Frederick sighed. *Focus on your voice, but not too hard. We'll need all the focus we can manage to put my memories back together.*

Eyes still closed, I imagined my voice as a bright spot in my brain, vibrating with sound. I imagined grabbing onto that spot and tucking it away, somewhere safe. After imagining that five times in a row, I tried speaking.

Hello, this is a test, I said. I heard only myself.

Splendid! Frederick crowed. *Now you, Henry.*

My name is Henry, and I don't like sharing.

Well, that's rather childish. Try opening your eyes. It might be disorienting.

Why? I wanted so badly to open my eyes. But what would I see when I opened them?

You will no longer be in Emerson Hall. Or rather, you will be, but not as you remember it. It will be as I remember it.

As he spoke, a feeling like fingers poked through the folds of my mind. Frederick was sewing our minds together into one giant, three-legged-race brain. Sounds began drifting toward us—voices, talking and laughing; rustling of clothes and feet; glasses tinkling together. I smelled people and musty fabric.

Oh, Frederick whispered, and everything he suddenly felt rushed through me—happiness, wonder. Sadness. Tears filled my eyes, but they weren't mine.

I remember now. Frederick sounded so small, like Nonnie wrapped up tight in her scarves. *It's all really here. Olivia. Henry. You can open your eyes.*

We did. At first, everything was spotty, like I had something stuck in my eyes. The more I concentrated, though, the clearer the picture became. And when it finally brightened enough to see where we were, I gasped.

We were in the Hall, and it was beautiful.

*C*HANDELIERS OF CRYSTAL AND CANDLES glittered from the lobby ceiling. Curling staircases gleamed with polished wood and rich red carpet.

And there were people—*everywhere*. They looked fuzzy, like we were in the middle of fog. Their voices echoed from faraway. They wore furs and silks, long gowns and sharp black jackets. Their boots shone; their coats fluttered behind them like wings. Glasses in their white-gloved hands caught the light and winked at me.

Most of them held concert programs.

To the left, through the main Hall doors, were rows upon rows of bright red seats. I took a lurching step closer. It felt like lugging two dead weights behind me, and four other legs.

Oof, Frederick grunted. *A little warning would be appreciated, Olivia. We must move together, remember?*

I hardly heard him. From this position, I could see the stage and the pipe organ, blazing with light.

"It's so *grand*, isn't it?" someone near us said, a silver-haired lady in furs.

"Indeed," said her companion, a tall man with a shining mustache. He looked upon the arched ceiling with puffed-up pride. "Unparalleled, architecturally speaking."

I stumbled over to a shadowy corner where it felt like I could breathe again.

What are you doing? Henry asked, crammed somewhere inside my ear.

Sorry. I got dizzy.

What I didn't tell him was that I didn't know how to handle seeing the Hall like this. It shouldn't look beautiful and impressive; it should look old and dirty, nasty and crumbling. That was a Hall I knew how to deal with, a Hall I could hate, a Hall I could blame.

Remember, Olivia, Frederick said gently, *that when sharing like this, it's easy for us to understand what you're thinking, if you're not careful.*

An embarrassed feeling crept through my stomach, but it wasn't my embarrassment. It was Henry's. I tried focusing on him and saw blurry, confusing images: a red-haired man; a white room; a battlefield. Henry's dirty brown jar. The lid was off. I could see things inside—papers, something metal and shining.

Then it was like Henry had shut a door. The images went black; I couldn't feel Henry's embarrassment. He was protecting himself so I couldn't see his thoughts.

I imagined snapping down the shades of my mind too. I felt bad for stepping into Henry's thoughts, but I couldn't help wondering what that white room meant, who the red-haired man was. Was it Henry? His dad?

Henry was blushing; I could feel it. *Sorry,* I whispered. *I didn't see much.*

He didn't answer.

"I say, van der Burg," said a voice very near us.

We all whirled, stumbling over ourselves—or, our *selves* inside our one, three-legged self.

This is so confusing, I said.

You're telling me, Henry said. He sounded like he was trying hard not to laugh.

I tried to kick him before I could remind myself that he wasn't actually *there,* and just ended up waving my leg around in the air. *I said, shut up!*

"Van der Burg?" the voice said again—a man standing nearby. "You don't look well, my friend."

Frederick recognized this man at once. Inside us, he gasped and said, *Thomas!*

What do we do, Frederick? I said. *He thinks we're you!*

You are *me,* Frederick explained patiently. *Or rather, you look like me. He only sees me. We're all me. This is my memory, after all.*

The man, Thomas, was looking at us like we were insane. We probably looked like it—Frederick standing in the corner, kicking himself.

Inside our head, Henry burst out laughing.

"Yes, I'm quite all right, Thomas," Frederick said, laughter in his voice.

I'm glad you two think this is so funny, I grumbled.

Frederick leaned toward Thomas. "Between you and me, I think I've had a spot or two more of wine than I probably should have."

He winked. We *all* winked. I'd never been able to wink before.

Thomas clapped us on the back. "That's my old Frederick. Now come on. Wine or no, you've got a concert to play."

A concert? I said to Frederick as we followed Thomas through the west lobby. *What's he talking about?*

But Frederick wasn't listening. *Look at it,* he said, dragging his fingers along the wall. *It's exactly as I remember. And tonight . . . I wonder which concert it is. There were so many.*

Were you a musician, Frederick? said Henry, his voice full of awe.

Frederick paused before the violinist fountain, which was working for once. I heard Frederick's thoughts, a jumble of things about ambition and talent, practicing until his fingers bled, stacks of paper covered with music notes. The memory images jumped out at me, one after the other: Frederick, a young boy, sneaking into a tavern to play the old broken piano. Frederick, a half-starved ten-year-old saving money so he could buy a violin.

"I was a musician," he whispered out loud, remembering, thanks to us. "I . . . played this instrument. I played the violin."

Thomas stared at us. "Frederick, you're completely off-kilter tonight, do you know that? What's the matter? Is there a problem?"

"No, no problem," Frederick said. We stumbled after Thomas, heading backstage. Our feet felt like metal weights.

Frederick, are you okay? I asked.

I'm not sure, Frederick said. *This is all very strange. I know what I'm seeing, but I also don't quite know it, at the same time. I only half remember. Does that make sense?*

Yes, said Henry.

No, I said irritably.

For example, Frederick continued, *now that I see him, I know that this man is Thomas, a friend of mine. A colleague. He also plays the violin. But I don't remember what concert this is, or what night this is, or even how old I am —*

Right at that moment, we passed a mirror — a huge rectangle of glass framed with golden swirls. I recognized the frame. It now hung on one of the walls in the west lobby without any glass in it.

We saw Frederick, and inside his mind, wrapped up in his thoughts, I felt the shock of seeing a real, flesh-and-blood face after so many years of ghostliness.

"I remember my eyes," Frederick whispered. He poked at his cheeks, felt the shape of his nose. "They were brown like this."

Brown eyes and dark hair. A crooked nose. A clean black tuxedo, a vest in a shiny fabric, and some sort of weird scarf thing around his neck. And when he smiled, it was broad and silly.

I felt myself smiling too. *You've got a great smile, Frederick.*

"I had forgotten," he said, touching his own cheek and then the reflection's cheek.

"Van der Burg." Thomas tugged on our arm, his eyes scanning the crowd. "Hurry up, man; you don't want to be late." His smile flashed. "This is your big break, after all."

Warning bells started chiming in our head. Thomas didn't seem so friendly anymore.

Frederick? Henry was thinking the same thing. *Is everything okay with this guy?*

Oh yes, said Frederick. *Thomas is an old friend. D'you know, we were in the Tenth Street Musicians' Guild for years, back from when we were boys.* Frederick sighed dreamily. *I remember now. I remember those hungry days.*

I frowned, inspecting Thomas's back as he led us downstairs toward the backstage area. I had no reason to suspect Thomas of anything—except for the fact that we were basically on the lookout for impending doom.

What's a musicians' guild? Henry asked.

Oh, it was an organization for us, shall we say, less-privileged musicians, Frederick explained. *We didn't have money, you see, or the connections to get into a real orchestra, so we just formed one ourselves. We played anywhere we could—on the streets, in pubs, anywhere. Sometimes we made money. Sometimes we didn't.*

But, Frederick, if you were in that guild, playing on the streets and stuff, I pointed out, *how are you here now? You're dressed up so nice, and Thomas said something about a big break?*

142

You know, I don't recall, said Frederick cheerfully, *but undoubtedly we're about to find out!*

We stepped into one of the backstage hallways, heading for the main rehearsal room. My heart jumped into my throat as we passed the area that would later be my and Nonnie's bedroom; right now it was just a brick wall. I dragged my fingers across the rough edges, wondering if my skin would feel a jolt of recognition.

I live here, I said, before I could hold it back. *Henry, this is where I live. In our time, this is a storage room. It's made of concrete. I sleep there, on a cot.*

I felt Henry pat me on the shoulder, which unfortunately made our physical arm—Frederick's arm—jerk like he'd been electrocuted.

"Frederick," Thomas snapped. "Really. Control your limbs."

"Apologies, friend," Frederick said. "I seem to be a bit overexcited. Big night, you know."

Thomas grunted. "Yes, I'm quite aware."

I know, Olivia, Henry was saying. *I try not to go back there, though. I know you don't like it. But you shouldn't be embarrassed. I think it's kind of cool, really.*

Cool?

Yeah, your family living back there to save the orchestra, giving up pretty much everything. It's so . . . noble.

Maybe when it isn't happening to you, I said as we turned a corner—and were nearly tackled by four giant men.

They slapped our back and gave us rowdy hugs. They

shouted "Good luck!" and "Old Frederick, you've really done it, haven't you?"

Frederick, I said, trying to catch my breath, *what is going on here?*

Frederick was laughing so hard he could hardly speak. *These are my friends! From the guild. They must have come to wish me good luck!*

I noticed that Thomas wasn't celebrating with the others. He stood off to the side, looking around nervously.

Henry, I said, *do you see Thomas?*

Oh, yeah, Henry said grimly. *Something's going on with that guy.*

Frederick? Look at Thomas. Don't you think he seems —?

"Come on, fellows," Thomas said, reaching into the chaos to grab Frederick's arm. He pulled us away, his face shining with sweat. "Let the great composer have some air."

Frederick, you're a composer? Henry repeated as Thomas led us away.

You know, I haven't the faintest idea, Frederick said, still grinning ear-to-ear. "Say, Thomas, tell me how I got here, would you?"

"What?" Thomas snapped.

"You said 'the great composer.' Am I a composer?"

Thomas laughed. "Very funny."

"I'm quite serious."

"Why, don't you remember?" Thomas stopped in the darkest part of the hallway. "How the Baron Eckelhart heard us playing on the street that beautiful autumn day? How he was so riveted by your solo that he invited you to his mansion for a private audience? How he brought you to the Maestro Seidl himself, who was so *enraptured* that he admitted you to the orchestra without even a formal audition?"

Frederick's mouth was gaping open. My insides crawled. I did not like the wild look in Thomas's eyes.

Henry? Something's wrong.

Henry agreed. *Frederick, we should get out of here.*

But Frederick wasn't listening. "Extraordinary," he whispered.

Thomas laughed again. "Indeed! And do you remember how, most wondrous of all, the Maestro discovered your *talent* and commissioned a concerto from you? It's said to be a masterpiece. Word on the street—with us *commoners*—is that you're to premiere it tonight, a surprise encore. That Mozart himself would weep to hear it. That you will be made unbearably famous because of it."

Thomas's eyes gleamed in the shadows. "Well? What do you have to say? Does that jog your memory, old boy?"

Frederick nodded, a smile spreading slowly across his face. His fingers curled, remembering the feel of the violin in his hands. His mind raced through the strains of the music he'd written; it echoed through our joined minds. My throat clenched, and Henry grabbed my hand.

Suddenly, we knew what it was to be a virtuoso violinist,

to compose music worthy of Mozart. We felt the mathematics of it swirling through our minds, just like the knowledge of how to tie our shoes.

Frederick, I said, overwhelmed by the rush of memories, *this is amazing . . .*

"I am a composer," Frederick murmured. Thomas looked disgusted. "I am a violinist in the City Philharmonic." He began to laugh. "I remember now . . ."

Thomas jerked his head, cutting Frederick off. Strong arms wrapped around us from behind—one around our waist, the other around our neck, choking away our air. Together, we clawed at the arm, but it wouldn't budge.

"All of that," Thomas whispered, "and you forgot about us, didn't you, Frederick? Your friends in the guild? Your entire *life* before this fame and fortune? Here you are in your fine clothes, with your wealthy patrons, and you forgot about us. About *me*. You left us out in the cold."

Frederick tried to shake his head, choking. "I didn't for-get—"

"Oh, it's too late, old friend." Thomas laughed. "Where is the music?"

Frederick didn't understand; I could feel his panic and confusion. I started to cry.

This is it, isn't it? I asked Henry. I reached for him, but I couldn't find him in our tangle of minds. *We're going to die, aren't we? This is his death.*

It'll be okay. Henry might have been crying too. It was

146

hard to tell. All I knew was my fear. *Remember? We'll wake up just fine. It's not real.*

It felt real.

"The manuscript, Frederick," Thomas hissed. "Your bloody brilliant music! Where have you hidden it?"

But Frederick didn't remember. I could feel that he had no idea. And with us so afraid, there was no way we could focus to figure it out in time.

"*Where?*" Thomas yelled.

Suddenly, something in my brain clicked into place. The manuscript. Frederick's music. A sense of *rightness* filled my every thought, and even though I was terrified, I wanted to laugh.

That's it! I thought to Henry and Frederick. *It has to be. That's your anchor, Frederick — the music!*

"D'you know, Olivia," Frederick said aloud, "I think you're right."

Thomas's face darkened. "You idiot. No matter. I'll find it myself." Then he jerked his head again and disappeared into the shadows.

The arms whirled us around, slammed us into the wall. A sound of sliding metal, a flash of silver, a veiled face scowling — and then Frederick said, "Oh," and thought to us, *I'm sorry*, and then it happened.

Something stabbed us in the gut. Pain ripped through us, hotter than fire. The killer slipped away, and we slumped to the ground. When Frederick put his hands to his stomach, they came away covered in red.

I was screaming, grabbing for Henry, but it hurt so much, and it kept getting worse. His arms slipped away from me. I yelled for him, but it hurt to yell. I fell to the floor of our joined brain, curled up in a throbbing ball of blood and guts.

Henry? I didn't recognize the sound of my own voice.

What does the world of Death look like? I thought, trying to keep my eyes open even though everything in the universe was pressing down on them. Maybe, if I tried hard enough, I would see Death. I would see stars and rivers, a flickering exit sign.

But I saw nothing.

I let my eyes fall shut.

CLAIRE LEGRAND

*W*HEN WE WOKE UP, FREDERICK LEFT US, drifting out of our bodies in gray tendrils. It felt like something was peeling my skin off my bones.

I threw up, and Henry did too. I was glad to see him right there beside me, in a huddle like me, wiping his mouth like me.

The pain in my stomach, where the murderer had stabbed us, began to fade. A tingling sensation rushed over my body as warmth seeped back in, melting away the cold of Death.

Igor burrowed under my arm, butting his head against my chest and meowing. *Such a foolish girl. Such a brave girl.*

"Olivia?" Henry said. "Are you okay?"

I nodded, and I didn't even care that Henry was still holding my hand, that he was squeezing it so tight it hurt. The pain meant we were both here, alive and safe.

Once I could stand to keep my eyes open, I looked around. We were in the Hall and it was old and crumbling again. Mr. Worthington was floating nearby, his mouth hanging open.

"That was *so* weird," Tillie and Jax whispered. Hovering

over us, they inspected us like we were some kind of crazy experiment.

"*What* was so weird?" I said.

"Frederick *melted* into you," Tillie explained, "and then the two of you sat there, holding hands, your heads tilted back and your mouths wide open. Frozen. Except your skin and the insides of your mouths were swirling. With Frederick, I guess." She grinned. "*So* weird."

Jax seemed less happy about the whole thing. "Did Tillie explain?" he said quietly.

I nodded. "Where's Frederick?"

Tillie pointed across the stage. "He's over there."

He was balled up like a kid in the corner, so see-through he was almost invisible. Since I didn't trust my legs just yet, I crawled over to him.

"Frederick?" I put my hand on his shoulder. My skin looked like ice, my fingernails blue and purple as I thawed out. "Are you okay?"

He turned toward me, his face drooping. At each blink, his eyes dripped down his face before sliding back up into their proper places. He could hardly hold himself together. His body wavered like something at the bottom of a lake, way down below the water.

"It took a lot out of me, but I'll be fine," he said. He tried to hug me, but when I started shivering, he pulled back. "Oh, Olivia. Henry. I'm so sorry. I didn't remember how badly it would hurt."

"Don't worry about that, Frederick," I said, even though my stomach still hurt. My whole *body* hurt. "Henry and I knew the risks."

"But you didn't know you would be murdered," Frederick said, shaking his head. It fell off with a soft, smoky *plop*, and he held it in his hands, looking back up at himself. "Thomas. My own friend had me killed. *Murdered*."

I shivered at the word. It sounded just like what it was—evil and angry, hidden in shadows where no one could see you.

"But we're here now, and we're okay," said Henry, coming up behind me. He seemed so different now, so quiet. Dying had changed us. I felt all mixed-up inside, and I couldn't meet Henry's eyes when he looked at me. Henry had been in my mind, and I had been in his. He had felt my hatred toward the Maestro and the Hall. He had seen my bedroom. He knew how every day Nonnie looked smaller, how every day I was afraid I'd wake up and find out she'd finally shrunk herself away into nothing.

And I had seen the white room, the redheaded man. The battlefield. The jar. It was almost like we had seen each other naked.

I realized I was looking at the world through tears. I needed to be alone; I needed to think.

Henry put his hand on my arm. *I don't want you to touch me,* I thought at him—before realizing he couldn't hear my thoughts anymore. How glad that made me feel, how safe— and how empty.

I shrugged his hand off me and took a deep breath. "But we did find out something important, Frederick," I said. "We know what your anchor is: the music you wrote." I walked to the edge of the stage, my toes hanging over the side. I crossed my arms over my chest and glared into the blackness, at that flickering exit sign.

There's no exit sign on the way to Death, I thought, and for some reason, that made me angry. *There's just nothing.*

"Now all we have to do is find it."

We agreed to wait a week to start searching for Frederick's anchor. He wasn't kidding when he said sharing took a lot out of you.

I felt like a sack of garbage that someone had taken out back and beaten with a hammer. Every bone in my body ached. Randomly, I'd feel like getting sick and have to run for the bathroom. Sometimes at night I would wake up, gasping, with this sharp pain in my stomach—an echo of the murder.

One time, when that happened, I woke up to find Mr. Worthington settled on the edge of my bed, staring at me.

I shot up into a sitting position, knocking an indignant Igor to the floor. "Mr. Worthington, what are you doing in here?"

Across the room, Nonnie rolled over and smiled at me. "Is one of the ghosts, Olivia?"

"Um. Yeah."

152

"Tell it I said hello. Oh." She hugged herself. "I wish *I* could see it. Do you think someday I will?"

"Him," I corrected automatically. "His name is Mr. Worthington. He was a businessman. And maybe. I don't know. They have to trust you first."

"I'm very trustworthy. *Molto fidato.* Does he like scarves?"

"Probably." I drew my blanket up to my chin. "Mr. Worthington, what are you doing here? I never gave you permission to come into my room."

Mr. Worthington took off his hat and turned it around and around in his hands. His face looked unusually distressed.

"You were loud, Olivia." Nonnie pulled out a scarf from the box by her bed and cuddled it. "You had bad dream. *Un incubo.* You have many now. You didn't always."

Igor shook himself irritably and glared up at me. *Obviously the old fellow was worried about you, in his own way. Now, if you'll excuse me, since I'm up, I'm off for a snack.* He slid out the bedroom door, invisible in the dark.

"Were you worried about me, Mr. Worthington?" I whispered to the frigid air swirling and shifting in front of me.

He didn't answer, of course, but he rearranged himself at the edge of my bed, stiff like a soldier, and when I went back to sleep, the pain in my gut wasn't so bad anymore.

The first time I fell asleep in class, Mrs. Farrity gave me a warning. The next two times, she gave me more warnings.

The fourth time, she sighed and beat her famous gavel on the metal underside of her desk until I bolted upright.

"Olivia," she said, frowning, "if you can't manage to stay awake in my class, then go stand in the corner."

I blinked at her, trying to wake up. People were laughing, Mark Everett the loudest of all, of course. I wished Henry were in my class. Mark Everett wouldn't mess me with if Henry was around. Or maybe he would have; he didn't seem too happy with Henry these days, not since he started sitting with me at lunch.

"Stand in the corner?"

"Yes. It'll be much harder for you to fall asleep if you're standing."

"Horses sleep standing up," Mark whispered at me as I stumbled to the corner, "and *donkeys*, too. Hee-haw, hee-haw." He made an ugly face and crossed his eyes.

"You're the one who looks like an idiot right now," I spat, "not me."

More giggling. More sighing from Mrs. Farrity. "*Olivia . . .*"

"Fine, I'll be quiet. Even though I'm just defending myself." I stood in the corner, determined to look as impressive as possible, like it was no big thing to stand up in the corner for the rest of class when all I wanted to do was curl up under my desk and sleep.

Right as Mrs. Farrity resumed her lecture about this book that I was supposed to be reading and wasn't, this sad-looking book with an old bearded man on the cover, I saw Joan

154

Dawson get out of her seat and march toward me with her head high in the air.

She took up position right next to me and clicked her heels together.

Mrs. Farrity was staring, everyone was staring.

"Joan, what on earth are you doing?" Mrs. Farrity said.

"Solidarity, Mrs. Farrity," Joan said. She lifted her eyebrow coolly. "Perhaps you've heard of it?"

Mrs. Farrity sent Joan to see Principal Cooper after that, but Joan caught my eye on her way out. She saluted me, and I smiled. Joan and I didn't talk much, not since the séance. I wasn't sure if we'd ever be friends again, or if we were even friends to begin with, but it was a nice thing, to have her come stand next to me.

Solidarity: when people stick together because they believe in the same things.

I liked that.

A week after sharing with Frederick, we all gathered on the catwalk during the Friday night concert.

It was the day before Halloween.

Below us, the orchestra wailed and shrieked their way through *Symphonie Fantastique* by Berlioz and *Night on Bald Mountain* by Mussorgsky. If I hadn't been so preoccupied with thoughts of ghosts and dying and murder, I might have actually paid attention to this music. It was dark and intense, designed to creep people out.

The orchestra was creeping people out, all right—but not the way they should have been. Already that night, I'd counted fifteen people getting up and leaving right in the middle of the concert.

Henry sat near the railing, watching morosely. "This is awful. It's like they're just going through the motions. No wonder they sound so bad. You can't just *go through the motions* when you're playing Berlioz!"

"Henry, calm down before someone hears you," I said. "Anyway, it's easier if you just ignore it. That's what I do."

"Your dad's conducting up a storm. Sweat's flying *everywhere*."

"Okay, ew. I do not need that mental image."

"He must feel so bad about what's happening to the orchestra," Henry whispered.

I did not want to think about the Maestro feeling bad. *I feel bad too*, I wanted to scream at the top of my lungs. *The orchestra might shut down. I could be homeless.* But I didn't have the guts to say that out loud. If I did, it might come true.

"Would you get over here? We've got a job to do."

Henry grumbled his way over, and I unfolded my map.

Tillie let out a low whistle. "Olivia, this is really good."

Jax beamed at me. "You drew this?"

My whole body flushed. Usually people didn't pay attention to what I drew. I mean, it *was* good—a complete diagram of the Hall, including every hallway, every room, every staircase. The angels at the entrance, the fountain in the lobby, the pipe organ—I'd drawn everything, framed with an elaborate border of curlicues and dragons and angels, just like the ceiling.

But I just shrugged. "Yeah. It was slow at The Happy Place yesterday."

Henry leaned over the map, inspecting it, but he didn't say anything. Probably too mad at me for not sobbing over the orchestra or whatever. But I could see in his eyes that he liked it. It's hard to fake things when you have sky eyes like that.

I pointed at the map. "Henry, you'll take the main Hall, your usher territory. Frederick, you can do the front offices because some of those are always locked. Tillie and Jax, you can take the attic, the ceiling, all the stuff we can't reach."

Tillie grinned. "Swinging through chandeliers never gets old."

"Let's see. Mr. Worthington, you get the grounds, if that's okay? Outside, the courtyards, the walking park?"

Mr. Worthington nodded, his eyes glued to the map.

"And I'll take the backstage area, the storage rooms, the basement." *Home*, in other words.

"Well, this map is indeed beautiful, Olivia," said Frederick. "But it will be futile for we ghosts to do any searching. We can't pick up anything we find, or move things."

"No, but you can see things we can't," Henry said. "You can float inside walls and underground. If you find something, come find us, and we'll figure out a way to get it."

We gave the ghosts icy high fives and split up to search our assigned areas, but we didn't find anything that night. I must have combed every inch of that rehearsal room, and I found lots of music, but not the piece I was looking for. Frederick couldn't remember much about his music — not a title, not what key it was written in, nothing. Just that it was a concerto, and that his name was written on it: Frederick van der Burg.

"A lot of good that'll do if the ink's rubbed off or something," I muttered to myself, climbing on top of the lockers to rifle through boxes. "Or if it's smudged or torn."

Igor didn't seem to care; he had found a piece of fuzz near the ceiling. *Fuzz, buzz, wuzz,* he purred to himself, batting at the fuzz with his front paws. *Linty, flinty, squinty.*

The others didn't have much luck either. I went to bed feeling frustrated and hopeless. How were we supposed to find one tiny piece of music in such a huge place, a place crammed full of music? And what if it had gotten burned in a fire or leaked on or crumbled into dust?

When I fell asleep, I dreamed of Mom. I always dreamed of Mom when my mind was too busy to remember that I didn't want to think about her.

The dreams weren't always nice.

This time, Mom was swimming in an ocean of music. I was high above her, soaring on the back of one of those origami swans she'd taught me to make. Dozens of others surrounded me, filling up the sky. I called to Mom, and she waved back, but then the ink started bleeding off the music, and soon she was lost in a cold, black sea. I couldn't find her anymore. Everything was dark.

The scariest part was, I didn't care. I searched through those crashing, thick black waves, looking for her blonde head, and the longer I couldn't find her, the more this hot, sharp feeling built up inside me. A satisfied feeling.

"That's what you get," I screamed into the inky storm. "You left us. You left me! That's what you get!" I pounded on the back of my swan. "I hope you never come back! I hope you *drown*."

Then the storm became stronger. The ocean of ink splashed up in tidal waves, drenching my swan's wings, making us too heavy. I started screaming for Mom, but she was long gone.

We crashed into the sea.

I woke up, sweating, to see Frederick floating beside my bed.

He put his hand on my leg. That frozen touch seeping through me was strangely comforting. "Forgive me for waking you," he said quietly, "but I think there's something you should see."

$\mathcal{I}$ FOLLOWED FREDERICK INTO THE MAIN HALL, my mind reeling from my dream. I couldn't shake the image of Mom drowning in blackness, the feeling of *gladness* that had filled up my chest. I didn't understand it; the longer I concentrated on it, the guiltier I felt. Glad? Glad that she *drowned*? What was wrong with me? As I followed Frederick up the narrow staircase that led to stage left, I tried to push all memory of the dream down into that deep, locked-away place where I kept everything belonging to Mom.

Frederick stopped me at the stage door, his hand trailing ice down my arm. "Look, Olivia."

I followed Frederick's ghostly fingers into the Hall. First, I saw a shade, just one, wandering around the ceiling. It seemed lost, or maybe just sad. It kept crawling across the ceiling from one end to the other, wagging its head.

Then I saw the Maestro.

The door at the back of the Hall opened, letting in pale light from the lobby. The Maestro's silhouette made its way down the center aisle. After a minute, he paused, peering into the darkness. I wondered if he had seen the shades move. But then he started walking again, waving his arms distractedly. As he approached the stage, I could hear him humming to himself. I recognized the melody: the scherzo from Mahler's Symphony no. 2. That symphony was nick-named "The Resurrection."

"What's he doing?" I whispered.

"I don't know, but he does this quite often," Frederick said. "He'll wander the Hall for hours, singing and conduct-ing, or talking to himself, or in complete silence."

At the first row of floor seats, right by the stage, the Maestro turned around and wandered back up the center aisle. At the back of the Hall, he started up one of the curling staircases that led up to the dress circle boxes.

"Sometimes, it seems as though he's searching for some-thing," Frederick said.

"Seems to me like he's just crazy." My cheeks were burn-ing. "I'm sorry you have to see him like this."

"Oh, I've seen much stranger things than a lonely man."

"Lonely?" I laughed. "If he is, he did it to himself."

"Perhaps."

"We've got to get you moved on." I watched the shade with my fists clenched. "We've got to get those shades out of here. They're making him nuts."

Frederick draped an arm around my shoulder. It felt like a scarf made of ice.

Desperate to change the subject, I remembered a question I'd wanted to ask, before the Maestro showed up. "You know how the only way you can see a ghost is if the ghost shows himself to you?"

Frederick nodded.

"Is it the same for shades?"

"No." Frederick paused. Then he said carefully, "In fact, the only people who can see shades are those who, like the shades, have experienced true loss."

During every class the next day at school, I tried to focus on my latest sketch. It was the ocean of melting music from my dream, Mom being tossed around in its waves. I thought maybe if I drew the nightmare out of my mind, I'd stop thinking about it—stop feeling glad, stop feeling guilty.

But concentration was impossible. Frederick's words stuck in my brain like thorns. *Only those who have experienced true loss can see shades.*

What counted as true loss? I guess Mom leaving was my true loss. Putting those words to it made me feel ripped open. Loss. I had *lost* her.

No. She had left me. You can't lose someone who knew exactly what she was doing when she left you behind.

I stabbed the paper with my charcoal, black dust flaking off the tip. This was my last piece of sketch paper. I tried not to think about that, coloring in the inky sea over and over, black as night, black as Death.

Another thought came to me as I worked, as Mrs. Farrity drew diagrammed sentences on the board and Joan shot disapproving looks at me for not paying attention:

Henry had also seen the shades.

He must have lost something too.

CHAPTER 20

*T*HAT FIRST WEEK OF NOVEMBER, WE WENT crazy searching for Frederick's music. Every evening after work at The Happy Place, I'd find Henry, wherever he'd camped out in the Hall working on his homework. The ghosts were usually hanging around him, so we'd set out an agenda for the evening, split up, and search.

We found nothing for a few days. I started to lose my patience. So did old Kepler. He kept whacking us with his broom and yelling at us for crawling around in the dirt like a couple of miscreants.

Finally, the only place left was the Maestro's bedroom.

During one of the first November concerts, while the orchestra fumbled through Dvořák's New World Symphony and the Brahms violin concerto, I snuck into the Maestro's room. Igor slid through, right on my heels. I shut the door behind me and switched on the light.

Music clogged every inch of this room — recorded music, music lying silent within the upright piano crammed into the corner, music in the old photographs of conductors plastering the walls.

"Well," I said, nudging trash around with my foot.

Igor yawned. *Well, what?*

"I guess we dig in."

Igor plopped onto the ground, tail twitching lazily. *We? I don't think so, friend.*

I rolled my eyes and began to search. I rifled through each stack of music one at a time — scores of symphonies, concertos, weird experimental music that the orchestra didn't play anymore. It was hard enough getting people to come hear the popular, classic stuff, much less weird experimental music. Weird experimental music didn't fly since The Economy.

Piece after piece after piece, and nothing by Frederick van der Burg.

I shoved the fifth giant stack of music aside, ready to give up, when I noticed the old cardboard box beside the Maestro's cot. It was full of used tissues, crusty plates, and moldy books — but at the bottom of the box, I found a hard plastic container.

Igor darted over and rubbed his head against the edge of the box.

"Oh yeah, now you're paying attention to me, because I actually found something interesting," I said.

Frederick's music would most likely not be at the bottom of some plastic box beside the Maestro's bed. But I opened the box anyway.

And inside, I found letters.

Bundles of letters, tied up with rubber bands. I recognized the writing on the front of the first letter: *Otto Stellatella, 481 13th Street, Apartment 4E.*

Mom's handwriting—loopy, dreamy, never the same twice.

I dropped the letters like they were actually a bunch of spiders.

Igor raised his kitty eyebrows. *What's the problem?*

"They're letters," I whispered. "Letters Mom wrote to the Maestro."

And some that he wrote to her.

Igor butted against my shoe. *Aren't you going to look at them?*

"No." But my hands were pulling them into my lap, and my fingers were undoing the string around the first bundle—the oldest one. The earliest postmarked date was almost twenty years ago.

My brain screamed, *No, I don't want to read this!* But my fingers opened the envelope anyway:

Dear Otto,

Thank you for your letter. I must admit, I was startled to hear from you. It was lovely to talk with you that night at the concert, but I never dreamed I'd hear from you again.

I'm blushing as I write this. Isn't that silly? But then, I blushed the entire time we spoke that night—on that terrace, in the breeze. I still have your jacket, by the way. Won't you need it before your next concert? Maybe we'll have to meet, if only so I can return it to you.

166

I'm blushing again! If you were here, would you touch my cheek like you did that night? Would you tell me how lovely I am when I blush?

I closed the letter and put it back into its envelope. My face was about to melt clean off. I couldn't even think about all that blushing and touching cheeks and cool night breezes on terraces without wanting to crawl under the Maestro's cot and hide. This letter was from when they first met. "I met your father on a starlit night," Mom would tell me when I asked, and smile at the Maestro. Back when she actually smiled at him.

I reached for the next letter, automatically, like a robot. It was from the Maestro.

Dear Cara,
 If I were there, lovely girl, and you blushed for me again, I would take you in my arms and—

Okay, no. None of that. I shoved the letter away.

Igor's tail twitched as he watched me. *What's wrong with you?*

"Nothing."

Igor blinked that slow cat blink designed to make you feel like a moron. *What did you think love letters were like?*

"I don't know, I've never thought about it." But I remembered how they used to look at each other—Mom and the Maestro. Their eyes would be so soft. Even when the Maestro was busy working, if Mom said his name, he would look up and smile, and he would become this whole different person.

"What went wrong, Igor?" I thumbed through the rest of the letters in my lap. I didn't stop to read any of them, but I saw flashes of words like *love* and *kiss*, *miss you*, and toward the end, my name—*Olivia*. Had they kept writing letters to each other after I was born, just for fun? "What happened to them?"

I didn't blame Mom for leaving. But when had *I love you* turned into ignoring each other, into all that shouting? I didn't understand that. Why had the Maestro gotten so busy? Why had he stopped eating dinner with us, paying attention to us, coming home even to sleep?

The only answer I could think of was the one I'd always known—the orchestra.

Looking around the Maestro's room at all that music stacked everywhere, I felt the old hate bubble up inside me. He had chosen this over Mom—this dusty, moldy music. I didn't understand that, either.

At the bottom of the letters were some that looked different than the ones I'd been reading. These letters were addressed to Gram's house. Mom's mom. They all had yellow "return to sender" stickers on them. The envelopes were sealed; they had never been opened.

"Does 'return to sender' mean Mom never got these letters?" I said, frowning.

Igor watched me steadily. *Mm-hmm.*

I examined the postmarked dates. December of last year to February of this year. "These are from after Mom left. There are tons of them."

Fifty-two, to be precise. Fifty-two letters over three months, all from the Maestro to Mom, all returned unopened and unread.

Why? Why had he written them, and why had Mom not answered? All that kissing and blushing and all those *I love yous*, and she didn't answer one single letter? I mean, I certainly wouldn't have. But Mom wasn't me. Mom wasn't supposed to not answer letters, to ignore us like we'd never existed.

I opened the first "return to sender" letter. It read:

Cara, dearest, dearest Cara,
Where have you gone? I tried calling your mother, and she will not talk to me. I tried every number I had. I tried your office. No one will speak to me, Cara. What have you done? Where have you gone? You cannot do this to me. I can change. "No, you can't," you will say, but I can. And what about Olivia?

I stopped reading. My eyes were thorny. I opened another one:

My Cara, my lovely Cara,
It has been two months, and still I have not heard from you. Where are you, Cara, where? The orchestra is — things are not going well. I need you, Cara. I need you, my dream.

That one, I shoved back into its envelope so hard that it ripped.

Igor's whiskers twitched. *Careful. You'll get a paper cut, and those can sting.*

"Shut up." I was not going to cry, and nothing I could find inside these envelopes would make me.

I opened the last "return to sender" letter. It said only:

Cara. Where are you?

I stared at those words for a good five minutes straight, and then put all the letters back in the box where I'd found them, and then I sat in the middle of the floor with my arms around my knees.

"Well, wasn't that interesting?" My voice sounded so calm, so outside of my head, like I was listening to a recording of myself.

Igor rolled over on his back. *Isn't my belly nice and fuzzy? Don't you want to give it a pet?*

I snatched Igor up into my arms and buried my face in his neck.

"Why wouldn't she answer him?" I whispered. "Where did she go? Why didn't she ever send *me* letters? She could have; I wouldn't have shown them to him. I would've kept it a secret."

Igor wiggled loose. *Maybe it was too hard for her to write you letters.*

"Too hard to keep in touch with her *daughter*? If I can sell my things and live on a cot and have to draw on napkins, then she could have sucked it up, you know? She could have written me something, anything."

From down the hall, the Maestro's voice boomed, probably yelling at one of the musicians. I jumped to my feet, dumping Igor to the floor. I hadn't even noticed that the music from the concert had stopped.

But it was too late. I ran out of the room and straight into the Maestro's stomach.

21

IMMEDIATELY THE MAESTRO CAUGHT ME BY the shoulders. Igor ran away down the hall toward the kitchen.

"What were you doing in my room?" The Maestro was in his full-blown post-concert state—skin flushed and sweating, hair wild, the permanent bags under his eyes even darker than normal. People didn't like to mess with the Maestro after concerts, especially not these days. But I could think only about those unopened letters, one after another after another.

"Cleaning," I said, glaring at him.

The Maestro looked past me at his bedroom. "And what a cleaning job. Perhaps you will tell me the truth now?"

"I told you. Cleaning."

"You shouldn't go in people's rooms without their permission, Olivia." The Maestro wiped his face with a stained handkerchief. "I give you your privacy. You should give me mine."

"That's what you want, isn't it? Your privacy. To be alone with your music. Well, you've got it now, don't you?"

I couldn't stop myself, even as I heard the words. Part of me screamed at myself to stop. The Maestro didn't deserve my anger, my energy. I had more important things to do.

But the other part felt sick after all those letters.

Why didn't you write me letters, Mom? Not even one?

Because of him.

"I don't know what she ever saw in you." The sight of him repulsed me. He was too sweaty and too skinny and too tired. "No wonder she left."

Something inside the Maestro snapped. I saw it in his eyes, like a light going out. He walked into his room and sank down onto his cot.

"No wonder," the Maestro repeated. He stared at his piano. "Did you know, Olivia, that it is possible to fall out of love with someone? That people can love one another very much, and then stop loving each other somehow?"

I didn't know what to say to this. The Maestro and I didn't talk about love. That was always Mom's thing.

"I loved Cara—your mother—very much," the Maestro continued. "But that's what happened. She fell out of love with me, Olivia. She fell out of love with our life together. And then she left us."

I didn't think mothers could fall out of love with their children. That's what I wanted to say to him. But I couldn't speak. I felt hopeless.

Then the Maestro's face crumpled, and he started crying.

I told myself not to look directly at him. I started backing toward the door. Then, when he buried his face in his hands and let out this awful gasping sound, I ran.

If I'd stayed there any longer, I would have ripped open that box and shoved the letters in his face and demanded an explanation. Either that or started crying right along with him, and that was unthinkable. The Maestro didn't get to see me cry.

I ended up in the basement, not stopping to notice how weird it was for the door to be left open. Kepler never left the door open.

I found a switch and paced in the dim light until I caught my breath. Old instruments surrounded me. Boxes of worn curtains. Seat cushions chewed through by rats.

Nothing made sense anymore. Letters and kisses, dreams and sobbing Maestros and missing moms—it all whirled about in my head like a sketch left out in the rain. It whirled so hard that I didn't see the hole in the floor until I'd already fallen through it, and I landed hard on my butt in the dirt.

"Ow."

I squinted up at the hole in the floor. I wasn't too far down, just a couple of feet. But it was still weird, for there to be this giant hole in the basement floor. The floor had been torn to shreds. I looked around and realized I was in a shallow tunnel that led back behind me into darkness.

The walls of the tunnel were grooved, like they had been dug away by someone's fingers.

I started exploring, running my fingers along the grooves

in the wall. They were icy cold, and they left behind black grit on my fingers. I brushed my hand on my jeans to wipe off the grit, but it didn't budge.

I looked closer. That wasn't black grit. It was tiny speckled burns, freckling my fingertips. Wherever I had touched the wall, my fingers came away burnt.

Automatically, I clutched the burn on my arm, hidden beneath my jacket. I knew then that shades had been here. Maybe shades had even dug this tunnel.

I should have turned around and climbed out, but I didn't.

A fat weight landed on my shoulder. Igor started hissing in my ear. *Must I constantly keep an eye on you?*

Something crunched beneath my left shoe, and I ran face-first into a cold, hard wall of dirt.

Igor tumbled off my shoulder.

"What is all this?" I knelt down to examine the wall, which was packed full of brick, old wiring, and garbage. The corner of a piece of paper caught my eye. I couldn't see anything on it but three letters:

"Urg."

Igor, irritably cleaning himself, meowed. *I do beg your pardon?*

"It says 'urg'. Look." I started digging into the wall. Mud caked beneath my fingernails. "It's almost like whoever was digging here stopped all of a sudden."

Igor wound himself between my legs, meowing louder.

"It's the concerto." I pulled out the paper as delicately

as I could. Twenty pages total, crumpled and filthy, but I could still read them. Frederick had written it in E major. How strange, to see his handwriting; it felt so personal. His real, nonghost hands had touched this. "Igor, *look* at it. Right here: It says Frederick van der Burg. We found it!"

When I whirled around, grinning like an idiot, I saw four long, black arms spring out of the tunnel floor. Their fingers, five times the normal length, curled around Igor and started dragging him toward an opening in the tunnel wall. Past the opening was swirling blackness and crooked, shifting shapes.

Limbo.

$\mathcal{I}$ CRAWLED TOWARD IGOR, SCREAMING.

"Let go of him!" Too angry to be afraid, I pounded on the shades' arms. Each thud burned my fists and sizzled like meat on a grill. But I didn't care. They would *not* take Igor from me.

Cold wrapped around me as shadow-fingers brushed against my clothes. Caressed me. *Pet* me.

Then they let go, like *they'd* been burned. They dropped Igor and darted away from me, back into the opening in the tunnel wall. I'd never heard anything like the sounds they made—these awful wails that made my teeth hurt. Even as they slunk back into Limbo, they reached for me.

I staggered back, and they were gone. I was alone, clutching a freezing Igor to me. His coat was matted with frost.

"You're okay, you weird, stupid cat," I whispered.

Igor grumbled cattishly to himself. *I almost get killed, and you call me stupid?*

Someone shouted my name: "Olivia!"

Henry jumped down into the tunnel and pulled me into a hug. The ghosts hovered right behind him near the tunnel's entrance.

"You're shaking so bad," Henry said. "What happened? Are you okay? Should I call 9-1-1?"

I let him hold on to me for a few seconds before pushing him off. "I'm fine. Just a little burned."

Henry whistled when he saw my fists, where I'd pounded on the shades. The sides of my hands were burned in twin black *C* shapes. "How will you hide those?"

"I don't know. Gloves?"

"Yeah, because that won't look weird."

"What were you doing down here, Olivia?" Frederick asked sternly. He, Tillie, Jax, and Mr. Worthington were almost completely transparent. The tunnel walls shimmered through their rippling bodies.

"Are you guys gonna be okay?" I said, reaching for them.

"Please don't touch, Olivia. We're quite fragile at the moment."

"That was Limbo, wasn't it? That opening in the wall?"

They looked at where Limbo had been. Frederick sighed longingly. Tillie folded her arms around herself, like she was holding herself back from something. Jax turned away.

Mr. Worthington kept shaking. It sent chills through the air.

"Yes," Frederick said. "That was Limbo. They were calling us to it."

"Those rotten, stinking—" Tillie muttered.

"Dirty, lying—" Jax mumbled.

"Thankfully, they didn't stick around with you and Henry close by, and we were able to . . . how shall I say it? Resist the temptation."

Henry whispered, "We can almost see right through you, Frederick."

"It takes a lot of effort to resist Limbo. One gets tired of fighting it, you see?" Frederick's face wavered. "Now, what were you doing down here?"

"Oh, your concerto!" I grabbed the papers and held them up like a flag of victory. "I found it. Frederick, we have your anchor."

Frederick's eyes widened as he reached for the music. I held my breath, and Henry grabbed my arm. This was it: When Frederick touched his anchor, he would fade. He would move on, and it was happening too fast. I hadn't prepared my good-bye, I didn't know what to say.

Even Igor seemed to be holding his breath.

When Frederick's fingers closed around the music, he straightened to his full height.

"But how are you touching it?" Henry whispered.

"Because it is my anchor." Frederick smiled and stroked one smoky finger down the first page. "I think I am meant to touch it."

I waited as long as I could stand it. "Why isn't anything happening? You're still here. Is it not working?"

"Henry, fetch me a violin, would you, please?" said Frederick calmly. "And then let's all reconvene onstage."

"Oh." I watched Henry climb out the tunnel and felt suddenly tinier than Nonnie, tinier than anything. "You have to play it, don't you?"

Frederick put his free hand through my shoulder. "Every anchor has a purpose, something it must do to be whole. What is music if no one ever hears it played?"

"Just some ink on a page," I said dully.

Tillie floated in midair on her side, squinting at me. "You okay, Olivia?"

At the same time, Jax said, "What's wrong, Olivia?"

"I'm fine." Even though I wasn't. First the Maestro crying, now Frederick leaving. Everything was happening so fast. I felt hollow inside, and tired. "Oh, and you spoke at the same time again."

Tillie spun around in a little circle; Jax smiled. They always liked when I told them that.

I tucked Nonnie into bed while Henry and the ghosts made sure the Hall was clear. As usual, music bled out the Maestro's closed bedroom door, rattling the walls. My mind automatically registered what it was: Mahler 2, again. At least he wouldn't be able to hear us.

When Henry met us onstage with one of the old basement violins, Frederick's fingers closed around it, just like a living person's fingers would have. His wispy gray fingers became more solid. He brought the violin up to his shoulder and

 180

Too angry to be afraid, I pounded on the shades' arms.
Each thud burned my fists and sizzled like meat on a grill.

rested it there, under his chin. This hum started, like when a television's on mute in another room, and the quiet electric buzz sizzles high up in your ears.

Frederick picked at the violin's strings. Tiny *pizzicato* notes plunked into the air. Frederick slowly drew his bow across the violin's strings.

A horrible, out-of-tune note *skrrritched*.

"Well," said Frederick sheepishly. "I'm a little out of practice, it would seem. Give me a moment."

We gathered around the Maestro's podium at the edge of the stage and waited while Frederick relearned the feel of the violin. Faintly, the memory of Frederick's talent came back to me. The night we shared with him, his talent had settled in my brain. It had felt like when I held a charcoal and sketchpad in my hands; that was my talent, my violin.

"I wish we could hear it for real," Henry whispered, scooting close to me. "You know, with a full orchestra. If I ever meet that Thomas guy in Death, I'll have a thing or two to say to him, that's for sure."

I nodded. It was all I could do. If I opened my mouth, I would ask Frederick to stop, to stay, and that wasn't fair.

After a few minutes, Frederick paused. "I want to thank you both. I don't know what's going to happen here, exactly, so I don't know how much longer I'll be with you."

He smiled at me, the kindest smile I'd ever seen. So what if it was dripping and black and deformed, like a melting jack-o-lantern? He was Frederick, my friend. And now he was about to leave, and I had to *hope* for him to leave, because that meant he would be safe and happy and wouldn't have to fight Limbo anymore. What a horrible thing, to have to hope for your friend to leave you.

"But I hope you'll remember me. I know I'll remember you. If that's even possible, in Death." Drops of black smoke rolled down Frederick's cheeks. "Goodness. I'm nervous all of a sudden. And I'm horrid at good-byes."

Jax sniffled and hid his face in Mr. Worthington's side. Tillie concentrated on her feet.

Henry said, "It's okay, Frederick. You can do it."

I stood there, trying to hold up this fake smile. My face felt close to breaking.

Then Frederick began to play, and I know I hated music and everything to do with it, but even I knew when a piece of music was really good.

Like this one.

It's this strange feeling, when you hear a good piece of music. It starts out kind of shaky, this hot, heavy knot in your chest. At first it's tiny, like a spot of light in a dark room, but then it builds, pouring through you. And the next thing you know, everything from your forehead down to your fingers and toes is on fire. You feel like the hot, heavy knot in your chest is turning into a bubble. It's full of everything good in the world, and if you don't do something—if you don't run or dance or shout to everyone in the world about this music you've just heard—it'll explode.

That's what I felt that night. And, judging by the look on Henry's face, he was feeling it too.

Frederick played through the entire concerto and finished the last note with a flourish of his bow. He said, "Ha!" and bowed. We gave him a standing ovation, and he beamed at us for a second, but then his eyes widened and he said, "Oh," and then, "Oh, dear." Then he sighed, and all the bits of him fell away like a gust of wind had blown through a cloud of smoke. There was a bright flash of light, so quick we almost missed it.

The high electric hum disappeared with a pop.

And then Frederick was gone.

The violin and bow crashed to the ground.

For a long time, we stared at the empty stage, at Frederick's music lying scattered across it. I was the first to move. I gathered up everything and put the pages in order, Tillie, Jax, and Mr. Worthington drifting silently behind me. They didn't say a word. When Henry and I left to go wait for his bus, I looked behind me. The ghosts were small and dark, floating onstage in a shivering huddle. They couldn't stop looking at the spot where Frederick used to be.

Outside, the sky was cold and starry. Henry and I didn't say much. This heavy thing sat between us now, soaking up all the air. We had helped a ghost move on to the world of Death. Had it worked? Was Frederick happy now?

"Well," Henry said, as his bus pulled up, "see you at school." His face looked about as sick as I felt.

184

I stared at the dark windows of The Happy Place, swallowing hard. "Yeah. See you."

Once Henry left, I added Frederick's concerto to the music library. It belonged there; it deserved to be played. I wondered what the Maestro would say when he found it — or if he would ever get a chance to find it, if the Hall would be around long enough for that.

After filing it away, I pushed my cot close to Nonnie's and crawled under my quilt and put my hand on her wrist, just to feel like I was still in this world.

With Frederick gone, everything suddenly seemed more real:

One ghost saved, three to go. Like a countdown.

  **23**

$\mathscr{T}$HAT NIGHT, I HAD THE STRANGEST DREAM. I dreamed that Tillie, Jax, and Mr. Worthington hovered over me as I slept. Tillie and Jax whispered back and forth to me, talking over each other. They told me that Frederick moving on had scared them.

"He just *vanished*," Tillie said.

"He *disappeared*, Olivia," Jax whimpered. Smoky black tears rolled down his face, carving lines in his cheeks.

"How do we know he really made it to Death?" they said together, their voices overlapping. "What if he went nowhere at all?"

Mr. Worthington groaned softly. I took that to mean he agreed.

But in my dream, I couldn't respond. My mouth was sewn shut, and so were my eyes.

"We're scared, Olivia," Jax whispered.

"I'm not sure we can do this, Olivia," Tillie said, folding her arms over her chest.

"It's nothing you did."

"It's not because of you."

"It's just because we're scared," Tillie and Jax whispered together. They were fading, drifting out of my dream like smoke out a window. "Don't feel guilty. It's okay."

"We just need time to think," Jax said.

"We just need to be alone for a while," Tillie said.

"Maybe it's not so bad being ghosts forever."

"We know how to be ghosts. We don't know how to be Dead."

Mr. Worthington stared sadly, twisting his hat in his fingers. Then they were gone.

When I woke up the next morning, I didn't think about my dream. It was just a dream, right? Besides, all I could think about was Frederick. How he'd disappeared in a flash, like he'd never been there at all. What do you do when a friend leaves you, even if it's for the best? I didn't know the answer to that. I still don't. But I already missed Frederick so much, it felt like my heart had been replaced with emptiness.

I stumbled out of bed, pulled on my boots, and trudged to the bathroom to brush my teeth. Igor followed me, meowing every couple of seconds.

"You're awfully talkative this morning," I said.

And then I felt it. That same emptiness in my chest was everywhere, like something important had been sucked out of the Hall itself. And, for the first time since the ghosts started hanging around me, I wasn't cold.

I breathed in and out. My breath didn't puff. I looked at my arms. No goosebumps.

"Tillie?" I clomped upstairs and out onto the stage, my bootlaces flying. "Jax? Mr. Worthington?"

Igor was right at my heels. *They're gone, pet. I don't know what happened, but I know they're gone.*

"They're not gone," I said, trying not to cry. My dream rushed back to me in shadowy images. Had it not been a dream at all? Had it been real? "They can't be gone. They're just hiding. Tillie? Jax? Mr. Worthington!"

Usually, the ghosts would appear as soon as I woke up, like they'd been waiting for me. Or if they were off floating somewhere in the Hall, I could just say their names, and they'd come right to me.

But not today.

"Tillie," I whispered, closing my eyes. "Jax. Mr. Worthington." I said their names over and over.

Nothing. The air remained still and my breath remained invisible.

"Olivia!" I could hear Nonnie calling from downstairs. "Where are you? Is breakfast time!"

As I stood there, looking around the empty Hall, anger flooded through me. They had *left* me, just like Mom.

"Fine," I said. "Fine, if that's how you're gonna be. If you're gonna run scared, then fine!" I kicked over the music stand from the night before, the one Frederick had used. It crashed to the ground, sending Igor darting back downstairs. "Stay invisible, then! *Cowards!*"

If they heard me, I couldn't tell. And I didn't wait to find out. I ran downstairs and slammed the stage door shut behind me.

"What do you mean, *gone?*"

I couldn't eat my lunch. I couldn't look at Henry. All I could do was stare at the back of my sketchpad, where I'd been doodling tiny pictures in a mural of scratchy ink.

"I mean they're gone. Invisible. Hiding."

I told him about my dream, which I didn't think had been a dream at all. I was pretty sure it had really been the ghosts, saying good-bye.

"After all that, after showing up and sharing with Frederick and everything, they're just giving up?" Henry couldn't believe it.

Down at the end of the table, Joan nibbled furiously on her sandwich, trying to watch us without being obvious. It didn't work.

I shrugged. It was easier to pretend I didn't care, with Henry getting so mad. "I guess so. Guess it really freaked them out."

"But they *want* to die!"

"Maybe they changed their minds."

"What, are they just gonna hide in the Hall forever until the shades drag them into Limbo?"

I forced myself to take a bite of potatoes. "Maybe. Who cares? If that's what they want, let them do it."

"You don't mean that," Henry said quietly.

"Henry, we did all we could for them. If they're too chicken to follow through, that's not our fault, and I've got too many problems to worry about scaredy-cat ghosts."

Henry didn't say anything after that, eating his lunch in silence, this miserable expression on his face. But the thing is, he was right. I didn't mean it. I didn't want the ghosts to be dragged into Limbo, to get stuck forever.

But apparently, they did.

That whole week, as I tried to ignore the ghosts' absence, the Maestro's words cycled through my head. Something about them nagged at me, but I couldn't figure out what.

I think that I see things, he'd said. *I think that I see her. But when I look again, it is just a trick of the shadows.*

On Thursday, after I finished wiping down tables at The Happy Place, Mrs. Barsky pulled me aside to give me my money for the week. Then she put her hands on my face and made me look her in the eye.

"Olivia," she said, "is everything all right? You look worn out."

"No. Yes." I stuffed the money into my pocket. "I don't know."

She and Mr. Barsky looked at each other in that way married people do, when they talk without actually saying anything. I know because Mom and the Maestro used to do it.

190

"You can always talk to us, *cher*," Mr. Barsky said. "Zat ees what friends do, no?"

"Really, Olivia." Mrs. Barsky eyed my gloved hands. I'd found an old-fashioned dressy kind at the charity store. They were a stained white satin. "We're here for you."

"Yeah. Thanks." I stared at my gloves for a long time, swallowing until I could speak again. A million things raced through my brain. My gloves. The burns. The ghosts. *Our* ghosts.

The Maestro. Mom.

"Can I ask a question?" I said.

"Of course," Mrs. Barsky said. "Anything."

"How do you fall out of love with someone? How is that possible?"

I don't think that was the kind of question the Barskys were expecting. They shared one of those looks again. Mr. Barsky said in his normal voice, "Well. That's a tough one, Olivia."

"People change," Mrs. Barsky said slowly. "They aren't always the same from year to year, or even from day to day. And sometimes when people change, the things in their life that they used to need or want, they don't anymore. Or things they used to think were beautiful turn ugly."

"Oh." I tried to wrap my head around that. "Have you ever fallen out of love with someone?"

"Yes," Mr. Barsky said. Beside him, Mrs. Barsky nodded

and took hold of his hand. "I imagine it's a bit like dying, in a way. It leaves you all cold and cracked open."

After I left, right before opening the Hall's backstage door, I sighed and squinted up at the roof. The Hall was missing shingles everywhere, like holes in the moon.

"Everything's cold and cracked open these days," I said to myself.

Then I felt something brush my arm. I turned around, expecting to see Mr. Barsky, making sure I got a cookie. Or Mrs. Barsky, saying I should come back and talk it out some more. Mrs. Barsky loved talking things out.

But it wasn't them.

It was a ghost.

Five ghosts, although none of them were mine. Dozens of ghosts, stretching down Arlington Avenue in an orderly line. Poking their heads through each other to get a better look. Whispering in excitement.

About me.

192

*I*T MADE SENSE: HELP ONE GHOST MOVE ON, AND others will want to be helped too.

Just not mine. Not the ones I really cared about.

I'm not sure why we never thought about the possibility of this happening. As I went inside to find Henry, the ghosts trailing behind me, I tried not to feel annoyed or freaked out.

"They could've given us a heads-up about this," I said to Henry through my teeth.

"Maybe they didn't know?" Henry said.

"Oh, come on. I'm sure they knew how many ghosts were in the Hall. Or at least had a guess."

I threw open the door of the green room. "Come on, everybody inside." I tried to make myself look and sound braver than I felt, like I was used to dealing with strange ghosts. They drifted in one by one. Some looked nervous. Some flashed me huge game-show-host smiles. That is, if the game-show hosts were missing chunks of face and had their heads on sideways.

Something cold tapped my shoulder. "Excuse me."

I turned around to find the ghost who'd touched me on the street. She was a woman, and the palest ghost I'd yet seen. Even for a ghost, she looked sickly.

"You *are* the girl who helps ghosts, right?"

I felt like when a teacher calls on me to answer a question, and it turns out I've been drawing and not paying attention. My skin goes hot and my mouth dries out while everyone waits for me to say something, only I don't know what to say.

Henry inched closer to me. It made me feel better. I took a deep breath.

"I guess, yeah. That's me."

Excitement rippled through the ghost crowd.

"I found Frederick van der Burg's anchor," I continued." Henry and I shared our minds with him and helped him relive his last memories. We reunited him with his anchor, and then he moved on."

I caught Henry's eye, and he smiled at me. It *did* sound pretty impressive.

The ghosts looked at each other and then back at us, almost completely in unison. Before I could think how spooky that was, they rushed for us, in a wave of grays and whites and blues and blacks. Their bodies blended together in a confusing mix of fog and smoke, faces and body parts. Their arms reached for us, grabbed at us. They shouted:

"Please, Olivia, you've got to help me!"

 194

"I'll do anything to move on. Anything!"

"Do you have any idea what it's like?"

"Me first!"

"No, please, help *me*!"

"Okay, *stop*," I shouted, "or neither of us will help you!"

Immediately, the ghosts retreated to the other side of the room, grumbling. One headless ghost reached over and slapped his hand over another ghost's mouth, sending up curls of smoke.

"You can't go nuts on us like that, okay?" I said. "If—*if*—we decide to help you, you have to swear it. Right, Henry?"

"Like no rushing at us, or touching us without permission." Henry pulled a spiral notebook from his bag and started writing. He pointed his pen at the ghosts, and they nodded furiously. "That'll be the number one rule."

"Rule number two: No hanging around in my and Nonnie's bedroom. That's my private space. And no following us around everywhere. That can get creepy."

One of the ghosts cleared his throat. "But the others went in your room, didn't they? And they were always with you. The kids and the old-timer."

Henry stopped writing. My throat closed up. "Yes, but only after they earned my trust," I said. *Tillie. Jax. Mr. Worthington. Where* are *you guys?* "You haven't earned my trust yet. Remember that."

Then a thought occurred to me. "You haven't seen them, have you? Tillie and Jax? Mr. Worthington?"

The ghosts looked at each other, but they wouldn't look at me. Their smoke drifted and twined together like a giant stormcloud.

"We can't tell you anything about them," an older ghost, dark as Mr. Worthington, croaked. "Ghost's honor. Confidentiality."

My heart sank. Henry bent over his notebook, frowning.

"It's not like we're trying to be difficult," the pale woman ghost said gently. "It's just—"

"Ghost's honor. Right. Got it." I turned away. Who cared what Tillie, Jax, and Mr. Worthington did? If they didn't want to have anything to do with us, then I wouldn't waste my time. "I figure we'll make a list. If we decide to help you, we'll have to share with each of you, one by one."

I shot a look at Henry. He looked nervous. To be honest, I was too. Sharing with one ghost had been bad enough. But dozens of ghosts? And maybe even more, if word got out and more ghosts showed up. Who knew how many people had died around the Hall over the years? Probably too many to count. And even the memory of sharing with Frederick was enough to turn my stomach.

But Henry just nodded at me in this determined way and kept on writing. I snuck a peek at his list: *Rules for the New Ghosts*.

"We'll make appointments," I continued. "Everyone will get a number, and then we'll draw numbers, and it'll be completely random, because that's the only way it's fair. Agreed?"

The ghosts nodded.

"I'll make a spreadsheet." Henry's eyes lit up. He *would* like making spreadsheets. "Everyone come give me your name, and I'll assign you a number."

The ghosts filed quietly by Henry, giving him their names.

Tabitha Jenkins was in two pieces, like something had sliced her right down the middle. She kept having to grab a half of herself and pull it back into place. Frankie James looked pretty normal until you noticed that his skin was bloated with water. Edgar Burroughs had no head, and his friend, who everybody called Geronimo, had to translate because he knew Edgar's hand signs.

Fifty-one ghosts in all. When we were done, their names, numbers, and descriptions took up a full page in Henry's notebook.

"We'll draw names tomorrow, onstage after the concert." I tried not to look at the overwhelming list of names. *Fifty-one* ghosts? "That's all for now."

"Does this mean . . ." The pale ghost woman was trembling, clutching the hand of a darker, frailer ghost beside her. "Does this mean you *will* help us, then?"

I made myself look at Henry's notebook, at the ghosts' names spelled out in his neat handwriting. This steady knot burned in my chest, and when I focused on it, pushing past my doubts I almost didn't miss my ghosts so much anymore.

Almost.

I caught Henry's eye, and he smiled and got to his feet.

"Yes," I said firmly, Henry by my side. "We'll help you. We'll help all of you."

The sound of their cheering and thank-yous followed me through the rest of the day, all the way into sleep.

With so many ghosts to get through, Henry and I agreed to share with a new ghost once a week. If it were completely up to me, I'd have done one a day, to get them moved on as quickly as possible.

But it wasn't up to me, it was up to my body.

As we'd already figured out, a human body can't take too much sharing before it starts to feel sick and tired. Sharing multiple times, though, and with only a few days between, quickly turned into a disaster.

The first time wasn't so bad.

"Number forty-three," Henry said, examining the spreadsheet on his clipboard. "Pearl Branson."

Pearl's number had been drawn first, and when she came forward for her sharing, the other ghosts in a semicircle around the stage to watch, she shook so bad that curls of smoke fell off her like rain. She looked about Tillie's age.

"It's okay, Pearl," I said, not very convincingly. I wasn't sure it *was* okay. What would sharing be like this time for me and Henry? However Pearl had died, I hoped it wouldn't hurt as much as stabbing did. "Just come a little closer."

"You have to kind of just *drift* into us," said Henry. "When

Frederick did it, he drifted closer and closer, until he was leaking into us, and then our bodies kind of slurped him up. Got it?"

Pearl rolled her eyes. "I'm nervous, but I'm not stupid. I know how this works."

Henry turned toward me, his legs crossed just like mine were. Our knees bumped against each other. "You really okay with this?"

"Sort of." I wiped my hands on my pants. The last thing I wanted was Henry feeling how sweaty my hands were. "We made our decision, though, didn't we?"

Henry looked around at the ghosts. Their faces looked ready to fall apart from excitement. "I guess you're right. It might be impossible to share this many times, though. You know that, right?"

I knew. But we had to try. The more ghosts showed up, the more shades would come. And who knew how much damage they would do to the Hall, to the Maestro?

For my answer, I took Henry's hands and folded my fingers around them. Together, we nodded at Pearl.

Pearl took a deep breath, her insides churning white, and drifted into us, like Frederick had done. Cold wrapped around us. Memories overwhelmed us. We *were* the memories: Pearl Branson, ten years old, who lived in an apartment on the corner. Pearl Branson, with the bad fever. Pearl Branson, with the weak heart.

Pearl started writing a story. She couldn't do much else with a weak heart. She liked to sit next door to her apartment in the Hall's gardens and write. But Pearl didn't finish. One sunny day, her heart gave out halfway through Chapter Six.

And that was it. Henry and I faded away with Pearl, and it was peaceful. Much better than being stabbed.

Until the sharing ended. The force of Pearl releasing us sent us skidding across the stage. Pearl flew back into the floor seats in a plume of white smoke.

As I lay on the floor recovering, my insides spinning and Henry gasping beside me, I actually considered chickening out. Saying, "Sorry, ghosts, but you'll have to recover your impossible-to-recover memories all by yourselves."

But then I realized something. As I lay there, clutching my stomach, I took in the sight of the ghosts, staring at us with those mangled, burned, smoky faces. Behind them loomed the shadowy rafters of the Hall, the rows of faded seats, the chipped angels and dragons on the ceiling, winking down at us.

My *home*, whether I liked it or not.

And if it wasn't my home, if I *hadn't* moved in here, would my ghosts have ever decided to trust me? Would *any* of these ghosts be here now? Or would they still be drifting around aimlessly, lost and forever soulless?

I pulled myself into a sitting position and took several deep breaths. I was tingling all over and not because of the ghosts' chill, but because I had recognized fate. This was *fate*; this was *destiny*. Maybe I was meant to help these ghosts. Maybe I was meant to move in here. I had a choice; I could quit now. Or I could keep helping them, even if it was hard. *Especially* if it was hard. And maybe then it would be like moving in here, losing our house, not having money or enough sketching paper, all of it—would be worth *something*.

"Olivia?" Henry whispered. "You okay?"

"It's a story," I said. My voice sounded strong, confident. The ghosts perked up. So did Henry. That made me feel even stronger. I struggled to my feet, the memories of Pearl's life turning solid in my head. "Pearl's anchor is a story. About two dozen pages long. The title is *The Resolute Steed*."

Each ghost was assigned to one of our zones, from the map we'd made for Frederick. Everyone helped search, so things would go faster—ghosts in the walls, ghosts in the basement, ghosts skipping through ceiling panels. It took us three days to find *The Resolute Steed*, buried in a tin box in the walking park outside. Once she had her anchor, Pearl Branson sat curled up in one of the ceiling rafters and finished her story.

Then she was gone. The pages of her completed book fluttered to the Hall floor like wings.

Henry checked off Pearl's name on his spreadsheet. "One down, fifty to go."

Resolute: seeing something through to the end. And that's exactly what I was going to do. Even if our ghosts, our *first* ghosts, didn't have the guts to do the same.

CHAPTER

25

$\mathcal{I}$T WASN'T UNTIL THREE GHOSTS IN—PEARL
Branson, Sue Han (heart attack), Reggie
Black (tuberculosis)—that things started
to fall apart.

Right before Thanksgiving week, we were supposed to turn in these essays to Mrs. Farrity. An expository
essay, to help prepare us for the end-of-the-year tests everyone in the state had to take.

I'd completely forgotten about mine.

When Mrs. Farrity stood by my desk, the other kids'
essays stacked neatly in her hands, I just stared at her.
Every time I blinked, my eyelids scratched together like
sandpaper. It had been a long couple of weeks. I was amazed
I wasn't puking my guts out in the restroom, much less at
school or even awake. How in the *world* were we supposed
to get through forty-eight more ghosts? That's all I could
think about. Had we taken on too much? Were Henry and I
insane for trying this?

And our ghosts—would they ever come back? Not only

was I exhausted from sharing with the ghosts, but I'd also stayed up late every night after Nonnie fell asleep, the old séance materials surrounding me and Igor in my lap. I whispered to my ghosts, asking them to come back. *Begging* them to come back.

So far, they hadn't listened.

I blinked up at Mrs. Farrity, my brain whirling with everything in the world *but* my essay.

Mrs. Farrity drew her lips tight. "See me after class, Olivia."

When the bell rang, I trudged up to her desk, trailing my hand along the top of each chair I passed. I hoped it looked casual. Really, I was just trying to stay upright.

"Forget something, Stellatella?" Mark Everett whispered as he shoved past. "Or did you just spend all your time drawing instead? Idiot."

One thing exhaustion does to you is dull your control center. Like, the part of your brain that tells you you should or shouldn't do something.

That's why I punched Mark Everett.

Or tried to, anyway.

At the last second, right before my fist connected with that stupid face of his, Joan grabbed my arm and pulled me away. I teetered back on my heels and almost fell over.

Mark ran out the door, laughing.

I yanked my arm from her. "Why'd you do that?"

"Because he's not worth it," Joan said calmly, shaking back her hair. "He's a lesser being. And you're welcome."

Then she left, and it was just me and Mrs. Farrity. Who stared at me like she was trying to dissect me with her brain.

"I'm worried about you, Olivia." If her lips got any thinner, they would have sucked her face inside out. "You've always been somewhat distractible, but you usually at least *do* the assignments."

I nodded. Coming up with words was so hard when all I wanted to do was keel over. Or hunt down Mark Everett and sic some ghosts on him. "Yeah. I know. I've just been . . . busy."

Mrs. Farrity eyed my gloves. "You've started wearing gloves a lot. Why is that?"

"I like them. They keep germs away."

Then she eyed my arm, the one with the burn. "And you're always wearing jackets these days. Even inside."

I shrugged. "Fashion."

Mrs. Farrity stacked some papers on her desk, straightened her pencils, cleared her throat, and looked right at me. "I've heard about the orchestra, Olivia. Things aren't going well, are they?"

"Things aren't going well for most people right now. With The Economy and all."

Something went out of Mrs. Farrity then, like someone had popped her. "I know. And I hate that for you kids. It's always the kids who suffer the most." She sighed and rubbed her eyes. "If you turn in your essay before Thanksgiving break,

 204

I'll just dock you a few late points. Okay? How's that?"

"Yeah. That's great, Mrs. Farrity. Thanks."

"And, Olivia, you know that the staff here is always available, if you need someone to talk to. Right?"

Now, that would be funny, to sit Principal Cooper and Mrs. Farrity down and tell them about my ghost problem. I pictured their faces and couldn't contain a snort, which I think hurt Mrs. Farrity's feelings, so I mumbled "Sorry," and thanked her, and left.

The next day, I tried to do some cleaning after getting home from The Happy Place. Backstage had turned into even more of a pigsty since the new ghosts came because I spent all my time sharing and searching for anchors and trying to sleep. But sleep didn't come so easy. I kept dreaming about the lives of the ghosts I'd helped, like their memories had latched onto my brain and wouldn't let go.

Nonnie watched me as I swept the kitchen. "So dim these days, *ombralina*," she whispered, rocking in her chair, weaving scarves into a braid. "You are darker than ever."

I tried not to pay attention to the ghost eyes I could feel watching from the doorway, waiting for me to join them. Waiting for me to save them.

"I don't know, Nonnie. I'm just tired, okay?"

Nonnie cupped her hands around her mouth and whispered, "Is it the ghosts? Are they bothering you?"

Yes. They're taking over my brain, they're taking over my sleep. "No. Just school and stuff, you know? And work. I worry about money."

"I worry too. Always worrying." Nonnie's lips twisted. "I worry about you every minute, *ombralina*, every day."

I dropped the broom and grabbed Nonnie's hands. They were cold as a ghost, and it terrified me. I rubbed them to warm them up.

"Don't worry about me, Nonnie. Okay? Worrying wears you out."

"You should have . . ." Nonnie looked around, spread out her arms. They were shaking and draped with scarves. "More. More than this."

"Yeah. And so should you."

The Maestro was out that night, uptown at some dinner party for orchestra donors. When I got to his room, I whacked the broom across his floor, knocking over stacks of music and heaps of garbage. It didn't make me feel much better.

Then I found the pile of mail shoved underneath his dresser, like he'd just walked in, dropped it to the floor, and kicked it out of his way, day after day after day.

I sorted through it. Bills and junk mail, mostly. Part of me hoped I'd find a letter from Mom. *It was all a joke!* it would say. *I'm coming home tomorrow! Surprise!*

No such luck. I did find some letters from school, though. Four of them. All unopened, all from Counselor Davis's office.

206

I opened the most recent one. As I read it, my stomach dropped to my feet.

According to her teachers, the letter read, *Olivia rarely pays attention in class and is easily distracted. She is consistently rude to other students and has even neared physical assault on multiple occasions. She lacks focus, and her schoolwork is suffering. She seems to have few friends, and we worry that the students she does associate with will follow her poor example. We are deeply concerned about Olivia's future. We are also concerned that our previous letters have gone unanswered, and urge you to call the counselors' offices and make an appointment for both you and Olivia before more severe action is taken. We suggest . . .*

I sank down against the wall, hugging the broom. So everyone at school, even the teachers, thought I was stupid, lazy, violent. Without a future. And friendless, too. And they were right. Well, mostly. I had Henry, but that was about it.

I didn't think ghosts counted.

"I have a future, though," I whispered. No one heard me but Igor, who slid in through the open door. "I have my drawings. I can . . . I can draw things, I can go to art school someday, maybe. I can figure out a way."

Igor wound himself around my ankles. *Oh? How?*

"The Barskys say my drawings are good." I could barely hear myself. The words kept getting stuck in my chest. *But the Barskys are just as crazy as I am.* "I'm not stupid." *But I don't make good grades; Henry's made the honor roll three years straight.* "I'm not lazy." *But I never pay attention in class.*

I hauled Igor into my lap and stared at him, nose to nose. "Well, of course I don't pay attention in class. I have to draw. My drawings are . . ."

Igor licked the tip of my nose. *Are what?*

Mom had always told me it was important to dream, to lie in my bedsheet fort and do nothing but stare at the paper stars over my head and make origami swans and let my imagination run wild across my sketchpad. My drawings were my dreaming, my secret thing that made my heart expand and scrubbed away the bad thoughts. And they reminded me of Mom.

But with that letter in my hands, the thought occurred to me for the first time: Maybe dreaming isn't enough.

The Monday before Thanksgiving, I went to Counselor Davis's office at lunch instead of to the cafeteria. I didn't know what "more severe action" meant, and I didn't want anyone showing up at the Hall, looking for the Maestro. They would see how we lived, and they might take me away—away from the ghosts, away from Nonnie.

So I turned myself in.

I walked right past Counselor Davis's assistant and into his office and set the four letters on his desk. "So, hi. Sorry I never answered these. Or showed them to my—to the Maestro. It's just, I was embarrassed. You know? But I'm doing the right thing now."

Counselor Davis leaned back in his green cushioned

chair and stared at me, his fingers steepled. His office was a million shades of green. I'd heard somewhere green was supposed to be soothing, but not, like, an explosion of green.

I clutched the ends of my jacket. "So. Let's do this."

"Do what?"

"Whatever counseling you think I need."

"But, Olivia, what about your father?"

I was afraid this would happen. "What *about* him?"

"I think it will be much more effective if your father is here for these sessions. Don't you?" Counselor Davis reached for a big binder behind his desk. "Why don't we give him a call while I have you here?"

"No!" I slammed my hand down on the phone. It was just a reflex. Not like the Maestro would pick up the phone anyway. But someone in the Hall offices might.

Counselor Davis watched me calmly. "Why don't you want to call him?"

Because I just want to get this over with.

Because he would have let the mail pile up until I got suspended.

Because . . .

"Because I want to just talk to you by myself first," I said. "It's less embarrassing."

Counselor Davis smiled. "That makes sense." He put the binder back. "How do you feel about your father, Olivia?"

I hate him. He made Mom leave, and now he won't stop crying. Now he's crazy and sees things that aren't there. He loves the orchestra more than me. I wish he had left instead of her. That's what danced between my teeth, waiting to be spit out. But I didn't let it.

Instead, I said, "I love my father very much."

That seemed to be the right thing to say. We talked for a while, about the Maestro and Nonnie and the orchestra, and my drawings, and Mark Everett. I don't remember much, though. I just remember lying through my teeth about most of it.

When we'd finished, Counselor Davis gave me a green candy from the dish on his desk and said this was a good first session and that we would meet again soon. He would set up another appointment for me with his assistant.

On my way out, bursting with the need to scream, I squashed my candy against his door, leaving behind a splat of green goop.

CHAPTER

26

THAT NIGHT, I CAMPED OUT IN BOX NUMBER five on the dress circle level while the orchestra rehearsed for the upcoming holiday concerts. Ghosts floated throughout the Hall, some in seats to watch the rehearsal, some talking in groups, others drifting through the walls, disappearing and reappearing.

A group hovered a few rows away from Henry, who was, as usual, doing his homework in the floor seats. They were probably trying to suck up or something. No way was Henry's homework that interesting.

Me, I had a stack of napkins and my charcoals.

Napkins were the new sketchpad.

"Humiliating," I muttered to myself. "Real artists don't draw on napkins."

Igor plopped down on the floor beside me, batting at the napkins with his paw. *I know what will make you feel better. Petting me. Better yet, asking for permission to pet me.*

I threw a napkin at Igor's face.

He chased it under the seats. *Villain! Scoundrel! Fiend!*

I smiled and returned to my sketch. We were scheduled for another sharing the day after Thanksgiving—Gregori Stevsky, ghost number fourteen—and I was determined to enjoy myself until then, even with the orchestra droning on below me. I mean, it takes serious talent to turn holiday music into something that sounded vaguely like a funeral march.

After about thirty minutes of this, the Maestro stopped and clapped his hands. "Stop! *What* are you doing?"

I crept to the railing on my stomach, looking through the posts for Richard Ashley.

"Do you want to lose everything? Do you *want* this place to close?" The Maestro's voice tripped over itself. It reminded me of the sound of him crying through his bedroom door.

Richard raised his hand, and I perked up. Igor climbed onto my back. *Oh, is that your boyfriend?*

"Shush." I pushed him away. "It's Richard Ashley."

"Maestro," Richard said, "this isn't working."

"You are saying something we already know, Mr. Ashley."

"No, I mean, it's not just us. Or you. It's just, it's *freezing* in here."

The other musicians nodded. Some of them were shivering. Their breaths puffed tiny clouds.

My breath was puffing tiny clouds.

I sat up. Igor slid off, grumbling. Henry was paying more attention now too. I hadn't thought about this. With all the ghosts flying around lately, the temperature had dropped. I was used to it, but the musicians wouldn't be.

I waved my hands at the ghosts. "Get out of here!" I whispered. "Go hide somewhere until rehearsal ends!"

Some of them hurried away. Some just looked confused.

"I don't care if it reaches arctic temperatures, you will *play*," the Maestro was saying.

"But something's not right," said Erin Hatch, one of the oboists. "It doesn't feel right in here. Can't you feel that?"

The Maestro was dumbstruck. "Excuse me? Can't I *feel* what?"

Right before I heard it, pain jolted across my burned hands and arm. I clamped down on a scream, and it's a good thing I did, because if I'd been screaming, I wouldn't have been able to hear the creaking sound in the ceiling right above my head.

I looked up.

Five shades gnawed on the ceiling, ramming themselves against the plaster.

Five shades reaching for me, shying away from me.

The ceiling right above me crashed to the floor.

I rolled away just in time, scooping Igor along with me. When I opened my eyes, I saw bits of broken ceiling to my left, dust wafting up from them.

The shades overhead scampered away, but one lingered above me, its face cocked to the side like a bird. It opened its mouth and groaned, this low, rumbling sound that made my ears hurt.

"Olivia!" someone shouted from below. I couldn't tell who. The shade darted away across the ceiling. I used the box's railing to pull myself up.

Igor wouldn't move from my chest, his claws digging into me. *I'm not scared. I'm only pretending, to make you look better.*

I watched the shades slink away into the shadows. Five this time. I'd never seen so many in one place. And that last shade . . . I could have sworn it was watching me. Trying to figure me out.

That couldn't have been good.

The ghosts nearest the shades scattered away in terror, except for three of them. Three of them barreled out of the walls and right toward me.

"Olivia," Jax cried, burrowing into my chest, right through Igor, who yowled but stayed put. "Are you okay? I'm so sorry, we should never have left you!"

Tillie raced around the ceiling, putting up her fists. "Where are they, huh? I'll punch 'em right in their slimy, shady, no-nose faces!"

Mr. Worthington slumped in a black puddle nearby, staring at me. He tried to smile, and it dripped all over the floor.

"You're back," I said, trying to hug Jax even though my arms kept falling through him. New ghosts? Shades? Crashing ceilings? Who cared about any of that? My ghosts were back.

"We had to come back," Jax said. "We saw the ceiling, the shades . . . Are you okay? Did you get hit?"

"I'm okay," I told him, even though my voice shook. "Mr. Worthington, go get Tillie. Make sure she doesn't do anything stupid."

"Olivia! Are you all right?" Several of the musicians tumbled out from the stairwell. So did Henry and the Maestro.

Henry nearly knocked me over with his hug. "Olivia! Oh my God. I saw it happen from downstairs. It was like slow motion, I couldn't move! Are you okay?" I saw his eyes dart over to the ghosts, who were hovering over the railing. Tillie waved, grinning.

"I think so." I put one of my arms around him. In that moment, *I* needed an anchor. Something to hold me in place. Someone who knew exactly what that crashing ceiling meant, and what it felt like to have the ghosts back. I had to remind myself not to smile. People who have almost gotten hit by ceilings don't sit there smiling like goofs.

Richard Ashley pulled us apart to feel my face and head. "Olivia? Are you injured? What day is it?"

Igor started purring. *I can see why he's your boyfriend. He has a nice smell.*

"The day before Thanksgiving," I said. "And your name is Richard, and you're *okay* at trumpet. I guess."

Richard ruffled my hair. "Harsh critic."

Past him, some of the musicians gathered at the railing, pointing to the ceiling.

"Did you see it?" Liesl Wilhelm, the harpist, said. "It was like a shadow, but it moved like it was . . . *real.*"

I caught Henry's eye. *Shades*, I mouthed to him. He nodded grimly. The ghosts inched closer to us, and Mr. Worthington put his arm around me.

Nick Chang, one of the trombonists, shook his head. "We must have been imagining it."

"I don't imagine things," said Liesl.

Riva Cull, the pianist, said softly, "I saw them too."

So. Liesl, Nick, and Riva. They had seen the shades, which meant they had experienced true loss. I wondered how many of the other musicians had seen them too, but just weren't saying anything. Maybe they didn't like to talk about their loss. Maybe they didn't yet know they had lost anything.

"You people aren't serious, are you?" That was Emery Ross, the associate concertmistress. She pointed at the ceiling. "It fell because this place is old, not because of *shadows*."

"Look," said Richard. "We've all had a scare, okay? Maybe we should take a break, get some fresh air. Maestro?"

Everyone turned to look at the Maestro. He examined the fallen pieces of ceiling, his face hidden in shadow, and it made me wonder: Had he seen the shades too?

"We can't tell anyone about this," the Maestro said at last. "No one. Not friends, not family, and certainly not Mr. Rue. They'll have an inspection and shut this place down."

"Maybe it's time, Maestro," said Riva carefully. "We don't want anyone to get hurt."

I could feel some of the musicians looking at me. I knew what they were thinking. I was thinking it too.

216

Would the Maestro ask if I was all right? Would he even look at me?

"It's not *time* for anything but rehearsal," the Maestro snapped. "We resume in five minutes."

"But, Maestro—"

"End of discussion."

Richard cleared his throat. "Sir, we won't be able to hide a giant hole in the ceiling."

"I'll hire workers. I'll repair it. I'll pay for it myself."

Anger boiled up inside me, melting away the happiness of seeing my ghosts back. That made me even angrier. "Yeah? With what money?"

The Maestro's eyes were cold and black. "With whatever money is required, Olivia."

Henry stepped closer to me and pressed his fingers into my palm. The contact made my eyes burn, so I ripped my hand away. No one needed to see me cry.

"Fine," I said. "I'll go find Kepler. He'll clean this up."

I crawled out of bed around lunchtime on Thanksgiving Day, feeling like . . . well, I would say death, but that seems like the kind of thing I shouldn't say, considering.

Every time I thought about the next day, when Henry and I would share with another ghost, my insides clenched up. I hadn't been able to sleep more than a few minutes at a time because every flicker in the dark made me think a shade was nearby, ready to crash the ceiling down on me again.

The shades overhead scampered away, but one lingered above me,
its face cocked to the side like a bird.

Still, I stumbled into the kitchen with a smile on my face, ready to cook Thanksgiving dinner. I heard clattering noises; Nonnie must have already been in there, getting out the dishes.

But it wasn't Nonnie making noise.

It was the Maestro.

He had set the table with our chipped yellow plates, our mismatched silverware, diet sodas from the vending machine. Baked potatoes, cooked so long they looked shrunken and wrinkled. Canned soup. A loaf of bread.

Nonnie was already seated. *"Ombralina!"* She clapped her hands. "You're awake! Look at this feast."

Feast? No. What we'd had at our old house was a feast. Turkey and dressing, spinach casserole and warm, buttered rolls. My stomach growled just thinking about it. I was so sick of baked potatoes and soup. The cheap kind too, which doesn't have much in it but broth.

"I thought I would help out a bit," the Maestro said. He straightened his sweat-stained shirt and smoothed down his hair. "To surprise you."

I took a seat. The Maestro was watching me. So was Nonnie, smiling and swaying from side to side.

So were my ghosts, crowding at the door, staring longingly at our food. I smiled, despite my bad mood. They were back, they were *back*. Everything—school, Counselor Davis, the new ghosts, the orchestra—seemed less scary now. Smaller. Quieter.

"Get back," Jax said, trying to shove the other ghosts away. Tillie kicked at them, puffing up clouds of smoke. "This is family time."

Family time. What a joke.

"Happy Thanksgiving, Olivia," the Maestro said quietly.

"Happy Thanksgiving!" Nonnie threw up her hands. Then she began to eat.

I didn't. Neither did the Maestro. He was too busy watching me.

"Olivia, I meant to ask you yesterday." The Maestro cleared his throat. "But in the confusion . . ."

"You forgot to ask me if I was okay?" I said. "After a ceiling crashed down on me?"

Nonnie stopped eating.

"Yes. I'm sorry, Olivia," the Maestro said. I couldn't look at him. "I suppose I was in shock."

I wouldn't say it was okay. It *wasn't* okay. "Fine. Great."

"Some in the orchestra, they were speaking of shadows. You remember hearing this?"

I hadn't expected him to say that. "Yeah. I think so." Of course I remembered. If he only knew. It was almost enough to make me laugh.

"Did you see what they were talking about?"

I shrugged, but my heart was racing. What did the Maestro know? What had he *seen*? *I think that I see things*, he'd said. *I think that I see her. But when I look again, it is just a trick of the shadows.* "Did I see shadows? Sure. There are shadows everywhere."

220

"No, not normal shadows. Shadows almost like . . . crea-tures." He laughed, leaned hard on his elbows. "That sounds insane, doesn't it?"

"Yes."

"Did you see them?"

Yes. "No. I'm not crazy."

We had a staredown then. The Maestro blinked first. "No," he said. "I didn't see them either."

Liar. He was so definitely lying. But then, I was too. I didn't want to admit what him seeing shades meant—that he had experienced true loss.

That he could hurt. That he could feel sad.

I didn't want to feel sorry for the Maestro. I didn't want to feel anything for him but anger.

Nonnie was playing with her fork, clinking it against her plate. "Let us take turns to say thankful things. Something glad."

After a minute, the Maestro cleared his throat. "I'm thankful that Olivia did not get hurt yesterday. That she is safe and healthy."

I stabbed my potato with my fork. "And I'm thankful for this food." I shoved a forkful in my mouth and glared at the Maestro. "Who knows how much longer we'll actually have any?"

His smile faded.

And just like that, Thanksgiving dinner went silent.

After I cleaned up, I ran outside to the corner pay phone. I couldn't be in the Hall for one more second.

I dialed, and waited. Not much traffic on Thanksgiving Day. The streets were quiet. A couple of cars, a truck, and a taxi sped down Arlington Avenue. When they passed by, it sounded lonely.

Someone picked up. "Hello?"

"Henry!" Like I was surprised to hear him, even though I'd been the caller. "Hey. Hi."

"Olivia? You okay? Are the shades back? Do you want me to come over?"

"No, it's not that. I just . . . I don't know. I wanted to talk to someone who wasn't here." Across from the pay phone, someone had painted MONEY IS LOVE in bright green across the brick wall at the edge of the Hall's property. "Sometimes when I'm here for too long, I feel like the Hall is all there is in the world. You know?"

"I think so." Henry paused. "We're kind of eating Thanksgiving dinner, Olivia. I don't want to get in trouble. I mean, if you're okay."

"Sure. I'm sorry."

"I'd ask you over, but I don't think I should. Family time and everything."

I didn't realize how much I wanted to go over to Henry's until he said it. Maybe they had turkey, and a house that was a real house. "That's okay."

"Hey, Olivia?"

"Yeah."

"It'll be okay. I'll see you tomorrow. Midnight, right?"

"Your parents are okay with that?"

The connection crackled. "Yeah. They won't even know I'm gone."

The next night, Gregori Stevsky tried melting into me and Henry five times before we gave up, gasping and shivering in pathetic heaps onstage. Our bodies just couldn't take it. We were too tired. Our minds were too full.

"You said you would help me," Gregori growled.

Igor was going back and forth between me and Henry, licking our skin back to normal. *Would you like me to claw his eyes out?*

"Hey, look," Henry said, "we're doing our best."

Tillie darted into Gregori's face. "Yeah, so back off or I'll—"

Gregori blew her off of him with a gust of icy wind. "Or you'll what, little girl? Kill me?"

Nobody laughed, but I don't think it was supposed to be funny.

"If you don't help us, what then?" another ghost said. He pointed at the ceiling. Shades had been there all day, alone or in groups of two or three. Coming close, but never too close. Darting. Watching.

Waiting.

The ghosts outnumbered them right now, and the shades hadn't bothered them yet, not with me and Henry around. But how long would that last?

THE *YEAR OF SHADOWS*

223

As it turned out, not long at all.

I didn't see how it happened because I had my head on my knees and my eyes closed, trying to swallow my nausea away. Then I heard cries from the ghosts.

I forced my head up.

"Oh, no," Henry whispered.

One of the ghosts had wandered away from the others toward the back of the Hall. A shade slithered there, back and forth across the floor. A black space behind it grew wider by the second.

Limbo.

"Don't listen to it!" one of the new ghosts cried.

"Stop!" Tillie and Jax shouted. "Please!"

But the ghost couldn't hear them, or maybe he did and chose to ignore them. Maybe he just didn't care at this point. Maybe he was too tired, and from here, Limbo looked like paradise.

The shade's arms grew to three times their normal size, welcoming the ghost in for a hug. A black smile spread across the shade's featureless face like tar. It shrieked softly, luring the ghost closer.

Some of the ghosts around me surged forward, wistful looks on their faces, but the others held them back.

The shade stretched out its hand—a clawed, long-fingered hand. The ghost smiled and grabbed hold of it. Then it screamed, and it sounded so human, so *scared*, that I felt sick and clapped my hands to my ears. The doorway to Limbo closed with an awful sucking sound, like a black hole collapsing on itself.

When they were gone, no one moved for a long time. A stone formed in my stomach, weighing me down. We had failed that ghost. He would be a shade now, because we couldn't save him.

I felt the other ghosts' eyes on me. They didn't say anything, but I knew that's what they were thinking too. Even Mr. Worthington seemed disappointed, or maybe just surprised, like he'd never considered we might fail.

Henry pulled me aside. His hair was dark with sweat, plastered to his forehead. "Olivia, what do we do? We're not going fast enough, but we can't keep on like this. Who knows, we might be giving ourselves permanent brain damage or something."

"You're right," I said. "We need help." And then inspiration hit me, as my brain searched frantically for an answer. "And I think I know just who to ask."

$\mathcal{T}$HE NEXT DAY, HENRY AND I MET AT THE HAPPY
Place, our ghosts right behind us.

"I don't know how I feel about showing
myself to another human." Tillie had been
muttering that all morning. "Who is this lady
again?"

"Her name is Mrs. Barsky," I said. "And she knows
things, apparently. She said so when we first mentioned
you."

"Everybody *knows* things."

"Yeah, but I think she knows things about ghosts."

We stepped inside, and Gerald squawked, pacing back
and forth on his perch. His neck feathers stood up. I wondered if he could see the ghosts no matter what, like Igor
could. Maybe animals were different in that way.

"I don't think she's going to be too happy about this,"
Henry said. "Maybe we should leave."

"And watch the ghosts get sucked into Limbo, one by
one?" I said. "Or kill ourselves trying to save them? No
way."

I hoisted myself up onto a stool at the counter. "Mr. B? Mrs. B?"

Mr. Barsky threw himself out of the kitchen with a flourish of an invisible cape. I sighed. Merlin today. He'd probably been peeking out from the kitchen, waiting for the best moment to make his entrance.

An older couple sitting by the window started applauding.

"Ah, young heroes," Mr. Barsky began, in this lofty, wizard-like voice. "You have journeyed far and wide, through many terrors, to arrive safely at my magical abode. I must reward such bravery, of course, as is my solemn wizard's vow." He bowed to us. "Whatever you ask of me, is yours." He stood back up, grinning. "Croissant? Green tea?"

Jax laughed. Tillie just stared. "This guy is nuts!"

"Actually," I said, "we need to talk to Mrs. Barsky. Privately. It's important."

Mr. Barsky's face turned serious. "Of course. Right this way."

Mrs. Barsky was in her office, jotting something down on a notepad. Today, her beads were bright purple. "Oh hello, you two! It's been a while since I've seen you around, Henry."

"Yes, ma'am," Henry mumbled. "Sorry, ma'am. I mean, yes, ma'am."

"You seem a bit out of sorts."

"The children wish to speak with you about something serious," Mr. Barsky said. He gave Mrs. Barsky this look I couldn't read, and then he left us and shut the door.

"All right." Mrs. Barsky settled back in her chair. "What's this about?"

And we told her—everything. The séance, the ghosts—both old and new—the shades. Sharing, the ceiling.

"And now there's too many of them," I said quietly. I felt ashamed to say it out loud. "We can't . . . It's not working anymore. It's getting too hard to share, and yesterday a ghost got sucked into Limbo. Right in front of us."

Mrs. Barsky put a hand over her mouth and closed her eyes. The ghosts peered curiously at her.

"We can't keep going like this. I'm missing assignments, and I can't keep up with the cleaning, and I can't sleep—"

"And I got a *B* in biology," Henry blurted all of a sudden, like he'd been struggling to keep it in. "A *B*!"

I rolled my eyes. "It's the end of the world."

Mrs. Barsky was still sitting there, her eyes closed.

Henry and I shared a look. "Mrs. B? What's wrong?"

After a minute or two, Mrs. Barsky opened her eyes. "Will you show me the Hall? The shades?"

"Sure . . ."

"Mrs. Barsky," Henry said hurriedly, "I'm not sure that's a good idea."

"No. A good idea would have been to come to me much sooner, when all this started. I could have helped you. But . . . then again, you couldn't have known to ask me. I never talk about it. Not anymore."

Henry's jaw dropped.

"What are you talking about, Mrs. B?"

Mrs. Barsky shook her head. "First, I need you to show them to me."

So we did, leading Mrs. Barsky across the street and through the Hall's main front doors in a solemn procession. We showed her the ceiling, which the Maestro was having a couple of handymen patch up. We showed her the basement, where the shades had dug the tunnel while searching for Frederick's anchor.

And we showed her the shades. The new ghosts huddled together in a tight group backstage, where at least the presence of Nonnie and the Maestro could help keep the shades away. But the shades hovered close by anyway, slinking around in the shadows onstage, curled around the organ's pipes.

"Oh my," Mrs. Barsky said calmly. "Yes, those are shades all right."

Tillie, Jax, and Mr. Worthington whirled around to stare at her.

"You've seen shades before?" I said.

"A long time ago." Mrs. Barsky sighed. "A long time ago, I was something like what you've become. A ghost talker, I guess you could say." She smiled crookedly at me as we headed back outside. "I spoke with ghosts, helped them find their anchors and move on. Lots of people do, you know, more than you might think. My mother taught me how. I did it from when I was a girl. Instead of playing with dolls and dressing up like little girls should."

"I don't play with dolls and dress-up," I said.

"No, you draw skulls and pirates and monster intestines," Henry said matter-of-factly. "Which is much cooler. You know, in my opinion."

"Anyway," Mrs. Barsky said, "one day, I failed to find a ghost's anchor, and she was pulled into Limbo. I watched it happen, right before my eyes. Just like you did."

I shivered, remembering. I didn't think I would ever forget that scream, and the awful sucking sound of Limbo.

"It was terrible," Mrs. Barsky said. "Horrible. I gave it up, after that. At first, the ghosts wouldn't leave me alone. I had to be firm. It's hard, ignoring them when they come to you with all these tragic stories. But I did it, and eventually they stopped coming around." Mrs. Barsky took a long, slow breath, and then let it out. "The sounds she made, the ghost who got pulled away . . . I felt dreadful, like it was my fault. I felt *responsible*. But I wasn't. And you two need to understand that as well."

We were back in Mrs. Barsky's office now, settling around her desk. Our ghosts watched Mrs. Barsky reverently, like she was a queen.

"But we *are* responsible," I said. "They asked for our help, and if we don't help them in time . . ."

"If you don't, then you don't," Mrs. Barsky said briskly. "You'll do your best, won't you?"

"Of course we will."

"Well, that's all that matters as far as you're concerned.

You said you would help, and that's a huge, important thing, and very serious. But ultimately, the ghosts' lives or . . . half-lives or . . . *whatever* you want to call it, are their own. And what does or does not happen to them is not the responsibility of two twelve-year-old kids."

Then, to my shock, Mrs. Barsky glared right at where the ghosts hovered. "Do you hear me, you three? Or is it four? I can't quite tell; I'm out of practice."

Impressive. I grinned at Henry. "There's three. Only *our* ghosts are here, not the other ones."

Mrs. Barsky raised an eyebrow. "*Your* ghosts?"

"Not like we own them or anything," Henry said quickly.

"I was gonna say!" Tillie said, crossing her arms.

"Just that they're our friends. The original ones, you know."

"Well? Where are they?" Mrs. Barsky snapped her fingers again. "Come on, show yourselves. I know it's hard, but if you care about your friends, you'll do it."

Tillie and Jax looked at Mr. Worthington, who nodded. I only knew when they appeared to Mrs. Barsky because she whistled at the sight of Mr. Worthington. "You're an old-timer if there ever was, aren't you?"

Mr. Worthington ducked behind Jax.

"Wow, you're a pro," Henry said.

"It isn't hard to understand that the darker a ghost is, the older he is. That's Paranormal 101." Mrs. Barsky examined each of the ghosts, and after they'd introduced themselves

(Jax spoke for Mr. Worthington), her eyes had this new sparkle in them.

"I swore I'd never do this again," she said, "but I can't very well let you handle . . . how many ghosts did you say?"

I grimaced. "Fifty-one, now that our ghosts are back."

"Fifty-one ghosts, all by yourself. What kind of person would I be if I did that? Bring the first one tomorrow," she said, turning back to her notepad, "and we'll see how it goes."

The next day, Sunday, The Happy Place didn't open until noon, so Henry, the ghosts, and I—plus Gregori Stevsky—showed up early in the morning.

Mr. Barsky let us in and led us through the shop to the office at the back. I wasn't sure about the expression on his face. I hoped he wasn't afraid, or angry at us.

"Do you help ghosts too, Mr. B?" I asked.

He laughed. Merlin again. "A wizard has many powers, Olivia, but ghost whispering is not one of them."

"Who is that?" Gregori asked. He was nervous about leaving the Hall, and even more nervous about showing himself to someone besides me and Henry.

"Mrs. Barsky's husband," I said. "Don't worry, he's cool."

"He seems a bit unbalanced."

"Mr. B, are you unbalanced?"

Mr. Barsky swung open the office door. "In all the best ways!"

Mrs. Barsky sat there on the floor, in the middle of a plush rug. Her nails were blue, her beads were blue, her slippers were blue. Candles surrounded her.

"We never used candles," Henry said. He whipped out his clipboard to take notes.

"They're not strictly necessary," Mrs. Barsky said, her voice serene, almost musical, "but they help calm me."

Gregori eyed her blue nails. "You're sure she has done this before?"

"Mrs. Barsky doesn't lie," I said sharply. To be honest, I was nervous myself. I'd shared four times now, but I'd never watched anyone else do it. And Mrs. Barsky was older than we were. Would it hurt her even worse?

"When you're in a room with me, Mr. Stevsky," Mrs. Barsky said, "you will speak to me directly. Now, shall we begin?"

"I'm really starting to like her," Tillie whispered to me.

Mr. Barsky dimmed the lights and shut the door. Gregori Stevsky ducked his head like a punished kid and started drifting toward Mrs. Barsky until they occupied the same space on the rug. It was like looking at Mrs. Barsky through a swirling charcoal-colored fog.

Then, her mouth flew open, wider than it should have been able to. Her head jerked back. Gregori Stevsky disappeared, and all we could see of him was this smoke curling out of Mrs. Barsky's nose, out of her ears and mouth and around her fingertips.

Henry grabbed my hand. I knew what he was thinking:

That's what we looked like while sharing? Disgusting. Disturbing.

And kind of fantastic.

"I'd forgotten how gruesome it can be," Mr. Barsky whispered excitedly behind us. "Just think how good this will be for business!"

Before I could ask Mr. Barsky how this could possibly be good for business. Mrs. Barsky's body jerked, and Gregori spat out of her mouth like a funnel cloud. The candlelight wavered. The beads marking the doorway to the private bathroom rattled softly. And just like that, it was over.

"That's it?" Henry said. "But did it even work?'

"Of course it did." Mrs. Barsky stretched and sighed, reminding me of Igor after catching a particularly fat rat. "Goodness, did that feel good. It's been far, far too long."

"Ethel, you are astonishing." Mr. Barsky hovered around her, patting her face with a cloth. "You're simply a star."

She kissed his cheek.

"Gregori?" Tillie waved her hand in front of his face. "You okay?"

"Yes." Gregori's figure shimmered like a veil, but he smiled anyway. "I am more than okay. I am hopeful."

"What happened?" Henry asked. "How did you die?"

Mrs. Barsky waved her finger. "That's only for the sharers to know, Henry. Privacy is important. And besides, the fewer death memories you have in your head, the better. I will tell you, however, that Mr. Stevsky's anchor is a set of marbles

234

in a black mesh bag. He was going to give them to his son and teach him how to play. I trust that, with fifty-one ghosts at your disposal, you'll find them quickly. And be careful. Be *watchful*." Mrs. Barsky turned and pointed one blue-nailed finger at us. "The more ghosts you help move on, the more shades will show up, and the angrier they'll get. Make sure the ghosts stay around people at all times. And they can come over here if they want, just as long as they don't haunt my customers."

While she spoke, Mrs. Barsky blew out candles and straightened up her office. Then she turned around and put her apron back on and clapped her hands. "Now. Who wants to help me make muffins?"

Mr. Barsky nudged me in the side. "Isn't she something?"

"Yeah," I said. "She is." I didn't look at Mr. Barsky, though, and I didn't stay to make muffins. I put our list of ghosts on Mrs. Barsky's desk and got out of there as fast as I could.

See, I had recognized the look on Mr. Barsky's face—the way his eyes had lit up, how his mouth had gone soft.

I knew it because the Maestro used to look at Mom that way.

That night, Henry, Tillie, Jax, Mr. Worthington, Igor, and I gathered in my bedroom for celebratory snacks. Well, Henry, Igor, and I snacked. Our ghosts *tried* to snack. But no matter how much Tillie rammed her head through my bag of chips, they didn't budge.

Igor watched her distrustfully. *She had better not try that with my tuna.*

"Yeah?" I poked him softly between the eyes. "And what'll you do? Claw her arm that doesn't actually exist?"

His whiskers twitched. *I'll think of something. Cats always do.*

Henry was licking cheese puff crumbs off his fingers. "Are you talking to your cat?"

I shrugged. "Sort of. Not really. It's complicated."

"Fair enough." Henry flopped down next to me on my bed. It was nice. It was comfortable. His tee-shirt lay right past my fingers, and I suddenly realized how freckles were quite possibly the cutest thing in the world.

Igor, purring, slid between me and Henry. *And I thought the nice-smelling trumpet player was your boyfriend.*

I almost said, "He's not my boyfriend!" but stopped myself in time and stuffed my face full of chips instead.

"I have a question," Henry said after a while, gazing up at the ceiling, where Mr. Worthington drifted in a hammock of his own smoke. "Now that you're back . . . I guess you want to move on pretty soon, huh?"

For a long time, none of us said anything. The words "move on" had this final-sounding feel to them, like the chords at the end of a symphony.

"Well, yes," Jax said slowly, "but we wouldn't have to do it right this very second, would we?"

"I guess not," I said.

"What'd he say?" Tillie asked, trying to smell an empty bag of chips.

I told her. She smiled up at me through the chip bag.

"Yeah. I mean, we could wait a while. Just a little while. You need all the help you can get to keep these new guys in line."

"And if the shades started up again, we'd obviously just go ahead and share as fast as possible, to get you out of here," Henry said, sitting up. The look on his face was like Tillie's, so happy and relieved that looking at it made my stomach hurt.

I felt it too, that relief. I didn't want them to go. Not yet.

"Mr. Worthington?" I waved at him. "What do you think?"

He smiled blackly at me and gave me a wavering thumbs-up.

"Good," Tillie said, settling happily next to me and watching as I ate. "I don't mind staying. Not too much, anyway. I like it here."

And right then, with Henry and Igor and my ghosts piled on my cot, I thought something for the very first time:

Maybe I liked it here too.

28

DECEMBER

*C*OUNSELOR DAVIS CALLED ME INTO HIS OFFICE for another session, right before winter break.

"How are we doing this month, Olivia?"

I thought about that for a second, and I guess he took that pause to mean I was struggling with some kind of awful emotion.

But for the first time in what felt like forever, I wasn't. I had ghosts for friends. The Maestro was keeping out of my way, which was just how I liked it. I'd found this great purple scarf for Nonnie at the charity store and already had it wrapped under our tabletop tree in the kitchen. The new ghosts were down to twenty-six. Mrs. Barsky was going through them like wildfire, but of course more kept popping up, so now she'd opened up this side business in The Happy Place, called The Ghost Room. She and Mr. Barsky had made it all official, turning their office into a space properly decorated for séances and conferencing with ghosts and meeting with sad people who'd lost their loved ones—candles, incense, floor cushions. And complimentary tea, of course.

And then there was Henry. Studious, organized, sky-eyed Henry. He'd started helping me with algebra after work most days. And he requested drawings—a drawing of Igor, a drawing of the ghosts, a drawing of him in a Superman costume. I made him a superzombie instead. He didn't seem to mind.

"The holidays can be a hard time of year for some people," Counselor Davis was saying. "Did you know that?"

I couldn't seem to stop smiling.

Counselor Davis seemed surprised. "You're awfully cheerful today. How is everything at home?"

"It's fine," I said. "It's going okay."

And I meant it.

This time, when I left his office, I didn't smash my candy on the door.

On the last day of school before break, the sky started spitting out pathetic little snowflakes while Henry and I walked to the Hall. The last holiday concert was that night, and we planned to binge on the leftover candy canes afterward.

At the corner, right outside the Hall doors, Henry started clearing his throat a lot and then pulled out a wrapped package from his backpack.

"Merry Christmas, Olivia," he said, grinning as I unwrapped it. Oh, he was so proud of himself.

And he should have been. I held the sketchpad in front

of me for a long time, staring at its perfection. The clean, unused white pages; the crisp corners; the endless worlds just waiting for me to uncover them with my charcoals.

"Henry, this must've cost you a lot," I whispered.

Henry rolled his eyes. "You're supposed to say thank you."

"Thank you." I swallowed hard, my throat hot and itchy.

"You're a real artist, and you've been drawing on napkins and newspapers for a long time now."

"Henry, I—" I kept swallowing. I thought I would choke. "I didn't get you anything. I don't have . . ."

"It's okay." Henry cuffed me on the shoulder. "I didn't expect anything."

That popped the whole moment right into smithereens. I shoved the sketchpad into my bag. "What, so I'm *that* poor and rude that you didn't even bother thinking I could get you something? Is that it?"

"No. I don't know, it's like . . . we've died together, Olivia." Henry frowned in that serious way of his. "We're way past needing to give presents and stuff. But I know you want to be an artist more than anything in the world, so I just had to do this."

Oh. "That's really nice, Henry."

Would he *ever* stop grinning? "I know, isn't it?"

"Idiot." I kicked him on the leg, but not nearly hard enough to hurt, and hugged my bag to me for the rest of the night. It held a new sketchpad inside it, like a precious egg.

CLAIRE LEGRAND

CHAPTER 29

ON NEW YEAR'S EVE, HENRY STAYED THE NIGHT. We watched the ball drop with the Barskys, and then they walked us back to the Hall.

"You've done a nice job back here, Olivia," said Mrs. Barsky, a cluster of ghosts trailing after her with these dopey looks on their faces. Ghosts were always following Mrs. Barsky these days. They were like her fan club or something. "It really feels like a home."

I stepped back and tried to look at the backstage rooms like I was seeing them for the first time. Then I tried to remember what they'd looked like the first day we arrived. I guess there was a big difference. I'd strung up paper birds across the kitchen ceiling and tacked up my drawings on the walls. For Christmas, I'd bought myself this nice round orange rug from the charity store and put it under the kitchen table. A sign on my and Nonnie's door said OLIVIA AND NONNIE, AKA, THE COOLEST, LIVE HERE.

"Yeah," I said. "I guess it's all right."

"Is your father around?" Mr. Barsky said.

I shrugged. "Who knows?"

The Barskys exchanged these looks that made me shrink inside my clothes. I didn't want them to feel sorry for me. I just wanted to return to the nice night we'd been having. My belly was bulging with cookies. Henry was wearing a pointy foil hat.

After I finally convinced the Barskys to leave, I helped set up a pallet for Henry on the floor of my room.

"Henry is sleeping here?" Nonnie sat on the edge of her cot, her knees up to her chest like a kid. She was practically drowning in her nightgown. "Is *una festa*? Party?"

"Sure, Nonnie."

Nonnie waved her hand at Henry. "Come here, boy."

Henry stood there like a champ while Nonnie turned him around and around, inspecting him.

"You are gentleman?" she asked.

Henry's eyebrows went up. "I think so."

"You *think* so?"

"I mean, yeah. Yeah, I am."

"You'll sleep by door? Watch for shades?" Nonnie looked past him to smile at me. "Olivia tells me about shades."

Tillie buried her head in my shoulder and giggled.

"Yes, ma'am, I will."

"You like scarves?"

Henry paused. Then he took off his hat, found a yellow

scarf from the pile on Nonnie's bed, and tied it around his head like a pirate. "I love them."

Nonnie clapped him on the arm. "He can stay."

Once Nonnie had fallen asleep, and the Maestro had stumbled into his bedroom from some party uptown and started up his music, Henry and I gathered onstage with our ghosts and a few of the others. We needed the backup.

It was time to share with Tillie and Jax.

We had planned on sharing with Mr. Worthington first, because he was looking darker every day. But he wouldn't let us. He kept pointing at Tillie and Jax and shaking his head, grunting like a caveman. So Tillie and Jax it was.

"Mrs. Barsky wouldn't like this," Henry whispered as we set up. "She'd want to do it herself."

"Yeah, but these aren't *her* ghosts," I said. "They're ours. Someone else helping them move on would be wrong. Besides, don't you want to see their memories for yourself?"

"Isn't that kind of selfish?"

"Look, do you want to do it or not?"

Henry sighed. "Just hurry before I change my mind."

Like the previous five times, Henry and I held each other's hands and braced ourselves for the cold and darkness of sharing, for the stifled feeling of not being able to breathe.

It had been a while. He had to be as nervous as I was.

"It will be okay," Jax said. But he kept looking around the darkened Hall. Other ghosts stood guard for us, hovering around us in a circle. They were twitchy, flinching at every noise. I didn't have to be a mind reader to know we were all thinking the same thing:

The shades had been awfully quiet since Mrs. Barsky had opened up The Ghost Room. They stayed far away from us, lurking in the corners, watching. It was like they had given up or something.

Only they didn't seem like the kind of creatures who gave up easily.

I set my jaw. "Just do it, guys. And hurry."

Tillie and Jax rushed into us, pouring through our skin, into our ears, under our fingernails. Everything in the universe was clamping down on me, trying to split me apart into pieces. When I breathed, it hurt, so I stopped breathing and thought I would pass out.

But then I found Henry's hand and squeezed. His hand squeezed back. It said, *I'm here, Olivia.*

When I opened my eyes, I was still me, Olivia, but I was also Jax. When I held my hands out in front of me, I saw a boy's hands, crisscrossed with scrapes and dirt. Across from me was a girl with wild braids and beautiful honey-colored skin. White dust, bandages, and strange markings—maybe burns?—covered her from head to toe.

Tillie? I whispered. *Or . . . Henry?*

The girl nodded. "Both of us are here," said Tillie's voice, but I knew it was really Henry speaking with Tillie's voice, because Tillie sounded gentler than she usually did. That thought startled me: Was Henry gentle? I tried to find him through the mask of Tillie's face. It was nice, the thought of a boy like Henry being gentle. Baseball stars who sat at popular tables weren't the kind of people you might first think of as gentle.

You're distracted, said Jax, from inside my head.

"Sorry," I muttered.

"What?" Henry-Tillie said.

"I was talking to Jax."

Henry-Tillie frowned. "This is confusing. It's like . . . okay, so Tillie is inside me, and Jax is inside you. And I'm kind of inside Tillie too. It's all mixed-up. When you talk, Olivia, I know it's you, even though it's Jax's voice."

"Same here, with you and Tillie. So . . . Tillie, can you see Jax? Er, me?"

Henry-Tillie paused, listening to the voice inside him. "She says she can't see anything. She says she's stuck inside my brain, and that it's gross and gray, just like she thought a brain would be. Thanks, Tillie."

That's how it is for me, too, Jax said quietly. *I thought maybe I would be able to see Tillie, in our memories like this. But it's just like always. I can't see her. I can't hear her.*

I'm sorry, Jax, I thought to him. *But I can see her. She's right here, I promise you.*

Does she look okay? Where are we?

"Tillie says this is stupid, because she can't see anything," said Henry-Tillie, putting his hands on his hips. "Also, when I put my hands on my hips just then, it was mostly Tillie moving them. That's completely weird." Henry-Tillie started waving his arms around and turning in circles like some crazy dance. "Okay, she's making me do this, too. Stop it, Tillie."

"We're . . ." I looked around as the memories surrounding us grew less fuzzy. "I don't know how to answer you, Jax. We're somewhere very gray."

Light gray flakes covered the world, as far as I could see. Some of them rained down from the sky like snow, but it wasn't snow. When I touched one of those flakes, it crumbled in my hand like feathery dust. In the distance, ruined buildings jutted up into a black sky.

I described this for Jax in my head. And I described where we stood—in a camp of some kind, with fences surrounding us, and shacks lined up in the center of the camp. Filthy people huddled by tiny campfires, or worked beside tables loaded down with supplies. Staircases stood attached to chunks of crumbling wall. Columns stood without a roof over them.

I felt Jax beginning to understand, to remember. *The war*, he thought. *There was a war.*

"What war?"

And there was . . . I was making something.

Overhead, a low, wailing sound roared out of the sky.

Me-Jax and Henry-Tillie threw ourselves to the ground and covered our heads.

"Jax, what are you doing?" I hissed, choking on a mouthful of dirt and ash.

 246

Quiet, Jax said. *The planes! Oh, no.* I could feel him curling up into a ball in my mind.

When I peeked up, I saw others around the courtyard doing the same thing we were: crouching in the dirt. Then everything was quiet, and we waited—one minute, two—and then everyone got up and went back to their business, like nothing had happened.

"I think you'd better explain what's going on, Tillie," Henry-Tillie said.

"Here, Tillie, you explain to Henry, and Jax'll explain to me," I said.

Well, walk around and act like you're talking to each other or something, Jax suggested. *Otherwise everyone'll think it's weird if you're both just standing there in silence, staring at nothing.*

He had a point. "Come on," I said, grabbing Henry-Tillie by the arm. "Can you feel that, Jax? I just grabbed Tillie's arm."

No, Jax said mournfully. *I remember what it felt like, though, to grab her arm. Like everything would be okay, and no one could hurt me.*

"So, explain," I said. I kept holding Henry-Tillie's arm as we circled the courtyard.

Basically, this is the end of the world, Jax began. *Or at least, that's what everyone said to us. I don't actually know what happened after we . . . well, you know. After we died. But there was a war, and it was bad. There were these dangerous weapons that destroyed pretty much everything.*

"Is that why everything's so gray here?"

Yeah. The weapons created these clouds that blocked out the sun, and people kept getting sick and dying from the inside out, and it was winter all the time, but the war didn't stop. Why didn't they stop? I didn't understand it.

I felt sick to my stomach. I'd never seen war before. It was just one of those things that I pretended to read about (and that Henry actually did read about) in history class.

"Jax?" I ran my fingers across the fence we stood beside. Something here was not right—besides the fact that I was inside a dead person's memories. "Where exactly are we?"

Jax frowned. *It's so hard to remember . . .*

"The future," Henry-Tillie blurted. His eyes widened, like he couldn't believe what he'd just said. "That's what Tillie says. We're in the future."

I had to hold onto the fence beside me to keep from falling down. "But how is that possible? You're *ghosts*. If you died in the future, before me and Henry were even alive, how can you be ghosts with us now, in the present?"

Jax shrugged. *Time works differently for ghosts. Once you start heading toward Death, all the rules change. All we know is, we're drawn to our anchors. Somewhere, in your present, are our anchors.*

"But you're older ghosts than Frederick was," I said. "Even though you died way after he did. How can you be older than him, then? Shouldn't you be the youngest of all?"

"Tillie says," Henry said after a second, "that they *are* older than Frederick, because they've been ghosts for longer, even though they died later, when you look at it in normal time. But in ghost time, it's just about how long it

 248

takes you to become a ghost. So, Tillie and Jax died in the future, but they've been ghosts for longer than Frederick, even though he died in the past, because it took him longer to become a ghost after he died than it did for them." Henry paused. "Does that make sense?"

"Not really," I said. In fact, my head hurt. "But enough for us to get this over with. How do we find your anchors?"

Jax shivered inside me. *There was a hiding spot. I remember that. There was a hiding spot where the organ used to be.*

"You mean the pipe organ?" I shook my head as if by doing that I could clear out my confusion. "This used to be the Hall, didn't it? That's why you can't leave the Hall in my time. Because this is where you died—in this camp, which is where the Hall used to be."

"Tillie says she doesn't remember the whole Hall being here when they were alive," Henry-Tillie said. "It was just this camp that some people set up for survivors. And some of the Hall is old walls."

There was a hiding spot, and a tree, Jax whispered. *Please, Olivia. Can we go find it?*

"Sure. Jax is saying something about a hiding spot . . ."

"Tillie is too, and she says they each had their own spot, separately."

"Well. That's a place to start, I guess."

It was over here. I could feel Jax's memories pulling me, like invisible strings. *This way, Olivia.*

But Henry-Tillie was walking the other way, and it gave

me a bad feeling in my stomach. I didn't want to leave him.

"Henry?" My voice, Jax's voice, sounded so small.

"It's all right," Henry-Tillie said, smiling at me. "We'll meet back here in ten minutes, okay?"

Then he turned and walked away. I watched Tillie's braids swing until they disappeared at the other side of the camp.

We found Jax's hiding spot in a ditch strewn with pipes and sludge. Shiny aluminum foil wrappers littered the ground. A deflated basketball, black with grime, sat against a gigantic old tree with bark scraped off its trunk.

"It doesn't seem safe to be crawling around in this junk," I said.

Well, just be careful, then. Jax sighed. *I love this spot. I liked to come here and think, or when Tillie was on duty.*

"On duty?"

We all had duty shifts. Just patrolling the fences with the grown-ups, you know. It was good to have lots of people watching the borders for raiders.

I wasn't even going to ask him what that meant. I didn't want to think about raiders and fence patrols; I just wanted to go home. This place was giving me the creeps.

Stumbling over a rusty pipe, I sliced my hand.

"Ouch!"

Oh! Jax started spinning around in happy circles. *My treasure chest!*

I sucked on my finger. Jax's memory-blood had no taste. "Your what?"

Open that box, that metal one with the jagged edge.

As carefully as possible, I tugged on the handle of a metal box shoved beneath a drainpipe—a drainpipe that looked strangely familiar. Maybe a pipe that had once been in the Hall's basement or our crummy bathroom.

"This is too weird."

Open it up! What's inside?

"You don't remember?"

I remember there were rocks.

"Seriously, rocks?"

The weapons did neat things to some of the stuff in the ground. The rocks would glow purple and green sometimes.

"You pick weird things for toys." I pried open the lid of the box, using the ends of Jax's shirt sleeves to protect my fingers. When the lid snapped open, I did see a bundle of rocks. A plastic sheriff's badge. A whistle, the boxcar from a model train, a few bars of something wrapped in foil.

Some scraps of . . . tree bark? And braided twine.

That's it. Jax was practically beating on the sides of my skull in his excitement. *Olivia, that's it!*

"You know, it's pretty hard to keep my balance with you shoving yourself around in my brain like that."

Sorry, but Olivia, this has to be it. I feel it in my . . . well, I'd feel it in my bones if I had bones. I was making this for Tillie—this has to be my anchor!

I gathered up the braided twine and the tree bark.

Someone had peeled away pieces of the bark into thin strips. "You were making her a bracelet?"

We were each working on one. Friendship bracelets, you know? Oh, I remember now! Olivia, this is wonderful. I remember everything. I remember so much.

I tried to hug him through my brain, which was a very wobbly sensation. "Keep going."

We wanted to make bracelets for each other so that if I was on duty and I got scared, I could hold the bracelet or rub it, like for good luck, and it'd be like Tillie was right there with me. And she was going to make one for me, and we were going to switch them, so it'd be like we had pieces of each other all the time, no matter what.

"And you think this is your anchor?"

Positive. It reminds me of Tillie. And I never got to give it to —

That low wail sounded again from the skies, louder this time, louder than thunder.

"Jax?" I could barely hear myself shouting over the racket. I clamped my hands to my ears, but it didn't help. The wail turned piercing, shrill.

Run. Hurry, run! Where's Tillie?

In the middle of camp, something exploded. Several shacks shattered. Dirt and rocks rained down on the heads of people running for cover.

I was one of those people, except I wasn't running for cover.

I was running for Tillie. And for Henry.

Find them, Jax sobbed, as the sky swarmed with black

252

planes. Explosion after explosion rattled the ground, throwing us down into the dirt. But every time, we pulled ourselves back up.

The half-finished friendship bracelet dangled from my fingers; the twine was turning dark.

I stared down at myself. Tiny red wounds dotted Jax's body, but I couldn't feel them. It was like my body was shutting down.

Run faster! Jax screamed. Together we ran, pushing aside anything that got in our way. We wouldn't be able to find her in time. I knew that. That was the point, that was why ghost-Tillie and ghost-Jax couldn't see or hear each other.

They hadn't been able to find each other before they died. They had never been able to give each other their bracelets or say good-bye.

Tillie? Jax's fingers were scraping my insides, digging for a way out. *Tillie! Where are you? Don't leave me here!*

In the split second before it happened, I saw a girl with braided hair running straight for us through the smoke. A bracelet dangled from her fist.

The next instant, the loudest noise I'd ever heard popped my eardrums. The ground between me and Tillie—and Henry—exploded. A red-hot light blinded me.

It wasn't like being stabbed to death; I didn't feel much.

WHEN WE CAME TO, GASPING ON THE FLOOR of the stage, Henry pushed himself to his feet, grabbed his backpack off the floor, and ran away.

"Henry?" I shook my head, trying to blink the fuzz from my eyes. My skin tingled. I had *exploded.* I felt sick and torn open. "Henry, where are you going?"

Igor was licking my neck. *Let him go. Meow. I was scared with you sitting there all frozen like that. Meow. I hate these sharing sessions. Look at me, I'm so upset I can't even speak properly. Meow, meow.*

Tillie and Jax were sad blobs of gray smoke near the back of the stage, but I had just been blown up for them; they could handle themselves for a few minutes. Something had to have been seriously wrong for Henry to just rush out like that.

So I followed him.

It was a bad idea. First of all, it was almost one in the morning. Twelve-year-old girls shouldn't be running around cities at one in the morning, unless maybe they have superpowers, and even then it's questionable.

Second, it was freezing cold, even through my jacket.

But I had to find Henry. I pushed myself faster than I'd ever run before. My throat burned with the cold, but I didn't care. I caught the tail end of Henry's legs racing around the corner onto Tenth Street and pushed myself to run faster. Moonlight shone on the black streets and the white traffic lines and the glassy skyscrapers. Everything was the colors of ghosts—except for Henry's red hair.

After running for ages, a stitch pinching my side, I followed Henry onto a smaller, quieter street I didn't recognize. His backpack jangled. I bet it was that jar he always kept with him, the dirty, rattling one from the séance.

"Henry!" A car raced by with people yelling out the windows. Henry had turned past a brick stoop and was climbing up a black iron gate. "Henry, wait!"

He froze, halfway up the gate.

"Why'd you leave so fast?" I said, bending over to catch my breath. "Are you okay?"

"You shouldn't be here." He jumped to the ground, trying to push me back the way I'd come. His voice sounded strange and closed-off. "Get out of here, Olivia."

"But why'd you—?"

"*Leave.* Why won't you listen to me?"

I stepped back. Henry had never talked to me like that before. Not since we'd become friends, anyway.

Before I could say anything, the porch light turned on, and five people piled out onto the porch. Two grown-ups and three kids. Only the grown-ups looked like each other, and none of them looked a thing like Henry. I realized then that I'd never actually paid much attention to Henry's parents before. They'd always dropped him off places from the car. I'd never seen them face-to-face.

Now I knew why.

They weren't his real parents.

"Henry," the dad said, coming down the stoop stairs, "this sneaking out business has got to stop. We talked about this." Then he looked at me and smiled a tired smile. "So. Henry's been sneaking out to see *you*, has he? I'm Ted Banks."

He held out his hand, and I shook it, this numb feeling taking over my body. "Hi. Olivia Stellatella."

Mr. Banks's eyebrows raised. "As in, Stellatella of the City Philharmonic?"

I flushed. "Yeah. That's me."

"You must know Henry pretty well, then. He's there constantly."

"Yeah." I risked looking at Henry, but he was just staring at his house. I couldn't even see his face. "We're friends, I guess."

But were we? He hadn't told his family about me, he'd been lying when he said they were okay with him staying the night. He hadn't even told me they weren't his real parents.

It was like he was embarrassed to even know me.

"Ted, can we just go inside?" Henry said.

Mr. Banks gave me some money and called me a cab, and after I got home and crept backstage, I curled up in my cot

256

with Igor and my ghosts, and tried to ignore the queasy feeling in my stomach.

Henry knew all of my secrets.

Why hadn't he told me his?

Henry didn't come to the Hall the next day. He didn't come for several days. I tried to call his house a couple of times, and I left these sort of coded messages with Mr. Banks. Henry would know they meant I wanted him to come help me search for Tillie and Jax's friendship bracelets. We'd decided those were their anchors, but we hadn't been able to find them yet.

Henry never showed up. I didn't see him until school started again.

At lunch the first day back, I sat down at my normal lonely table in the cafeteria and pretended to be incredibly interested in my cheese sandwich. After a few minutes of dedicated chomping, I peeked out from beneath my hair at Mark Everett's table.

Sure enough, Henry sat there, laughing at some doofy face Nick Weber was making with his milk straws.

Joan sat down at her normal seat, way at the end of the table. She looked at me, and at Henry's empty seat, and scooted along the bench with a very serious expression until she was right across from me. Where Henry should have been.

"So, what happened with Henry?" Joan asked, but it

wasn't snotty or gossipy or anything. It was solidarity, I think. She patted my arm, and something about that made me spill everything—about the ghosts, about the shades, about Henry and Mr. Banks. She didn't say a word for a long time, just nodding instead. I liked that she took me seriously. She accepted everything I said like it was something people said any old day.

I guess that's why the ghosts decided to trust her and show themselves to her the night of the séance. Joan was the kind of person you trusted, protest posters and all.

When I was done, Joan said, "You mean you didn't know Henry lives with foster parents?"

Her tone made me defensive. "No. How was I supposed to know that?"

Joan shrugged. "Well, I mean, they come to open house sometimes. And to the baseball games." She made a face. "My dad loves baseball. He'll go to any game in town."

"I don't know," I said. "I guess I never paid much attention." Maybe I didn't pay attention to a lot of things like I always thought I had, or at least not to the right things. I started doodling in my sketchpad. That made me feel better.

"Well." Joan scooted closer. "Daddy knows everything about everyone in this town, right? I mean, he's pretty important and all. And I don't mean that in a snobby way."

"Sure, I guess."

"He told me, once, about Henry. You know, because Henry's a good pitcher. Daddy pays attention to him."

Henry was a good pitcher? I'd never gone to a single game. I felt myself shrinking down into my seat. I felt like the most awful friend who had ever lived.

"Anyway, Henry's dad went overseas a few years ago because he was in the military, and he had to go. But he never came back."

"You mean . . . he died?"

Joan nodded gravely. "And after that, Henry's mom just kind of . . ." Joan looked around to make sure no one was watching us. "Well, she got really depressed and stopped taking care of Henry, and then she had to go to a hospital, and then she never came back either. I think she's still there, but I don't know what hospital it is. So Henry lives with foster parents now."

I didn't know what to say to that.

"Oh, Olivia." Joan sighed. "You must be so distressed to have Henry abandon you like this."

"He didn't *abandon* me. He just . . . got mad. Even though I don't know why."

"Well, obviously, sharing with Tillie and Jax, and the whole war thing, reminded him of his real dad. So he got upset and ran away. And also obviously, he's embarrassed about living with foster parents, although I don't know why he's so funny about it. I've met Mr. Banks, he's really nice. So he wasn't mad at you, just mad that you saw what he didn't want you to see."

"Well, if he hadn't just run away like that, I wouldn't have been so worried," I said, sawing my sandwich into pieces. It felt good to destroy something. "He could have just gone home like normal, and everything would be fine, and he'd be sitting here right now instead of you."

"I understand you didn't mean that to sound as rude as it did, Olivia. I understand that you are under great emotional stress."

I stabbed a piece of sandwich and shoved it in my mouth. "Whatever."

But the truth is, she was right.

When Henry finally showed his face at the Hall that night, I nearly jumped on him.

"Henry, I'm so sorry," I blurted. "I didn't mean to follow you home the other night, but I was worried because we had just died with Tillie and Jax, and I thought something was wrong, so I just ran without thinking, and I don't care that you have foster parents. How could you think that, anyway? I should punch you for thinking that."

I stopped to take a breath. "That came out wrong. I just meant that it doesn't make me like you less, and I don't think it's stupid or anything. But I am mad that you didn't tell me and that you were hiding me from them." I paused, scuffing the carpet with my shoe. "Sneaking out to come see me. You're embarrassed about me, aren't you? Because I live here. That's why you didn't tell your foster parents you were visiting me, isn't it? And please don't sit with Mark Everett at lunch anymore. That guy's a jerk. Come back and sit with me. Please? And, I'm so sorry about your dad. And your mom. I really am."

Henry stared at me in stony silence, not even moving when Tillie started drifting up underneath his chin with her hands clasped at her throat and this puppy-dog expression on her face. She tried to bat her eyelashes, but she did it so hard her eyes popped out and hung there by ghostly strings.

That made Henry laugh. "Tillie, you're disgusting."

Tillie hooted in triumph and pushed herself up above our heads.

I could have slapped her, I was so nervous. "Well?"

"I'm sorry, Olivia," Henry said. "I was gonna tell you about everything at some point. It's just . . . I don't know, it's weird. I don't talk about it with people. And I'm not embarrassed by you. I just thought you wouldn't want them to know you live at the Hall. Not that I care, but you do. So I didn't tell them." Then he grinned. "Besides, it's kind of fun sneaking out."

So he didn't hate me after all. I could have pushed off the ground and started flying like Tillie. But Henry didn't need to know that.

"Well. Okay. Fine, then. But still, you should have told me about your parents sooner," I said.

"You didn't show me your rooms backstage until you absolutely had to," Henry pointed out.

"But I had to find out from *Joan*. She knew more about you than I did." *That hurt*, I didn't say aloud. But it wasn't all his fault, and that hurt too. I could have paid better attention. I could have paid better attention to a lot of things. I hugged my sketchpad close.

Henry took the jar out of his bag—that crusty, brown glass jar that was always clanging around in his backpack. The jar from the séance.

"Would it help if I showed you what was in here?"

"Is it important to you?"

"It's the most important thing in the world to me," Henry said firmly.

"Then, yeah. It'd help"

We went outside into the walking park, the trees purple and soft in the sunset. We sat under a looming black tree beside one of the bug-filled lampposts, and Henry opened the jar.

Inside was a whole lot of junk—crumpled-up pieces of paper, tags that I knew meant something military, some weird-looking coins, an ancient music tape with the name rubbed off it, photos so old they folded up like fabric. Strange jewelry made of stones and wood.

"This is my parents," Henry said, wiping some grit off his hands. "It's all I have left of them."

As I sorted through everything, Henry explained. The crumpled pieces of paper were old concert tickets and concert programs. The weird-looking coins were foreign money that Henry's mom used to collect when she was a little girl and her parents traveled with the army. That's how his parents had met. The photos were of them—and Henry, when he was little.

"You were a fat baby," I said.

"You know, if you're not gonna be serious, then—"

"Fat, but cute."

Henry ducked down to stack the photos back together. "Thanks."

"And this jewelry?"

"My mom always wore it. She got it when they were on base somewhere. Like in Africa or something. I don't remember."

"What's this of?" I held up the cassette tape. "I didn't even know they made these anymore."

"They don't. It's super old. It doesn't even play. But I have a new copy. Hold on."

And then Henry pulled some headphones out of his bag and played the music for me. I knew it immediately—Beethoven's Seventh Symphony, second movement.

"It was one of my parents' favorites," Henry said quietly. "They were big music people. All kinds, not just classical stuff. This one always made me feel like, I don't know, bigger than I actually am."

I closed my eyes, nodding along with the music. After a while, Henry pulled the headphones off me.

"That's why I like it here," he said. "Music reminds me

of them. I remember the good days, and then I remember the bad days too. After Dad died, Mom would just sit there and stare at nothing. She wouldn't even look at me when I played music for her. That's why I study so much. There wasn't much else to do. And good grades are important, you know. For college and all that. I've gotta get scholarships."

My cheeks burned as I watched him bundle everything away. I should have said something meaningful about his parents, but all I could say was, "I don't make good grades."

"Yeah, but there's still high school. Plus, you can draw. You could go to art school or something."

"You really think that?"

"Sure! You're talented, Olivia." He yawned and leaned back against the tree. "Everyone knows that."

"They do?"

"It's totally obvious."

I leaned back against the same tree, right next to Henry, and closed my eyes. This tiny happy feeling was buzzing around in my chest, and I didn't want to lose it.

It was still buzzing around when the sun went down and Henry and I headed inside. His backpack jingled with that jar, and I bet he'd never showed anyone before—only me.

My chest was going to explode, but in a good way. I threw back my head and laughed into the dark. I was happy.

Then we entered the Hall, and everything changed.

CHAPTER 31

M R. WORTHINGTON MET US IN THE WEST lobby, wringing his hat in his hands. It reminded me of Nonnie.

"Nnngh," he moaned. "Nnngh."

I was in too good a mood for this. I slapped my hands on my knees. "Come on, boy! Who's a good ghost? Show me what's wrong! Can you show me what's wrong?"

Mr. Worthington frowned and pointed at one of the doors leading into the main Hall.

"That was kind of rude," Henry said.

"Sorry, Mr. Worthington. What is it?"

He led us inside. Mr. Rue was there, and the Maestro, and someone else I didn't recognize—a tall man in a nice suit. They were walking around the Hall, and Mr. Rue had a bunch of papers in his hands. A group of ghosts floated behind them. They always liked spying on new people.

"Oh, man." Henry pulled me down behind the seats. "That's Mayor Pitter!"

Tillie and Jax zoomed up behind us. "What's he doing here?"

"Nnnnnngh!" Mr. Worthington said, pointing at the mayor.

We followed them, creeping through the seats as close as we dared.

"You have to understand, Otto," Mayor Pitter was saying, "I didn't want to have to do this. But I'm under enormous pressure from City Council. The fact is, your orchestra's a dying business, and Emerson Hall sits on a huge patch of land. I can't just let it sit here, taking up space and losing money, while so many people are out of work. I could build shops here, apartment buildings! Businesses that would actually make money."

By this point, they had stopped moving, and so had we. Henry and I crouched in the seats, hardly breathing.

"Are they saying what I think they're saying?" Jax whispered.

Mr. Worthington curled himself up into a ball of black smoke and moaned softly.

The Maestro threw his arms up in the air. "I can't believe you're just standing here listening to this, Walter!"

"Walter?" Tillie said.

"That's Mr. Rue," Henry whispered.

I couldn't say anything. That happy feeling buzzing around in my chest? Sinking fast.

"He is talking about shutting down our orchestra," the Maestro said. "And we're the only one the city has! My musicians will be out of work. *I* will be out of work. I'll be a laughingstock, mocked across the world because I couldn't keep my orchestra alive. *Pitied* for it."

Mr. Rue looked up sadly from his papers. "Otto, maybe it's time. Our numbers aren't getting any better. And the mayor's right, the land could be put to better use."

Then the Maestro spat out an Italian curse word—one of the really bad ones—and shoved Mr. Rue away, hard.

"Really, Otto," said Mayor Pitter, frowning. "Get control of yourself, or the police will. Have some dignity, man."

"What if someone came up to you, Mayor Pitter," the Maestro said, "and told you he was about to take away everything you'd worked for your whole life?"

"I'd be angry at him." Mayor Pitter put a hand on the Maestro's arm, which I thought was pretty brave, considering. "I don't want to tear down my city's only music hall. I used to play the trombone, actually. In school. Did you know that?"

The Maestro just stared at him. I knew that look. I shot that look at people when I was secretly imagining stomping them into a pancake with my boot.

"But times are tough," the Mayor said, "and your orchestra's not cutting it."

He started walking away, and then stopped and turned back. "If you don't raise your ticket sales by one thousand percent by the end of March, then that'll be it. We'll tear down the Hall in the spring. Unveil a development plan in the fall. It'll boost city morale. People will get excited about something again." Then he paused and said, "I'm sorry," and I could tell he was.

But that didn't make things any better.

"I'll do it," the Maestro said quietly, once the Mayor was gone. "Somehow I'll raise the money. I'll make it happen, Walter."

"No, you won't, Otto. We've *been* trying, haven't we?" Mr. Rue's frown was the saddest I'd ever seen. "It's over, my friend. It's over."

Then Mr. Rue put his arm around the Maestro's shoulders, and they left, the Maestro's head in his hands.

"Olivia?" Henry got to his feet and helped me up too. "Are you okay?"

"Tear it down?" Tillie looked around at each of us, and for the first time since I'd met her, it looked like she might cry. Her eyes were these big shaking black pools. "What does that mean?"

"What if we can't find our anchors before they do it?" Jax whispered. "What'll happen to us?"

"Olivia." Henry shook me a little. "Say something."

I ran for the door.

Out the front lobby and across the street, not even waiting for the walk signal. I heard brakes screeching and cab drivers cussing me out, but I didn't care. I slammed open The Happy Place door so loud that Gerald got spooked and started flying around the shop.

Henry and my ghosts were right on my heels as I barreled

into The Ghost Room. Mrs. Barsky was there, counting money.

Just looking at it made me want to be sick.

"Mrs. Barsky," I said, "what happens if a ghost's haunt is torn down before they can find their anchor?"

"What?" Mrs. Barsky put her hand to her mouth. "Is the Hall going to be—?"

"Just answer me!"

"If a ghost's haunt is destroyed, the ghost has no home. The haunt is protection. Without the haunt, a ghost will fall prey to shades almost immediately. He won't be able to move on. He won't be able to find his anchor." Mrs. Barsky squeezed my hands. "Baby, is something going to happen to the Hall?"

Yes. Something was going to happen. They were going to tear it down, and without it, my ghosts would be homeless. They'd be out in the world, alone and unprotected.

And so would I.

PART THREE

CHAPTER 32

I COULDN'T SLEEP FOR A WHILE AFTER THAT. I kept having too many nightmares.

In the nightmares, there were storms. They weren't storms that made sense, because even though there was wind and rain and hail, you could still see the stars. The stars were giant, hurtling closer and closer to where I stood with Igor, Nonnie, and the ghosts. And the closer the stars got, the harder it was to stay together.

We were holding on to the Hall, to the columns that held up the staircases in the main lobby. But then it turned out the Hall and the storm were actually this giant, swirling black hole, and that's what was sucking the stars toward us.

Nonnie was the first to fly away from me. Then the ghosts and Igor. Then me.

The Hall sucked us into Limbo, and then it collapsed, and we were stuck in cold nothingness.

Forever.

One night, instead of trying to sleep, I settled in one of the Hall's floor seats with a candle from Mrs. Barsky and drew.

The ghosts stayed in my room with Nonnie. It was safe enough in there with her. Anyway, the shades had basically disappeared in the last few days. I hadn't seen even one creepy shadow-fingernail.

Maybe they figured they didn't have to hunt my ghosts anymore. After Mayor Pitter tore down the Hall, the shades would have all the ghost victims they wanted—mine and the countless others who kept showing up, asking Mrs. Barsky for help.

"This is stupid." I scribbled out the sketch of Nonnie being sucked away from me by my nightmare and wiped my eyes on my pajama sleeve. "We should just find me a cardboard box to live in and get it all over with."

Igor massaged the cushion of the chair beside me with his claws. *Funny. I never thought of you as a quitter. Human, yes. Therefore somewhat of a simpleton, yes. But never a quitter.*

"I'm not quitting, I'm just . . . scared."

Igor pushed his paws against my leg. *Being homeless isn't so bad, you know.*

"You're a cat, Igor. I'm a human. I can't live on the streets."

His whiskers twitched. *See? Simpleton. My point exactly.*

Then I heard someone humming from across the Hall. At first, I saw only a dark figure walking across the stage, and I grabbed Igor, ready to run.

But it was just the Maestro. And it was too late to run from him. He'd seen me.

"Olivia?"

I settled lower in the seat, like preparing for battle. "What? I'm drawing."

When the Maestro reached me, he stood there silently for a second before sitting down. Maybe he was waiting for me to say something else, but I wouldn't. I wanted him to speak first. I'd been waiting for him to tell me about Mayor Pitter and the Hall, and maybe he was finally going to do it.

"That's, uh," he said. "Your drawing. I like it. What is it?"

I glared up at him. "A black hole of death."

"Oh. Well. That's good."

I rolled my eyes and kept drawing.

"Did you know that, when your mother and I first met, it was because of the orchestra?"

So I guess he wasn't going to talk about our soon-to-be-homeless problem after all. I dug the tip of my charcoal harder into my sketchpad and said nothing.

"She said the sound of their music—of *my* music—was like someone calling her home at last. She said she'd never heard anything so beautiful. Did you know that?"

"Whatever."

But he kept going like I wasn't even there. He settled back against the chair and gazed at the pipe organ. "If I can make them play beautifully enough, and loudly enough, and just right, I think she will find her way back home again. It will be like before, only it will be right this time, no mistakes. She will come back to us, Olivia."

Now that, I couldn't stand. I slammed my sketchpad

closed. "No, she won't. She's never coming back. And anyway, soon there won't be anything to come back to." I got out of my seat so I could feel taller than him. "Will there?"

He looked at me for a long time, and then tightened the sash of his robe. "I know I saw something, Olivia. The day the ceiling fell. I know I did."

Then he wandered away through the Hall, taking his time and humming. Mahler 2, again. Waving his hands to an invisible orchestra. Peeking into the shadows.

When he'd slipped backstage again, I felt it—a presence, somewhere behind me. Without turning around, I grabbed my sketchpad under one arm and Igor under the other, and pretended I was made of stone.

Stones were brave. Stones didn't break. I turned around.

A shade stood there, a tall piece of darkness in a dark room. One of its long-fingered arms was reaching for me.

"Get away!" I hissed, kicking at it. "Get away from me! Go home!"

It shrunk a little, and groaned and darted away, like I'd scared it. I hoped I had.

Then, just before the shade disappeared into the east lobby, color flickered across it. White, and blue, and gold.

For that one second, I thought I saw a familiar face. A face I hadn't seen in over a year.

"Mom?" I whispered.

But then the color was gone, and the shade was just a shade, slithering out the door on its belly.

I cuddled Igor close. "Did you see that?"

He flicked his tail. *I'm a cat, pet. I see more things than you can imagine.*

The next day, I got to school early and headed straight for the library.

Henry was already there, holed away at a table in a corner with a bunch of textbooks.

"Olivia!" he whispered, waving me over.

"Sorry, Henry. Can't talk."

I found a free computer, opened a search engine, and typed the word "Cara."

A bunch of suggestions popped up for me to try, most of them names, and most of them Italian, and none of them Mom's. A sour knot twisted my stomach.

When Mom first left, I searched for her everywhere. I liked to pretend that she had had to leave us for some noble purpose, like she was a spy who had to go away on some urgent mission, or she was secretly a scientist and one of her experiments had gone wrong.

That was a long time ago, though. Then I realized she'd left because of the Maestro. And then I stopped looking for her, period. It gets depressing after a while, trying to track down your own mom.

So why I was searching for her now? She obviously didn't want to be found. She hadn't said good-bye, she hadn't answered the Maestro's letters, nothing. She might have even changed her name, for all I knew.

The word "Cara" stared at me in that harsh computer-screen light. The first bell rang, but I didn't move.

If Mom didn't want to be found, then I wouldn't look for her. That weird-looking shade the night before didn't mean a thing. Probably the shades just wanted to trick me, make me think things that weren't true.

"Olivia?" Henry had snuck up behind me, arms full of books. "What's wrong?"

"I don't know."

Henry peered at the screen. "Cara. Your mom?"

"No." I turned the monitor off. "She's nobody."

CHAPTER

33

$\mathcal{T}$OWARD THE END OF JANUARY, WE STARTED TO feel pretty desperate. We were no closer to finding Tillie and Jax's bracelets, and soon it would be February.

Only about a month to go until the Hall would close.

Or, as I liked to think of it, the end of everything.

"That's pretty dramatic," Henry said. We were at lunch, and it was a Wednesday.

"Pretty dramatic?" I slammed down my lunch tray. "Yeah. It is. Because I'll be *homeless*."

"Maybe the Barskys will let you live with them. Or one of the musicians."

"Yeah. Maybe Richard Ashley." I fluttered my eyelashes. "He's dreamy."

"He is?" Henry looked at me kind of funny. "Do you think he's dreamy?"

"Sure. Who cares?"

"So you *do* think he's dreamy?"

"Henry, focus. Besides, I can't just go live with someone.

I have Nonnie. Whoever takes me in has to take her in too."

"Oh." Joan, at the end of our table, slammed down her lunch tray. "*Oh*. Don't even get me *started* about how we treat the elderly in this society."

Henry sighed. "Nobody asked you that, Joan."

"Yes, well. If you *did* ask me, I'd have a lot to say on the subject." Then Joan turned back to her food. I noticed she sat closer to us these days, scooting closer an inch at a time.

For the rest of lunch, Henry and I went back over our map of the Hall for the hundredth time, trying to figure out where we hadn't looked for Tillie and Jax's anchors. I could feel Joan watching us anyway, stealth-like. You could tell she was thinking really hard about something, but I didn't pay much attention at the time. Joan was always thinking really hard about something.

For the second series of January concerts, the orchestra was playing *The Pines of Rome* by Ottorino Respighi. The Maestro had always loved Respighi because they shared first names.

Henry loved Respighi because he said his music sounded like flying.

"Close your eyes and imagine it," he whispered to me. We were in the floor seats during a Tuesday night rehearsal, the map spread out on our laps. "Come on, the third movement's the best one."

"Henry, get real. We've got anchors to find."

Henry made a pouty face. "Please, Olivia?"

I rolled my eyes, but that face was pretty cute. "Fine." I closed my eyes, leaned my head back against the cushion, and listened.

It wasn't good because, well, it *was* our orchestra. And the Maestro had been out every night, visiting donors and City Council members, so he was cranky and had ticked off pretty much every musician onstage. But after a couple of minutes, I felt the music take over anyway. Each of the movements of *The Pines of Rome* is supposed to take place in a different section of pine trees in Rome. The third movement happens near a temple at night. And as I listened, I could feel nighttime soaring over me—sunsets and the first stars twinkling, and maybe a cool river nearby. Even nightingales singing. And yes, just like Henry said, it felt like flying. I was in a forest, a dark, cool forest of pines, drifting lazily through the branches like a bird, like the wind, like a ghost . . .

I bolted upright. My brain wobbled at the edge of something important.

"What is it?" Henry said.

Images raced through my head. Ghosts. Bracelets. The tree by Jax's hiding spot, with the bark scraped off. Henry's mom's jewelry.

"Henry," I whispered. "That jewelry your mom wore . . ."

"Yeah?"

"It was made out of rocks and wood and stuff like that, right? It came from stones and trees."

"Sure . . ."

280

Claire Legrand

"And Tillie's and Jax's bracelets were made out of bark . . ." The orchestra's music soared over our heads, out of tune and lifeless. I laughed, feeling a little crazy. "Maybe even from a pine?"

Henry's eyes widened. His binder crashed to the floor. "It's . . ."

". . . a tree." The Maestro was glaring at us over his shoulder. "That's why we haven't been able to find those bracelets. It's because their anchor is a tree."

Pure adrenaline zipped through me from head to toe, and Henry and I laughed like idiots all the way backstage. I knew the musicians could hear us, but I didn't care.

But when we got Tillie and Jax outside and told them to touch every tree on the grounds until they found the right one, the tree that held their anchor, they couldn't.

They floated up through every branch, just like I'd imagined when listening to *The Pines of Rome*. They wrapped themselves around every trunk and swam underground through every tangle of roots.

"Nothing." Jax slumped glumly next to me, and I tried my best to put my arm around him, even though it made my arm crackle up like ice.

"Stupid!" Tillie screamed, zipping through the trees like an angry shade. "Stupid, stupid!"

"I was so sure that was right." Henry slumped against a trash can. "It made total sense!"

Jax hid his face in my arm and started to cry.

I forced myself to sound cheerful. "Well, we'll just have to come up with something else, won't we? We'll figure it out."

But, a little voice whispered in my head, *what if we don't?*

I couldn't eat lunch the next day. Henry couldn't either. He just sat across from me with his head propped up in one hand, making mountains out of his mashed potatoes.

I pounded the table with my fist. "I want to smash something."

Henry tossed his chicken patty at me. "Here, take this. I'm not gonna eat it."

Before I could grab it, Joan rushed up out of nowhere and slammed a big notebook down on top of it.

"I," she declared breathlessly, "have a brilliant idea. It's so brilliant that sometimes I can't even stand it."

"Whoa, Joan," Henry said. "Your eyes are lit up kind of weird. Are you sick?"

"Sick with *brilliance*." Joan put her hands on top of ours. "Don't despair, friends. Like my historical namesake, I've come to your aid, to defend the innocent and weak against the injustice of the corrupt."

Henry blinked. "The what?"

"Joan, spill it already," I snapped.

"I know how to save Emerson Hall."

"You . . . what?"

"It's simple, really." Joan slammed open her notebook.

282

"We just need some fliers, a petition or something. A *message*. I've been doing this my whole life, you know. People just need to know what's going on. What the *issue* is. We need to make ourselves *visible* to the public."

"'We'?" I asked. "You know, I don't remember telling you about any of this. Were you eavesdropping?"

Joan stared at me. "Well, of course I was eavesdropping. I sit at your table, don't I? Besides, what does it matter? I'm going to help you. Let's look at"—she paused to draw a box in the air—"*the bigger picture.*"

"She has a point," Henry said.

I blew my hair out of my face. "Fine. What's this about a petition?"

"Well, I was thinking we make a petition and get lots of signatures. Then we can show Mr. Rue and your dad and Mayor Pitter and everyone how many people really care about the Hall." Joan slid some papers out of her notebook and shoved them at me. "See? Here are some sample ones."

"*Petition for Putting Seat Belts on All School Buses*?" I read. "Really?"

"It hasn't worked yet, but I won't give up." Joan grabbed the papers back. "So, we get all these signatures. Then we make fliers. You can do that, Olivia." She smiled shyly. "Since you're such a good artist."

Henry kicked me under the table. "See? What'd I tell you?"

"Ow." I kicked him back. "Jerk."

"We'll put them up all over town, and I mean every-where," Joan was saying. "All the telephone poles, every building we can find. The libraries. The only problem is, it has to be something more than just saving the Hall. People have to feel like they're getting something out of it too."

"Something to make them buy tickets." Henry was get-ting excited, flipping through Joan's sample petitions like they were sheets of gold. "That's the important thing. We need the money, the numbers."

As they kept talking, I started doodling fliers on my sketchpad to help me think. I halfway listened to them and my mind wandered, and so did my pencil. After a few min-utes, I looked down and saw that I had doodled ghosts. Four of them. Even Frederick.

Bingo.

I had to stand up and walk around and then come sit back down. The inspiration that had just hit me was too big for me to sit still.

Henry and Joan watched me. "What is it, Olivia?"

"I know what our message could be," I said slowly. "Besides saving the Hall, I mean. Something cool, some-thing to get people's attention and fill seats. We could tell them about the ghosts."

CHAPTER 34

Henry and Joan were quiet for a second. Then Joan's face lit up.

"That," she whispered, "is brilliant."

I wasn't used to people calling me brilliant. "Is it?"

"Yes. *Yes.* It's the perfect angle. Everyone loves ghost stories and being scared . . ."

". . . and the Hall is kind of creepy, too," I said, "with everything so old and broken-down. It's the perfect setting. We could spread rumors around the city. Maybe your dad could help, Joan. People will listen to him. And it wouldn't even be lying because it's the truth, there really *are* ghosts. People might think it was just a rumor, but they'd come anyway, to see for themselves."

Henry leaned forward. "We could coach the ghosts to show themselves every once in a while, to show people that something really is going on . . ."

Joan picked it up from there. "And people would tell their friends about what happened to them, and more and more people would come . . ."

"And pretty soon we'd have an audience again," I finished.

Joan leapt up out of her seat and danced.

"Olivia," Henry said, "you're a certified genius." Then he spun me around in this big hug, but I couldn't even enjoy it. Up in the air, I'd just had a horrible thought.

"Guys . . . wait." Henry put me down, looking confused. I backed up, shaking my head. "Actually, I don't know if we can do this. Isn't it kind of like . . . *using* the ghosts? Making them work for us? What if they don't want to?"

Henry's shoulders dropped. "Oh."

"Of *course* they'll want to, Olivia," Joan said patiently. "You've helped them all this time. The least they can do now is help you. It's like you were meant to help each other." Her eyes shone, and she leaned forward. "That's what they call—"

"—destiny?" I smiled. Joan was right. We *were* meant to help each other. My skin tingled. "They call it destiny."

35

FEBRUARY

*T*HE FLIER I DESIGNED LOOKED SOMETHING like this:

ATTENTION CITIZENS:
HELP SAVE THE GHOSTS
OF EMERSON HALL

The City Philharmonic needs your help!
The City Philharmonic is one of our city's
oldest, most honorable institutions.
AND IT'S IN TROUBLE.
We need *5,000 signatures* by March 1.
We need *increased concert*
attendance by 1000%.
Otherwise . . .
EMERSON HALL WILL BE DEMOLISHED.
The Hall desperately needs repairs,
but repairs cost money. We know times
are hard these days, with The Economy,

but what's more worth saving than
the culture of our city?
AND THE GHOSTS OF OUR CITY'S PAST,
WHICH ARE HAUNTING IT?
Please sign below if you want to
save the Hall and its ghosts.
And please come attend City Philharmonic
concerts in February,
and meet the ghosts of
Emerson Hall . . .

The flier had a border of music notes and wispy shapes that looked like typical Halloween ghosts. I had drawn the letters in a swirling, official-looking font.

Henry whistled when I showed him the finished copy. "Olivia, it's beautiful."

"You think so?" The way Henry said "beautiful" was so nice, I couldn't stop smiling.

"Yes, absolutely. Don't you think, Joan?"

Joan kissed it. "It's completely *marvelous*, Olivia. It looks so impressive, and everything about the ghosts is so intriguing. People won't be able to resist."

But it turns out, they could.

We started early the next Saturday morning, and when I say early, I mean seven in the morning, loaded up with backpacks full of pamphlets and clipboards, photographs of the Hall and musicians, and old recordings I'd found stashed backstage—recordings we hadn't been able to sell.

The ghosts trailing behind us, we set out down Arlington Avenue in raincoats and boots because it was, of course, raining. It just figured. I scowled at my feet as I squished through the gutters, kicking around gobs of wet leaves. The worst part was that I'd had to borrow a raincoat from Joan. It was so nice, so stylish and sophisticated—yes, a sophisticated raincoat—that I felt like I shouldn't be allowed to wear it.

"Is there some kind of limit to how far you can go from your haunt?" Henry asked.

The ghosts shrugged. Raindrops sizzled through them.

"I hadn't thought of that," I said. If they got a certain distance away from the Hall, would the ghosts pop out of existence or something? Would they fade away or be in some kind of pain? Could ghosts even *feel* pain?

"Well," said Joan, "maybe they should stay at the Hall—"

"No," Tillie wailed. "We won't have anything to do! We're so bored."

Jax cuddled close to me. "Don't worry, Olivia. We can go pretty far. We'll let you know when it starts to hurt."

I gaped at him. "Hurt?"

"Well, yeah. Our anchors only let us go so far."

"That doesn't make me feel any better."

"Oh, come on, Olivia," Tillie huffed. "You've risked a lot for us. Let us risk something for you."

"Fine." I yanked my raincoat shut. "But you'll let me

know the *second* you start to hurt. Understand?"

The ghosts saluted me in unison. I couldn't help but smile.

We headed uptown to the park and, for the next few hours, did what Joan called "pounding the pavement," which is when you walk around and try to shove your business on everyone. It was about as fun as it sounds.

"Excuse me, good sir!" Joan ran up to a man decked out for bike riding, wearing a slick bodysuit and goggles. Henry jogged after her, holding our umbrella over her clipboard. "Might I have a moment, sir?"

The man looked around in surprise. "Uh, what now?"

"Hello and good morning." Joan shoved herself forward for a ferocious handshake. "My name is Joan Dawson, and these are my associates, Olivia Stellatella and Henry Page. We attend Killough Intermediate School, and we're here to talk about Emerson Hall."

"Actually, I've got to—"

"All we need is your signature, sir."

"Right here on this petition," I added, trying to smile as widely as Joan. It felt more like a scowl.

"This is saying that you don't want the city to tear down Emerson Hall," added Henry.

The man glanced at the petition while adjusting his goggles. "Isn't that the crummy old music hall down on Wichita and Arlington?"

Once upon a time, I would have agreed with that man.

 290

Instead, I found myself getting ready to punch the guy. Henry had to hold me back.

Tillie growled under her breath. "I know I'm not supposed to attack fleshies, but can I attack *this* one?"

"No, Tillie," Henry hissed.

"With due respect, good citizen," Joan said, her nose up in the air, "that is not a polite thing to say about your city's cultural—"

"Look, I'm sorry, kids, but I've got a schedule to keep, huh?"

And with that, the bike man zoomed off into the rain.

"You know, I don't think he even *read* the petition," Henry said.

"Well, of course he didn't, he thinks the Hall's crummy." I kicked another leaf gob, and it stuck to my shoe like a molasses creature. I made a note to sketch that later: Glorbit the molasses man. "Lots of people are gonna think that, I bet. Maybe we're just wasting our time. And it's *raining*."

"Oh, Olivia, don't be such a gloomy Gus," admonished Joan. "Come on, where's your intrepid spirit? Onward, friends!"

But by ten thirty that morning, even Joan had lost her intrepid spirit. We were wet, cold, weighed down with soaked clothes, and had asked (Henry kept a tally) sixty-seven people for their signatures.

Only six of them had actually signed.

"That last woman was simply wretched," Joan fumed, as we stomped into a coffee shop on Reginald Square to warm up. "No one believes in free speech more than I do, but there's no need to *curse* at people."

"My toes are frozen," Henry groaned.

"Here, have mine," Tillie said gleefully, plucking off her toes one by one and dropping them down Henry's shirt, which made him shudder and dance around.

"Thanks for making me look like an idiot," he said.

Tillie turned slow, grinning circles in the air. "You're welcome."

As they argued, I watched a white-haired man, sitting by the window with tea and a newspaper, look up at us, look back at his newspaper, and then look up again. His face paled. He squinted and shifted his glasses.

He was looking right at Mr. Worthington.

"Guys," I whispered, elbowing Joan. "Look."

"Mr. Worthington?" Henry said under his breath. "What are you doing?"

Mr. Worthington shrugged and smiled. "Grrflt."

"What's that supposed to mean?" I said. "He's gonna start a panic or something!"

The man stumbled out of his seat, pointing at us. He started to talk, but the words got stuck in his throat. His chair crashed to the ground. A woman nearby snapped, "Hey, knock it off, will you?"

"It's a— It's a—!" he croaked.

Joan put on her most dazzling smile and marched up to him with her clipboard in hand. "Good morning, sir. Would you like to sign our petition to save Emerson Hall?" Then she leaned close and whispered, "It's *haunted*, you know."

The man went even paler and hurried for the door, barreling into a server. Plates full of food came tumbling down.

I rummaged around in my backpack and shoved a piece of paper at the man right before he squeezed out the door. "Here's a concert schedule!"

"That . . . was amazing," said Joan. "Just the kind of publicity we need. Except, like, hundreds of more times."

The coffee shop was a mess. People were staring. The server, mopping up the mess, was *glaring*.

"People are looking at us," Henry said through his teeth.

"Exactly!"

"What'd you do to that poor guy?" said the woman from before, laughing. "He looked like he saw a ghost."

I grabbed the petition from Joan. "Maybe he did, maybe he didn't," I said. "But if you come see a concert at Emerson Hall, you might find out."

"And you could sign this petition, too," Henry added, hurrying over. A line was forming behind the woman, people shoving each other to get a closer look at us.

"Mr. Worthington," I whispered, "you're a genius."

He grinned lopsidedly at me.

As the woman scribbled her name on the petition and read over the flier, Joan grinned at me and gave me a thumbs-up.

Our seventh signature. And *maybe* one of the thousands of people we needed to buy tickets.

It was a start.

We were wet, cold, weighed down with soaked clothes, and had asked
(Henry kept a tally) sixty-seven people for their signatures.

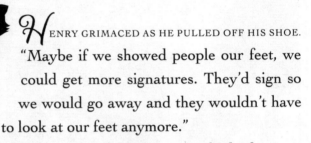

CHAPTER

36

$\mathcal{H}$ENRY GRIMACED AS HE PULLED OFF HIS SHOE. "Maybe if we showed people our feet, we could get more signatures. They'd sign so we would go away and they wouldn't have to look at our feet anymore."

Our feet were looking pretty bad after two hard days of pounding the pavement. I myself had three blisters, one of which looked ready to pop. And even Joan, who was wearing some kind of fancy cross-country shoes, had sores rubbed up and down the sides of her feet.

"How many signatures did we get, Joan?"

Joan compiled our clipboard lists. "Thirty-three."

"That's *it*?"

"I'm afraid so. Obviously our citizens suffer from cultural deficiency."

"Either that or we're bad salespeople," said Henry.

I yanked my shoes back on, gritting my teeth against the blister pain. "Well, we'll just have to try harder."

"*How?*" said Henry.

"We'll go out every day, before and after school, and

we'll talk to people in the cafeteria at lunch, and in the halls between classes, and we'll go to The Happy Place, too, and we won't stop until we've gotten five thousand signatures, or ten thousand. Not until we've plastered every square inch of this city in fliers and pamphlets and posters and *whatever it takes*. Easy as that."

"Oh, right." Henry had slumped over, massaging his legs. "Easy."

Joan was lying flat on a bench outside the Hall, humming what she called her zen exercises. "I admire your spirit, Olivia. Although my feet don't."

"Maybe this is unrealistic." Henry put his head in his hands. "Are we crazy for trying this?"

"Absolutely," I said.

And we were. But I liked it. It was hard work, and it kept me too busy to worry, and too excited to doubt.

Every day that next week, before, during, and after school, and every spare moment we could find, we kept working, tacking up fliers on every telephone pole, every bulletin board in every laundromat, recreation center, apartment building, and restaurant we could sneak our way into. We left huge stacks of fliers on shop counters and in the magazine sections at the libraries.

By the end of the first week of February, we had 241 signatures. It was Friday night—concert night.

This was the ultimate test.

How many people would show up? And how would they react to the ghosts?

"You remember your instructions, right?" I asked the ghosts. Our ghosts and about a dozen others we'd recruited huddled around me on the catwalk. Tillie kept nervously plucking ribs out of her chest and then shoving them back in topsy-turvy. Jax drifted back and forth across the catwalk, mumbling his part over and over to himself.

Mr. Worthington, naturally, stared at me. He would not let go of Joan's arm.

"Of course," said Tillie. "Once the concert starts, Jax and I will each take a side of the Hall. Me the west side, Jax the east side. Every now and then, we'll show ourselves to someone and look pitiful."

"And why will you look pitiful?"

"Because people are less likely to be frightened by ghosts and start some sort of stampeding panic if we look like innocent, tragic children," recited Jax.

"Right. And you won't ever stay visible for too long. Just long enough for people to think they saw something but not be totally sure."

Tillie saluted me. Jax nodded solemnly.

"And Mr. Worthington?"

Mr. Worthington stuck his hand through Joan's stomach and then pulled it out again.

"Merp," Joan squeaked.

"Sorry, Joan. And yes, that's right. You'll try to touch as

many people as possible." I paused. That sounded so wrong. But if enough people felt the strange, cold sensation of Mr. Worthington nearby, then rumors would begin. People would talk. And talk meant publicity. "Well, you know what I mean. And what about you guys?"

The other ghosts, most of whom were part of Mrs. Barsky's latest fan club said, their voices overlapping: "We do what the second-in-commands tell us to do."

Jax's chest puffed up like a balloon.

"Right," I said. "And if you see signs of shades coming to crash the party?"

"We'll fly right into the center of everyone and cause a mass panic," Tillie said brightly.

A flash of red caught my eye, and I looked down through the catwalk railing to see Henry, waving his arms to get my attention. The musicians were walking onstage. Soon the concert would begin.

Ed and Larry dimmed the lights. I peered down into the half darkness until I found Henry leading people to their seats on the mezzanine. In one of the dress circle boxes, Mr. Rue was shaking hands with Mayor Pitter and his wife.

Joan crouched down next to me and pointed. "Olivia, look."

Throughout the audience, flashes of yellow flickered like fireflies. Clusters of people here and there whispered to each other, looking up at the ceiling, pointing.

Could they be looking for ghosts?

"Our fliers," I whispered.

Joan grinned at me. "Olivia, this might really work."

I clamped down on the bubbly fluttering in my chest.

"We'll see," I said, and then applause, a little louder than usual, broke out as the Maestro took to his podium and bowed. Trying to count the number of heads in the audience, I kept getting too excited and losing my numbers, and finally just gave up. Instead I found Richard Ashley's head in the orchestra and thought good-luck thoughts at him.

When the opening notes of Wagner's *Tristan and Isolde Prelude* began, I whispered to the ghosts, "It's time. Go."

My ghosts swooped away in three different directions—Jax to the east, Tillie to the west, and Mr. Worthington right down the middle of the orchestra floor. The others split up and followed them.

With the lights off, their smoky bodies blended in well with the shadows. Tillie slunk past Henry, who was leading a mother and her two children to their seats. As Tillie passed, she dragged her arm through theirs, but so fast that by the time they looked to see who was there, they couldn't find anyone.

Except for the smallest kid, a blond boy. He watched Tillie float up onto the mezzanine with a smile on his face.

I found myself smiling too.

And Jax, over on the other side, settled in gently beside an older woman sitting alone. When he brushed a kiss

300

against her cheek, the woman flinched and clapped a hand to her cheek.

But Jax was already gone.

And Mr. Worthington? He glided through the orchestra floor like an eel, snaking through people's stomachs and then out through their mouths and ears, trickling softly like candlelight smoke. People shifted in their seats, putting hands to their stomachs, frowning.

"You okay?" I saw a man mouth to the woman beside him. She nodded, peering out into the dark aisle beside her, like she could find whatever had made her suddenly feel colder, nauseated, tingling with ice.

It was working—slowly, of course. If the ghosts did too much too fast, it could start a panic. We had been very specific with them about that. But it was working.

From down below, Henry flashed me a quick thumbs-up. I thought my heart would twist itself into permanent knots.

"Olivia?" Joan whispered after a long time. "Do you always watch concerts from up here?"

"Yeah. I mean, most of them, anyway. When I can stand it."

Joan turned to me, her eyes wide and bright. "I don't know how you *do* stand it. It's so beautiful up here. I had no idea."

"Beautiful?"

"With this tragic music playing, and the paintings on the ceiling. And the chandeliers, and the curtains draped everywhere, and, oh, Olivia. Just look at everyone down there."

At first I just rolled my eyes. Joan could be so dramatic. But then I saw it.

Have you ever watched people when they don't know you're watching them? Like in a movie theater or a concert. When people get caught up in watching something, their faces change. The lines on their faces get softer, because whatever they're watching has made them forget how they think they're supposed to be looking. Instead, they just *are*— just sitting there, listening and watching and being real.

Goosebumps broke out on my skin. It was about four minutes into *Romeo and Juliet*, when those spooky notes start out low in the strings and then drift up high, and the harp floats right on top of it. The orchestra actually sounded decent for once. I don't know why, or maybe I was just imagining things, but I think the audience heard it too.

"It is beautiful," I whispered, and I meant it.

Joan clutched my hand. "Oh, Olivia, we have to save this place."

"We're working on it, Joan."

"No, but we *have* to. Not just for the ghosts, but because . . . oh, never mind, it's getting louder and I want to listen."

And we did. I listened like I hadn't ever listened before, and I got that soaring, bursting feeling in my chest like when Frederick had played his concerto. But it of course

CLAIRE LEGRAND

wasn't Frederick doing it this time; it was an orchestra, led by the Maestro. And like it or not, we shared blood.

How strange, I thought, watching him wave his arms around onstage, sweat on his forehead; watching the musicians blow red-faced through their parts. Their eyes darted up every now and then to catch the Maestro's movements. Invisible wires connected them, and the wires vibrated with electricity so thick that by the end of the piece, I had to remind myself to breathe. The Maestro lowered his arms. The audience clapped, yellow fliers forgotten in their seats.

Henry was clapping too, and the ghosts dashed up to wrap me in ice-cold hugs that left me feeling light-headed.

"It's working!" Tillie squealed in my ear. "We were really messing with people. They were shivering and a couple of people had to go to the bathroom and get sick!"

Together, we peeked through the curtains. Instead of bolting out of the Hall like people usually did after a concert, the audience had stayed in their seats. They pointed up at the ceiling, some of them looking through binoculars. They read their programs, they read their fliers. Their whispering and chattering rose up to us in a low roar of excitement.

Henry ran out onto the catwalk, making it shake. "Look!" he said, yanking down his sleeve to show us tally marks scratched up and down his arm in black ink. I'd never seen him smile so big. It was like the sun; I couldn't look directly at it.

"This is how many times I heard people talking about

ghosts, or the fliers, or the petition. All the stuff we've been doing. It got to be so many, I stopped counting. But, Olivia." He grabbed my arms and it was like there was no audience, no Joan, no ghosts. It was just me and Henry, and his sky-colored eyes, and all of our secrets that no one else knew.

"Olivia, I think it's going to be okay. I think *we're* going to be okay."

Then he hugged me. And I held on for what felt like forever.

$\mathcal{E}$VERY DAY, WHENEVER WE HAD A SPARE SEC-
ond, Henry, Joan, and I flew around town
pinning up new fliers and replacing old
ones. Joan got her dad to come see the Hall,
and we gave him a tour. He was this towering,
skinny guy with really good skin, and he loved
the Hall, our petition, the whole thing. He thought it was
charming and *quaint* and *a treasure. Romantic. Noble.*

I could see where Joan got her dramatics. But Mr.
Dawson could be dramatic all he wanted, as long as he kept
bringing reporters.

Yeah. *Reporters.*

They started coming to concerts—quick, speedy people
with tape recorders and notepads, photographers with flashing cameras. People the Maestro had been trying to get to
concerts for months, to write reviews and take photos.

Now, they were crowding him for interviews after concerts like he was some sort of sports star. I watched from a
distance as the lights flashed, as reporters and news crews
hovered around him.

"Maestro Stellatella," they would say, "tell us about the ghosts! People are saying it's the hoax of the century!"

"Maestro! Is it true the orchestra is in danger of bankruptcy?"

The Maestro fumbled over his answers, but the reporters didn't seem to mind. They loved him. They loved *this* — the ghosts, a haunted music hall, a struggling maestro overwhelmed by something he didn't understand.

All I could think was how the camera flashes lit up the Maestro's pale, sweaty face. It made him look old and frail, like Nonnie.

One night, the reporters dragged me into these interviews, musicians and audience members all jammed into the lobby with us.

"Maestro! This is your daughter, huh? The marketing whiz? What's her name?"

"What's your name, kid?"

I searched frantically through the crowd for Henry, for my ghosts. Camera flashes blinded me. Sweating, smiling faces hovered wherever I turned.

The Maestro put his arm around my shoulders. "Her name is Olivia," he said, "and if you touch her again, you'll regret it."

I shoved him away, blushing. "I'm not a baby, okay?"

The reporters just laughed. "That's great, that's just great. Dad and daughter, the dynamic duo."

"No *way*," I said before I could think about it. "We're not a duo. It's just biology."

The reporters kept laughing, but the sound didn't make me feel good. The Maestro's arm slid off my shoulders, and I hurried away before I had to look at him.

During concerts, the ghosts kept making their appearances. Each night, they skulked and drifted and slunk around. Each night, I looked out for shades, but they were nowhere to be found.

That made me more nervous than if they *had* outright attacked.

Meanwhile, the audience grew. And grew. And *grew*. Henry and I camped out in the box office during intermissions, watching Mrs. Bloomfeld tally up all the receipts.

The first night of the second February series, she finished counting and threw up her hands with a choking sound.

Henry immediately started thumping her back. "Are you dying? I know CPR."

"No, sweetie." Mrs. Bloomfeld smiled at us, her eyes shining. "Ticket sales are up four hundred percent. Can you believe it?"

"You know what this means?" Henry said as we hurried back to the catwalk for the second part of the concert. "It means we've only got a six-hundred-percent increase to go!"

I shoved him. "Thanks, genius. I *can* do some math, you know."

"We can do that in a week and a half, no problem. Have you *seen* how crazy people are for this ghost stuff? You're a genius. Joan's a genius. We're *all geniuses*." Then he took my hands and spun me around in a circle. I couldn't stop giggling, no matter how hard I tried.

In that moment, it felt like nothing could ever go wrong. We were on top of the world. We had fought fate and won.

Then, as it tends to do when you start thinking things like that, disaster struck.

It was the first night of the second February series, and there were 1,032 people in the audience.

Let that sink in for a second, before I talk about the disaster.

1,032. That was 800 more people in the audience than at our most popular holiday concert. That means the Hall was almost precisely halfway full. Still pretty pathetic, but less so than before.

Maybe it was how glorious this made us feel—me, Henry, and Joan, up on the catwalk, toasting each other with peanut butter sandwiches and tap water in paper cups—or maybe it was that we were doing just a little too well for the shades to feel comfortable with what was happening.

Whatever the reason was, about halfway through Rachmaninov's *Rhapsody on a Theme of Paganini*, two awful things happened.

First, one of the three huge chandeliers that hung over the main part of the Hall began to swing back and forth.

"It's a shade," Henry whispered. "There, see it? Riding right there in the middle. Tugging on the chains."

He was right. A shade straddled the chandelier with eight

legs, one for each of the chandelier's prongs, an enormous black spider creature. Eight sets of long fingers wound around the gold wiring holding the chandelier in place.

Two lightbulbs shattered and rained down onto the audience.

The orchestra faltered for a moment—a couple of cracked notes, a screech in the second violins—but the Maestro didn't seem to have noticed anything. He waved them furiously onward.

Then, before either we or the audience could figure out how to react to the swinging chandelier, someone screamed from the back of the Hall.

The orchestra abruptly stopped playing. The solo pianist covered her mouth with her hands. The Maestro whirled around, peering into the blackness.

"What the devil?" Ed murmured, pushing aside the curtains from the lighting control station.

It was a little girl, running into the Hall from one of the west side doors and screaming something about a demon, or a ghost, maybe, she didn't know—and then she found her father and dissolved into tears.

The west side. Tillie's territory. But I could see her, way down by the stage.

"Wasn't me," she mouthed, shaking her head up at me.

"Henry, you stay here with Joan," I said, and rushed for the stairs before he could start arguing with me. I had to talk to the girl myself; it was my responsibility, whatever had happened to her. *Please let it not be what I think it is*, I thought, bounding down the utility stairs two steps at a time.

In the confusion, it took me a while to get to the girl. Everyone wanted to speak to her. The reporters were pushing through from the back of the Hall, their photographers' cameras flashing. The Maestro was yelling something onstage about this deplorable breach in concert protocol.

I thought to myself, *be a shadow, be* ombralina, and turned quiet and small enough to slink my way through.

The little girl clung to her father's side. Everyone was trying to get a closer look at her and talk to her father.

"Is she okay?"

"Was it really a ghost?"

"Is she hurt or anything?"

My stomach turned to ice. If she *had* encountered a shade, and if the shade had burned her, then this wouldn't just be fun and games anymore. That was evidence you couldn't just ignore.

It was like the girl read my thoughts. On the other side of her father, hidden by the press of people surrounding us, she caught my eye and mouthed: "I saw one."

I mouthed back: "A ghost?"

She sniffled and shook her head. "Something else."

"What is the meaning of this?" The Maestro had arrived in the midst of the crowd, flourishing his baton like he was trying to conduct everyone back into order. Behind him stood Mr. Rue and Mayor Pitter.

 310

I hid between some excited college kids snapping photographs.

"Can you not control your child, sir? We are in the middle of a concert!"

Something over our heads sizzled. Crackled. Exploded.

The lights went out.

Sparks showered off the chandelier. The smell of burning and electricity filled the air.

The lights came back on, flickered off, and came on again, and off again, and finally they stayed on.

The chandelier had stopped swinging. It now hung by a mere thread, a single golden chain.

Around the room, the shadows churned with shades, and I'd never been more afraid in my life.

"Out of the way, everyone back up!" I found myself screaming, waving my arms around. I didn't care if the Maestro saw me. Audience members getting creamed by a falling chandelier was not part of the plan. "Move, people, get out of the way!"

Once everyone had backed up sufficiently, I sank into the nearest chair, my knees shaking. This was getting serious.

But not to the audience, apparently. Because there was a strange sound drifting to me through my retreating panic: applause. They were *applauding* whatever had just happened—the screaming girl, the exploding chandelier, the interrupted concert. Some people whistled. Others hollered, "*Encore!*"

The Maestro looked like someone had just told him he

had somehow transformed into a cow overnight. Mayor Pitter just looked confused. Mr. Rue found one of my fliers on the ground. He picked it up, read it, and scratched his head, frowning.

"Fantastic effects," I heard someone say.

"How did they do that?"

"Better than a haunted house."

"That poor kid. Must have been a great costume, to scare her like that."

"Are you kidding? Kids eat that kind of stuff up."

"Hold on, I gotta go call my sister. She loves freaky things like this."

"Dude," I heard one of the college kids declare solemnly to his friend, "I didn't think coming to the symphony could be so fun."

I glared at him. *This isn't the symphony*, I thought. *The symphony is the music you were listening to. Idiot.*

"Olivia," Henry whispered, pulling me out of the crowd. Joan hovered behind him, wringing her hands, mumbling, "Oh my gosh, oh my *gosh*."

"What do we do?" Henry said. "That was close. Too close."

"Tell me about it. That girl saw a shade."

"What?"

"She told me."

Henry teetered, off balance. "If it touched her . . ."

"It didn't."

"How do you know that?"

"Even if it did and she tells someone, who'll believe her?"

"What do we do? If this happens again . . ."

"We just keep going as planned. Nothing changes. The ghosts keep doing their thing, and we keep doing ours."

"But what if the chandelier actually falls next time? Or something even worse?"

I clenched my fists. "That's just a risk we'll have to take. And . . ." I glanced behind him, at Tillie, Jax, and Mr. Worthington. I caught Mr. Worthington's eye, and he nodded.

"And we have to find Tillie's and Jax's anchors. *Fast.*"

Henry buried his face in his hands. "Are we gonna have to die again? I don't want to blow up anymore."

I didn't either. I didn't want to have anything to do with that future place, the war that reminded Henry about his dad, with everything gray and dead and shriveled—

Like that tree. The giant, shriveled tree in Jax's hiding spot.

"Say that again, Henry," I whispered. If I moved a muscle or spoke too loud, I'd lose the careful thought burrowing its way out of my brain.

"I. Don't. Want. To. Blow up. Anymore."

"Technically, you should say, you don't want to blow up *again*," said Tillie. "You've only done it the one time."

"That tree. The . . . future . . . Oh. Oh my— It's not planted yet. Because it's in the future." I started jumping up and down. I grabbed Joan's hands and pulled her along with me.

"Olivia, why are we bouncing?"

"Henry. Listen. The tree. It was in the future, and this is in the *now*, so maybe the reason why we can't find their bracelet tree is because—"

"It hasn't been planted yet." Henry slapped a hand to his forehead.

"*We* have to plant it. We plant it, and then in the future, the tree is there, right there by Jax's hiding spot! Come on!"

I grabbed Henry's hand, and he grabbed Joan's, and the ghosts *whooshed* alongside us.

"Where are we going?" Joan cried, as we burst out onto the street.

Henry answered for me, laughing. "Tree shopping!"

$\mathcal{T}$HERE WAS ONLY ONE NURSERY CLOSE ENOUGH to bring Tillie and Jax to, on the south side of town, at Wichita and 1st Avenue. It stayed open until ten on Friday nights, so even after taking the bus, we had about a half hour to search.

"There are approximately one billion trees here," Henry said.

We stood at the end of the tree section—aisles upon aisles of tiny saplings all the way up to decent-size oaks.

"How are we ever supposed to find the right one? And how are we supposed to pay for it? Do you *see* how expensive these are? And how are we gonna even get it back on the bus?"

I frowned. "I hadn't thought about all that."

"Obviously, when it's the right tree, we'll *know* it," said Joan. "Isn't that how it was for Frederick's music?"

"Well, yeah," said Henry, "that, and it said 'Frederick van der Burg' on the top."

"Don't worry," said Jax, "I'll know the tree. Both of us will."

So we started looking, each of us taking an aisle and touching each tree one by one. By the end of it, scratches covered my cheeks and arms.

Then I found it.

I couldn't even see it at first, it was so far back. Joan had hold of my shirt, keeping me upright as I balanced on bags of dirt to stretch as far back as I could into the stacked trees.

When my fingers brushed the trunk, I knew.

A jolt of memory shocked me, as white-hot as a lightning strike.

In a flash, I saw the gray war camp in the bones of the Hall. The gray skies and the black planes. That shriveled, exhausted-looking tree with some of its bark freshly scraped off.

"I found it," I gasped. "Guys! Over here!"

The next thing I knew, I was lying on the ground, my head spinning, my palms sweating. My head was in someone's lap. Two blue eyes stared down at me.

Henry.

I closed my eyes. If Henry was there, everything would be okay.

"What happened?" I said.

"You passed out a little," Henry said. "Memory overdose."

"Great. Did we get the tree?"

"You're the Stellatella girl," someone was saying, leaning over me.

"Yeah. And who're you?"

Henry helped me up. "Olivia, be nice. This is the tree guy."

"Tree *specialist* is the term," said a man with a rumpled red cap. "But you *are* the Stellatella girl, right? The ghost girl?"

Ghost girl? That was a new one. "Yeah, I guess that's me. Why?"

The man thrust out his hand. "Name's Gary. Boy, I gotta tell ya—I got tickets to tomorrow night's concert, and I kind of can't stop thinking about it."

"Really?"

"Well, yeah! The ghosts of Emerson Hall. Everybody's talking about it. My sister, Linda, she went to the show couple weeks ago. Said it was phenomenal. She couldn't see the ghosts herself, but other people could, she said, and she got this awful, cold feeling. She said things were *movin'* by themselves."

Gary winked at me. "It's a hoax, right? If you tell me how they're doing it, I won't tell anyone, I swear."

I looked at Henry, who nodded. I took a deep breath. "It's not a hoax. It's all real. In fact, the ghosts are with us right now."

And then Jax held his nose and swan-dove into Gary's chest. Tillie wrapped herself around his back like for a piggy-back ride, giggling into his ear.

Gary began to shiver uncontrollably. Gary's arms turned white and crackly.

Then Gary gave us a free tree.

He gave us shovels, too, and even sent along one of his employees to help us get the tree back to the Hall.

Gary wouldn't come himself. Too spooked. Too fascinated by the coldness of his skin. Too wrapped up in the ghost story book he'd just been inspired to write.

Oh, brother.

So his employee, Nancy, helped us dig the hole, even though it was almost eleven at night. By the time the tree was in the hole, covered with mulch, and watered, it was midnight, and Nancy bolted out of there while we had our backs turned.

Igor watched everything from the low branch of a nearby tree. *She didn't last long, did she?*

"So much for Nancy," Henry said.

"Guys?" Tillie whispered.

"Can you blame her?" I said. "We basically made her boss go crazy."

"What if his ghost book turns out to be a bestseller?" Joan pointed out. "He'd better dedicate it to us."

"Guys!"

"*What*, Tillie?"

Tillie pointed right at where Jax stood.

"Is that . . . I see . . ." Tillie slapped herself across the face, knocking her nose sideways. "Come on, Till. Pull it together. Is that Jax?"

"Tillie?" Jax whispered. "You're just a blur. Is that really you? Why can't I hear her?"

"What can you see?" I said.

"I see . . . gray. Gray, like the color's been sucked out of that spot. But it hasn't, has it? It's because Tillie is there."

"What's he saying?" Tillie burst out, shrilly.

"He says he can see a gray blur where you're standing, but that's it," Henry said. "He can't hear you, though."

"We have to hurry, then." Tillie rushed at me, grabbed my shoulders. "Find us knives. Hurry, oh, I can't stand it!"

I didn't get it. "Knives?"

Tillie started punching her fists through my chest, sobbing. "Knives, *knives*, hurry up . . ."

Henry shoved his hands in his pockets, looking tired all of a sudden. "For cutting the bark."

"For making our anchors." Tillie sniffled.

"For our bracelets, Olivia," Jax said, smiling at me.

Joan gasped.

I stared at him. "Already? Right now?"

"I guess now that the tree's planted, it's gotten the anchor started, so they can see each other," Henry said. "Well, barely. We can't make them wait anymore; that's like torture."

"*Torture,*" Tillie cried.

"Okay," I said. I felt numb, like I was watching myself go through the motions of talking. It was happening again. I was going to have to say good-bye, just like I had to Ferderick, and this time was worse. Tillie and Jax . . . we'd gone through so much together.

I blinked, hard. Clenched my fists, hard. "Fine. I'll get knives."

I found two dull kitchen knives and raced back outside. The second I got close enough, Tillie and Jax blasted toward me and grabbed them away. They didn't even stop to think about the fact that they could *hold* things now.

Not even a *thank you*, huh, guys? Not even a *see ya*?

I guess they had more important things to worry about.

Like how, once they started scraping away at the bark of the tree, they turned brighter, more solid. They were starting to see. They were starting to hear.

"Tillie! Are you there?" Jax's face squinted in Tillie's direction.

"I'm right here! I'm right here!" Tillie screamed. She could barely hold the knife straight.

Joan said, "Oh, you poor thing," and reached for them, but Henry held her back.

"This is private," he said. "Let them figure it out."

I just stood there. I couldn't think anything but *They're leaving me*. I felt Mr. Worthington's eyes on me, but I ignored him. I couldn't deal with his staring right now.

Igor wound around my ankles. *Pay attention. Soon they'll be gone. You won't want to miss anything.*

So I forced my eyes open, and Joan whispered, "Oh, Olivia, it's going to be all right. Don't cry," and I couldn't even tell her to shut up.

"Tillie," I tried to say. "Jax?"

320

But they weren't listening to me. They were each braiding three strips of bark together. They were starting to look like real people, like the memories we had seen. You could almost believe they were real kids when they lunged at each other, when they tied their new bracelets around each other's wrists.

"I can see you!" Tillie was laughing and crying at the same time. She yanked Jax into a hug, and their heads knocked together. "Jax, can you see me?"

"Clear as day," Jax said, grinning. He pulled Tillie's braids, and then, over Tillie's shoulder as he hugged her, Jax caught my eye. And he said, "Good-bye."

Two silent pops of light, and they were gone.

Two crude bracelets made of birch bark plopped to the grass.

Mr. Worthington drifted toward the tree and wrapped himself sadly around it.

"Bye," he said, his voice croaky. "Bye-bye."

Joan clapped her hands to her mouth. "Did Mr. Worthington just *talk*?"

But Henry and I couldn't answer her. There was too much to say, too many fists squeezing my chest. So we listened to the leaves rustle instead, and after Mr. Dawson picked up Joan in his shining black car, Henry brought one of the bracelets to me.

"We should wear them."

I snatched the bracelet away, the bark digging into my palm. "I don't want to wear it."

"You want to just let them sit here and rot?"

"I don't know, Henry." I kicked the dirt. It didn't make me feel better.

"They would have wanted us to wear them, I bet."

He was right, of course. Especially Tillie. Tillie would have just *loved* me and Henry exchanging bracelets.

I rolled my eyes. "Fine."

Henry tied his bracelet onto my wrist, over my glove, and I tied mine onto his. Overhead, the tree's leaves rustled.

"There." I turned away, kicking the dirt some more. "You happy now?"

"Yeah, actually. Are you—?"

I flung my arms around him, cutting him off. I didn't know what to say, so this would have to be good enough.

"Oof. That was your elbow."

"Sorry." His shirt smelled like gym and mulch and freckles. This was mortifying. But I didn't want to let go. "Henry?"

"Yeah?"

I pulled back and punched him in the arm. "You'd better not take that off."

"Ow! Jerk. Of course I'm not gonna take it off." He held up his wrist. "For life?"

"Well, through eighth grade, anyway. Okay?"

Henry grinned. "Okay."

We thumped wrists.

"Thump," Mr. Worthington said happily, nodding at us. "Thump."

322

That night, right before I went to bed, I took out my school planner, doodles covering it in a charcoal wonderland.

Three down, one to go.

My ghost countdown was almost over. And in a week and a half, it'd be March.

In a week and a half, we'd know the Hall's fate.

No, not its fate. Its *destiny*.

I liked that word better. It sounded softer, like something Mom would say. It sounded like stars.

CHAPTER 39

THE MONDAY AFTER TILLIE AND JAX MOVED ON, I sat next to Mrs. Barsky while she wiped down the counters. She wore a new collection of yellow beads. The Ghost Room was doing good business.

"Hello, Olivia. Long time, no see."

"Yeah." Suddenly I couldn't look her in the eye. "Sorry about that."

"Oh, that's all right. You've been busy, I've noticed."

"Yeah."

"It's really quite fantastic, Olivia. You know that, don't you? I know this year has been tough, but what you kids have done—"

"Am I gonna see ghosts my whole life?" I twisted my umbrella around and around in my hands. "Because I don't know if I can stand that. They're gone, Mrs. B, and now there's only one left, and—will I just keep meeting them and helping them and then having to say good-bye?"

Mrs. Barsky set down her rag and leaned forward on her elbows. "Olivia. Look at me."

I did, and she wiped my cheeks.

"I don't know if you'll keep seeing ghosts, if they'll keep coming to you. But you can always decide whether or not to help them. You can always tell them to go away. This is your life. *Yours.*" She smoothed my hair. It made my chest ache. "And no one else's. You're a strong girl, Olivia."

I made a noise like *phbtchya.*

"I'm serious. You've endured things a lot of grown-ups never have to." Mrs. Barsky tipped up my chin. "And yes, it gets easier every time, to say good-bye. And that's not just true for ghosts. That's for everything."

I kicked the counter wall. "Maybe it'd be better if I'd never met them."

"There's a song you should listen to, Olivia," said Mr. Barsky, sailing out of the kitchen. "*Mais oui*, it's by Edith Piaf, a wonderful French *chanteuse.* It's called "*Non, je ne regrette rien.*" Do check it out, *ma petite belle.*"

"What's he saying?"

Mrs. Barsky shook her head. "He's talking about a song. It means *No, I regret nothing.* Don't ever wish you hadn't met them, Olivia—or anyone, for that matter. It's who we meet that makes us *us.* Does that make sense?"

"Yeah. I think so." I tried out the word *regrette* on my tongue, the way Mr. Barsky had said it, but the r's got stuck in the back of my throat.

"*Regrette, regrette,*" Mr. Barsky corrected, bustling back into the kitchen with dirty dishes.

Mrs. Barsky booted him on the butt. "So, how is the

oldest one, the quiet one with the hat?"

"Mr. Worthington? He's the only one left. Of *my* ghosts, I mean."

"And you'll help him quickly, I assume?" Mrs. Barsky nodded over my shoulder at the Hall. "I also assume you've seen that?"

I didn't even have to turn around. I knew the shades had been swarming through Emerson Hall the last couple of days, since Tillie and Jax had moved on. Like an anthill that's been kicked.

"Yeah. I know they're there."

"It's catastrophe waiting to happen, Olivia. You must move quickly."

I slammed the umbrella down on the table. "I *know* that, I'm just . . . strategizing."

"Yes, slam away, that's the kind of fighting spirit you'll need. Now, off with you! Go on!"

As I stormed out and across the street, I could feel the shades watching me with their invisible eyes. Watching, and waiting.

But for what?

That evening, Henry, Mr. Worthington, and I gathered in my bedroom. It was too open onstage, too vulnerable. Shades writhed in the shadows like countless black holes, chewing on the ceiling, barreling through the rafters. The Maestro had locked himself in his room; Mahler 2 blared down the hallway. I was glad, for once. It meant we couldn't hear the shades.

"Do you think they'll rip another hole in the ceiling?" Henry whispered to me. "There are two more concerts to go, you know."

I ignored him. I couldn't think about that. I shut the door firmly. "Nonnie, you'll keep watch?"

Nonnie bobbed her head. She had constructed a turban of her yellow, blue, and purple scarves to celebrate the approach of spring.

In just a couple of days, it'd be March. Would we have done enough? Or would we all be out on the streets come summertime?

"I watch over you all," Nonnie shouted, spreading her arms wide.

"Nonnie," Henry said, "it might look weird while we're doing this. You understand what we're doing, right?"

"Mr. Worthington will smoosh you!" Nonnie clapped her hands together. "So you can see through his eyes."

"Okay, yeah, basically."

"I'm ready!"

"I wish I were that ready," I muttered, sizing up Mr. Worthington, who waited patiently at the edge of my bed. "To be honest, I'm a little freaked out about this, Mr. Worthington. You're . . . well, you've always been . . ."

"Disturbing?" Henry suggested.

With his thumbs, Mr. Worthington pulled up the corners

of his mouth up into a smile. It was too much effort to do it the normal way, apparently; with the shades around, Mr. Worthington had gone almost completely see-through. Luckily, they hadn't attacked him . . . yet. During the day, he stayed at The Happy Place. At night, he sat at my feet.

But we couldn't keep doing that forever.

"Reluctant," Mr. Worthington said over his thumbs. "Reluctant."

"Yes, we're reluctant, all right," I said. "And how about you don't talk? You need to save your energy for us, you know."

"Ready, Olivia?" Henry held out his hand and smiled. "One last time?"

I held up an imaginary glass. "To the world of Death."

"To the world of Death," Henry agreed, clinking our hands together. "Well, sort of."

We sat down, our knees touching, and laced our fingers together. We turned to Mr. Worthington.

"Ready," I said.

And Mr. Worthington swooped low, spread his mouth wide, and poured gently into us, slowly, like tar.

When I woke up, I was lying under a roof of cardboard. Trying to sit up, I realized I couldn't. A sharp pain stabbed me in the stomach. For a second, I thought we'd been murdered again.

Henry? I gasped, blinking to clear my vision. *Where are you?*

Olivia, I'm right here, came Henry's voice from somewhere deep inside my mind.

I latched onto it. *Keep talking, almost anything. I'm almost there.*

Seven times seven is forty-nine. O what a brave new world, to have such people in it! Your name is Olivia, and you don't like people very much.

Shut up. I like you, don't I?

I dunno. Henry sounded like he was smiling. *Do you?*

My brain blushed. *Whatever. What were you saying about a new world?*

It's Shakespeare. The Tempest.

Oh, *Mr. Honor Roll. Of course it is. Where's Mr. Worthington?*

Look down, said a soft, kind voice from inside our heads, *and you'll see my hands.*

We did. They were thin and tired-looking.

I'm sorry I haven't been able to speak much. Mr. Worthington sighed. *Once upon a time, I had a lot to say.*

Where are we, exactly?

I'm not entirely certain. Let's find out, shall we?

Together, we crawled out of the cardboard house, across a pile of damp newspapers, and into a gloomy winter's day. Across from us was another cardboard hut, and another beyond that, and another. Beside the huts towered the Hall. When I peeked inside the doors, I saw rows of beds on the floor and people huddled over bowls of soup.

Farther off, through the light rain, I saw buildings that looked vaguely familiar.

Is that downtown? I asked.

Yes, I believe so. And this is . . . this must be Gladville. Yes. Yes, that's it.

Gladville? Henry said. *Doesn't look very glad to me.*

It wasn't, said Mr. Worthington. *It was . . . yes. A nickname. The city put us here.*

What is it? I asked. *And what happened to it?*

It's a shanty town, said Mr. Worthington. *One of several. There was . . . there was trouble, you see, with the banks. They had to put us all somewhere. There was Gladville, and Sunnyville, Peace Park . . .*

I could feel Henry's mind whirring through months of schoolwork. *Are you talking about the Great Depression? In the thirties?*

There wasn't anything great about it, Mr. Worthington said. He was in my mind, crawling through a swamp of remembering.

I was . . . a businessman, he said sadly. He tightened what remained of his ragged tie, he straightened his shirt. *An honorable man.*

It was The Economy, I whispered. *Wasn't it?*

Then something slammed into our stomachs.

"Hi, Daddy, look! I got us lunch!"

We looked down and saw a tiny girl with dark hair and dark eyes. She was hugging us, and she had a pail in her hands.

"Tabby?" Mr. Worthington's voice creaked on the words,

330

and then we were kneeling and burying our face in the girl's hair. "Tabby, Tabby . . ."

"Daddy, come on, I'm hungry! I waited in line for *hours*. What's wrong?" The girl put her hands on our face and kissed our nose. "Did you have a bad dream?" She kissed our nose again. "Your nose is so cold!" Kiss. "Like a reindeer!" Kiss, kiss.

"Yes," Mr. Worthington said. I could feel the lump in my throat from where he was trying to smile. "I'm afraid I did, a terrible nightmare."

"Well, I have soup, so it's time to eat," Tabby said, tugging on our hand. "Sit, and I'll serve you, monsewer."

"*Monsieur*," Mr. Worthington corrected.

Tabby giggled, and it turned into a nasty, wet cough.

Henry, it's his daughter, I whispered.

I know. Her name is Tabitha.

Tabby for short. Together, along with Mr. Worthington, we were remembering. His memories floated through us, like leaves on the wind.

She was born in April.

Her mom got sick. Lydia.

Tabby likes cats.

The image of Tabby and Gladville swirled away, and then it was a different day. A stormy day.

We were inside our cardboard house, and Tabby was in our arms, coughing. Each cough jolted her body like an electric shock.

"Someone help us!" Mr. Worthington screamed, and there it was again—that sharp, stabbing pain in our gut. I realized it was hunger.

I doubled over, gasping. *Henry, I'm gonna pass out.*

No, you're not, it's okay, came Henry's voice, but he didn't sound much better than I felt.

"Someone, please!" Mr. Worthington tore open the door and stood in the rain, Tabby in his arms. People watched us from their own shacks. But no one helped us. Tabby wasn't the only one coughing.

Everything swirled again. When we came to, we were walking down an aisle of shacks. In our hand, wrapped in grimy paper, we held two slices of bread.

This'll help Tabby, Mr. Worthington told us cheerfully. *She'll be on the mend soon, with this food in her belly.*

I could barely open my eyes. My stomach was going to cave in. And it wasn't just my hunger; it was Henry's, and Mr. Worthington's, which he was trying to ignore. He wanted this bread for himself—but he would give it to Tabby. Everything was always for Tabby.

Mr. Worthington? I whispered. We couldn't possibly go on like this.

You'll see! Everything will be better soon.

But when we reached our shack, it was empty.

"Tabby?" Mr. Worthington shouted, digging through the garbage. We ran all through Gladville, searching, yelling. "Tabby, where are you? Tabby!"

332

"They cleaned everything out earlier," someone said, a hunched-over woman with yellow, drooping eyes. "The policemen. They took the bodies. Got to take out the rot, they said. They came with wheelbarrows."

"But Tabby will be all right; she's not a body!" Mr. Worthington shook the woman, even though Henry and I tried to pull his arms back. "I've brought her bread; it'll help her! Tabby!" We were running again, digging through the garbage. "Tabby, I'm coming, sweetheart! I won't leave you!"

The world turned over, swirling. When it stopped, we were lying on the floor of our shack in wads of newspapers.

"She's gone," Mr. Worthington was saying, over and over. "Tabby, my poor, sweet Tabby."

He reached for a doll propped up on a pile of garbage in the corner. It reminded me of Joan's doll, Magda. Above it hung a tacked-up cross made of twigs.

I wanted to throw up, but there was nothing left to throw up.

Henry, make it stop. I clutched my stomach. This was worse than being stabbed, worse than blowing up. We hadn't had enough food for weeks. Our fingernails were cracking from the cold. We'd been drinking filthy water, we hadn't bathed, we couldn't find work. We hadn't eaten, we hadn't eaten . . .

It'll be over soon. Henry whispered. *I promise.*

I closed my eyes and listened to his voice. That's what I died listening to: Henry whispering. The last thing I saw before everything faded was the lonely, lumpy doll in the corner.

We came to slowly, just like we had died.

"*Bravi, bravi, bravissimi!*" Nonnie cried, applauding us. Igor blinked slowly from her lap.

For a long time, I just lay there. What do you do—how do you move again—after something like that?

"Sorry." Mr. Worthington stretched out his hand to us, a dark, shimmering, barely-there splotch in the air. "Sorry."

"Was it like a roller coaster, *ombralina*?" said Nonnie. "Did you zoom through the air?"

Henry had turned away from me, and his voice sounded funny. "Yeah, Nonnie. We zoomed."

"A doll" was all I could say, because it was obvious. "That's his anchor. We'll have to find Tabby's doll."

MARCH

WE KEPT MR. WORTHINGTON CLOSE WHILE WE searched. Shades followed us everywhere, every day, their black jaws clacking. At night, while we slept, I heard clawed things clattering across the roof. Soft groans. Crashes from the attic, where the floor was too weak to store anything.

"The ceiling, it will fall! *Una catastrofe!*" Nonnie declared one evening after dinner, while I attempted to dust. The Maestro sat at the kitchen table, head in his hands as he studied the Mahler 2 score.

"Don't worry, girls." He smiled up at us. His eyes were red and watery. I wondered if he'd been sleeping, if he could hear what I'd been hearing. "The noises lately. Don't worry about them. It's only rats. I've already called an exterminator."

I raised an eyebrow. "Rats?"

"No, no!" Nonnie shook her head. "Not rats. *Shades.* Olivia told me. They come, they drag you away!" She yanked her scarf through her fingers.

I couldn't tell what the Maestro was thinking as I stood there, clutching the dust rag. I figured even the shades, crashing across the roof, could hear my heart pounding.

"Anyway, it doesn't matter." The Maestro returned to his music. "This . . ." He pointed at Mahler 2, his notes scrawled across the pages. His fingers shook. "This will make all the difference. She will come back. She will."

I backed away as quietly as possible. When I'd reached the hallway, I made a run for it, straight for Mrs. Bloomfeld's office up front, and locked myself in. I picked up the phone, almost dialed Henry's number—and stopped.

What exactly would I say to him? *The Maestro's officially lost it. The Maestro thinks some symphony will bring back my mom.*

I hung up the phone and started to pace, Mr. Worthington right beside me.

"I mean, he's insane, right?" I kicked one of the file cabinets. It made a satisfying boom. "What, like some music he plays will magically call her back from wherever she's gone? She could be halfway across the world, for all we know."

Mr. Worthington nodded. "Halfway."

"Right. So whatever. I don't want to think about this anymore. He can think whatever crazy things he wants to, just as long as he keeps conducting."

I flung open the door, marched back into the lobby—and stopped dead.

A single shade had curled around one of the marble

columns, peeking out at me. Its fingers had dug black grooves into the stone.

Something inside me boiled up at seeing it standing there, just waiting to attack. I rushed at it, baring my fingers like claws.

"Go away!" I screamed. "Get out of here!" I saw a stack of programs, freshly pressed and waiting for the next concert, sitting by the door. I grabbed them and flung them at the shade, hitting it square in the back as it scampered away. And for a second, I thought I heard the strangest thing—a sick little sound, like from a hurt dog.

Then it was gone, leaving me shaking in the middle of the lobby. Mr. Worthington hovered behind me, muttering, "Halfway, halfway," over and over, like a prayer.

One day, I was so tired from searching for Tabby's doll and going to school and work and practicing algebra (which had actually gotten kind of fun) that I fell asleep right after getting home from The Happy Place and didn't wake up until two in the morning.

Mr. Worthington stood on his head in the middle of the room. He enjoyed trying different sleep poses.

I told him I needed a drink of water, made sure he was safely near Nonnie, and padded out of the room in my socks. Something pulled me through the silent backstage rooms. Instruments—a piano, a harp—stood silently in pale light streaming in from the windows. Some of the musicians had

The Maestro had fallen asleep on his cot, right on top of—I tiptoed closer to look—the score for Mahler's Symphony no. 2: "The Resurrection."

left their jackets hanging on chairs. The light coming in from outside froze dust particles in place like snow.

When I shuffled past the Maestro's bedroom, I saw his door standing open, just enough for a thin ray of light to escape.

I peeked inside.

The Maestro had fallen asleep on his cot, right on top of — I tiptoed closer to look — the score for Mahler's Symphony no. 2: "The Resurrection." What a surprise.

The Maestro rolled over onto his back, blowing the score open to the first page of the fourth movement, the *Urlicht*. He started to snore.

"Gross."

Igor jumped into the room and onto the mattress. *At least he doesn't drool.*

"Oh, ha-ha."

That's when I saw the plastic box lying open between the Maestro and the wall, the letters lying in smashed piles underneath the Maestro's cheek. I recognized those letters and the loopy handwriting that read: *"Dearest Otto . . ."*

Strange, how different the Maestro looked while sleeping. In fact, he looked about five years old with his mouth hanging open like that. Had he been reading these letters before bed?

Out from under his arm poked a triangular scrap of paper — the corner of a newspaper clipping.

I slid it out. The Maestro's greasy fingers had smeared

some of the ink, but I could read it just fine. There weren't a lot of words. But there were enough:

Waverly, Cara. Waverly was Mom's name, before she married the Maestro. My fingers shook. I thought I might drop the paper. Igor sat up on his haunches and put his paws on my wrist.

I took a deep breath and read on:

Waverly, Cara. Passed away 2/15. Memorial service to be held 3PM 2/21 at Pine Ridge Baptist, 5144 Grandison Road.

My brain couldn't get past the words "Memorial service."

"That's right here in town," I said. "She was here? But . . ."

Then I saw it, the ugliest, most unforgivable word I've ever known:

OBITUARIES.

I didn't need Henry or Joan there to tell me what that meant. I knew. The realization sank into me, collapsing my insides.

It meant Mom was dead.

PART FOUR

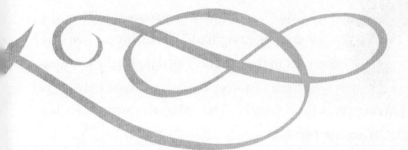

CHAPTER 41

"I DON'T UNDERSTAND," I WHISPERED.

Igor meowed softly. *Yes, you do. I think you've understood all along.*

"But . . ." The newspaper fell to the ground, floating like Tillie swinging her way down from the rafters. The date on the newspaper was from just over a year ago. Last February.

"Olivia? What's wrong?" The Maestro was yawning awake, reaching for me.

"Get away from me!" I slapped at his hands. "Don't touch me!"

"Olivia, what in the world—?"

When he saw the obituary on the floor, a heaviness fell over him.

"Oh," he said.

"*Oh.*" I snatched the clipping and ran out to the stage, tumbling over my own feet. The Maestro followed me, and Mr. Worthington was right behind him, fretting.

"Olivia, allow me to explain—"

I thrust the obituary at his face. "How did it happen? How did she die?"

He flinched. Good. Let him flinch. He could flinch himself into a coma, for all I cared. That wouldn't change the fact that Mom was dead—dead, *dead*—that I had found out like *this*.

"It was a car accident," he said simply. "They said—" He cleared his throat. "Olivia, they did say it was quick. She would not have felt tremendous pain. Cara's mother—you remember Gram."

I did. She'd never liked the Maestro, and I don't think she'd ever liked me too much either; we looked too alike.

"She called me with the news. That's how I found out."

"I don't care about that. Why didn't you tell me?"

The Maestro put up his hands. "Olivia, you will wake your grandmother."

"Oh, like you care about Nonnie."

"But of course I—"

"Why didn't you tell me? You've been lying to me. There was a memorial service. She was *here*, in this city, at that church. You kept her from me. All of you did!" My head spun. They must have known. The musicians, Richard Ashley, maybe even the Barskys. They all must have known.

"Kept," Mr. Worthington muttered, pacing behind the Maestro. "Kept."

"Olivia, you wouldn't have wanted to go to that."

"How do you know? You don't know me at all."

"She did not look like herself, Olivia, not at the end. She was broken all over."

I tried to imagine what that would look like. I was an artist, and artists had to examine even the awful things —*especially* the awful things —to find the truth.

"Olivia, how was I supposed to tell you?" The Maestro's voice was thin, wavery. "On top of everything that's happened to us, how could I tell my daughter that her mother had died? That she had lost her again? First because of me, and then because of this?"

What would a broken Mom have looked like? Would her nose have shattered into bone splinters? Would there have been a great, black gash across her stomach where the windshield sliced her open? A spiderweb of scars?

The Maestro reached for me. Igor put his paws on my legs. I shoved them both away and found the Maestro's eyes —those black, wet, pathetic, red-rimmed eyes.

I whispered, "I wish it had been you instead of her."

He nodded. He was suddenly a thousand years old. "Sometimes I do too."

Then the air filled up with this horrible croaking sound. Mr. Worthington moaned and rushed across the stage, his arms reaching out for something.

Toward a shade. With a doll in its arms.

Igor dug his claws into my foot. *The doll, Olivia!*

Tabby Worthington's doll.

But it was too late. Because the shade was opening a dark, shadowy slit right beneath the exit sign. Unzipping it with its spider-fingers, like a tent flap. Through the slit, I could see teeming shapes of blues, reds, and blacks. The shade slipped back through the opening, the doll in its arms . . .

. . . and disappeared into Limbo.

Mr. Worthington let out an awful cry.

I ignored him. I ignored the Maestro, who stood like a statue, watching me. He hadn't noticed a thing. He whispered my name. I even ignored Igor, until I realized I was back in my room, that I had marched there like a robot, that I was scribbling exploding cars and broken faces in my new sketchpad, the one with Henry's name on the inside.

For Olivia, it read. *My favorite artist. From Henry.*

Igor slammed his head into my hands, knocking my pencil away.

"Is a storm?" Nonnie murmured, rolling over in her sleep.

"Igor, I can't breathe," I whispered. There was a hot river building inside me, and I was drowning in it.

Igor started licking me. *I can clean you, if you like. Would that help? You look messy. You don't even have to pet me. Although I wouldn't stop you or anything.*

I tucked Igor into bed with me and rocked him, and rubbed the friendship bracelet around my wrist, and shoved the twist in my throat down, down, and down.

Dead. Mom was dead. Not just missing, but actually dead.

Maybe if I said the word enough times, it would stop being so awful.

DEAD. DEAD. *DEAD.*

I wasn't sure where to go from here. I shut down. I went dark. "Radio silence" is the term. At lunch the day after I found the obituary, I said only enough so that Henry and Joan would understand.

"I found an obituary in the Maestro's room last night. My mom is dead. She left, and then she died a couple months later. About a year ago. It was a car crash."

Joan dropped her sandwich and covered her mouth with her hands.

"Olivia . . ."

I was fine until I heard Henry's voice. Then the river started swelling up in my throat again, so I kept talking.

"Also, the shades got a hold of Tabby Worthington's doll and took it into Limbo. So I'm not sure what we're going to do about that."

"Olivia." Henry grabbed my milk carton, and I glared at him.

"I was drinking that, Henry."

"*Olivia*. Are you okay?"

"What do you think, Henry? Give me my milk carton."

"Fine. I just . . . you can talk about it if you want."

"I don't. I just wanted to keep you updated." We didn't have time to talk about mothers. I pulled out our clipboard and our pounding-the-pavement plans for that evening, ignoring Henry and Joan's shared look of concern. There were only two concerts left. We had to make the most of it. "Now. We've got work to do."

That Friday, the Maestro called a surprise rehearsal. Normally, the orchestra wouldn't rehearse the afternoon before a concert, so everyone was curious and more than a little grumpy. Somehow, I found myself sitting in seat H15 with my sketchpad, Henry on one side and Igor on the other. I was drawing, but not anything in particular; I just let my pencil wander.

"What do you think this rehearsal is for?" Henry asked.

I shrugged. "Who cares?"

Henry didn't say anything more after that. I think he was afraid to talk to me, afraid that I would crack. He might have been right. All I knew was the tip of my charcoal on my sketchpad, like I was sewing myself back together.

Once everyone was onstage, the Maestro clapped his hands. "I'm sure you're wondering why I've called you here."

From behind me, I heard a door open. I looked over my shoulder and saw Mr. Rue, Mayor Pitter, and two men I didn't recognize enter the Hall.

"First," the Maestro was saying, "I wanted to announce that for our finale concert in May, we are going to adjust the program slightly. And, yes, we are going to go forward as though the Hall, and our orchestra, will remain intact. Instead of the Bach, Mozart, and Elgar, we are going to perform Mahler's Second Symphony."

The musicians looked surprised and impressed. I saw Richard Ashley elbow one of the other trumpet players with this huge grin on his face. Trumpet players loved Mahler.

Henry let his algebra textbook fall to the floor. "Mahler 2," he breathed, like it was something to worship.

I was still watching the group of men. The two men I didn't recognize were talking with Mayor Pitter, pointing at the damaged chandelier, at the crummy ceiling repairs the handymen had done for a discount.

Mr. Rue looked miserable, his arms crossed, his shoulders hunched.

"Henry, what are they doing?" I said.

Henry turned. "Uh-oh. That doesn't look good."

"Second," the Maestro was saying, "I wanted you all here to congratulate my daughter, Olivia, with me."

I spun around. "What?"

"Our ticket sales are up—you will not believe it—one thousand percent. *One thousand*. Exactly what we needed." The Maestro held his arms out toward me. "And you have helped get us there, Olivia. You and your friends and those beautiful posters. My little ghost girl." He kissed his fingers and then threw the kiss at me. "My little shadow."

I hoped the Maestro didn't think this changed anything. I was still furious with him. I still felt sick when I looked at him and thought about the secret he'd kept from me. But the musicians were smiling, cheering, raising their instruments to me. Richard Ashley smiled the biggest of all. For a few seconds, I soaked it up, gulped it down—this flushed, proud feeling. I had done good work.

It didn't last.

The Maestro had noticed Mr. Rue and the others. He waved the musicians silent and squinted past the bright lights. "Walter? What is this?"

Mr. Rue walked slowly toward the stage. "It's over, Otto. It's over."

I hadn't ever heard a room go so silent so fast. "What do you mean?" the Maestro said. "Who are those men? Mr. Mayor?"

"I'm sorry, Otto." Mayor Pitter cleared his throat and held out a paper to read. "After the incident at that concert with the chandelier, I sent in some people from the engineering department to inspect the building. Otto, this place is dangerous. It shouldn't be open, not even for another day. I'm not sure how it's still standing." He took a deep breath and looked around for a long time, like he was making himself look the musicians in the eye. Then he gave the papers to the Maestro and stepped away. "I've got a notice here I can't ignore. A notice to condemn."

Condemn: to say that something can no longer be used; can no longer be open for business.

To say that something should be destroyed.

Immediately, the stage erupted into chaos. The musicians demanded to read the papers themselves. They demanded meetings with the mayor, with City Council.

Henry chased after Mr. Worthington, who was wailing in agony. Other ghosts flitted around, shouting to each other, making a mad rush for The Ghost Room so they could share with Mrs. Barsky as soon as possible. They were jumping off a sinking ship.

The Maestro stared silently at the papers in his hands. He seemed small and shrunken, like a kid in too-big clothes.

His mouth moved. I couldn't hear him, but I could read his lips.

They said *Cara*.

Then he said, *What do I do?* and looked up at the ceiling.

I followed his eyes to the ceiling, and I tried to scream, but nothing came out.

Shades swarmed up above the stage, maybe drawn there by all the chaos of the ghosts flying around. A big knot of shades hovered right over the Maestro's head, hanging from the ceiling like a cluster of bats.

They were chewing on the ends of a big, curved wooden beam. Clawing at the ceiling in a frenzy, chipping away the painted angels.

I knew what would happen right before it did happen.

And I couldn't do anything about it.

I couldn't move fast enough to get to the Maestro, to push him out of the way. I couldn't get my voice to scream, "Watch out!"

So when that stretch of ceiling crashed down, it landed right on top of him.

I watched his body buckle under the weight of all that wood and plaster.

 350

I saw his head smack the edge of the stage.

I saw him topple off the stage to the Hall floor, and the wreckage pin him there.

I saw his arm, bleeding. It was the only part of him I could see.

It didn't move.

42

I WAS ZOOMING SOMEWHERE, FAST.

There were blue lights, and red lights. People rushing around, uniforms floating in the air. Hands touching me, hugging me.

"Olivia?"

Colors blurred, surrounding me. I was being poked, prodded, patted. Why wouldn't they just leave me alone here? Why did they keep talking to me?

"Olivia? Look at me."

Two hands cupped my face. A man with sandy brown hair.

"It's Richard, Olivia," the man said. "Richard Ashley."

I nodded. I knew Richard Ashley.

"We're on the way to the hospital. Do you understand? Your father's in an ambulance. He's hurt, Olivia. We're following the ambulance in a cab. Do you understand?"

Of course I understood. Why did he keep asking me that?

"Olivia, say something. Hilda, do you have any water?"

I blinked and looked around. Richard Ashley. Hilda Hightower. A water bottle.

"Here, drink some of this, sweetie," Hilda said.

I tried to drink some water, but it didn't go down right because something was choking off my air.

"Henry," I said, and my face was wet. Richard Ashley was hugging me. His jacket was around my shoulders. I smelled the valve oil he kept in his pocket. That's what trumpet players use when their valves go dry. There are seven valve combinations: open, 1, 2, 1-2, 2-3, 1-3, 1-2-3. The Maestro once showed me. I was sitting in Mom's lap. The Maestro made a weird sound on the trumpet that sounded like a horse neigh. You can do that, you know, if you hold the valves down only halfway and shake the horn around.

It made us laugh, me and Mom.

"Where's Henry?" I kept saying. "Henry."

"He's right here," Richard Ashley said.

"I'm here, Olivia," came Henry's voice. I felt him grab my hand. Nobody grabbed hands like Henry did. "I'm right here. It's okay."

*T*HEY PUT THE MAESTRO IN THE ICU. THAT means Intensive Care Unit. That means You've Been Hurt Bad.

I let Richard Ashley and Henry lead me around. I was still in zoom-land, where everything but Henry's hand in mine and Richard's hand on my shoulder was a blur.

He will be okay, they kept saying. The doctor was a tiny, serious man who reminded me of a bird. His touch on my arm was light, like feathers. He darted everywhere, like he was gathering twigs.

When I started imagining drawing Dr. Birdman, the genius half man, half sparrow neurologist, I finally snapped out of it. The things that make you the most *you* can do that. When everything else is zoomy and hazy and doesn't make sense, you at least have that. Your hobbies. Your dreams. You at least have your sketches, or your trumpet playing, or your homework in its neat, color-coded folders labeled HENRY PAGE, SEVENTH GRADER.

They're kind of like anchors, those things.

"Do you want something to eat?"

I found Henry standing in front of me. Past him, the Maestro lay in a beeping, wired-up bed.

"Richard gave me ten bucks," Henry said. "I can get us food from the cafeteria. It's always open, they said."

I pried the words out of myself, like I hadn't spoken in centuries. "What happened?"

"Oh wow, finally," he said, and sat down next to me, on the ugliest couch in the world—gray and pink and faded blue. "You've been so quiet. They said you were in a state of shock."

"Yeah."

"Your dad was hurt pretty bad, Olivia. Broken bones, a major concussion. And he was bleeding on the inside. They had to operate."

"Yeah."

"But they think he's gonna be okay."

"Is he sleeping?"

Henry hesitated. "He's in a coma. They said it's because he hit his head so hard."

"Why? What does that mean?"

"It's like his body shut down, so it can heal."

"When will he wake up?"

"They don't know."

I took a deep breath. When I let it out, I felt like crying. "It's my fault."

"What? No, it was the shades."

"I said it," I whispered. "I said, the other night: I wished it had been him instead of her."

"Olivia—"

I grabbed Henry by the shoulders. "Don't you get it? I bet the shades heard me. How could I have been so *stupid*, to say something like that? They heard me, and they're mad at me because of everything we've done, so they decided to give me what I asked for."

Henry grabbed me by the shoulders right back. "Olivia, he's not going to die."

"Did Dr. Birdman say that?"

"Who?"

"I mean the doctor."

"No, he didn't say that, *exactly*. He said he's hopeful, though."

"Hopeful doesn't mean squat." I drew myself into a knot, the couch making my legs itch. "Don't tell me things you don't know. And what is this couch, porcupine?"

"Richard decided it was hedgehog."

"He's here?"

Henry smiled. "Olivia, everyone's here."

"What do you mean?"

He helped me to the door of the ICU, and I peeked out into the lobby.

The entire orchestra was there—sitting, standing, spread out with blankets on chairs pushed together to make beds. Cups of coffee, food wrappers, and music on the ground. A couple people praying in the corner. Grace Pollock,

356

principal violist, listened to something on her headphones, her head bowed. Richard Ashley sprawled out on the floor, snoring.

"They've been waiting for news," Henry explained.

I slipped back into the Maestro's room, my throat too full for talking. The beeps of the machines keeping the Maestro alive pounded in my head like some giant, evil clock.

"What are you thinking?" Henry asked, following me.

"Do you think he'll die?"

"No," Henry said firmly. "I think he'll wake up any minute with a really bad headache."

"What if he doesn't wake up?"

"He will."

But we didn't know that, did we? "And what about the Hall?"

"Closed, but still standing. Everything's postponed, indefinitely. It would be too disrespectful, Mayor Pitter said, to destroy the Hall with your dad in the hospital and . . ."

Henry's voice trailed off. *And possibly dying*, I finished for him.

"So the Hall's safe for now," I said slowly.

"For now, yeah. Olivia, there were reporters and everything. The whole city's talking."

"Where's Mr. Worthington?"

"He's hiding on the roof. The hospital weirds him out. Plus, I think sick or dying people can see ghosts better. This one lady, she had all these tubes in her, and she pointed right at him, screaming. People thought she was nuts."

I put my hands over my ears to drown out that stupid beeping. "Tabby's doll is in Limbo. With the shades."

Henry tried to pry my hands loose. "Are you okay?"

"I have to go."

"What?"

I hurried toward the door. "I have to go into Limbo."

Henry spun me around. "Are you crazy?"

"Look, if the Maestro dies—"

"He *won't.*"

I pointed at the Maestro, lying there in his bed. So small, so tubed. Things like that shouldn't be in a person. "He might, Henry."

Henry couldn't look at me.

"If he does die, he might become a ghost. And if he becomes a ghost, he'll obviously haunt the Hall. And the Hall will get torn down, and the shades will come after him next. They'll wait around the Hall until his ghost shows up, and then they'll take him away."

Henry sank down onto the porcupine couch. "I didn't think of that."

"We've got to get them out of here, Henry. We've got to get Mr. Worthington out and show the shades that they can't just stick around here until they get what they want. Make them never want to come back here again." I drew myself up tall. "I have to go into Limbo. I have to find that doll."

"And how will you do that, exactly?"

I marched toward the door. If I stopped for even one second, I might chicken out. "I haven't figured that out yet."

Henry stopped me. "Olivia, you don't know what the shades will do to you."

"Whatever it is, they'll fail."

Henry put his hands on my face, just like Richard Ashley had done. His cheeks turned red. He dropped his hands.

"I'm coming with you," he said, swallowing hard. "I can't let you go alone."

"No, you're staying here with the Maestro. Someone has to keep an eye on him. And besides, I won't be alone. I'll have Igor."

Henry put his hands in his hair. "Man, Olivia, for the last time, that cat is *just a cat*."

"Nonnie says he's a very weird cat."

"Is that supposed to be better or something?"

"Just watch the Maestro, okay? And make sure no one sees me leave."

"No way, I'm not going to just—"

I needed to shut him up, to distract him. That was the only reason I did it, why I leaned up on my toes and kissed Henry Page's cheek. Twice, for good luck.

"You have sandwich breath," I told him.

Then I grabbed the ten-dollar bill and left him standing there, his hand on his cheek.

The Hall was empty and dark, wreckage from the caved-in ceiling swept to the side in a pile blocked off with ropes. The holes in the ceiling gaped down at me.

I stood there for a minute, trying to figure out how to go about this. I'd spent months avoiding Limbo. But I didn't know how to find it. All I knew was that shades came from Limbo. The only times I'd seen it, they'd been around.

Maybe it was as simple as that.

Igor bounded toward me out of the dark. *And what exactly do you think you're doing?*

"Um, hello?" I called out. My voice bounced around the Hall. "Shades? I've come here to—"

A blast of cold air knocked me to the ground. Mr. Worthington's face appeared in the seat cushion above my face.

"Stupid," he boomed. "Stupid."

"I'm not stupid," I said, glaring up at him. "I've just got to find your daughter's doll, thanks very much."

Mr. Worthington patted me anxiously. "Safe. Please. Stay."

That's when my arm started to burn, colder than it had ever burned before, and I knew, instinctively, what was about to happen. I smiled at Mr. Worthington.

"Can't stay," I said.

Igor growled, jumped onto my shoulders, and dug in his claws. *Olivia . . .*

I turned to see dozens of cold black hands reaching for

360

me, then jerking away like I'd burned them, then reaching for me again. Behind the hands, a door to Limbo swirled.

"Okay." I turned toward Limbo, spread my arms wide, and closed my eyes. Igor was meowing in my ear. "You can take me. I'll go with you."

The hands grabbed me. None of them could hold on for very long. It was like Frederick had said—they wanted to be like me, but they also hated me. I was painful to them. One hand snaked around and clamped over my mouth and nose, choking my air away. Another hand reached under my shirt and pressed itself over my heart.

"Blood," a rattling voice wheezed. "Fresh blood."

They dragged me through what felt like a pane of glass. It smashed to pieces around me. Mr. Worthington's thundering screams vanished, sucked away into nothingness.

Abruptly, the hands let go of me.

To make sure I was alive, I took a breath. Two breaths. I could feel it puffing, freezing in the air like a cloud of ice.

I clenched my fists, fingernails pinching my palms.

Igor shook against my stomach, his claws digging into my skin. I felt the warm sting of blood.

Alive, then.

But where?

I opened my eyes.

CHAPTER

44

I WAS IN THE HALL, BUT NOT THE HALL I KNEW.

It was Limbo's version.

The pipe organ here was black instead of silver, and five stories tall. Its pipes slithered in the air like seaweed underwater. Instead of dusty red fabric, the Hall floor seats were covered in skin, stretched tight and bolted into place with teeth. They loomed in the darkness, big as houses. Black water covered the floor, knee-deep. My hair was wet and frozen. So was Igor.

Igor tried to meow. *Well, I hope you're satisfied with yourself.*

"I could have drawn this," I whispered, looking around at the curtains made of old spiderwebs, at the craggy mountaintops that burst out of the Hall's ceiling. Up past the tops of the mountains, black stars blinked in a dull, white sky.

That didn't seem right.

Colors swirled everywhere, like when you close your eyes at night and see entire worlds behind your eyelids.

Blues, purples, reds, pale yellows. I started to shiver. When I rubbed my hands up and down my arms, my skin felt crackly, old, like the bark of a tree, or . . .

A burn.

I looked down.

Igor noticed it at the same time, yowled, jumped into the water, and climbed onto one of the giant chairs. His claws pulled on the chair's skin, yanking out long, gummy strands.

What have they done to you?

I turned my arms around, marveling at my newly black, glittering skin. I gleamed and glistened like volcanic rock.

"Whoa," I whispered.

Igor's tail flicked back and forth. *Whoa? That's all you can say?*

"Whoa, I look awesome?"

I leaned down to touch the surface of the black water. My skin sizzled at the contact, and I jerked back. I took an experimental couple of steps forward. *Tsssss, tsssss,* the water sizzled around my legs.

Igor was crying on his chair. *This is not happening.*

"Sure it is," I said, sizzling toward him. "Come on. We've got a doll to find."

He shrank away from me. *Aren't you at all disturbed that your entire body seems to have changed its texture and color? That you're sizzling when you walk? That you look like a shade?*

Actually, I was incredibly disturbed. But what can you do when you've decided to do a thing—like go into Limbo to find a dead girl's doll—and it ends up being more terrifying than you thought it would be?

You keep going.

So I did, with Igor wrapped around my shoulders. He couldn't sit still, like if he kept his paws in one place, my skin would burn him.

"Igor, I won't hurt you. Sit still."

Igor sneezed in my ear. *You don't know that. For all I know, this could be the first stage of shade transformation.* He sneezed in my ear again. *And that's what I think about this whole catastrophe. Mucus.*

Shades slunk through the water beside me, crawling along the giant chairs, peering down at us from the mountaintops.

They followed me as I pushed through the water, but they didn't touch me. They talked to me, though. Or about me, anyway.

"Once there was a shadow named Olivia," they rasped.

I shivered. My skin cracked open along the seams of my veins. I was a walking earthquake.

"She had a father," one of the shades wheezed, slinking between my ankles. "And a grandmother. And a motherrrr . . ."

"And a friend," another shade said, laughing. "A much smarter, much more pleasing to look at friend than she was."

One of the shades started scampering beside me, running across the top of the water. "And no one loved her. You can't love something that isn't there."

I was in the Hall, but not the Hall I knew.
It was Limbo's version.

Igor growled deep in his throat. *I should like to claw its face off, if it had a face.*

I ignored them and kept walking—toward what, I didn't know. I started scanning the darkness for a doll. Where would you hide a doll in this land of black water, with the chandeliers hanging down from the ceiling like giant upside-down carousels, and doors on all sides, barred like a jail?

"She never paid attention in class," a shade hissed, chomping its toothless mouth at me.

"She got into fights with people."

"Olivia the shadow girl."

"She tried to draw things, but they weren't very good."

The shades began to laugh—high, piercing, grinding sounds.

Igor swiped at a shade and almost lost his balance. *Olivia is an excellent artist.*

"Oooh, kitty's got claws, kitty's got paws," sang a shade, swinging its head from side to side. "Kitty might die tonight, just because."

"But what about the girl?" hummed one of the shades.

"Ah yes, the girl," slithering through the water beside me.

"Olivia, the mean-hearted," floating overhead with great, leathery wings.

"Olivia, the stupid."

"Olivia, the talentless."

"Olivia, who nobody loves."

 366

Don't listen to them. Igor batted my face with his paws. *They're trying to distract you.*

But with each sentence the shades moaned at me, it became harder to move. My steps grew heavier. The water turned to tar.

"Mean-hearted," a shade whispered, a few inches from my ear.

Part of my ear flaked off and crumbled, dropping into the water like sizzling embers.

"Stupid," another whispered.

"Talentless."

"Unloved."

Tears filled my eyes, black tears to match the rest of me. That made it hard to see. I tripped and fell into the water. Shades swarmed at my heels, their jaws clacking.

"I don't know where I'm going, Igor," I whispered into the water. I opened my mouth, let the cold rush in.

Igor tugged at my hair with his claws.

"Ow."

Yes, that's right, ow. Now get up.

I did, somehow, and started to climb.

A foothold here, in the side of this chair. Another, there. I pulled myself up, and then again, and again. Igor, perched on my shoulders, weighed me down like a sack of rocks, but I couldn't leave him.

Behind me, a black wave of shades followed me up. The giant chairs turned to cliffs and then mountains, rising up out of the Hall into clean, cold air. The shades stampeded each other to get closer to me, digging their long fingers into each others' backs.

"Mean-hearted," their yawning voices echoed up at me.

"Stupid."

"Talentless."

"Unloved."

It was harder to breathe up here. The sky grew whiter as I climbed, dotted with black stars. I saw, in the distance, faint outlines of pipe organ forests. There was a road in a valley. People floated along the road—gray people. Ghosts. They were running from the pitch-black shades chasing after them. The shades jumped. The shades engulfed them, slurping, chomping.

And when I looked again, there was a shade where the ghost had been.

I kept climbing, up and up the mountains made of black snow. Everything was reversed, here.

A shape reared up beside me.

"Henry?" I slid down a ridge and landed in a pool of black water that started climbing up my arms like it was alive. Igor sliced me free. "Henry, what are you doing here?"

"Olivia?" Henry said, but it wasn't Henry. It couldn't have been. Oh, I hoped it couldn't have been. He was shrinking, shriveling, into a treelike creature of black crusty limbs and black fungus spots where his freckles used to be.

"Olivia," the Henry-creature moaned, reaching for me. "I'm so hungry. Help me?"

I turned away, shimmying back up the glassy black slope. Stomach pangs flooded through me. Tabby Worthington's wet coughs echoed through the mountains like thunderclaps.

"Why won't you help me?" the Henry-creature called out. "I'll die. You can't leave me here! Find me something to eat!"

"Igor?" I whispered. My sweating hands kept slipping on the snow.

Igor dug his claws into my crackling skin. *Keep going. He's not real.*

I suddenly felt very small. I let myself drop. Curled into a ball, I let black snow rush into the cracks of my skin. "Are you sure?"

Olivia, this is not how I want to die.

I took a deep breath, and then another one. "No. Me neither."

I pulled us up, inch by inch, flat on my belly. Igor rode on my back. *I think I've counted one hundred and forty-seven shades so far.*

"Thanks," I panted. "That's helpful."

"You are such a disappointment." Nonnie sighed, appearing suddenly to my right. I gasped at the sight of her — frostbitten, white and blue and black, her fingers and nose and skin dropping off. Her bones were as black as the snow. "I'm always so cold. So lonely. So frightened. And you just let me stay that way."

"No," I said, gritting my teeth. "I try to take very good care of you, Nonnie."

"Not lately. You've been too busy. Too worried about yourself. What about me? I'm so old. So . . . *old* . . ."

I ran from the black Nonnie-skeleton chasing me, so high up now that my lungs started to burn. Finally, the Nonnie-skeleton crumbled and fell, back into the oncoming surge of shades. They gobbled up the bits of her like starving wolves. Below them, the Hall stood open to the skies.

Igor was purring. *Keep going.*

"I can't," I whispered, because my tears were freezing over, making hard lenses over my eyes. I took a step, another step, another, impossible step. "I can't do it."

But you are doing it.

"Olivia," an awful creature croaked next to me, half Richard Ashley, half beast. "You've let us down."

"Olivia," a three-headed giant moaned, reaching down to breathe stinking air on me. One head was Counselor Davis, another Principal Cooper, another Mrs. Farrity. "You're such a disappointment. Why can't you be smarter?"

"Why can't you work harder?"

"Why can't you be nice?"

"I'm smart," I whispered, "or I try, anyway."

"She tries and she fails." The giant laughed.

"Leave me alone." I pressed my cheek into the snow,

pulling myself up by handfuls of ice and grit. The cold was peeling off scraps of my clothes. "Please leave me alone."

"Olivia," boomed a voice.

The Maestro. Covered in tubes—up his nose, under his fingernails, into his scalp. The tubes spurted blood.

"You've killed me," he moaned. "Why did you kill me? Why couldn't you forgive me?"

My tears froze before they even reached the ground. I could barely move my face.

"I'm sorry," I sobbed. "I can't breathe."

Igor was warm on my back. *You're doing it. You are, you are. And I'm here.*

So I kept climbing. And, finally, I reached the top.

This was the tallest of the mountains.

I lay at the top, panting, and looked around. The other mountains were anthills far below. Even farther down, the Hall gaped open to the sky. The shades circled beneath me like a rushing black river.

It was only me and Igor up here, and the howling, biting wind, and the black stars, so close I could almost touch them. Black, purple, and shining.

"Olivia?" a new voice said.

Oh, no. I'd thought we were alone. Wrapping my head in my arms, I tried to burrow into the snow to hide.

"Leave me alone." My frozen tears shattered like glass. "Please, no more."

"Olivia," the voice repeated, full of disbelief. And I recognized it then. That voice had made birds for me. That voice had told me to dream and made up stories late at night for me, with only a flashlight and a bedsheet.

"Look up, Olivia."

I looked up.

Even though she was dark as night, even though she had no face—or at least, not the face I remembered—I knew it was her. I knew because when she pulled me into her arms, I wasn't afraid, and Igor didn't hiss, and even though she was made of shadows now, her hug still felt warm, just like it used to.

A flash of color flickered across her darkness—white, and blue, and gold. The same colors I'd seen in the Hall that day, on that strange-seeming shade.

"Mom," I burst out. "Where did you go?"

She didn't answer. She just rocked me, up there on that mountain in the wind, beneath the black stars. And I said her name a million times over, because I couldn't get enough.

It would never be enough.

CHAPTER 45

How long we sat there, I have no idea. After a few minutes or a few hours, I forced myself to look at Mom's face.

Black and crisped, shimmering like fairy dust. Without eyes, without nose, with a hole for a mouth.

"How long have you been here?" I whispered.

"Here?"

I closed my eyes, wrapping myself up in the sound of her voice, even though shadows scratched through it. "In Limbo."

"Is that where this is?" She sighed, looked around. "You know, I'm not sure. I'm not sure of a lot of things, these days."

"Mom, you do know . . . you know you're dead, right?"

"Dead?" She tilted her head. "Is that what this is? It's difficult to remember."

I reached for Igor. He crawled into my lap.

"You left us." I tried to sound casual about it. "The Christmas before last, you left me and . . . and the Maestro, and then about a year ago, you died."

She stared at me in silence.

"There was a car crash, Mom. And a memorial at Pine Ridge Baptist. And the Maestro didn't tell me. I *just* found out."

"Car crash?"

"Why didn't you say good-bye? Huh?" Suddenly I was mad. Boiling mad. Burning mad. I punched her arm. It was like punching stone, and I started to cry. "Why couldn't you just have explained? You fell out of love with him. With us."

"Never." Mom leaned close to me. Her breath smelled of lightning and dark places. "*Never* you, Olivia."

"Then why?"

"I was scared, and angry."

I kicked the ground. Black snow flew everywhere. "Yeah, well, I'm scared and angry too. A lot. And I'm only a kid, you know?"

"I never said I had a good reason. But it's a reason. And more time passed and more time passed, and then I was really scared. I couldn't come back to you. You would hate me."

I ground my fists into my eyes. "I never hated you."

"But you hate your father."

"He made you leave."

"Nobody made me leave but me. I was unhappy. I left. I didn't do it right. But I can't change that now." Mom looked out over the mountaintops. "So, Limbo, is it? It's a strange sort of place. Isn't it? Surely I was alive only yesterday. It can't have been long."

"You died, Mom," I whispered, "and you never said good-bye. You were just . . . *gone*."

"I know, baby."

"We live at the Hall now. Me and the Maestro and Nonnie. He sold all our things."

"Oh, honey."

"I hate my clothes. They smell like smokers because I have to get them from the charity store."

And I couldn't stop talking. I told her everything, a whole year of everything. Counselor Davis and Principal Cooper and the notes from school. Green candy. The petition. The Economy. Richard Ashley and how he let me cry into his jacket on the way to the hospital. My sketches, and art school.

Henry.

That color flickered over Mom's face again. For a second, I thought I saw her real eyes. "Henry. He sounds like a nice boy. Is he cute?"

"Mom."

"Well. I'm supposed to ask these things."

I squinted up at her. "You are?"

"I think so. Well? Is he?"

Suddenly, my crackling black shoelaces seemed very interesting. "I don't know, he's got freckles and whatever."

Igor snorted. *Ahem.*

"You've seen him, though, right?" I looked up carefully. "I mean, you and the shades have been all over the Hall.

You've been attacking everything—the ceiling, the ghosts, even me."

Mom leaned back. "We have?"

"Don't you remember? For months, you've been coming to the Hall. You . . ." I swallowed, hard. "You hurt the Maestro. You crashed the ceiling down on him. He's in the hospital."

"Oh, Olivia . . ."

"You *have* to remember that. Why'd you do it?"

"Oh, I don't, though." She started to wring her hands. "I remember . . . light and warmth. I remember searching. I remember . . . feeling angry and lost, and so alone. I remember finding others. I remember searching for . . . fresh blood."

Fresh blood. One of the shades that brought me here had said that to me. What if that shade had been Mom, confused?

Perhaps, Igor suggested, *they are all confused.*

"Maybe they don't know what they're doing?" I murmured.

Igor bent to smooth out his tail. *Like moths to flames.*

"Instinct."

Frederick had said shades didn't know who or what or where they were, once in the world of the Living. *They become hardly more than mindless beasts, confused and vicious.*

I scooted closer to Mom, took her hand in mine. My head ached, my heart ached. "Mom, are you telling me that you *weren't* trying to eat the ghosts?"

"I beg your pardon?"

"You weren't trying to attack them, or us, or make the Hall come crashing down?"

Mom shook her head, shrinking into a black stump of shadow and snow. "I don't know what you're saying, Olivia. Please slow down."

"All you saw was fog, you said? Light and warmth?"

"So warm." She looked up at me. "Do you know where I can get more of that? It's that other place, outside. That's where the warmth is. We like it there. We want more of it."

I lay back on the snow, staring at the inside-out sky. "You didn't mean it. You were confused."

Mom lay down beside me, shadowy tendrils tickling my wrist. "This is nice. I lie here a lot, but not with friends."

Tears filled my eyes, turning the sky wobbly and black. "Mom. I'm not a friend. I'm your daughter, Olivia. Remember?"

She placed her hand in mine. "They can be the same thing."

After a few minutes, Igor nudged my cheek. *Olivia? We need to go.*

Yes, we did. But how? I had found her at last.

"I have so many questions," I choked out.

"So do I," Mom murmured, wonderingly. "Like why the sky is white here, and the stars black. I'm sure if anyone hurt you, Olivia, they didn't mean to. We don't mean to do a lot of things here."

Igor was peering over the mountainside. *Olivia, we really should go.*

I joined him. The other shades were inching toward us, pulling themselves up by their sharp, black fingernails.

"I thought they didn't mean to hurt us," I said.

Igor backed away, his fur standing straight up. *Remember what Frederick said. To them, you are warmth and light and blood, the very things they want and don't have—and* can't *have. Think about that. They might not mean it. But they want it.*

"Mom, we need your help."

"Anything, baby."

"There's a doll here, somewhere. A little girl's doll. We need to take it back with us." My throat tightened, but I shoved through it. "And we need to go back. Now."

"Oh! That. Why, Olivia, it's right here."

Mom dug through the snow, and the next thing I knew, she handed me the doll. A tiny rag doll, covered in years of dust. I could barely see its smile.

"See? I found it for you. I found it before. I thought it was warm, but it turned out to be just a toy. A fake you."

"We need to take it back. Do you understand? Back to the other place?"

"The warm place." Mom nodded. "I can do that. And then we have to say good-bye?"

"I think so, yes."

Mom smoothed my hair, sending tiny dark icicles flying. "Good-bye again. I don't like that."

"Me neither."

"Promise me this, Olivia." And Mom leaned close, and the

color flickered across her face, and it stayed. She was her old self, smiling down at me, pale hair in her eyes and shadows around the edges. "Try to forgive your father. He's a good man. He showed me many beautiful things. But sometimes even beautiful things fade and change. Do you understand?"

"Yes." I tried to memorize her face. I wanted to draw this moment. "I'll try."

She flashed me a brilliant smile. "That's fine. I know you try hard."

Shadowed hands reached for us. Long, thin heads with drooping mouths slithered up over the edges of the cliffs surrounding us.

Igor hissed at them. *Olivia! Action, please!*

"Mom, we have to go."

"Very well. Hold this."

She folded the doll into my arms. Then she scooped me and Igor up against her chest and leapt out into the wind.

I squeezed my eyes shut. We were going to fall to our deaths. "Mom? Mom!"

"Open your eyes, baby."

I did.

We were flying.

Mom was still made of shadows, but they were beautiful and strong, streaming behind her like wings. The stars had turned into birds, like us, flapping and soaring beside us. We dipped and darted, we dove and danced, and they matched us. They were swans. Mom's swans.

She folded the doll into my arms. Then she scooped me and Igor
up against her chest and leapt out into the wind.

"Mom." I laughed. "You taught me how to make these. You put them all over the house."

"I remember. You liked making things. Hold on tight, now."

She kissed my head, and I grabbed Igor tighter. My skin was melting away, becoming normal again.

"Is this it?" I whispered.

"Yes. You see?"

Following Mom's eyes up to the very top of the sky, I saw the birds gathering there, a storm cloud of wings. And then they weren't birds at all, but an opening. Warmth rushed toward me, flooding my mouth. I saw beautiful lights.

"Is that home?"

"Live." That was her answer, whispered at my cheek. "Live, for me."

Then, she threw me out of her arms and pushed me up, up, up . . .

I reached for the birds, for the tips of their wings, for the warmth. I would see Henry soon. I had kissed his cheek. And the Maestro. He needed to wake up.

Once, I turned back.

Mom was there, waiting in the middle of the white sky. She waved. I waved back. I took a deep breath and reached for the birds.

And right then, right before I pulled myself out, I saw Mom close her eyes. The shadows faded from her, and she was a woman, all smiles and fingers and hair and warm arms, and she sighed, and was gone.

So was I, tumbling out.

I was home. I was in the Hall, on the stage. Tabby's doll fell at Mr. Worthington's feet. I couldn't hold myself together anymore. My skin felt fresh and raw, tingling all over, and it *was* warm here, and so, so bright. I got sick, careful not to get it on the doll. I lay there on the ground and cried so hard that not much came out but gasps.

Mr. Worthington tried to hug me, his arms slipping right through me. "Okay? Yes?"

"I don't know," I said. "Have you been waiting here for me?"

"Yes."

I pushed myself up and tried to hug him. It didn't work, and I screamed in frustration. "I wish . . . I'm going to miss you."

He paused. "Yes."

"Just do it, okay?" I stepped away from him, even though it hurt. "Do what you have to do."

"Okay?"

"Is it okay? Yes, it's okay. Do it."

Mr. Worthington hesitated, staring at me with those drooping, shimmering eyes. He didn't have much time left, I would bet.

"Do it!"

My shout still echoing in the Hall, Mr. Worthington

crouched by his daughter's doll. His fingers hovered over her tiny hands.

"It's okay," I whispered. "It's time."

He looked back at me, his hat dripping down to his feet. "Friend?"

"Yes." I nodded, squeezing Igor to my stomach. "Now, hurry up."

With both hands, he picked up the doll, holding it like it was made of glass instead of rags and dirt. He kissed its head.

A tiny bright cloud shimmered around him. I saw the figure of a girl, smoky and soft like a ghost, but better. Something better than a ghost. Something happier.

Tabby threw her arms around Mr. Worthington's neck.

"Tabby," Mr. Worthington gasped. He picked her up, swinging her around till they were a blur of color and smoke. As they moved, he started to come apart. First his hat flew off. Then his tie.

He looked up at me, right at the end.

"Thank you," he whispered.

Then Tabby's light swallowed them up. I had to look away, it was so bright.

For half a second, the doll hung in midair. Then it plopped to the floor. Its head slumped heavily onto its chest.

And that was it. He was gone.

All of them were gone.

CHAPTER

46

ENRY FOUND ME IN THE MORNING. I'D FALLEN asleep onstage. Thank goodness he found me before anyone else.

"Olivia?" He shook me awake.

"Henry?"

"Yeah, it's me."

I stood up, my knees wobbling. "What time is it?"

"Seven a.m. It's Saturday. Ted brought me here last night. You know, my . . . Mr. Banks. I kept him out of here, let you get some rest."

I nodded, leaning on the conductor's podium to find my balance.

Henry put out his arms, then stopped and stepped back and put out his arms again. Then he dropped them.

"What's wrong with you?" I asked.

"I just . . . I don't know. Are you okay? What happened?"

"It's done, Henry. They're gone."

"Mr. Worthington? You found the doll."

"Yeah." I felt like everything had been sucked out of the world. My head ached, and my arm felt . . . strangely naked. When I pushed up my sleeve, I saw why.

My burn had disappeared. Henry nodded and pushed up his pant leg. "Yeah. Mine's gone too."

"It's done," I said. "All of them."

Henry looked out into the Hall and shoved his hands in his pockets. "I should've been there with you."

"No, you shouldn't have." *That was just for me and Mom.* And I would explain that to him. Someday, maybe.

"Well. Okay. I'm here, though, just . . . well, you know. In case."

"Yeah. I know."

Igor grumbled. *Such profound conversations you two have.*

"Richard Ashley was so mad when he figured out you came back here. But he said he understands. He might come by after a while. Ted's camped out in the office, in case we need anything."

The mention of Richard Ashley had triggered the memory of Mom leaning close, asking me for a promise. "Henry?"

"What's wrong?"

"The Maestro. How is he?"

"Oh!" Henry slapped his forehead. "I'm such an idiot."

"I've been saying that for years."

"Ha-ha. I should've told you right when I came in. I mean, I was going to, but I saw the doll, and . . ." Henry shook his head. "Anyway. Olivia, he woke up. He's going to need a lot of recovery time, but he's going to be okay."

A rush of something filled me. It was like I had been

chained down and then set free. It scared me, a little. I wobbled where I stood.

Henry found my arm. "Whoa, you okay?"

"Yeah." I smiled at Henry. Something twisted in my chest where Frederick, Tillie, Jax, and Mr. Worthington used to be. But it was a good kind of twist. "I think I am."

Henry and I went out to the grounds and found Tillie and Jax's tree, swaying silver and pink in the morning light. Right there in the shade, in the cool, dewy dirt, we buried the doll.

When we were done, I lay flat on my back, looking up at the sky through the leaves above me. Closing my eyes, I spread out my legs and arms and fingers, airing myself out. Henry did the same.

We lay there quietly for a while. It was cool in the dirt.

"I'll miss them," I said at last.

"Yeah," said Henry. "Me too."

I stretched out the tiniest bit more, so I could touch the tip of my pinkie to the tip of his thumb.

His thumb poked me back, gently.

Well. At least, after everything, we had that.

CHAPTER 47

*L*ATER THAT DAY, RICHARD ASHLEY DROVE ME back to the hospital. I settled into the chair next to the Maestro's bed, drawing up my knees to my chin and watching him.

He looked better today. Not as many tubes.

I squeezed my eyes shut, trying not to remember the bleeding tube monster from Limbo, but I couldn't forget it.

You've killed me, the monster had moaned. *Why did you kill me? Why couldn't you forgive me?*

I wiped my eyes on my jeans. I rocked and rocked. I wished they allowed cats in hospitals.

"Because I was mad at you," I whispered. "I still am, you know."

And that was the truth. Yes, I made Mom a promise, and I *would* try. But it wasn't like I could snap my fingers and do it immediately, and I wasn't sure I even wanted to.

I lifted my head so I could see the Maestro's face—his eyes closed, his hair greasy and falling over his forehead, his mouth slightly open, the tubes in his nose.

So small. All of us, we were so small.

"You should've told me," I whispered to him. He probably couldn't hear me, they had him so pumped full of drugs. But I said it anyway, over and over, and lay my head down on the edge of the mattress, and found his hand under the thin white sheet.

APRIL

CHAPTER
48

*F*OUR FLUTES. FOUR OBOES. THREE CLARI-
nets, two E-flat clarinets, four bassoons,
ten French horns, ten trumpets, four trom-
bones, one tuba, seven percussionists, a huge
choir, harps, one pipe organ, and, as it instructs
in the score: "The largest possible contingent of strings." So,
basically, a string army.

As many people as you can cram onto one stage is the
general idea for Mahler's Symphony no. 2.

And somehow our orchestra had to do it without a conductor. The Maestro was still at the hospital, in no condition
for rehearsals. Dr. Birdman had prescribed four weeks of
bed rest, or at the very least, minimal activity.

That wasn't going to stop us.

Richard Ashley was the one to call the meeting. Two
Wednesdays after the Maestro got hurt, the entire orchestra gathered onstage without their instruments. Some of our
old donors had put together just enough money to get the
Hall in working order for one last concert, and it had been

approved by the city's department of engineering. Nonnie and I had been staying with some of the musicians, and the Maestro had started making calls from his hospital room to Gram. Even *I'd* talked to Gram. I didn't recognize her voice, but she recognized me. She burst into tears right when I said, "Hello?"

We were good to go for what may have been the Hall's most important concert ever.

Richard stood on the podium with a clipboard in hand. Henry and I sat at his feet, Igor in my lap. Richard had requested we be there, front and center.

"Many of you suggested we meet today," Richard Ashley said. "It wasn't just me. But I'm up here right now because I have something to say before we get started planning this farewell concert. I want you to look around you. I want you to really look."

The Maestro had said that the first day we moved in. Now Richard was saying it. Both times, when I'd looked around, I'd seen the same thing: faded chairs with threadbare cushions. Gaping holes all across the ceiling. Paint the color of grime and dust.

It wasn't the prettiest of sights.

"Ugly as mud, isn't it?" Richard Ashley said. "Or something worse."

A few people laughed.

Igor started cleaning himself. *Typical trumpet player. Always putting on a show.*

 390

"Hush," I whispered.

"Now look again, and remember."

That's all Richard Ashley had to say: *remember*. And I did remember, looking around the Hall, two hundred pairs of eyes looking around with me. I remembered sitting with Mom in the dress circle to watch rehearsal. She would pay such close attention, never taking her eyes from the stage. "It's like magic," she whispered to me once, holding me in her lap and pointing out the different instruments. Sometimes the Maestro would whirl around and blow us a kiss with both hands.

The musicians would whistle and hoot, and Mom would hide her cheeks in my hair.

I remembered when I first discovered the catwalk and declared to Ed and Larry that this was now my official hiding spot. They helped me make a flag for the railing so everyone would know.

I remembered spying on Henry from the catwalk through a paper towel roll. Hiding in the basement to draw. Lying on the stage and trying to perfect the tentacles of pipe organ monsters.

I remembered thinking this could never be my home. And then somehow it had turned out to be just that.

The musicians were smiling, chuckling, wiping their eyes. Gazing up at the curtains, the ceiling, the balconies, like they'd never seen anything quite like it.

"This has been our home," Richard said. "Some of us for

years. And it deserves a good send-off. So a few of us have been working hard the last couple of days, making phone calls, pulling some strings. And now it's time to get to work. Olivia?"

I turned around, surprised. "Yeah?"

He smiled, holding out his hand to me. "Come up here with me."

Scrambling up into place beside Richard on the conductor's podium, I almost reached into my bag for my charcoals, and then I stopped. It was an automatic sort of thing, but I stopped anyway. Balled my fingers into fists. Put them down straight at my sides. Stared out at the orchestra and didn't look away.

Dreams—even ones you were good at—weren't for hiding yourself in.

"Olivia, what you've done for us—and what you've done, Henry, and your friend Joan, too—you need to know how much it means, to all of us. You helped us get through a hard time. You brought life back to this place again. And we're family here. I promise you, no matter what happens, we're not going to let you fall. Our homes are your home. Okay?"

"Okay," I whispered. I blinked down at my feet. "Thank you."

Richard tilted up my chin. "We want to give your father an ending, Olivia. A finale."

"Mahler 2?"

He nodded. Out of the corner of my eye, I saw some of

the other musicians smiling and nodding along with him.

"But how?" I said. "He's . . . the Maestro, he can't . . ."

"No, he can't. Not right now, anyway. So we're bring-ing in help." Richard turned toward the side of the stage. "Okay! We're ready."

A tiny parade of smiling people headed out onto the stage. I recognized them vaguely, like they were from another life.

"Oh . . . my gosh," Henry breathed, trying to flatten his hair. "Are you kidding me?"

"Maestro Ogawa," I whispered, as the first man reached me, his black hair flecked with gray. He smiled and shook my hand with both of his.

Henry whimpered.

"Olivia, it's good to see you again," Maestro Ogawa said. "I'm very glad to be here."

He moved to the side and the curly-haired man behind him stepped forward.

"Maestro . . . Thompson?"

He grinned broadly. "I'm impressed you remember me, Olivia. You were only seven or eight years old the last time I saw you."

"Mom helped me remember everyone's names," I said quietly.

Richard squeezed my shoulder.

"I'm sure she did," Maestro Thompson said, smiling, and then moved aside. One by one, they stepped forward to shake my hand. I tried to remember, concentrating on the memory of Mom's voice, fresh in my mind, thanks to Limbo. They were conductors from New York (that was Maestro Ogawa) and Chicago (Maestro Thompson) and Philadelphia, San Francisco, Cleveland, Boston. They used to be our friends, before the Maestro lost his friends, before I lost mine, before we both lost Mom. And now . . .

"Why?"

Richard bent low. "What's that, Olivia?"

"Why are they here?"

Maestro Thompson said, "To rehearse, Olivia. Someone's got to hold down the fort until your father's back on his feet. And Mahler 2's no picnic."

I sat back down, right next to Henry. "Oh."

"I volunteered to run rehearsals myself," Richard said, clapping a hand on Maestro Ogawa's back, "but no one seemed too excited about that idea."

Everyone burst out laughing, and I did too, or at least I tried. Mostly I just tried to keep breathing.

Igor was trying to squirm out of my arms. *These people look like promisingly good petters.*

"Isn't this amazing, Olivia?" Henry asked.

I stepped back to take in the whole stage. Richard Ashley was saying something, and so was Maestro Ogawa. The musicians were laughing, hurrying backstage to get their instruments, tuning the timpani, blowing warm air through their horns, tightening their strings. The parade of conductors set up chairs and stands, pulled out pencils, opened their

394

scores. Maestro Thompson took the podium and helped me and Henry up.

"It might be better if I had some more room by my feet," he said kindly. "I tend to jump around a lot. Mahler 2 is one of my favorite works."

"Mine, too," gushed Henry. "Mr. Thompson, sir—er, Maestro Thompson—I'm a huge fan. Do you think you could sign my algebra homework?"

"Won't you have to turn that in?"

"No way, sir. I'll take the zero."

While Henry worshipped at the feet of Maestro Thompson, I took the chance to slip away. I wanted to hear the rehearsal, but there was something I needed to do first.

Ted—Mr. Banks—was sitting at the back of the Hall to watch rehearsal. He jumped to his feet when he saw me.

"You all right, Olivia?" He put his hands on his hips and grinned at the stage like the happiest guy alive. "Isn't this great? This is going to be something else. Your dad's gonna love this."

He wasn't Henry's real dad, but he had the same huge smile. I was going to like him, I could tell. "Mr. Banks? I need a ride."

*O*NCE THE NURSES GAVE ME THE OKAY, I WALKED into the Maestro's room, right up to the side of his bed. I wouldn't avoid him anymore. Not now, not ever again. If my ghosts could face Death, I could face this.

He stared at me, his mouth full of pudding.

"Sir," I blurted. "Er. Maestro. I mean . . . hi."

The Maestro swallowed and put down his spoon. "Hello, Olivia."

"How are you feeling?"

"Much better, now that I have had some pudding."

"Yeah." I twisted the edge of his sheet between my hands. "The orchestra is rehearsing. I thought you should know."

"Rehearsing? For what? With whom?"

"With friends." That was the easiest way to say it. "And for . . . well, for you. I think it's supposed to be a surprise, but I thought you'd want to know. To cheer you up."

The Maestro folded his hands in his lap and stared at them. "What are they rehearsing?"

"Mahler 2." I took a deep breath. "For a farewell concert. For you and for the Hall."

The Maestro nodded slowly. "Yes. Perhaps it is time after all."

"I guess." I tried to swallow and it came out this shaky-sounding hiccup. "I'll miss it."

"Olivia, I'm sorry."

Shadows don't cry. Someday-famous artists don't cry. I twisted the sheet as hard as I could. "Yeah?"

"For everything, Olivia. I know I haven't been a good father. Not since your mother left, and maybe not for a long time before that too."

Sometimes it isn't okay when people say they're sorry. At least not at first. "Yeah. I noticed."

"You notice many things, don't you?"

I looked up at the smile in his voice, but then I saw his arm. "When do you get those tubes taken out?"

"Soon, I hope. Why?"

"I don't like them." I kept twisting the sheet, but it didn't help. I burst into tears. "I don't like them at all."

The Maestro took hold of my hand. He held it for a long time and didn't say anything until I had finished. I was glad. I needed to finish.

"This might be my last concert ever, Olivia. You know that, don't you? Not just with this orchestra, not just at the Hall." He leaned back in his bed and winced. "It's been a hard year. I'm not sure I'll be the same now, if that makes sense."

I wiped my nose with my arm. "Yeah. It does. I've changed too."

"Have you?" The Maestro considered me for a long moment. "How are the ghosts, Olivia?"

Was he making fun of me? Was he angry? Or did he really want to know? Had he believed me this whole time? I couldn't tell, and I didn't care. "They've gone home."

The Maestro nodded, settled back more comfortably. "I see."

"I saw Mom."

"You—" He turned to me, his face going all strange. "Where?"

"You saw her too, didn't you? That's why you walked around all the time at night. You thought you saw her, and you kept looking for her."

"Perhaps," he said slowly.

"I helped her to move on. At least I think so." *I was her anchor*, I thought, because I'd been thinking it a lot. Sometimes it made me cry to think it, but more often it just made me feel light inside. "She said she was sorry, and that you showed her beautiful things. She said you're a good man."

"Did she?" The Maestro smiled then, the biggest I'd seen him in a while. We had the same smile, I noticed. I'd forgotten. "Well. I'm glad."

I'm not sure he believed me. But I think he liked what I said anyway. I think it was nice to imagine.

Sometimes that's how you get through things.

*T*HE NIGHT OF THE MAHLER 2 CONCERT, ON THE first weekend of May, I settled down on the catwalk with Igor to keep me company. Technically, I wasn't supposed to be up there, especially now. But it was the last time, and I knew this catwalk like I knew my sketchpad, inside and out.

Far below us, the Hall crawled with people — in jeans, in furs, kids and college students and grown-up people, and reporters. A lot of them, with cameras and notepads and flashing lights, the whole deal. Mayor Pitter and a group of important-looking people, surrounding him in suits and ties. Mr. Rue, smiling like a kid. The Barskys in greens and yellows, and their ghost entourage, of course. Joan, with her parents. She waved up at me like I was a rock star.

Igor jumped down from the railing. *Where's your sketchpad, by the way? I would think this would be terribly inspiring.*

"It is, but not tonight. Tonight is different. Tonight is just for this."

Henry hurried up the stairs and settled next to me with

his jar. When I raised my eyebrows, he shrugged. "I want them to see this."

He didn't need to explain who "them" was, not to me. How completely wonderful and strange.

"What are you smiling about?" Henry said.

"Everything."

"You're freaking me out. Where's the scary Olivia, with the attitude and the crazy pictures?"

"She's still there. This morning, I drew a man made out of bloody tubes. And a giant with three heads. And I might have accidentally slipped something stinky into Mark Everett's backpack."

"See, that's more like it."

"Henry?"

"Yeah."

I threaded my fingers through the grated floor. "I'm going to talk to Counselor Davis about art school. You know, for later. I want to get started looking into it now. Do you think that's crazy?"

"No." Henry lay back and propped his feet up on the railing. "I think it's great, Olivia."

"That's not very proper behavior for an usher."

"If I don't lie down, I'll fall over. I'm so nervous."

"You shouldn't be." I looked over the edge and found Richard Ashley's sandy brown head. He gave me a thumbs-up. I waved back. "They'll be fine. They'll be better than fine."

And they were. From the moment the lights went down

400

(Ed kept pulling at his collar and Larry kept muttering how he'd never been more nervous in his whole life) and the Maestro stepped out onto the stage with his cane (he had to walk with one now), everything was better than fine.

Because nobody cared that a month ago, there'd been ghosts here, scaring people, and shades crashing down ceilings. They didn't care about our petition or the fact that I lived backstage or the rumors that had been flying around.

Not once the orchestra started playing.

They just watched, and listened. In the pauses between movements, you could have heard a shade slithering around, it was so silent. But shades didn't come around here anymore. I wondered if it was because of Mom.

"This is incredible," Henry whispered, about halfway through the finale. It was the first time either of us had spoken. You couldn't speak, not with the strings soaring like they were, all the musicians' arms sweeping at the same time. Not with the cymbals crashing, and the timpanist thundering on his drums, mallets flying. Not with the trumpets blaring their fanfare way up high, and the rest of the orchestra rumbling underneath them.

I peeked over the railing as the orchestra quieted down to a lullaby—the horns crooning, the violinists' bows kissing their strings, the chimes ringing like a clock. When I looked down at the audience, I saw that open, soft look on their faces. People watched with hands over their mouths, people clutched their neighbors' arms. A boy on his father's lap stared at the choir, eyes shining.

That's when I realized all that was happening behind the Maestro's back. He wasn't seeing it. He *couldn't* see it.

I watched his arms stroking the air, guiding the piccolo player up and up. His shoulders bunched up near his ears. *Quiet.* That's what he was saying to the orchestra: *Quiet, here. Quiet, now. Hush.*

The musicians watched him, just as attentive as the audience. They could see his face.

But I couldn't.

And suddenly, I needed to.

"I've gotta go," I whispered to Henry.

"What?" Henry grabbed my arm. "Are you kidding me? They're at *Etwas bewegter*!"

I stared at him. "Henry, please don't tell me you speak German, too."

"No, but I did memorize the lyrics. And the major tempo markings."

I rolled my eyes. "Oh, well, if that's all. But seriously, I have to go."

"Where are you going?"

"To the organ loft." It seemed like the best place. "I want him to see me."

After a second, Henry nodded and let go of me. "You should."

"Come with me?"

"I don't think your dad cares about seeing me."

"Maybe not. But I do."

402

Henry beamed and took my hand. "Yeah?"

"Yeah. Come on. Igor?"

Igor thumped his tail at me. *Oh, so you* were *going to ask. That's nice to know.*

"Igor . . ."

He stretched out in that lazy way only cats can do. *I'm far too comfortable here. Besides, organ lofts are dusty.*

As the alto solo continued, Henry and I crept across the catwalk, past Larry and Ed, who watched the concert with the goofiest smiles on their faces. I don't think they even noticed us walk by. We hurried down the utility stairs and backstage, past my empty bedroom.

Toward the end, when the choir stood up in one quick motion, we heard it boom over our heads.

"We should hurry," Henry said.

Nonnie sat backstage, bundled up in her scarves and watching the concert on the monitor.

"Oh, Olivia!" she cried, waving at us. "I'm watching, with my favorite scarf! *Molto stupendo, assolutamente perfetto!*"

I stopped long enough to kiss her cheek. "That's great, Nonnie."

We climbed up the zigzagging loft stairs as they vibrated with the force of the organ over our heads. The pipes surrounding us shook my teeth, making it hard to stay balanced, but finally we made it to the organist's door. Past that loomed the entire, glittering, packed Hall.

And the Maestro.

Together, we opened the organ loft door. I stepped out first, into the blinding light.

With my hand on the doorknob, I hesitated.

"What's wrong?" Henry had to bellow to be heard.

Lots of things, really. Mom was dead. The Maestro had to walk with a cane. I didn't know where we would be after the next few days, what would happen to the people playing onstage, to the Hall, to us. Would donations increase? Could we save the Hall after all? Or was it too late?

I didn't know how to keep my promise to Mom, how to forgive the Maestro. What I was about to do stung a little, deep in my chest. That deep, stinging part wondered if the Maestro really deserved it.

But then Henry took my hand. "Come on, it's all right."

And it was. Or at least it would be, somehow.

Together, we opened the organ loft door. I stepped out first, into the blinding light. Betty Preston, our organist, didn't even notice me. It was the very end of the symphony, where it's pretty much impossible to notice anything but the organ thundering and the choir singing their brains out and the trumpets and horns climbing over the top of it all.

I crouched behind the chipped wooden railing and found the man on the conductor's podium, waving his arms in gigantic sweeps, mouthing the German words along with the choir, pointing at the trumpets — *You there, it's your turn. Strong, now. Be strong.*

I stared at him until my eyes burned.

"Look at me," I whispered. "Please, Maestro. Please. *Dad.* Look at me. I'm here."

And he did, right at the end, when the choir sang their last words. He found me, and his eyes locked with mine. Behind me, Henry squeezed my hand.

I held on tight, to Henry's fingers and to Dad's eyes. They smiled at me, only for me, and I didn't let go

 406

Author's Note

For readers interested in learning more about the music mentioned in The *Year of Shadows*, I've included below the City Philharmonic's full concert schedule for the year of Olivia's adventures. Just like a real-life Maestro Stellatella would strategically plan his concert programming, I also tried to be strategic in planning the music of *The Year of Shadows*, selecting musical works that fit well, thematically, with Olivia's story.

For example, the first series of concerts, in September, all deal with either fate or ghosts. *La Forza del Destino* means "the force of destiny." Tchaikovsky's *Francesca da Rimini*, as Olivia explains, tells the story of people condemned to Hell, stuck there forever as ghosts and tormented by the memories of their former lives. (If you've read *The Year of Shadows*, that should sound familiar!) And Tchaikovsky's Fourth Symphony opens with a brass fanfare—the "Fate" theme—that occurs regularly throughout the rest of the symphony. *Fate* and *ghosts* are both ideas to which Olivia is introduced early on in the book.

(Of course, sometimes I simply selected pieces that fit well with the time of year. For example, the February concerts feature romantic works in honor of Valentine's Day.)

One more quick note: You'll notice that I've listed programs for the April and May concerts, even though, in Olivia's story, April and May don't turn out the way anyone originally planned. I thought interested readers might want to see what pieces the original concerts were scheduled to include, just in case they wanted to go find recordings of all the music the City Philharmonic plays in *The Year of Shadows*. I know I, as a former trumpet player—yes, just like Richard Ashley— would have done that, if I were in your place, reading this book for the first time.

SEPTEMBER

First Series:
La Forza del Destino Overture—Verdi
Francesca da Rimini—Tchaikovsky
Symphony No. 4—Tchaikovsky

Second Series:
Leonore Overture No. 3—Beethoven
Violin Concerto No. 5—Mozart
Symphony No. 3 "Eroica"—Beethoven

OCTOBER

First Series:
Overture to *The Flying Dutchman*—Wagner
Toccata and Fugue in D minor—Bach
Symphony No. 5—Beethoven

Second Series:
Night on Bald Mountain—Mussorgsky
Bachianas Brasileiras No. 3—Villa-Lobos
Symphonie Fantastique—Berlioz

NOVEMBER

First Series:
Violin Concerto in D Major—Brahms
Symphony No. 9 "From the New World" —Dvořák

Second Series:
Hungarian March — Berlioz
Cello Concerto — Dvořák
Pictures at an Exhibition — Mussorgsky

DECEMBER

First Series:
Suite from *The Nutcracker* — Tchaikovsky
Pavane — Fauré
"Hallelujah Chorus" from *Messiah* — Handel

Second Series:
Skater's Waltz — Waldteufel
In terra pax — Finzi
A Christmas Festival — Anderson

JANUARY

First Series:
Overture on Russian and Kirghiz Folk Themes — Shostakovich
Piano Concerto No. 1 — Tchaikovsky
Suite from *The Firebird* (1919) — Stravinsky

Second Series:
Divertimento for Orchestra — Bernstein
Fantasia on a Theme by Thomas Tallis – Vaughan Williams
The Pines of Rome — Respighi

FEBRUARY

First Series:
Prelude and Liebestod from *Tristan und Isolde* — Wagner
Butterfly Lovers Violin Concerto — Chen Gang and He Zhanzao
Romeo and Juliet Fantasy-Overture — Tchaikovsky

Second Series:
The Water Goblin — Dvořák
Suite from *Der Rosenkavalier* — Strauss
Rhapsody on a Theme of Paganini — Rachmaninov

MARCH

First Series:
El Salon Mexico — Copland
Piano Concerto, op. 67, "Memo Flora" — Takashi Yoshimatsu
Sinfonia No. 6 — Carlos Chávez

Second Series:
Roman Carnival Overture — Berlioz
Adagio for Strings — Barber
Ein Heldenleben — Strauss

APRIL

First Series:
Piano Concerto — Schumann
Symphony No. 7 — Bruckner

Second Series:
Sensemayá — Revueltas
Violin Concerto in D — Stravinsky
Concerto for Orchestra — Bartok

MAY

First Series:
Overture from *Egmont* — Beethoven
Valse — Ravel
Symphony No. 4 — Ives

Second Series:
Brandenburg Concerto No. 2 — Bach
Symphony No. 1, *Jupiter* — Mozart
Enigma Variations — Elgar

SPECIAL SEASON FINALE

Symphony No. 2, "Resurrection" — Mahler